MW00850120

Citations:

Federico García Lorca. "It's True (Es verdad)." Originally published in *Canciones*, 1921-1924. Translated by A.S. Cline in *Poems of Love and Death*, 2007-2023. Public Domain.

Henry Wadsworth Longfellow. "The Lighthouse." *The Seaside and the Fireside*. Boston. 1849. Public Domain.

A PACK FOR AUTUMN

A COZYVERSE NOVEL

by
Emilia Emerson

For anyone who's been told you're too prickly, too much,
or that you feel too deeply—

Starlight Grove welcomes you home with open arms,
just as you are.

AUTHOR'S NOTE

Welcome to Starlight Grove! If you picked up this book because of the super cute cover, I want you to know that this is a cozy, small town romance that's also *very spicy*. This book is for adults!

While this is a sweet, low angst read, there is some content that some readers may find upsetting, including the loss of parents and grandparents and the grief that follows. Additionally, one character discloses a history of child abuse/neglect. Our main female character has a hormonal disorder that is omegaverse specific, but has similarities to PMDD and PCOS and impacts her physical and mental health. There are also a few scenes that depict some challenges of living in a plus-sized body and challenges of living with dyslexia.

This book ends in a happily ever after!

A Pack for Autumn is part of the Cozyverse shared universe with Emilia Emerson and Eliana Lee. Our books can be read as standalones, but all take place in the charming town of Starlight Grove with crossover characters.

For more detailed information on the content in this book, please visit
emiliaemerson.com

INTRO TO OMEGAVERSE

This is a Why Choose Omegaverse.

Why Choose means that our female main character doesn't have to choose between her guys for her happily ever after.

While each omegaverse is different, in general, it's an alternative world where society is composed of three designations: alphas, omegas, and betas. People are born into a designation, which influences biology and personality. All these characters are fully human—they do not shift into animals!

Alphas are physically large and often dominant, and they are highly attracted to omegas' scents. Male alphas have a knot at the base of their penis that swells during sex, allowing them to lock inside of an omega. Alphas can also "bark," which means injecting their voice with a certain tone that omegas feel compelled to obey. Barks are generally only used within trusting pack relationships, and omegas can resist them if they choose.

Omegas are the rarest designation. They are typically physically small and have a high need for physical touch. Starting in early adulthood, omegas go into heat. During heats, they are ruled by their instincts. They have a strong urge to nest, gathering soft and cozy items into a bed for comfort. Omegas need to be knotted by alphas in order to avoid pain and physical harm during heat. During heats, alphas can go into rut, which means they are overwhelmed by their alpha instincts to sate and care for their omega. If omegas want to avoid their heats, they can take a daily suppressant pill.

Omegas are physically compatible with alphas and able to take their knots, although some betas can train themselves to take an alpha knot. Omegas are often the center of pack life, the glue that holds the pack together.

While this omegaverse doesn't have fated mates, some alphas and omegas are uniquely compatible with each other (scent-matches). Alphas and omegas can bond with each other through a bite, which forms a connection that allows them to sense the others' emotions.

Betas are essentially what we would consider "normal" humans. They don't have strong scents. Betas can be a part of packs and alphas and omegas can bite them to form a bond.

1

EASTON

I AM NOT A STALKER.

I am not a stalker.

I am definitely *not a stalker.*

I chanted the phrase to myself as I wound through the aisles of Mariposa Market, stealing covert glances at the dark-haired beauty on the other end of the aisle.

I'd looked it up—the definition of stalking. This definitely *did not* qualify. Stalking required a pattern of repeated *unwanted* attention or harassment.

I wasn't harassing her, and how would I even know it was *unwanted*? Okay, she might have turned me down when I asked her out on a date—*twice*—but I wasn't *stalking* her. It just so happened that the adorable lighthouse keeper and I were often at the market at the same time. Like today, I'd had an urgent need for baking soda.

Urgent.

I'd seen a video about how baking soda could deodorize your fridge. How was I supposed to last another minute without it after hearing that?

I jolted when I realized she wasn't in the aisle anymore. She was heading to the checkout.

Olive.

The first time I heard someone in town speak her name, it felt like the clouds had parted and sunlight was streaming down on me. A great achievement since it had been pouring down rain, but that was the power of Olive. She was sunshine on a rainy day, and I needed to be by her side forever.

I just had to figure out how to win her over first.

I slipped in behind her in line, a bright orange box of baking soda clutched tight in my fist.

The cashier, an idiot teenager named Jack, smiled at her. I coughed to cover the rumble of a growl in my chest. Olive deserved all the smiles in the world. *I* just wanted to be the one to give them to her.

To give her everything.

"Your name is Olive, right?" Jack asked.

"Umm, yeah," she responded.

There was a slight frown on her luscious pink lips. A little crease between her big, brown eyes.

Jack chuckled as he scanned her first item. "So, does that mean your parents are olive farmers?" He paused his scanning as if waiting for uproarious laughter.

She fixed him with what could only be called a withering stare, and my heart pounded with excitement. Olive was shy and quiet, but sometimes she let out her snarky side, and it always delighted me.

"I don't know, Jack. Were your parents super into changing tires?"

"Umm... what?"

"Or growing magic beans?" she deadpanned.

Jack blinked, looking totally lost, before busying himself with scanning the rest of her items. I, on the other hand, coughed again, this time to cover my laughter. My girl was so fucking funny.

She turned towards me. Our eyes met, and the world slowed. Her beauty was the kind that made it hard to breathe. The way her bangs fell across her forehead was so cute I could hardly stand it. She was wearing a forest green sweater that draped gently over the luscious curves I wanted to bury myself in.

Just then, the market door opened and Hank—Starlight Grove's quintessential cranky old man and bookstore owner—walked in, sporting a deep frown as he leaned heavily on his cane. The noise distracted Olive and she looked away. My jaw clenched against the urge to beg her to look at me again.

Hank's interruption did bring one good thing—a gust of wind that blew into the market through the open door, catching Olive's hair and ushering her scent in my direction. My irritation vanished as I inhaled deeply. She smelled like a pumpkin spice latte, all warm and comforting and sweet with an edge of bitter coffee. My cock stiffened immediately, and I shifted my stance. This was why I tried to resist breathing around Olive. I didn't want to scare her off by sporting a hard-on every time I was around her but fuck, it was pretty much impossible. She wore a sort of deodorant to mute her scent, but the faint whiffs I got were enough to feature in my dreams. I wanted to roll around on her adorable chunky sweaters, wanted to drown myself in her. Maybe the wind would blow little particles of her scent onto my shirt, and I could curl up in bed with it later.

My scent, however, was out full-force, declaring to all in the vicinity that I was completely obsessed with this omega. Olive stared straight ahead, but I thought I caught a tinge of pink on her cheeks. It gave me a tiny spark of hope that she wasn't as unaffected by me as she acted.

All too quick, Jack was reading out her total. She paid for her items, grabbed her two cloth bags, and headed to the door.

I wanted to run after her. I could offer to carry her bags so she didn't have to balance them on her bike handlebars as she rode back to the lighthouse. Or I could carry *her* if she wasn't feeling up to biking today.

But my feet stayed rooted to the floor. She already felt like mine, but I was terrified of messing this up. After she'd practically run away from me the second time I invited her to dinner, I realized I needed to rethink my strategy.

I'd been told repeatedly that I came on too strong, and that, according to the last woman I'd gone on a few dates with, my attention was *suffocating*. And my Olive was skittish. She only came into town when she'd run out of her stash of ramen and TV dinners. She never initiated conversation. I'd never even seen her smile. I had to play this right. I couldn't scare her off. I wouldn't survive it.

I watched her through the large market windows as she got on her slightly rusted bike and set off down the road.

"Umm, are you going to buy that?" Jack gestured at the crushed box in my fist. A dusting of baking soda spilled onto the floor. *Shit.* I looked around furtively to see if Marisol or Carmen were around. They would kill me for getting their floors dirty. I let out a little sigh of relief when I didn't spot either of the sisters. This was another reason I had to be careful with Olive. I'd never gotten used to my alpha body—the way I towered over pretty much everyone, especially omegas like her, and how I constantly bumped into things and broke them with my clumsy limbs.

I never wanted to break her.

I mumbled an apology as I handed Jack some money. By the time I left the store, Olive had already disappeared down the winding road that led to the bay. I hated that she didn't live closer to town. What if something happened to her out there, all alone?

My legs were heavy as I headed back to the house I shared with my packmates.

Finn was making lunch when I entered the kitchen. His eyes flicked to me and the still-leaking box in my hand. "Are you going to tell me why you sprinted out of the house like it was on fire?"

I'd been hovering by the window all morning, knowing Olive usually went to the market on Thursdays. My heart had almost exploded when I saw her coming down the street. But saying that would make me sound like a stalker, and I definitely wasn't.

"We needed baking soda," I grunted. I opened the fridge and set the sad little box on the shelf.

Finn looked like he wanted to press me, but he just turned back to his sandwich. I wanted to tell him about the woman I dreamed of making our omega, but Finn was still lost in his grief after the death of his grandparents, and Lars was still obsessed with an omega he'd scented years ago.

I took a deep breath. First, I would convince Olive to give us a chance. Then, I would convince the guys.

2

OLIVE

I CRINGED AT THE SQUEALING BIKE BRAKES AS I approached my house. I'd found this bike in a small shed on the property when I moved in a month ago, but it wasn't in the best shape. I needed to figure out how to fix it so the chain stopped popping off and the brakes stopped sounding like a siren. Still, I wouldn't complain. It made transporting groceries back home much easier.

I parked by the front door, pausing for a moment to breathe in the salty sea air and listen to the crashing waves. A meow alerted me to the presence of Sir Cat, the fluffy orange, white, and brown stray who had been sitting by my front door the day I moved in. He'd walked right inside, making himself at home as I'd hauled in my sparse possessions consisting of a suitcase and a couple of boxes.

"Hello, Sir," I said, bending down to scratch his head. He didn't have a collar, so I had no idea what his real name was. I'd tried out several, but he had fixed me with a deeply disapproving expression, so I just stuck with "Sir Cat." He was regal enough to warrant the name, anyway.

When I interviewed for the lighthouse keeper position, I'd been told the house came furnished. I'd arrived with a rental car packed with my limited possessions and opened the door to an almost empty house. There were some dishes in the cabinets. A small wooden table in the kitchen. Some books on lighthouse-keeping on the built-in bookcases. I'd purchased an air mattress to sleep on and a few other small things at a thrift store, but that was it. I was so close to paying off my credit card debt and needed to save every dollar. My new job came with free housing, but the salary wasn't much.

I'd been relieved to have Sir Cat with me that first night. A small storm had blown through, howling and rattling the windows. He'd kept me company in the lighthouse watch room, purring the night away on my lap as I acquainted myself with the lighthouse manual and storm protocols.

We'd quickly fallen into a quiet routine. He rarely left my side, trailing me through the cottage and lighthouse like a fluffy shadow. I'd found a basket for twenty-five cents at the thrift store and put one of my own blankets in there for him. He certainly couldn't keep sleeping on the floor.

"That alpha was at the market again today," I said, my voice almost a whisper as if we would be overheard.

Easton.

The golden-skinned, curly-haired alpha with thick forearms, a broad chest, and stubble on his jaw. We kept running into each other, but he hadn't asked me out again after I'd absolutely panicked the first two times he'd tried. He'd obviously come to his senses and given up, which was for the best. I'd moved to Starlight Grove to be alone. I couldn't think of many jobs more solitary than lighthouse keeper.

So then... why did it feel like my heart was breaking at the thought of Easton giving up on me?

I moved inside, holding the door open for Sir Cat, and unloaded my groceries. One day, I'd learn how to cook. Pasta with jarred sauce was about as advanced as I got, and that's what I was planning for dinner. Although, the only thing I was craving right now was croissants filled with Nutella and thick slabs of chocolate cake. I sniffed my sweater, unsure if I could actually catch a hint of the alpha's rich, chocolate hazelnut scent or if it was just wishful thinking. My inner omega let out a forlorn whine, but I drowned her out with the kitchen radio, turning the knob until the static faded and music filled the room. My heart ached as I recognized the song. It was by one of me and my mom's favorite artists—a semi-local singer we'd seen play at a bar before he blew up. Mom and I had played this album on repeat on the boat until my dad banned it.

Until the next day, at least. He could never refuse us anything.

I swallowed the lump in my throat as I drained the pasta. What would it be like to have a love like they'd had?

"What kind of music do you like?" I asked Sir Cat. He cocked his head. "Something sophisticated, right?"

Meow.

I grinned. "Do you want some pasta?" I held a noodle out for him and he took it neatly from my hand.

After I dished up my dinner, I headed to the door that connected my cottage to the inside of the lighthouse. I trudged up the winding metal stairs to the very top, emerging onto the balcony. I loved sitting up here, even as the wind turned cold with the start of fall. It made me feel more alive.

I sat down, and Sir Cat immediately settled on my lap. I shoveled down my pasta before the wind could turn it stone-cold and then set my bowl aside so I could focus on scratching Sir Cat and enjoying his soft purr.

"Have you always lived by the ocean?" I asked. "I know you don't like the water, and here I am, unable to live without it." He nudged my hand, urging me to continue petting him.

I peered out into the darkness, the flashing beacon from the lantern illuminating the waves. "I should be out there."

I had grown up on my parents' lobster boat, spent most of my days there before I could even walk. By the time I was ten, I was helping my dad check traps and learning about weather patterns and navigation. My dad was a fifth-generation lobsterman, and I thought I'd be the sixth generation. But nothing had turned out how it was supposed to.

Sir Cat and I stayed outside until my fingers grew too frozen to continue petting him. I crept back down the stairs, set my empty bowl in the sink, and crawled into my nest, wondering if I would always feel this empty.

3

OLIVE

I peeked out the curtains in my bedroom. It was still dark outside, but the slight shift in the color of the sky promised that sunrise wasn't far away.

I took my morning pill before pulling on a sweatshirt, grabbing a towel, and slipping on my shoes. Sir Cat met me at the door.

"Good morning. Hope you slept well."

He just butted his head against my leg.

While Sir Cat clearly felt this was his house to enter and exit whenever he pleased, he never tried to enter my nest. In fact, he avoided my bedroom completely, content to curl up in his makeshift basket bed. Probably a good thing since I was sleeping on an air mattress. Wouldn't want him to puncture it with his claws.

"Let's go, then," I said, opening the door.

He led the way down to the small beach by the lighthouse. The sand was rocky, and it was freezing out, but I didn't care. Watching the sky slowly turn pink and purple every morning made me feel connected to *something*. The universe, I supposed, or just something bigger than me.

I placed my towel on a large flat boulder higher up the beach and started stripping.

"You know, cold plunges are really good for you. Very rejuvenating, gets your blood pumping."

Sir Cat looked at me like I was an idiot, like he did every morning. Once I was undressed, he curled up on my towel to wait for me.

"One of these days, I'll get you in the water," I called over my shoulder. I swore he rolled his eyes.

I raised my hands out to my sides, embracing the morning as I ran into the ocean. The freezing waves stole my breath as I plunged in, but they also stole all my anxieties.

My anxieties about my lie on my job application.

My grief.

My dark days.

My uncontrollable body.

Everything that piled on so heavily disappeared in the water.

I floated on my back, buoyed by the gentle waves as the sky brightened above me.

I'd come here to start fresh, to create some sort of life for myself away from the town that held all the memories of my life *before*, of the Olive who had parents and a community and a laid-out plan for her future. I had no idea what this new life would look like, except for small and isolated, but this morning, in the waves, it felt like I'd made the right decision with this move.

I turned to head back to the shore and let out an excited noise when I saw Sir Cat. He'd left his spot on the towel and moved closer to the water. Keeping complete eye contact with me, he reached out a single paw to touch an incoming wave. He withdrew it with a shake and a disgusted look before scampering off.

"I'm proud of you for trying something new!" I shouted after him with a grin.

Yeah, maybe this would be okay.

4

OLIVE

A BELL RANG AS I OPENED THE DOOR TO THE GROVE Bookstore and slipped inside. My heart pounded as I closed the door behind me, desperately hoping I hadn't been followed.

This was absurd. I was acting as if an ax murderer was chasing me when it was only the overly friendly townspeople. Four people had stopped me on the short walk from the pharmacy where I'd picked up my monthly prescription to the entrance of the bookstore. I'd been too overwhelmed to remember most of their names, but they had stopped me to say hello, give me unsolicited advice about what flowers I should plant in my window boxes, and press a small container containing Arepa Dulce—a type of Dominican cake—into my hand. That last one was from a woman named Marisol, who owned the market. I'd slipped it into my tote bag. I wasn't about to turn down dessert.

Everyone seemed excited to have someone new in town, but I was waiting for them to get bored of me when they realized I was the least interesting person to ever walk the planet.

Most people would love this kind of small-town charm, but I hated that I couldn't move around anonymously. Social situations didn't come easily to me, unlike my dad who had been one of the most outgoing men I'd ever known. He'd been right at home when we'd visited Starlight Grove six years ago for a rare off-season vacation. Sometimes, I wondered if he would have been happier to live in a town like this instead of spending most of his days on the boat. But he had grown up on the water, expected to take over the family lobster business, and then he'd fallen in love with a painfully shy beta who was at home on the sea, away from the bustle of coastal towns.

When I'd seen the lighthouse keeper position posted online, I'd felt a little tug of something inside me. My mom would have said it was the call of the universe, but I wasn't so sure. I'd spent the years since my parents passed feeling lost, and there was something alluring to the idea of returning to a place I'd been happy with them... like maybe I would find some of the happiness we'd had.

I wandered through the cramped bookstore aisles, careful to avoid tipping over the precarious stacks of books and wondering if I should have looked for a more remote lighthouse position. One where supplies needed to be specially shipped in and I wouldn't be bombarded by overly friendly townspeople.

Then, I would be totally alone.

A tall man appeared in front of me and I shrieked. My breaths were ragged and I clutched my chest before realizing it was Hank, the elderly bookstore owner I'd seen around town.

"Oh, hello," I said weakly.

He lifted his chin at me, a faint scent of old books wafting in my direction. "You're the new girl."

His voice was gruff. Grumpy.

I nodded.

"Name's Hank. I own this store."

"Yes," I said.

I groaned internally. This was why I hated talking to strangers. Everything inside me froze up, preventing me from forming a complete sentence.

When I said nothing further, he asked, "Are you here to buy or just take up space?"

My throat tightened and all I could do was blink. Why was I like this? Why couldn't I just say *yes, I want a book*?

"I don't have time for this," he muttered. "My hip says a storm is coming."

I glanced down at his cane. His hip was right. The forecast was calling for bad weather.

I took a deep breath, trying to compose myself enough to speak, but the words wouldn't come. My cheeks grew even redder until I couldn't handle it anymore. I spun on my heel and booked it for the front door. It was fine. It didn't matter that my e-reader had broken and all I had at my cottage was a stack of nautical books left by the former lighthouse keeper. It didn't matter that my favorite author had just released a new book. All that mattered right now was getting home.

The wind whipped my hair as I emerged back onto the street, another sign that the storm was fast approaching. My hands shook as I fumbled with my bike chain that had popped off again. My eyes burned with tears and that, more than anything, told me an episode was starting. Darkness plucked at the edges of my soul, ominous and exhausting. Maybe if I just ignored it, it would go away.

"Olive!" A bright voice called my name just as I got the chain back on its track. My heart pounded as I looked over my shoulder. A smiling blonde woman who looked to be close to my age was sprinting towards me, her pale green dress rippling in the wind. "I can't believe I ran into you! I've been dying to meet you!"

I pushed up from my crouched position.

"I'm Lucy," she said, panting heavily as she came to a stop in front of me. A wave of her bright spring floral scent washed over me, telling me she was an omega.

"Hi," I mumbled.

"Whew, I need to do more cardio. I hate that I haven't introduced myself before now. I'm the head of the Starlight Grove Welcoming Committee! I stopped by your house a couple of weeks ago, but you must not have been home."

Or I'd heard the knocking on my door, panicked, and hid in my nest.

I was so pathetic.

"Oh, yeah. Sometimes I'm up in the lighthouse and can't hear," I said.

Lucy's smile never faltered. "Of course! I think it's so cool we have an omega lighthouse keeper. We all loved Fredrik and Carina and were devastated when they passed, but I'm so happy such an amazing person has taken their place."

My brow furrowed. She didn't even know me. Why would she say I was amazing?

"Do you have a minute?" she continued. "I'd love to buy you a coffee and welcome you to Starlight Grove."

"Well..."

I trailed off, and Lucy seemed to take my non-answer as a yes. She looped her arm with mine and set off for the coffee shop across the street. She effortlessly carried the conversation, telling me about the history of the town and all the gossip about the shop owners, not seeming to mind or even notice how stilted my answers were.

"What would you like? My treat," Lucy asked once we were at the front of the line.

What I really wanted was a pumpkin spice latte, but I hated when people made comments about my scent, so I typically just got plain coffee. Although, I was wearing a new industrial-strength deodorant. The name had made me roll my eyes—*No-NonScent Deodorant*—but it seemed to be doing its job. It had better, since it cost double the generic drugstore one I usually bought.

"Just a regular coffee," I mumbled.

"Are you sure? The pumpkin spice lattes here are incredible. I dream about them. I've tried everything to get them out of season, but they refuse." She fixed the cute beta barista with a glare, but the girl just grinned back. "Just try it," Lucy said. "If you hate it, you can have your coffee." Her tone made it clear that plain coffee was a travesty.

Thanks, Lucy, that's really kind of you. You're right, coffee tastes like dirt and I hate it. But "Um, sure," was all I could say in response.

We found an empty table in the corner and sat down with our lattes. I took a sip and in that moment, my life changed. I swear to god, I perfumed a bit.

"I told you," Lucy said, triumphant. "Best thing you've ever tasted, right? I've tried to recreate the recipe at home, but nothing ever gets close."

"It's really good," I said, hiding my smile behind another sip.

"You have to meet my friends Ivy and Summer. They're omegas, too. We all grew up here and sort of knew each other, but weren't in the same grades. But we all made our way back here as adults and are besties now. And, as an omega, you're officially a part of our group now. We just need a great group name."

I blinked. Lucy wanted me to be part of her friend group? When all I'd given her was blank stares and a dozen choked out words?

"Oh, and my brother, Lars, lives on Main Street," Lucy said, looking out the window as if he would materialize out of thin air. "He's thirty-one and single." She turned back to me with a twinkle in her eye. "If you're into alphas."

An image of Easton's face floated in front of me until I blinked it away. I made a noncommittal noise.

"I get it," Lucy said with a sigh. "Most of the time, they're more trouble than they're worth. But Lars is a good guy. Even though he always stole the last piece of cake growing up."

Just then, the coffee shop door flew open and Marisol walked in. "It's getting chilly out there," she said, unwinding her neon green scarf. "My knee's been acting up all day."

"Oh, that means a storm must be coming," Lucy said, giving me a conspiratorial look.

Marisol waved at Lucy and made a beeline for us. "Lucy, doll, I was hoping I would run into you. Have you seen Felix? I barely see him around these days and I'm getting worried."

Lucy frowned. "Now that you mention it, I haven't. But we have a town meeting coming up."

"That's right," Marisol said. "I'll give him a good talking-to after the meeting. He can't just vanish like this and think we won't worry about him."

I had no idea who Felix was, but right now I was more focused on getting home than asking questions. I wanted to enjoy this time with Lucy. The idea of having friends was tantalizing. But even sitting here, in this cute cafe, surrounded by cheerful people, I could feel it coming on—the edge of darkness looming over my mood, trying to sink its tendrils inside me.

I took a big gulp of my latte. "I should probably get going if it's going to rain."

Lucy's face fell, and her disappointment looked so genuine. "Of course. I'm sure you want to get back before the rain starts. Let's set up a better time to hang out! And the welcome committee still needs to bring your basket."

I smiled and nodded as I said goodbye to Lucy and Marisol, my expression plastic. By the time I got to my bike, the rain had started, pelting my face and chilling my skin on the ride back to the lighthouse.

My depression rolled in with the storm clouds, and I quickly headed inside, pulled all the curtains, and dragged my favorite blankets into my nest. I would head up to the lighthouse watch room in a bit to monitor the storm. Just as soon as I worked up the energy.

A pit of loneliness swallowed me up like a gaping hole in my chest as I prepared to spend the next few days in darkness. My mom used to sit with me during my dark days, braiding my hair and telling me stories of mermaids. But she was gone, and I could never ask anyone else to be with me when I was like this. Could never bring them down into this despair with me. The fantasy of forming a pack with someone like Easton, or even going on a date with him, was just that: a fantasy.

I scrubbed a tear from my cheek and closed my eyes, pulling the blankets tighter around me.

5

LARS

"ALL I'M SAYING IS SOMETHING IS GOING ON WITH HIM," Finn said as I pushed open the door to Beans 'n Bliss. "He's been to the market twice this week. Since when does he go grocery shopping? Or care about deodorizing the fridge? Like, what the fuck is that?"

I just grunted as we stepped out of the drizzling rain. I was pretty sure the root of Easton's distraction for the past few weeks was a crush. He was acting like a love-sick puppy, and it filled me with dread. Was he trying to pursue someone without Finn and me? Was he... considering leaving our pack for a woman? I shoved the thought aside. It was impossible to think he would ever consider it. We were a family.

But that part of me who worried I wasn't doing a good enough job leading our pack poked and prodded at my chest.

I didn't say any of this out loud, though. Better to wait and confirm my suspicion.

The weather had driven everyone inside. We waited in the slow-moving line, Finn grumbling about Easton the whole time.

When we finally got to the counter, it hit me.

Pumpkin spice.

Rich, mouthwatering sweetness with a sharp edge of coffee.

The same scent I'd smelled six years ago, that had haunted me ever since.

I stumbled and gripped the counter. My alpha roared and I whipped my head around, trying to find the omega who the scent belonged to. The coffee shop was bustling—young people with laptops getting work done, older couples sharing an afternoon coffee together, a small playgroup of moms with their babies laughing in the corner. My heart pounded. She wasn't here. *Again.* I couldn't handle losing her a second time. Wouldn't.

Finn smacked my arm, and I jolted. "What's going on? I've been talking to you. It's our turn to order."

I faced him and gripped both his shoulders, hard. "Pumpkin spice."

Finn raised his eyebrows as he glanced down at where I was holding him. "Umm, didn't know that was your drink, but sure." When I didn't release him, he added, "You good, bro?"

"I smell her," I said urgently. "Pumpkin spice. The omega from all those years ago."

Finn looked around skeptically before turning back to me. "You do know this entire coffee shop smells like pumpkin spice?"

Hope soared in my chest. "You scent her, too?"

He shoved my arms off him. "It's the signature drink." He gestured at the decorative sign on the wall with a dancing pumpkin on it.

"No, you don't understand." My eyes were wild as I scanned the cafe again. I whipped my head to the door. She must have left. I would follow her scent until I tracked her down and convinced her that she was mine, *ours.*

Finn's shout followed me out the door. I took off down the street, my shirt quickly growing wet as the rain came down harder. I spun around, my heart pounding. The incoming storm masked all the scents in town, leaving nothing but damp earth. The street was empty. I wanted to knock on every door in town until I found her, but even through my panicked haze, I understood that would be inappropriate.

I trudged back to the coffee shop, not caring that I was soaked.

Had it all been a figment of my imagination? My alpha snarled. *No.* The scent had been faint, but it had been there. There was no way my mind could make up something so perfect.

Finn was standing under the coffee shop's striped awning, a pinched expression on his face. "Here's your omega," he said dryly, handing me a pumpkin spice latte.

I fought the urge to throw it in his face. "You're not taking this seriously," I growled. I wanted to roar at the sky. How dare the universe be so cruel to dangle my omega in front of me again?

"Taking what seriously, Lars? You've been obsessed with some omega you scented *once* years ago. You never even *saw* her. And now you're chasing a ghost around town? What am I supposed to do with that?"

I bit my tongue, unwilling to say anything hurtful to my brother. Finn and Easton were my world. I loved my family, but these two were the brothers I had chosen. We had built a life together, a business, and had dreamed of bringing an omega into our pack. But things had felt shaky with us for a while. Finn had been struggling these past six months since his grandparents died, and Easton was a distracted mess. I'd felt unsettled in my role as head of the pack, but all that vanished now. Scenting the omega I lost years ago filled me with certainty as we headed home. The universe had sent her back to me, to *us*.

And this time, I wouldn't let her get away.

6

EASTON

IT WAS THURSDAY, AND THERE WAS NO SIGN OF OLIVE. I'D been sitting by the living room window for hours, waiting to see the cute omega coming down the road on her bike. The one time I'd had to go to the bathroom, I'd sprinted there and back to make sure I didn't miss her.

But the sun was setting, and she still wasn't here.

I knew how much she bought at the store. It wasn't much—just what she could bring home on her bike. She didn't have enough food to skip her grocery shopping. Memories of staring down an empty pantry as a child flooded me, and my alpha roared for me to go get her. Feed her. Love her.

I waited another few anxious minutes, and then I'd had it. I couldn't go a full week without my Olive sighting. A realization struck me—this was the *perfect* excuse to ask her to dinner. Showing up at her house would show her how committed I was, and taking her to dinner would show her omega I could provide for her.

My chest filled with excitement. This was it, my chance to win Olive over. I could feel it.

I pulled on a jacket and bounded out of the door. I jogged down the path to the lighthouse, even though my body wasn't quite built for running, and I tripped a few times. Was this path even safe for

Olive to bike on? My chest squeezed until it was hard to breathe, but I pushed myself to run faster. Images of Olive being hurt flashed through my mind. What if she'd injured herself, and that's why she hadn't come into town?

I turned around the bend and the lighthouse came into view, along with the silhouette of three figures. For a moment, I thought Olive was in the group, but as I got closer, my heart sank. It was a group of omegas from town—Ivy, Lucy, and Summer. Lucy was Lars's sister, so I knew her the best of the three. As I grew nearer, I saw they were dragging a wagon filled with food and other house-warming gifts.

"Good afternoon, ladies," I said, trying to sound calm. "What are you up to?"

"Oh, hi, Easton," Lucy said, a bright smile on her face. "We're bringing Olive her welcome basket." She bit her lip. "We should have brought it weeks ago when she moved in, but I couldn't quite get it organized in time."

I knew from Lars that Lucy had been going through a lot with her recent breakup.

"What are you doing here?" Summer asked, arching an eyebrow.

I opened my mouth and then closed it. What could I say to avoid sounding like a stalker? "I wanted to ask Olive to dinner," I finally said.

Lucy squealed. "Oh my gosh! Are you interested in her? What about Lars and Finn? Are you planning to court her?"

"He might want to keep that private," Ivy said gently.

Lucy crossed her arms with a huff that made me grin. She shared my impatience.

"I just want to get to know her better," I said. *Liar liar liar* my alpha chanted, but it wasn't like I could say *Olive is mine even though she doesn't know it yet and I'm going to bite her and fuck her and take care of her forever.*

"We should probably get moving before it gets dark," Summer said, eyeing the pink streaks in the sky above the churning ocean.

I hadn't been back to the lighthouse since Finn's grandparents passed away and had forgotten how breathtaking it was out here.

The lighthouse carried so many happy memories. It was where Lars, Finn, and I became a family—those long days swimming and playing at the beach, helping Fredrik with lighthouse maintenance and Carina with the garden.

I hoped Olive found this place as comforting as I did.

I took the wagon and pulled it the rest of the way to the door. Lucy knocked, practically brimming with excitement as she waited for a response.

None came.

Her smile fell a little. "I caught up with her last week in town, and she said sometimes she's up in the lighthouse and might not hear the door." She knocked again, louder this time.

My heart pounded faster. The panic that something catastrophic had happened returned full-force. What if she'd hit her head on a rock? Tripped and broken her ankle? Been taken by a riptide out to sea?

A ferocious *meow* sounded behind the door, and then it slowly creaked open, revealing Olive. I immediately knew something was wrong. Olive was always dressed nicely. I'd never seen her in town without an outfit so fucking cute it made me want to squeeze her body and rumple her perfect little clothes. Today, though, she was wearing baggy sweatpants, her fingers twisting in the cuffs of her sweatshirt. Her hair was limp, she had dark circles under her eyes, and her scent was strong and acidic with distress. My chest seized, and the world seemed to grow dark. There was no sunshine when Olive was unhappy.

Lucy seemed to falter for a moment before smiling widely. "Hey, Oli. I hope we're not disturbing you. We just wanted to bring you your welcome basket." She gestured wildly at the large basket sitting on top of the wheeled cart. "And this is Ivy and Summer. Ivy teaches at the school." When Olive didn't say anything, she continued. "And Summer is a great cook. She added some food to the basket so you know it's going to be good. Not like when I cook." Lucy forced a laugh.

Olive's eyes flickered to my face before she looked down at the ground.

"Oh, and this is Easton," Lucy said, her chipper tone just slightly strained. "He's *not* part of the Welcoming Committee."

Olive's shoulders hunched in even more, and she swallowed hard but still said nothing. The omegas shifted uncomfortably, and Lucy's eyes flitted to mine.

I cleared my throat. "You okay, Olive?" I asked. *Tell me what's wrong, baby. I'll fix it for you.*

Olive took a deep breath. "I'm fine," she said, tone harsh and eyes on the ground. "I just don't need any intrusions."

And with that, she stepped inside and shut the door on us.

A long beat of silence followed as the four of us tried to make sense of what had just happened.

"I'm not going to say 'I told you so,'" Summer said. "Wait, no. Actually, I am. *I told you so.* Not everyone wants a whole welcome committee at their door."

"Was it something I said?" Lucy asked quietly.

Ivy rubbed Lucy's shoulder. "I don't think so. But maybe this was too overwhelming. We can just leave the basket and maybe try another time without a whole group of us." She looked at me, but my eyes were still fixed on the closed door. I was fighting my instincts hard—my alpha was screaming at me to go after Olive.

The omegas left the basket on the doorstep. When I didn't move to leave with them, Lucy spoke up. "Are you coming, Easton?"

I rubbed my neck. "Umm, I think I'm going to stay. Check out the ocean."

Summer arched her eyebrows, and Ivy hid what looked like a smile behind her hand.

"Check out the ocean?" Lucy spoke the words slowly as if they would make more sense that way.

"You know, the waves." I cleared my throat. "Sand." I gestured at the shore.

"Come on, Lucy," Summer said, fixing me with a look that was a little too perceptive for my liking. "How about we get some pumpkin spice lattes?"

Lucy perked up at that and followed her friends down the path, turning to look back at me multiple times until they made it around the bend.

I took a deep breath and turned back to the door. I knocked again, hoping Olive would answer if there were fewer people. But there was still no response.

Helplessness washed over me like the choppy ocean waves. How could I fix whatever was going on with her if she kept the door shut? My heart pounded, and I had to practice the breathing exercises I'd learned in therapy.

Breaking down her door was probably too much, so I forced my feet to head down to the water. I sat down on the large flat rock I'd spent hours on as a kid. I'd even slept on it for a couple of nights when things got too bad at my house. Carina had found me one morning, horrified, and told me I would be sleeping inside with them. No arguments.

I missed her and Fredrik. I wished I could talk to Finn about them, but he shut down anytime I brought them up. I twisted my fingers in my sweater. I just wanted all the people in my life to be happy, would do anything to make it happen.

Stars dotted the sky as the sun sank below the horizon. I sighed and got up, making my way up the path to the lighthouse. My heart leapt when I walked around the front of the house and saw the welcome basket was gone. A smile spread across my face. Olive was inside and had food for dinner.

Maybe gifts were the key to winning her over. Omegas loved presents, at least according to the online articles I'd read. I broke out into a sprint back to town. What could I get her? Definitely more food, and not just the staples she usually got. She deserved all the treats. And what about cozy things? I could get her blankets or even a new jacket for winter. One that smelled like me.

Main Street came into focus, and I tripped as I ran to Lucy's shop, Spring in Your Stitch. She tailored and sewed clothes and was the perfect person to help me find Olive a jacket. I growled when I saw her shop was closed. I whirled around, scanning the street. Almost everything was closed. Damn these small-town hours.

I trudged to the market. At least I could get her food. Omegas liked sweet things, right? I should buy one of everything until I figured out what her favorites were.

The market door opened and Carmen stepped out, her hands full of papers. I quickened my pace so I could hold the door open for her.

"Thanks, honey," she said. "I just remembered I told Stanley I'd get him this paperwork by 5:00 p.m."

"It's almost seven," I said with a wry grin, which Carmen returned.

"It's good for him. Helps him loosen up. I don't know how Harry deals with that man—" Carmen was cut off as Felix darted in front of her, causing her to trip. I threw my arm out to prevent her from falling, but all the papers flew from her hands.

"Felix!" she shrieked. The cat fixed her with a sharp expression, meowed, and ran away.

Carmen huffed as she crouched down to gather the papers. I joined her, chasing after some that the wind was carrying off.

"I don't know what's gotten into Felix lately," she said. "I barely see him in town anymore and now he does this?"

Now that she mentioned it, I hadn't seen Felix around for weeks. He was a Starlight Grove mainstay, keeping a sharp eye on things and selecting one lucky person's house to sleep at each night.

I glanced down at the papers in my hand and furrowed my brow. "Historic Lighthouse Restoration Grant Application?"

"Yeah, we won a government grant to restore the lighthouse. I was surprised your pack didn't apply for it."

"I didn't even know this was a thing." My heart raced, and I could see everything coming together like magic, like *destiny*. "When's the deadline to apply?"

"5:00 p.m. today," Carmen said.

I fixed her with my most charming smile. "Have I mentioned how radiant you look?"

Carmen pursed her lips, but there was a twinkle in her eye. "What, are you interested in applying?"

"You know how much I care about the lighthouse." *But especially the lighthouse keeper.*

Carmen fixed me with a piercing expression as if she could hear my unspoken words. "How about this—I was going to drop these off and head to Rosie's for dinner, but I could inconveniently leave them in my office, forcing me to come back here after dinner to give them to Stanley."

"You are an angel, Carmen." I took all the papers from her hand and ran inside the store to her office.

This was it. I would apply for the grant. We would get it, *of course*. Finn was a literal restoration architect, and Lars and I covered woodwork and electrical.

I started filling out the forms with a shaking hand. I couldn't believe Finn hadn't heard of this application. My pack brothers would be so excited when I told them I won this grant for us, and it would perfectly position them to fall in love with Olive like I had. Then we would be a pack, and everything would be perfect.

7

OLIVE

I HUFFED AS I PULLED ON MY SWEATER. I HATED TODAY.

My calendar app had rudely reminded me of tonight's event: *Town Meeting, 8pm.*

I'd been trying to ignore it ever since that guy—Stanley?—had showed up at my door. He had introduced himself as the mayor of Starlight Grove before telling me that the town had received a government grant for lighthouse restoration, and they would decide which company would get the job at an upcoming town meeting.

I'd told him I would just do the work myself, but he had hand-waved my suggestion. Apparently, I didn't hold the proper qualifications to take on a historical restoration. Which, okay, might be true, but I still hated the idea of anyone entering my space. The restoration was focused on the lighthouse itself, but since my cottage was connected to it, I wouldn't be able to avoid whoever they hired. They would invade my space, get it all dusty and messy, leave their scents lingering around, and probably want to *talk* to me.

I reached for my glass of water on the counter and accidentally knocked it over. Water splashed on the front of my sweater, and bits of glass littered the floor.

Perfect.

When I'd asked if I had to attend the town meeting, Stanley had

sputtered before jumping into a never-ending lecture about community involvement and town pride. I didn't care about any of that—I
didn't *want* to be involved in the community—but he'd also said if I
didn't attend, I wouldn't have any input on which restoration team
they chose. So now I had to drag myself out of the safety of my new
home.

I quickly cleaned up the spilled water and bits of glass, promising
myself I would sweep the floor more thoroughly when I got back. I
locked the door behind me and looked around for Sir Cat. It was
silly, but I wished he was here with me, giving me the courage to face
the townspeople. I hadn't seen him all day and hoped he was okay.
I'd gotten unexpectedly attached to him.

I got on my bike, awkwardly holding a flashlight under my chin.
The path from the lighthouse to town was unlit, and fall's shorter
days meant I would be biking in the dark. It seemed a little ridiculous
that the town was focusing on lighthouse restoration when they
couldn't even be bothered to light this path. I switched the flashlight
to my hand as I made my way into town, clenching my teeth at every
dip and bump in the road. I wasn't afraid of the dark *exactly*. I just
didn't like it.

I let out a sigh of relief as the town lights came into focus. I had
to admit, it was pretty like this. Old-fashioned gas lamps lined Main
Street, and the storefronts were lit up with string lights and decorations for the upcoming Harvest Festival, which just happened to be
on my birthday.

Another day that would just come and go.

My brakes squealed as I parked in front of Town Hall, garnering
curious glances from the people mingling outside. I broke out into a
sweat as I locked my bike. I hated being perceived.

I wrapped my arms around myself and ducked my head as I
entered the building. It wasn't like anyone in town had been mean to
me—quite the opposite—but I felt like I was being constantly
watched. And in my experience, being perceived eventually led to
being judged. How long would the kindness of the Starlight Grove
townspeople last?

The town hall meeting room was already packed at 8:02, so I slipped into an empty row of seats in the back.

Stanley called the meeting to order and launched into the evening's agenda. Most of it had to do with preparations for the Harvest Festival, including arguments on whether they needed a hot chocolate stand and an apple cider stand (in my opinion, *yes*). I focused on keeping my breathing steady, refusing to give into my panic at being surrounded by so many people. Now, an elderly woman named Mrs. Cassini was arguing passionately with a younger beta about what alternatives to grass should be allowed for lawns.

I'd known Starlight Grove was cute and charming from when I visited with my parents, but I hadn't quite realized how involved everyone would be in town things. Growing up on the docks, there had always been a sense of support and camaraderie between the lobstermen. When something happened to one of our own, we rallied. But most days, we kept to ourselves. Spending our days out on the boat, checking traps. Maybe grabbing a quick bite to eat before heading home to shower, sleep, and do it all again. But in Starlight Grove, someone deciding to plant a clover lawn instead of grass was apparently momentous enough to merit a full-town discussion.

I jolted when Stanley banged his gavel. "It's time for our final agenda item of the night. As many of you know, the historic Star Lighthouse has been an essential part of our town for over two hundred years. The lighthouse is a beacon of hope for all those weary souls lost at sea. In the words of the great American poet Henry Wadsworth Longfellow: 'Sail on, ye stately ships! And with your floating bridge the ocean span; be mine to guard this light from all eclipse, be yours to bring man nearer unto man!'"

Stanley ended the reading with his arms raised in the air, voice triumphant. The audience was silent besides some awkward throat-clearing.

The mayor rolled his eyes. "Does no one value poetry anymore?" With a sigh, he continued. "Starlight Grove has been given the *prestigious* honor of receiving the National Historic Lighthouse Restoration Grant for Historic Lighthouses on the Eastern Coast, or

NHLRGHLEC for short. The grant pays for a restoration team to make repairs in the areas of electricity, plumbing, woodwork, and plasterwork to ensure this magnificent beacon of light remains standing for another two hundred years. But before we cast our votes to see who wins this project, let's all give a warm welcome to Olive Autumn Harvest, our new lighthouse keeper!"

All eyes in the room followed Stanley's outstretched arm to the back of the room.

Noooooo.

Death, please take me.

My cheeks burned and sweat trickled down my armpits as I prayed for someone, *anyone*, to wake me from this nightmare.

Movement towards the front of the room caught my eye, and I realized it was Easton. He was standing and waving wildly at me, a huge grin on his face. I wanted to shrink further down in my seat. Not only had I rejected him multiple times, I'd been so freaking rude when he came over with the omegas the other day. I didn't understand why he looked so happy to see me. He should despise me for how I acted.

I despised myself sometimes.

Stanley cleared his throat. "Our fine city council members narrowed down the applicants to two businesses. The first is Legacy Corporation out of Briar's Landing." There was censure in Stanley's voice as he spoke the name of the neighboring town. "The second is our very own Moonlight Restoration company, who apparently have the correct qualifications for this project even though they're hoodlums with a penchant for TP-ing homes, egging cars, and stealing garden gnomes."

My lips twitched in an almost smile, but then Easton stood again and waved at the crowd. "Allegedly," he called out with a chipper smile.

Ohmygod noooo. Easton was on one of the teams? He looked completely unbothered by Stanley's statement as he gave me a wink and sat back down.

I couldn't let this happen. I already got too flustered around him, and my omega was *way* too interested. I couldn't let myself get involved. The more time Easton spent around me, the more he would realize that I was dull and boring. Absolutely not the right one for someone bright and fun like him.

The Legacy Corporation team—composed of two older betas—did a quick presentation focused on their qualifications and how they would source their materials. They came across as a bit pretentious, slipping snide comments about Starlight Grove's crumbling infrastructure into their presentation. Even so, I cast my vote for them—filling out the little paper form and dropping it in the collection bucket at the end of my empty row—before Easton even started his presentation.

Easton didn't have anyone with him as he presented his proposal for the restoration, but apparently there were two other people on his team. He talked about how one of the guys, Finn, had grown up in the lighthouse because his grandfather was the former lighthouse keeper.

Now I felt bad for not voting for them. I chewed my lip, wondering if I should swap out my slips, but my anxiety won out. I was too overwhelmed by the idea of Easton being in my space for weeks on end to complete the extensive renovation. All I'd wanted was to move to a town where no one knew me. Being alone was the only way to avoid heartbreak, and I could see Easton breaking my heart way too easily.

There was a low murmur of conversation as everyone cast their votes. Carmen took all the slips of paper and tallied them up before handing the result to Stanley. A deep frown settled on his face. "People, must we do this *every* time? I'm convinced you're colluding to do this on purpose." He scrubbed his hand over his face. "It seems we have a tie."

The room erupted in excited chatter as everyone peered around as if looking for something. I caught whispers of the name "Felix."

"He's outside, Stanley," Carmen said, a wide grin on her face.

"Open the door, then," Stanley said, looking utterly defeated as he waved his gavel towards the door at the back of the room.

This was all *really* weird.

I turned in my seat as someone opened the back door and in

walked Sir Cat. The anxiety I'd carried all day at his absence eased but was quickly replaced with confusion. He was wearing a plaid bow tie and heading straight to the front of the room. His head swung towards me, and I could have sworn he winked.

"Bring out the cards!" Carmen said, clapping her hands.

A young kid—maybe ten or eleven—rushed out with two laminated cards that said *Option A* and *Option B* in bold letters.

"Thank you for being here, Felix," Carmen said. "We are deciding between two companies for the lighthouse restoration project. The first option is Legacy Corporation, and the second is Moonlight Restoration."

Sir Cat is choosing the restoration company?

I looked around, jaw dropped, to confirm this was *unhinged*, but no one seemed remotely confused. People watched attentively as he peered at the two cards.

Okaaay. I guessed *Felix* was deciding my fate. Maybe this wasn't a bad thing. As sad as it was, Felix knew me better than anyone in town. I'd grown to love him, and he seemed to at least tolerate me.

His head turned, glowing eyes fixed on mine.

Not the alphas. Not the alphas. I tried to send the message to him telepathically. An expression came over him that could only be described as smug. He turned back to the cards and lifted a decisive paw up to Option B. Moonlight Restoration.

My heart pounded as betrayal washed through me. It was ridiculous to feel this way—Felix was a *cat*. He didn't understand what was happening. But as he swaggered back down the aisle, I couldn't help feeling that his actions were intentional. I scowled at his swishing tail as he disappeared through the door.

Stanley banged his gavel, finalizing the decision. Easton stood in his seat, his gaze landing on me, and I couldn't handle it anymore. Couldn't handle any more eyes on me. Couldn't handle more judgement or rejection. My bitter scent broke through my deodorizer, and that finally pushed me to get out.

Felix was nowhere to be seen as I ran out of Town Hall. My hands were shaking as I unlocked my bike.

"Olive!"

A slight whimper slipped through my lips as Easton bounded up to me. My omega wanted to crawl into his arms, and that was exactly why I needed to get away.

"Isn't this exciting?" he asked, grabbing my bike's handlebars to steady it as I stood up.

His massive body was crowding mine, my eyes level with his chest. His broad, muscular chest. God, I wanted to press my face into his button-down shirt and cover myself in his chocolate hazelnut scent. My omega was begging me to climb this alpha like a tree, to invite him into my nest and get his scent everywhere while he had his way with me.

I swallowed hard and breathed in and out of my mouth steadily to stop myself from bursting into tears. I was letting myself fall into a ridiculous fantasy because I was overwhelmed.

"I have to go," I mumbled, grabbing my bike from Easton.

8

EASTON

She was trying to run away from me again.

She pulled a flashlight out of her bag and started biking towards the lighthouse.

I wasn't letting her get away this time. I knew I was being too overbearing, too *everything*, but I could tell Olive was upset about something. She was always standoffish and skittish, but tonight she seemed exceptionally fragile. Whatever deodorant she was wearing masked her scent, but I would bet anything that it was all twisted and bitter right now.

I jogged after her, easily keeping pace. She glanced over at me and her expression made my heart stop. Fuck, Olive looked close to tears. She quickly turned back to the street and biked faster. I wasn't much for cardio, but I would run to the ends of the earth if I were following Olive.

She was fumbling with the flashlight, managing to keep balance as she turned it on and clenched it in her hand.

I swore as I realized why she had it. "There aren't lights along the path."

It wasn't a question, but she gave me a little nod, anyway.

She had been riding back and forth to town in the fucking dark? That was unacceptable. As we neared the small path to the lighthouse, I placed a gentle hand on her shoulder. She inhaled sharply and slowed her pedaling.

"I don't like the idea of you biking in the dark. How about I take the flashlight and run next to you? That way, you don't have to focus on holding it."

She stared straight ahead, but her lower lip trembled as she spoke. "Why would you do that?"

I'd never wanted to hug someone so badly, but I had the feeling that she couldn't handle that kind of affection right now.

"I need to get my workout in," I said. "You know, I was the star cross-country runner of Starlight Grove High."

She blinked, briefly meeting my gaze. "You were?"

I snorted. "Fuck no. I played hookey from gym class as often as I could."

Her lips quirked into an almost-smile.

"I know you don't *need* a knight to rescue you, but just let me pretend. It will make me feel a lot better to know you got home safely." That sounded good, right? Because what I actually wanted to say was, *how about I follow you around at all times and implant a tracker under your skin just in case we ever get separated?*

I was killing this whole *taking things slow* thing.

Olive let out a little huff and it was the cutest fucking sound. "Fine." Her tone didn't give anything away, but I spotted the little smile on her lips and the pink of her cheeks.

I bowed with an exaggerated flourish. "Excellent, my lady. Let us go forthwith."

I took the flashlight from her and pointed it down the pitch-black path. Stanley was going to get an earful about this tomorrow. As I kept pace with Olive, all the times Lars, Finn, and I had run down this path together in our childhood came back to me. I'd forgotten how we'd always had a stash of flashlights to light the way. It hadn't seemed like a big deal back then, but this was *Olive*. She was precious. And she deserved a lit path to her home.

My chest tightened at the thought of my pack brothers. I needed to tell them we'd won the grant.

The grant I had applied for without telling them.

I was sure they would be excited about it. Well, *pretty* sure. That annoying voice of reason in the back of my head said that this wasn't how we ran our business—we made decisions together. But even if they were initially irritated, they would understand once they met Olive. She was perfect for us, the omega we'd been waiting for. This restoration project was going to bring us together, I was convinced of it.

The gentle roar of the ocean waves beckoned us to the lighthouse and we arrived much too quickly. Olive got off her bike and crossed her arms like she was trying to hold herself together.

I tried to give the flashlight back to her, but she didn't take it.

"You need it to get back," she said softly.

My heart was going to explode at her concern for me. "The three of us will come by tomorrow to start planning the restoration. I'll bring the flashlight back then."

She shifted her weight and looked down at the ground. I couldn't stop my eyes from taking in her lush, curvy hips. They would look even better with my fingerprints pressed into them.

I cleared my throat. "Does 11:00 a.m. work for tomorrow?"

She shrugged and nodded at the same time. I caught a hint of her scent—twisted and stressed—and I couldn't stop myself from brushing my fingers down her face. When she didn't move away, I gently tilted her chin up so she met my gaze.

"Sweet dreams, Olive."

Her lips parted and I wanted to kiss her more than anything in the world, but I'd already pushed my luck tonight. I would practice patience for her.

I stepped back, giving her a soft smile, and gestured at the door. She seemed dazed as she unlocked it and slipped inside.

9

LARS

THE TENSION WAS SO THICK IN THE HOUSE, HANGING IN the air like a tangible thing, that it was a relief when we walked out the front door. I took a deep breath, the slightly salty tinge to the air clearing my mind.

Finn was pissed at Easton. For good reason. I loved Easton, but he could bulldoze over the people in his life. Sometimes it was the necessary push we needed to do something, but this time he had overplayed his hand. Finn's face was fixed in a permanent scowl, but his expression masked the deep hurt I knew he was feeling. Finn had been heartbroken when his grandparents died. He hadn't been back to the lighthouse since his grandpa passed, and now he was returning, but not on his terms.

I clasped his shoulder and gave it a squeeze, trying to lend him some support, but his body remained rigid. I removed my hand with a sigh.

What could have possessed Easton to bid on the grant? Historic restoration jobs were competitive, but we weren't hurting for money. Besides, Easton was the worst person in the world with a budget. Last week, he'd come home from his now-frequent market trips with four types of name-brand ice cream. No, this move had been motivated by something else.

Finn trudged slightly behind me, as if he were being led to his execution.

I wasn't thrilled Easton had pulled this either—we were supposed to be a team, and he had decided without us. But I loved the lighthouse and was excited about this project. I had happy memories there, of visiting Fredrik and Carina, and there was no one more qualified to do this restoration than my brothers and me. Certainly not anyone who cared as much as we did.

For all of Finn's anger, he never would have been happy with anyone else doing this restoration. He was too lost in his grief to have willingly applied, but he would have been heartbroken to know someone else was doing the job. And in that way, Easton had given him a gift.

We turned the bend and the lighthouse came into view, stretching high to the sky. There was a slightly rusted bike leaning against the cottage, and I recognized it as the one I had learned to ride on. Shit, that was over two decades ago. There were new flowers in the flower boxes under the windows, and the tension in my chest eased. I didn't know anything about the new lighthouse keeper, but they were taking care of the house, and that mattered to me.

Easton was practically vibrating in anticipation as he waited for us to catch up to him at the front door. He beamed at me before knocking.

I strained my ear to see if I heard any rustling or movement from inside, but there was nothing.

A few tense moments passed, and Easton knocked again.

Still no response.

Finn huffed, arms crossed. "Glad to see how seriously she takes this."

Easton's smile fell. "Maybe she just got the times mixed up. Or she could be around the back?"

The three of us walked around the cottage to the lighthouse entrance, but the door was closed. I could feel Finn's rising agitation.

"Maybe today isn't the right day," I said, glancing between a crestfallen Easton and an angry Finn. "We can arrange to come back another..." I trailed off as Finn spun around and stormed back to town.

"Her phone number isn't on the information form we got," Easton said. "But maybe she's in town and just lost track of time. I'm going to go see."

Before I could say anything, he was already jogging back down the path.

Well, that went about as poorly as expected.

I didn't have it in me to follow my brothers, so I headed down to the beach. We'd been so busy the past year with restoration projects that I'd barely had time to just *be*. Every step closer to the water soothed me—the sound of the waves, the salt in the air. The coast was rocky here, but still beautiful.

My booted feet hit the hard-packed sand as I strode down to a little cove I used to go to when I was younger. Except, as I approached, I saw someone else sitting on the large, flat rock. As I got closer, I realized it was a woman. She wore a large charcoal gray sweater, her arms tight around her bent knees. Even under the sweater, I could see how deliciously curved she was. I clenched my jaw. I was not going to be a creep and approach this woman with a hard-on. I turned around to leave when I caught a hint of it on the wind—pumpkin spice. I whirled back around, my heart pounding so hard I could barely stay upright.

She was here. The omega from all those years ago.

And she was staring at me.

A strangled sound I was sure I had never made before emerged from me, and she bit her lip, looking anxious.

Fuck.

I needed to get my shit together. Put her at ease.

"Hey there!" I said with a chipper wave.

Hey there??? What the fuck was that? And why was I waving like I'd only just discovered I had arms?

"Um, hello," she said softly.

She didn't look like she was going to run away—at least not yet —so I continued my slow walk towards her. The closer I got, the more I could see how perfect she was. Her dark brown hair was a mess in the ocean breeze. Her bangs framed her dark eyes and golden skin. My eyes flitted to her plump pink lips before I ripped them away and forced myself to look out at the ocean.

I swung my arms at my side. "Nice waves we're having today."

Fucking kill me.

Now I was the one about to run away in fear. I was making the worst possible first impression on the perfect omega who had only been the sole focus of my dreams for the past six years.

A smile tugged at her lips. "Yes, very nice waves."

I couldn't stop staring at that little curve of her lips. It wrecked me. *Destroyed* me. Any other goal in life I'd ever had was gone and was now replaced with the need to see this omega smile every day for the rest of my life.

I cleared my throat. "I'm Lars." I stepped close enough to extend my hand. Her small one slipped into mine, and a wave of calm washed over me. Then I frowned. "Your hand is freezing."

She shrugged her shoulders. "They're always cold."

My alpha hated that. I quickly took off my light jacket, wishing I'd brought mittens...and a hat, scarf, and blanket.

The omega's mouth fell open as I wrapped my jacket around her.

"Oh, you don't need to do that." She went to take the jacket off, and I stilled her hand.

"Tuck your hands under the jacket." I tried to keep my tone light, but her slight shiver told me I'd failed. "If you want," I added in an awkward mumble.

There was a pink tinge to her cheeks as she tucked her hands under my coat. "Thanks." She chewed her lip, looking uncertain for a moment before she spoke again. "Do you want to sit down?"

The rock she was sitting on was a pretty good size, but I would still crowd her on it.

I sat down.

My thigh pressed against her leg, and I held my breath to see if she would move away or show any other signs of discomfort.

"I'm Olive, by the way." She was looking out at the water but didn't seem uncomfortable.

It would be so easy to put my arm around her. Pull her into my lap. Of course I wouldn't, but I could imagine how soft and perfect she would feel against me.

"Are you here for vacation?" I asked.

"No. I'm actually the new lighthouse keeper."

God, if I had more than one functioning brain cell in her presence, this would have been obvious. Everything was making sense now. Olive was the woman Easton had been secretly obsessed with, the reason he'd applied for this job. I'm sure he was convinced we would all fall in love with Olive the moment we met her, and he would be fucking correct.

"I should have guessed that," I said.

She met my gaze, surprise on her face. "Yeah? I feel like most people don't think an omega is the right person to run a lighthouse."

I shrugged. "Don't know what designation has to do with it."

I was rewarded with a real smile, and I swear my heart skipped a beat.

I meant it. Of course omegas could do anything they wanted. My sister and moms proved that. But the idea of her being isolated from town in the lighthouse put my alpha on edge.

"I'm actually one of the guys on the restoration team."

Her smile disappeared and she turned back to the waves. "Oh, right. Did you come looking for me so I could unlock the door?"

Her scent soured with something like shame and I fucking hated it. I couldn't stop myself from putting my hand on her shoulder.

"Nah, I came out here because I didn't really feel like working today."

She kept her face hidden.

Shit.

"Was there a reason you weren't there?" I asked gently.

She shrugged. "I'm sorry. We can reschedule."

"Hey," I said, gently touching her face and tilting her chin towards me. "I'm not upset."

Her eyes met mine—deep and dark. "I'm not good with strangers in my space," she whispered.

My heart ached. Olive was *shy*. Of course it would be overwhelming to move to a new place and have three alphas immediately in her space.

"Good thing I'm not a stranger now."

She swallowed hard, but her scent turned sweet again.

"And I think you've already met my packmate, Easton?"

The blush on her cheeks was back. "We don't really know each other," she said. "I've just seen him at the market."

I couldn't stop a grin from spreading across my face. Another mystery solved. Easton must really care about her if he had tried this hard to restrain himself. It made sense, though. Olive was skittish. I could picture her leaping into the ocean and turning into a mermaid if she got overwhelmed.

And I'd fucking follow her. Even if it meant drowning.

10

OLIVE

Growing up in a fishing family meant early mornings. During peak lobster season, we were on the boat by 3:30 a.m. every day. Night owl, I certainly was not.

But tonight, I couldn't fall asleep. My mind kept flitting to those brief minutes with Lars on the beach. I'd ended up running away from him because, apparently, that was what I did when faced with amazing-smelling alphas who showed any sort of interest in me.

His scent was all pine and bonfire, earthy and masculine like the alpha himself. I'd had to stop myself from climbing into his big lap and running my hand through the strands of blond hair escaping his bun.

He'd made me feel instantly safe.

I clung to my bike handles as I navigated the dark path into town, hoping no one would be around this late. I needed something to drown out my omega, who kept shouting at me to track down Easton and Lars, scent mark them, pull them into my nest, and then sit on their knots. I'd tried distracting myself by re-reading one of my favorite romances, but the love interest was an alpha who reminded me of Easton, and I'd put the book down. There hadn't been a TV in the house when I moved in and I didn't have the money to buy one yet. So here I was, parking my bike by the Hollywood Cinema at 9:30

p.m. I'd seen on the sign outside the theater that they did a late-night showing for $3, so I thought it just might be the perfect distraction.

The small lobby was lit when I walked in, and I was hit with the overwhelming smell of movie theater popcorn, but it was completely empty. A small sign announced that the owners weren't about to stay up late and to drop money for tickets and concessions into a small box sitting on the counter.

The sign brought a smile to my lips. It reminded me so much of the grumpy lobstermen I grew up with and the sense of trust we had in our small community.

I pulled a couple of crumpled bills out of my pocket. I bit my lip, wondering if I should splurge on popcorn and soda. It was only another $3. I decided to go for it, dropping my money in the box and helping myself to the concessions before heading into the small theater room.

I let out a little happy squeak when I saw it was empty, not quite believing my luck. I'd never heard of the movie that was showing tonight—*Beyond the Bleachers*—but I wasn't very up to date on my pop culture. I settled back in my seat as the pre-movie trailers started playing.

11

FINN

THE DOOR OF THE HOUSE SLAMMED CLOSED BEHIND ME AS I stormed down Main Street.

If I stayed inside for one more second, I would murder Easton.

I still couldn't fucking believe he'd done this. The three of us had run our business together for years. We didn't make decisions without consulting each other, and certainly nothing on this scale. He'd applied for, and accepted, a massive government project that would take weeks, if not *months,* to complete.

I headed down the empty street with no destination in mind.

After our disastrous visit to the lighthouse this morning, Easton had returned home, discouraged that he couldn't find the lighthouse keeper. I'd lost my shit on him, yelling that this was not how we ran the business. Lars had stepped in and told me to calm down. In that moment, I wanted to punch Lars, too. I'd escaped to my room, and that's where I'd stayed the rest of the day.

I was embarrassed by my behavior. Easton was particularly sensitive to yelling. What he'd done was wrong, but he didn't deserve that. It was just easier to yell than admit I was fucking devastated to have to witness, up close, someone else living in the lighthouse.

The town had offered me the lighthouse keeper position after my grandpa passed, but I had a job, a business to run, and... I'd been scared of what it would be like to live there without my grandparents. Would it always feel like their ghosts wandered the halls? Now I felt like I'd let him down. Someone else was in their space, in *my* home, and there was nothing I could do about it.

I didn't understand why Lars wasn't as angry about the situation as I was, but he'd returned from the lighthouse in a surprisingly good mood. And that just made it worse. I was alone, even in my own pack.

I wasn't ready to talk to either of them, but I was going stir-crazy in my room, hence the current wandering around the quiet town.

The illuminated marquee of the Hollywood Cinema caught my eye. I was just in time for the 10:00 p.m. showing. Hopefully a movie would help me calm down so we could all have a more productive conversation tomorrow.

I headed inside, threw some money in the box in the lobby, loaded up on a shit-ton of snacks, and headed into the theater to watch whatever atrocious film Missy and Herbert had dug up. I'd never known people with such a talent for finding borderline-unwatchable movies.

The previews were already playing when I entered. I came to an abrupt stop when I saw a lone woman sitting right in the middle of the theater.

In my favorite seat.

I was about to turn around and walk out—I didn't want to be around anyone right now—when the woman spotted me, let out a little startled squeak, and knocked over her full bag of popcorn.

Her soft "oh no" reached my ears, and she sounded so distraught I couldn't leave. My alpha, who'd been dormant for a while, perked up as I moved to her row. I set down my large popcorn bucket and stack of candy boxes.

"Sorry for startling you. Let me help you with that."

The woman was trying to pick up the spilled popcorn but paused to look up at me. The light from the screen illuminated her face, and my heart skipped a beat. She was stunning. My mouth grew dry, and in the back of my mind, I knew I was looming over her and should move, but my feet were rooted to the spot.

She straightened up, hands filled with popcorn. "Oh, it's not your fault. I'm just clumsy." She laughed a bit, but it sounded forced. "Is there a broom or something I could use to clean this up?"

My brain couldn't quite catch onto what she was saying. Nothing mattered when the most gorgeous woman was in front of me. I couldn't catch any trace of a scent—not for lack of trying; I was a fish gasping for air—but I was pretty confident she was an omega.

"A broom?" she asked again, shifting slightly from side to side. The light from the movie screen dimmed, and I couldn't fully take in the shape of her round hips and stomach and breasts, and I held in a growl. I wanted to see her in the brightest light so I could take in her every curve, every freckle, every strand of hair.

She met my gaze. Did she feel the connection, too? The electricity in the air between us?

"Or not?" She broke eye contact and put the bits of popcorn into her small popcorn bucket.

Fuck. She'd asked me a question. I furiously tried to get my brain functioning again.

"There's a broom out in the lobby," I blurted out. "I'll grab it for you. I know where the supply closet is."

I practically sprinted away, my alpha clawing at my chest with every step. I was breathing heavily by the time I located the supply closet and pulled out the broom and dustpan. No one had ever made me feel this off-kilter. The strength of my feelings made me want to keep running straight out the door, and at the same time, urged me to wrap that little omega up in my arms and pull her to my chest so no one could ever take her away from me.

The broom handle snapped in my hand, and I swore. I needed to get myself under control.

She was just a woman. An omega. This wasn't a big deal.

I kept a measured pace as I returned to the theater. The woman went to take the broom from me, but I didn't want her to comment on the broken handle, so I quickly swept up the popcorn.

"Thanks," she said, her voice practically a whisper. Did I make her uncomfortable? Should I leave?

Just then, a loud sound burst from the speakers and the screen showed the movie's title.

"It's starting," I said unnecessarily.

We both stood, staring at each other for what felt like approximately three hours before the woman sat down. Should I sit next to her? Or move far, far away? She probably didn't want company.

I sat in the seat next to hers.

"You can have my popcorn," I said.

"Oh, no, that's okay."

I placed the bucket in my lap so she could reach it if she wanted. All my muscles were stiff, but not with irritation. I'd wanted privacy tonight, but now I was having to hold myself back from getting to know this omega... from touching her.

I focused on the film instead of the storm of emotions inside me. Two high school sweethearts broke up to go to college. Years later, they were meeting back up at the school to see if they could make their relationship work. I munched on the popcorn as the couple on the screen started making out under the football bleachers. I definitely did *not* allow my mind to imagine what it would be like to kiss the cute stranger beside me.

The production quality was shit, but this was definitely the most *normal* movie I'd ever watched in this theater.

Famous last words.

Flashing lights filled the screen as something descended onto the couple with a loud mechanical noise. The screen went black, and then an alien appeared. A group of green aliens. I furrowed my brow in confusion, but I should have known. Herbert and Missy were incapable of showing a normal rom-com.

The head alien told the couple that the only way they could be together was if they went back in time and never broke up in the first place. If they didn't, the world would explode in three days. I scrubbed my hand down my face. Who even made these movies?

The couple agreed to go back in time, and then the aliens broke out into a fully choreographed dance with song.

"What the fuck is happening?" the woman whispered, and that

broke the tension between us. I let out a bark of laughter and settled back in my seat.

"The movies here are always unhinged." I held out my large popcorn bucket, and she took a handful. "Candy?"

"Yes, please." She also relaxed back in her seat, putting her legs up on the chair in front of her as she ate some Junior Mints. Satisfaction ran through me that I had provided for her.

She started humming along to the alien's song. "This is pretty catchy."

I laughed again. My chest felt bright and light... and I realized I was *happy*. The past six months, my chest had been so heavy with grief I'd forgotten what happiness felt like... had stopped believing I would ever feel it again.

The couple in the movie was rocketing through space until they landed back at their high school. "You think they're going to save the world?" I asked.

"With dancing skills like that? Probably not."

I snorted out another laugh, and this time, it was my popcorn flying all over the place.

"We can't be trusted with popcorn," she said as she grabbed another handful.

The movie continued to devolve into something increasingly incomprehensible, but I loved her snarky commentary. Every time I moved, my shoulder brushed against hers, and it made me feel like I was on fire. And then a weight rested on my shoulder. I glanced down and saw the omega had fallen asleep curled up on her chair. I slowly shifted down so my shoulder was a better angle for her to rest on. It wasn't very comfortable with the armrest digging into my ribs, but I didn't care. I would stay frozen in this position all night just to watch her sleep. Her eyelashes were dark and long, her cheeks pink and round. I could picture myself running my hand through her hair, kissing her face, and tucking her into my bed.

My chest turned cold at the intimacy of the fantasy, and I shifted away from her. I'd decided six months ago that I would never bond an omega. I'd always wanted a love like my grandparents had, but after seeing what it was like for my grandpa at the end, I knew I couldn't do it. Easton and Lars still wanted an omega and to be a true pack, but it was becoming more clear to me that I wouldn't be a part of it. Bonding an omega was too risky.

She startled as I moved her off my shoulder and sat up straight, cheeks flushing red. "Sorry." She rubbed her face. "I usually go to bed a lot earlier than this."

"No worries," I choked out. Fuck, why had I done that? Now I wanted her head back on me. I wanted her entire body on me.

"Did I miss much?" she asked.

I blinked. I hadn't been paying the slightest bit of attention to the movie.

"No," I grunted.

I turned my focus back on the screen. The couple was being torn apart by the space-time continuum. I scrunched my face as the camera and boom mic appeared in the frame.

The thought of saying goodbye to the omega after the movie seemed... unacceptable. Maybe she would be open to a casual hookup?

"Oh good, another song."

I hid my grin behind another mouthful of candy. My movie partner was funny. She bopped back and forth as the aliens and couple did a dance. Then she jumped and let out a little squeak as an explosion erupted, turning everything dark and gray. Words displayed across the screen: *Not every mistake can be fixed.*

"The end?" the woman shrieked, sitting forward in her seat. "That was the end?" She turned to me, lips parted in shock.

"I'm guessing this is your first time watching a movie here?" She nodded as she fished out the last of the Junior Mints. "One thing you can count on is that every movie at the Hollywood Cinema will be the most bizarre thing you've ever seen. Missy and Herbert are staunchly against showing anything resembling a Hollywood movie."

She let out an adorable snort. "Interesting choice of theater name."

I grinned. Having her eyes on me was like magic. The lights were dim as the credits played, and the air between us was electric.

Nothing felt real in here. It was just me and her, wrapped in the darkness as dramatic electronic music played.

I wasn't sure who moved first, but then our lips crashed together. Her fingers gripped my shirt, trying to pull me closer, and my hand cupped the back of her neck. I growled at the armrest keeping us apart. I gripped her waist, lifting her to place her on my lap. Her core pressed against my hard cock, and we both let out a moan.

"You need this, sweetness?" I asked as she ground against my hard-on.

She let out a sweet little moan. "What can I say? Aliens and the end of the world get me really hot."

I pressed my smile into her throat. My mouth watered with the urge to bite her, mark her as mine, and I pulled away quickly. This was an anonymous hookup, nothing more. I wouldn't let my alpha instincts push me into something I didn't want.

I tugged on her leggings as she unzipped my pants. We were a flurry of desperate movements and gasping breaths. Her small hand surrounded my cock right as my fingers sank into her heat, and we both groaned.

"So fucking drenched," I gasped.

"All for you. Well, you and the aliens."

I snorted a laugh but was quickly cut off as she squeezed my dick, spreading precum down my shaft. I was going to come embarrassingly quickly but refused to come before she did. I roughly thrust two fingers inside her, curving them until I hit her omega spot. She cried out, throwing her head back, and fuck, she was beautiful. My other hand gripped her hip, my fingers digging in tight as I rocked her in a steady rhythm.

"That's it, ride me, pretty girl."

I swore as she ran her thumb along the tip of my cock, pleasure shooting through me like lightning.

She was whimpering now, grinding her clit against the palm of my hand as she continued working my cock, and then she let out the sweetest cry, her pussy gripping my fingers hard. Her eyes were closed, lips parted, and she looked like an angel as her orgasm washed over her in waves. Seeing her come pushed me over the edge, pleasure rocking through me with my release. I soaked her hand and the front of her sweater in my cum.

My alpha was fucking thrilled that she was marked with our scent.

She collapsed into my chest, and we lay there, breathing hard. My fingers were still inside her, and I didn't want to pull them out. My other arm was wrapped around her back, keeping her tight to me. A burst of sweetness filled my senses, complex and spicy and mouthwatering. In my post-orgasm haze, it took me a minute to identify the scent: pumpkin spice.

The omega pulled back enough to meet my gaze, her expression soft as a smile played on her lips, but I felt like I was going to throw up.

This was just my fucking luck. Here I was, trying to have a casual hookup with a woman, and she happened to be the omega Lars had been obsessed with for years. He would want us to be a pack, and I just *couldn't*. The presence of this omega in our town meant the end of my pack life with my brothers. They would choose her over me. I'd known this outcome was inevitable. I just didn't realize it would happen so soon.

I pulled my fingers out of her. I wanted to lick her slick off them, but resisted, reaching down instead to grab a crumpled napkin. She must have sensed the change in mood because she moved off my lap, pulling up her leggings.

I busied myself with picking up my trash, doing my best not to look at her, but I still caught her wiping up my cum with some napkins. Her scent was fading, but what lingered in the air had a bitter note to it. My alpha urged me to fix it, to pull her into my arms and take her home. Instead, I looked around to make sure I had all my trash.

I cleared my throat. "It was nice meeting you." And then I fucking fled like a coward.

12

OLIVE

THE LIGHTS IN THE MOVIE THEATER CAME ON AND I WAS still standing there, holding cum-soaked napkins.

I didn't understand what had changed. The alpha had seemed to be into what we were doing... into *me*. But his abrupt departure left me cold and unsure.

This was only what I deserved after I'd run away from Easton and Lars. At least, that's what I told myself as I got on my bike, feeling decidedly wobbly. I'd had anonymous hookups before, but none of them had left me feeling like this.

It didn't matter that the alpha didn't want anything more with me.

It didn't matter.

Didn't matter.

Tears blurred my vision as I made my way down the unlit path home.

13

LARS

Finn's footsteps sounded on the stairs and then he slipped into the kitchen, heading straight for the coffeepot and pointedly avoiding looking at me.

I leaned back in my chair, staying quiet as I sipped my coffee. Finn would speak when he was ready.

Finally, he ran out of things to pretend to add to his coffee and turned to me.

"Where's—" Something caught in his throat and he paused to clear it, taking a sip of coffee. "Where's Easton?"

"He ran out to get coffee and breakfast for Olive before we head to the lighthouse."

"Olive?" he asked.

I wanted to roll my eyes but contained myself. The fact that he hadn't been bothered to learn her name was unreasonably irritating to my alpha, who wanted to climb to the top of the lighthouse and shout to the world that she was mine.

"The new lighthouse keeper."

"Right." He looked down at the floor. "I'll apologize to Easton when he gets here."

I nodded slowly. "Good." I took another sip of coffee, wishing it was a pumpkin spice latte. Hopefully Easton remembered to get me one. "He needs to apologize to you, too."

Finn's eyes widened, and I huffed a deep breath. "What he did was shitty. We don't work like that. We're a team."

A flash of emotion crossed Finn's face before he covered it by chugging his coffee. My brothers were a mess. I had to remind myself that they hadn't been as lucky as me growing up. I had four amazing moms who were bonded in a committed pack. Finn's mom had died when he was little. He'd had amazing grandparents in Fredrik and Carina, but he lost them, too. And Easton's parents weren't worth a shit. We'd thrown a party when his mom finally moved out of town.

The front door clattered open, and Easton rushed in. I leapt up to grab the drink carrier out of his hands before he dropped it. Easton had grown about a foot in a month after he revealed as an alpha, and he'd never quite gotten used to his body.

"We should leave," he said. "I don't want to keep Olive waiting." He realized Finn was in the kitchen and froze.

The two of them stared at each other and both said, "I'm sorry" at the same time. Easton threw the bag of pastries aside and pulled Finn into a hug.

"I thought you'd be excited about the grant. I just want you to be happy," Easton said.

"I know," Finn said. "I'm sorry for yelling."

They clapped each other on the back and pulled apart.

"So you're okay with this? If you're really not, maybe we can back out of the contract."

Finn scrubbed his face. "No. You got one thing right—it would kill me to see those idiots from Briar's Landing doing the restoration. I'll get through it."

I snuck a sip of one of the lattes Easton got. He whipped his head towards me and fixed me with a glare. "Those are for Olive."

I raised an eyebrow. "All four of them?"

"I got all four of their specialty flavors. I didn't know which one she'd like best."

I turned the coffee cup to see I had gotten the pumpkin spice latte. Perfection. I took another long sip.

Easton huffed. "Fine, let's just go."

I grabbed the cooler with the lunches I'd packed for us and pulled on my jacket, sticking a pair of mittens in my pocket. Just in case Olive was outside again and got cold.

The sun was shining brightly and there was a light chill in the air as we walked to the lighthouse, but I got overheated quickly. The drawback of being so massive. By the time we got to the front door, I'd pulled off my jacket.

Easton knocked, and this time, the door opened. Olive was there, dressed in a rust-colored sweater that looked more like a crop top. I couldn't stop staring at the little strip of skin between the sweater and her leggings. I wanted to unwrap her like a present.

"I brought you a latte and breakfast," Easton said excitedly, thrusting the drinks and bag of pastries at her. I'd put the pumpkin spice latte back in the drink carrier, and my alpha roared when she picked up the cup I'd been drinking out of and took a sip. Her lips touched the exact spot mine had been. Her cheeks turned pink, and she mumbled thank you. Then her eyes flitted to me and her blush intensified.

"These are my pack brothers," Easton said. "Lars and Finn."

Olive's smile fell and her eyes widened when she looked at Finn. She opened her mouth to say something, but before she could, Finn spoke.

"It's nice to meet you."

She blinked, and a blank mask fell over her face. "Right." She turned back to Easton. "I can show you around back?"

An uneasy feeling wormed in my chest. What was going on between her and Finn?

I followed behind our group as Olive led us around the side of the house to the entrance to the lighthouse. Easton was chatting away, unbothered that the shy omega offered only quiet one-word responses. Finn's shoulders were hunched and I wanted to pull him aside to ask what was wrong, but I had a feeling I wouldn't get an honest answer. Maybe I was just imagining the weirdness between them. If coming back here brought up memories for me, I couldn't imagine what it was like for Finn. It had to be hard.

Olive opened the door to the lighthouse and gestured for us to go in.

I scowled. "You should keep that locked. It's not safe to leave it open."

The omega met my gaze with her big brown eyes. I wanted to sink into them. "I just unlocked it because I knew you were coming over."

Easton and Finn disappeared inside the lighthouse. I paused at the entrance and cupped her chin. "Good girl."

Her cheeks pinkened, and I got the slightest whiff of her scent. My chest rumbled with a growl that I didn't even try to cover. I wanted her to know how much she affected me.

We packed inside the base of the lighthouse, the space a little tight with the four of us. These first few days would be all about planning the restoration. The lantern had gone through a major repair about a decade ago, but the interior masonry and woodwork were deteriorating from the salty ocean air.

"We'll start our restoration plan, but we'll make sure to stay out of your way as much as possible," Finn said, eyes fixated on a rusty path on the wall. Olive's shoulders curved in and she crossed her arms.

I narrowed my eyes. Only a lifetime of knowing Finn told me this wasn't his normal standoffishness. My alpha wanted to pin him to the wall and make him be nicer to the sweet omega who was wilting beside me.

Easton was looking between Finn and Olive, obviously catching on to the odd tension in the space.

"I'll just leave you all to it, then," Olive said.

Before I could respond, she slipped through the door that connected the lighthouse to the inside of the cottage.

Easton looked crushed, Finn looked irritated, and all I wanted to do was stand by the door, inhaling deeply in an effort to get Olive's scent.

14

OLIVE

I GROANED WHEN I REPLAYED HOW I'D AWKWARDLY FLED from the three alphas who were currently working inside the lighthouse. Easton, Lars, and *Finn*.

Finn, the large broody alpha with big hands, angular jaw, and dark hair that fell lazily in his face.

Finn, whose fingers had been inside me mere hours ago.

Finn, who had pretended *not to know me*.

My little omega heart was all pathetic and crushed. I'd run to the living room, plopped down in an outdoor chair I'd found in the shed, and wrapped myself in blankets until only my eyes were exposed. My omega wanted to be closer to the alphas... even *him*, which told me everything I needed to know about her judgement.

Last night I'd stripped off my clothes the second I got home, throwing the dirty sweater in the trash.

And then I'd burst into tears.

My omega had panicked, needing the mystery alpha's scent on us. So I'd fished the sweater out of the trash and tucked it into my nest. I didn't want to admit that I'd slept better than I had since I'd moved here, surrounded by the sweet scent of maple candy. Now that alpha was just feet away, separated from me by a single door.

The moment he'd looked me straight in the eye like I was a

complete stranger replayed in my brain, and my tears quickly morphed into fury. How dare he treat me like that? Discard me after he'd gotten what he wanted? My omega was incensed, too. Finally, we were on the same page.

Something vibrated against my leg.

And again.

I groaned when I realized it was my phone. Hardly anyone contacted me except for the occasional scam call or political fundraising text. It took me a minute to free my arm enough to grab it out of my pocket.

> **UNKNOWN NUMBER**
>
> Hi Oli. This is Lucy. I hope it's ok that I got your number from Easton. I wanted to apologize the other day for the welcome wagon.

I stared at the text. It was a group chat, with two other numbers.

> **UNKNOWN NUMBER 2**
>
> Yeah, that was probably really overwhelming.
> (This is Ivy)
>
> **UNKNOWN NUMBER 3**
>
> Did you like the pho?
>
> **LUCY**
>
> ^ that's Summer

I chewed my lip. Why were they texting me? They didn't have to do that. Unless... unless Lucy had been serious when she said she wanted me in their group. To be *friends*. I had no experience with this. I'd always been painfully shy, and kids could be mean. Once I hit third grade, the bullying had intensified. My classmates made fun of me for being quiet. They stole my stuff, shoved me at recess, and laughed at me in class. After coming home crying for weeks in a row, my dad announced he couldn't stand seeing his girl cry for one more second and that I would not be going back. I'd done an online school program, and my parents helped teach me as much as they could. They'd asked several times if I wanted to try school again, but I didn't. Online school allowed me to spend my days on the boat, which was the only place I really wanted to be. But it meant I didn't have practice with real friends.

OLIVE

The pho was amazing. Thank you

After living off instant ramen, the soup Summer made me had literally featured in my dreams.

OLIVE

Also you have nothing to apologize for. I'm sorry I was so rude.

LUCY

Oh my gosh not at all! I just hope you still give us a chance. Omegas need to stick together!

Oh god, that was so nice. Suddenly, a craving to not be alone hit me. It shocked me with its intensity. I'd barely left my crappy studio apartment the past five years, had moved to this lighthouse to be alone, and yet... maybe that's not what I wanted. Was I allowed to change my mind?

I stared at the group chat, anxiety rising in my chest. I needed to say something. Something friend-like. I remembered reading a research study ages ago that said people viewed you as a warmer person if they held a warm beverage while talking to you. Maybe that's why Lucy liked me. She'd had a warm beverage at the coffee shop. But that strategy wouldn't work over text. I did a quick search to get more tips on how to make friends. One article said that you should ask people for a favor. It seemed counterintuitive to me, especially growing up in fishing communities where self-sufficiency was viewed as a strength. But the article said people would feel more connected to you if they did something for you.

OLIVE

I need help p

Shoot. I sent the text before I finished writing it.

LUCY

Oh my gosh what is it? We'll do anything!

OLIVE

Plotting revenge

Our messages came through at the same time, and I cringed. Maybe I should have started with a more normal favor. Fuck, I should have just asked for more pho.

Seconds ticked by without a response and then...

SUMMER

Well this just got interesting. I'm in. What's the revenge?

Okay, that was a promising start. I pushed forward.

OLIVE

I need ideas for how to get revenge on Finn

IVY

Oh no, what did he do?

My cheeks heated, and I wasn't sure what to say. I decided to keep it vague.

OLIVE

We met last night at the late-night movie showing. Today he came to the lighthouse to start the renovation and he pretended not to know me

SUMMER

What a jerk

IVY

That seems unusual for Finn. He's usually really sweet. He's been going through a hard time lately, though

LUCY

That's no excuse to treat Oli like that! We ride at dawn!

OLIVE

Where are we going?

LUCY

lol to revenge land. Ok, I pretty much grew up with Finn since he's been best friends with my brother for ages. He hates pickles and Pride and Prejudice, the movie

IVY

The guys were all in the class ahead of me, but one time we all went on a field trip together and Finn's socks got wet and he had a bit of a meltdown about it

SUMMER

When was that?

IVY

2nd grade. Maybe he's gotten over it by now

LUCY

No one likes wet socks

Visions of me tying Finn to a chair and force-feeding him pickles while I doused his socks with water and played *Pride and Prejudice* at full volume danced before my eyes. The image was equally hilarious and satisfying.

OLIVE

Umm ok. I think I can work with that

SUMMER

If those ideas don't work, we can always just throw him off the top of the lighthouse

I snorted a laugh, my chest feeling lighter than it had in ages.

LUCY

Summer! No murder

SUMMER

Boring

IVY

> We should get lunch sometime. Oli, have you been to Rosie's?

OLIVE

> Not yet

I didn't admit that I'd barely stepped foot in town besides the market.

LUCY

> How about the day after tomorrow?

IVY

> I'm there! We have a half day at school

SUMMER

> I'll be there

OLIVE

> That works for me

That sounded nonchalant, right? Something a normal person would say to a lunch invite.

I let out a startled shout when Felix jumped onto my lap.

"Oh my god, where did you come from?"

He just stared at me, and I frowned.

"I'm mad at you. Those three alphas are here because of you," I hissed.

Felix looked completely unbothered. He nudged my hand until I showed him the group chat with a huff.

"I need revenge on Finn. Something pickle-related."

When Felix stayed silent, I continued. "How am I supposed to trick him into eating pickles? They brought their lunch today. I saw Lars carrying a small cooler. Also, I'm a terrible cook. Although... maybe that's a good thing in this instance."

Felix fixed me with an expression that was a mix between *this girl is helpless* and *must I do everything myself?*

He jumped off my lap and pranced away.

"Okay bye," I said, rolling my eyes.

A few minutes later, I heard shouts outside. I frowned and ran to the window, making it just in time to see Felix. He was a streak of orange and white as he ran past the house towards the water, the cooler in his mouth. Easton ran after him, shouting, until he stumbled on the sand and rolled down the embankment.

My lips twisted in a smile when Easton popped back up the hill, looking sandy but unharmed. Felix had somehow stolen a cooler twice his size and run away with it, all for *me*. I couldn't stay mad at him after that.

I took a deep breath and headed out the door. The three alphas were all outside, peering out at the beach where Felix seemed to have vanished.

"What happened?" I asked.

Easton spun towards me, a broad smile spreading across his face. "Olive!"

My cheeks heated. I couldn't believe he was always so happy to see me.

"Felix ran away with our lunch," Lars said, shaking his head. "He's been acting so weird lately." He looked down at his watch, and I couldn't help but notice how thick his forearm was. He was in a black t-shirt that spread tightly across his huge chest. I bet I would feel so tiny in his arms, and I usually didn't feel tiny.

"We'll just have to head into town to get lunch," Lars continued. "Want to join us?" The way he said it was so hopeful, like he actually wanted to have lunch with me, and it was almost enough to make me forget my plan.

But I couldn't let Felix down now.

"I could make lunch," I blurted out.

Lars's lips parted, Finn furrowed his brow, and Easton jumped up with a whoop. "You would do that for us?"

"We don't want to inconvenience you," Lars hedged.

"Umm, it's not a problem. I mean, I can't cook anything fancy."

Shit shit shit. Easton and Lars seemed so excited at the idea of me cooking for them. Probably because they'd never eaten anything I made. Now I had to make sure I made them something really good.

My eyes flicked to Finn. He was standing in silence, a shocked expression on his face. When he caught me looking, he glanced away.

"Just give me thirty minutes?" A realization crashed over me: if I was making them lunch, it would make sense to invite them inside. Into my space. I wasn't ready for that. Felix was the only one who had been inside my home.

"It's a nice day. We can eat outside," Easton said. My lips parted as he winked at me, and I had the strange feeling that he'd read my mind. Or maybe he'd just noticed my body language. My omega wanted to preen at how much Easton seemed to *see* me.

Before I did anything ridiculous like run into the alpha's arms and scent mark him, I turned and went back inside. I leaned back on the door and took a deep breath. One day, I would stop running away from people.

THE THREE ALPHAS sat on the sandy bank leading down to the beach. They all looked a little more rumpled and sweaty than when they arrived this morning, and I felt a warm spark of something deep inside me. I took a deep breath, steeling myself as I balanced the plates on my arms. I walked over to them slowly, carefully, giving me more time to take them in.

Lars's hair was tied in a topknot, and he laughed at something Easton said. Finn was sitting a bit apart from them. Had he told the other two about the movie theater? Based on how he was sitting, all hunched over and silent, the wind ruffling his somehow-perfect dark hair, I doubted it.

All three guys looked up as I got closer. I nervously handed Easton his plate first. He looked down at his sandwich with what could only be described as stars in his eyes. I'd made him and Lars grilled cheeses. Nothing fancy, but I added tomato and bacon to it and two types of cheese, so it was basically the fanciest thing I made.

I gave Lars his plate next, mumbling, "I hope you like it."

Then I handed Finn his lunch, which consisted of two cold slices of bread. And sandwiched in between? Three large dill pickle spears. Unsliced.

Finn looked at the sandwich and then back at me, finally meeting my gaze. I arched an eyebrow. Lars and Easton took in our silent standoff.

"Oh, Finn doesn't like—" Easton started to say, but was cut off by Lars elbowing him in the side.

Finn picked up the sandwich, slowly bringing it to his lips. His gaze locked with mine, and he took a large bite. The pickle crunched loudly and his eyes watered as he chewed. And chewed. Apparently, the pickle sandwich didn't quite want to be swallowed. Finally, he did it.

"Thanks," he croaked.

I smiled sweetly, feeling seconds away from letting out an evil cackle. "You're welcome."

I turned around, flipping my hair dramatically over my shoulder. "Enjoy your lunch." And I flounced away.

15

FINN

Our front door shut behind us, and Easton and Lars both turned to face me, arms crossed.

"Want to tell us what the fuck that was about?" Lars asked.

"What do you mean?" Pretending to be ignorant wouldn't get me far, but I was desperate to put off the inevitable. The moment I told them I wasn't interested in pursuing Olive, it would be over for me. I would be out of the pack. Actually, I might just be kicked out if they found out what I had done to her... leaving her alone in the theater like that.

"There was something going on between you and Olive," Easton said. "Why did she give you a pickle sandwich? And why did you *eat* it?"

I had to fight the bizarre urge to *smile*. I swore my lips twitched. I had no idea how she'd found out about my hatred for pickles, but it was a fitting revenge for how I'd treated her. Actually, I deserved much worse punishment. Olive would never be my omega, but that didn't lessen the sick feeling of guilt in my chest.

"I don't know why she did that," I mumbled with a shrug.

Easton let out an exasperated noise that sounded like *ungrr,* and Lars just scrubbed his hand down his face.

"Olive is the omega I scented years ago," he said. "My alpha knew she was ours back then, and I feel it even more strongly now."

Easton threw his arms around Lars's shoulders with a *whoop*. "You're kidding me. You're *kidding* me. I knew she was perfect for us. It's meant to be!"

My heart sank as Lars confirmed what I'd suspected when I scented Olive. It was all coming to an end, and I wasn't sure my heart could take it. Losing my grandparents was one thing, but losing my brothers?

I should tell them. Come clean and let them know I wasn't interested in bonding with Olive or any other omega. That I *couldn't*. My alpha rumbled in disagreement. He wanted Olive. But the grief of seeing my grandpa fade away after the loss of his bonded was a heavy stone in my chest.

I ran my fingers through my hair. "I don't *know* her yet. And neither do the two of you, really."

Easton bounced on his toes. "This restoration is the perfect time to get to know her. To court her."

I pursed my lips, confident this had been Easton's plan all along.

"You'll be nice to her?" Lars asked, his voice deep and serious. "Give her a chance?"

My throat closed up too tight to form words, so I just nodded before escaping upstairs to my room.

I threw myself onto the bed and screamed into my pillow. I was a mess. My brothers had put up with my terrible moods the past six months, had been so understanding, but I sensed their patience was coming to an end. *Well, maybe if you just communicated with them, you idiot.*

Exhaustion weighed heavy on me. Who knew grief made you so tired?

I lay there for a while before forcing myself to sit at my desk and open my laptop. I started pulling up sites for the restoration materials we would need, but somehow ended up looking at homes for rent in other towns. Jobs, too. I would have to tell my pack brothers the truth soon, and needed to have a place to go to when they inevitably kicked me out.

For just a moment, I allowed myself to imagine what it would be like if we all bonded Olive. To come home to her looking all rumpled and cozy at the end of a long day. To have someone to hug, cuddle, *love*. The image of it was so powerful and filled me with such intense longing, it took my breath away.

I clutched at my chest. How could I risk it, giving so much of myself to another person when I could lose them, too? I just... I couldn't. Even though my cowardice would cost me everything.

16

OLIVE

I TRIED TO STAY INSIDE MY HOUSE WHILE THE ALPHAS were working. I really, truly did. But the minutes ticked by soooo slowly, and my omega was whining about needing to be close to them.

Finally, I broke.

I looked at the clock. Great, I'd lasted forty-five minutes since they arrived this morning.

I rolled my eyes, frustrated with myself. My omega had been quiet these past few years, ever since the *incident*, but she seemed to be blossoming now and had lots of opinions about what I should do with these alphas. And her fantasies revolved around sitting on thick knots and having endless orgasms.

I headed to the door but stopped and turned to check myself in the full-length mirror. I'd put on fishnet tights and a brown plaid skirt with a rust sweater tucked into the front. I twisted from side to side. Did it look like I was trying too hard? I thought the tights were cute, but did they too obviously shout, *Hello, I'm fishing for dick*? It had been a while since my last hookup. They'd never been amazing—I'd stuck to betas and never trusted them enough to say what I actually wanted—but they'd scratched an itch. My *thing* with Finn in the theater, for how shittily it ended, had awoken... err, my pussy for lack of better words.

I sighed. I just wanted to feel good.

I tugged at my sweater. It did a decent job hiding my round belly, but there wasn't much I could do to cover my wide hips or thick thighs. I'd always been curvy, but my medical condition made it almost impossible to lose weight. My mom had never spoken poorly about her own body or mine or anyone else's. My eyes flicked to the picture of me with my parents that I kept on the mantel, and I blinked quickly to keep my eyes from watering. My parents had taught me I was worthy and valuable, and I wasn't about to let anyone convince me otherwise.

I flipped my hair over my shoulder and marched to the front door. It was another bright, sunny day, but the air was still a little chilly. Winter would be here before I knew it, and as soon as I figured out how to work the fireplace, my little cottage would be nice and cozy.

I rounded the lighthouse, coming to a stop when I saw Lars leaning over a table they had set up outside.

Shirtless.

The alpha was *shirtless*.

My brain turned completely blank while a dramatic slideshow of shirtless Lars flashed before my eyes. His chest was so broad I didn't think I'd be able to get my arms around him, but I was desperate to try. There was a dusting of blond hair leading my eyes down to his low-slung jeans. The table was blocking me from seeing anything lower. I shamelessly stood on my tiptoes to see if that would give me a better view. His arms flexed as he leaned over the table. My breathing sped up and warmth shot down my stomach into my core. I swear my mouth was practically watering.

As if he sensed my eyes on him, he looked up. A slow grin spread across his face, and his eyes were dark and heated.

"Want to see, sweetheart?"

I froze. Was he talking about his chest? Or something *lower*? He chuckled and gestured at the papers on the table. "It's a blueprint of the lighthouse."

My cheeks heated until they felt like they were on fire, but I stumbled forward until I was standing in front of Lars. I had to tilt my head back to meet his gaze. His eyes were so blue it was like the whole ocean was in there. The wind blew my hair over my face and he brushed it away, cupping both my cheeks. I caught a hint of my perfume in the wind. It seemed the No-NonScent Deodorant didn't stand a chance against Lars.

His hands moved to my shoulders, and he gently turned me so I was facing the blueprint, which was pinned to the table by rocks. He placed his hands on the table, caging me in with his body.

His lips brushed my ear. "We try to get as much information as possible about the original design and materials before we start any restoration work."

He continued explaining their process and I was sure whatever he was saying was very important, but I didn't absorb a single word. His chest brushed my back, heat radiating off him like a furnace. I shifted my weight to my other leg, *accidentally* scooting back a tiny bit in the process so I was more firmly pressed against him. Lars's arms moved closer together until I was trapped between them. He smelled so good, like enchanting forests and bonfires on cool nights. I tipped my head back and ran my nose down the column of his throat.

"How're you doing today, sweetheart?" His deep voice rumbled through his chest.

"Good." I wasn't about to admit that I'd *missed* him last night. That I'd dreamed of him tucking me into my nest before wrapping his arms around me.

His hand collared my throat from behind, gently holding me in place as he leaned down and kissed my jaw. The move was so intense, so fucking *possessive*. My legs felt like jelly, and I leaned more of my weight into Lars.

"You smell so good, little omega. So sweet." He inhaled like he was about to say something, but we were interrupted by the door opening. Easton stumbled out of the lighthouse, his eyes fixed on us.

"Well, well, well, what do we have here?"

I jumped and tried to move away from Lars, but his arms kept me in place. And then Easton was there, bringing a mouthwatering wave of chocolate hazelnut over me. Lars rotated me so I was facing Easton and I was pressed between their bodies.

I swallowed. "Lars was showing me the blueprints."

Easton grinned. "Yes, I can see a lot of really important work is being done here." His hands dropped to my hips, and I inhaled sharply. I wanted them closer, needed to be pressed tight between them until I couldn't breathe anything except their delicious scents. Easton was wearing a shirt and I wanted to tear it off with my bare hands and lick his skin.

His fingers trailed up my side, tracing my curves and rolls, until they gently gripped my chin. "Oh, Olive."

My chest squeezed. He said my name like it was something precious.

He lowered his forehead to mine. "Please, Olive, I'm *begging* you. Put me out of my misery. Just one kiss, one taste of your sweetness. I won't survive without it."

My lips parted and I brushed my cheek against his, his stubble rubbing against my skin. My breath hitched. Was I dreaming?

Well, if this was a dream, I might as well take advantage.

"Yes," I murmured. "Easton, *yes.*" The voice in the back of my head piped up, telling me I would regret this, that it would only cause me more pain and rejection down the road...

Easton ran his strong fingers down my jaw. Ever so slowly, he tilted my chin up, and then his lips were against mine. I'd expected Easton's kiss to be as exuberant as the alpha, but it was slow, gentle, and exactly perfect. As if he knew exactly what I needed. I leaned into him, wrapping my fingers in his soft brown curls. When he pulled away, I was breathless and desperate for more, all thoughts in my head silenced.

"Even sweeter than I thought." Easton placed little kisses down the side of my face. His lips dropped to my ear. "I wonder if other parts of you are this sweet." I shivered in pleasure, and then Lars's hands were on my waist as he turned me to face him. His eyes crinkled with his smile.

"Now you've done it. He might say he just wants one kiss, but

I've never known Easton to just want one of anything." He ran his fingers through my hair and twisted it around his hand, giving him control. "Especially something as perfect as this."

He tugged on my hair, sending a shiver through me. Before I could overthink my actions, I ran my hands up Lars's chest, feeling every ridge of muscle. We both groaned.

"Fuck, sweetheart," he said before pressing his lips to mine. I melted into him, parting my lips to deepen the kiss.

Easton was pressed to my back, his hard cock nestled against me. And then his hands were gripping my ass hard.

Lars tightened his hold on my hair, tugging slightly to break our kiss. I whined, and he chuckled. "Our little needy omega. What should we do with her, Easton?"

"I say we strip her down right here and make her come on our cocks before filling her up. Preferably more than once."

A whimper slipped through my lips.

"Do you want that? Will you let us make you feel good?" Lars asked.

I bit my lip and glanced at the lighthouse. "Where's Finn?"

"He went to Briar's Landing to source materials," Lars said. "Won't be back for the rest of the day."

I should be grateful he wasn't here. It was easier not to face him, but I couldn't shake the feeling that Finn was intentionally avoiding me, and it made me feel strangely crushed. I should walk away from this, from them. The last time I got involved with someone in this pack, it ended up with me feeling discarded. But the swirl of scents around me made it hard to think clearly, and my body *craved* them.

Easton pressed a kiss to my shoulder, and I wished I wasn't wearing such a thick sweater. "What's going on between you and Finn, sunshine?"

I shook my head.

What happened was between Finn and me. He'd accepted my revenge. Ate my pickle.

Fuck. Even that sounded dirty right now.

"Mmm," Easton said, sounding like he didn't believe me. I tensed, waiting for him to insist I tell them, but his fingers trailed under my skirt. "These fucking tights. So sexy. Did you wear these just for us?"

Lars groaned when I nodded, pressing his face to the top of my head and breathing in. His hand moved down to cup my breasts, his large hands covering them as he squeezed. "Will you let us make you feel good, sweetheart?"

"You want to?" My voice came out high and insecure.

Easton and Lars growled in unison, pressing their bodies tight to me until I could barely breathe. I loved it. They were both rock-hard against me, and slick drenched my underwear.

"Now that we've answered that question," Lars said, his fingers kneading my hips, "do you want to move inside?"

My breath hitched as I was filled with unexpected anxiety at the thought of bringing them into my house. It was stupid. I should just do it. Invite them inside. It wasn't a big deal.

Shouldn't be a big deal.

But my personal space was sacred to me, and if I let them inside and this didn't work out? It might not feel so safe anymore.

"Wait," Easton said. "I have just the thing." He took off running —flinging the lighthouse door open and coming back seconds later with a large blanket. "I brought it so we could have a picnic." He was breathless as he slid to a stop in front of us. "I didn't know omega would be on the menu." He waggled his brows.

Lars and I both crinkled our noses.

"Bro, you could have worded that better."

"Yeah, now I'm worried about cannibalism," I said.

"Oh, I do want to eat you. But you'll like it," Easton said with an exaggerated wink as he tried to lay the blanket down.

"Fuck's sake," Lars muttered. "At least I have better game than him." He leaned down and fixed the corner of the blanket.

I covered my smile with my hand. In my experience, sex was serious and stressful. This already felt so different.

I let out a squeal as Easton pulled me down, making sure I landed on top of him. My breasts pressed against his hard chest, and he moved his legs in between mine so my hips were spread wide.

"This is the fucking best view I've ever seen." Lars's deep voice behind me was the only warning before he flipped my skirt up and palmed my ass. His large hands gripped me hard. "I think she's trying to kill us. Wearing this tiny little thong that barely covers anything."

Easton swore. "You should see the view from down here," he said, his eyes fixed on my breasts.

My omega started taking over, another whine rising out of my throat as I became desperate to feel their skin against mine.

"Okay, baby, I've got the hint." Easton laughed as he brushed my desperate hands aside and pushed himself into a seated position, keeping me tight against his lap. The change in position meant my pussy was pressed right against his cock. My breathing sped up and a burst of slick soaked the inside of my thighs. Lars's hands were there, slipping under my skirt and gripping my inner thighs and slick-drenched tights.

"I need these off." His voice was a growl, feral with want, and I knew exactly how he felt. Easton and Lars moved me like I was a doll, stripping me of all my clothes until the three of us lay on our sides, naked on the blanket. I was pinned between them too tightly to see much of their bodies, but the feel of their skin against mine was *everything*. They ran their hands down my body and I tensed, wondering how they would react to seeing me naked.

Easton let out a moan and pressed hot kisses down my neck. "You're perfection. Straight out of my dreams."

He kissed my breasts and then took a nipple into his mouth. I arched against him, letting out a low moan when he gently bit down. The spark of pain went straight to my core. I threw my head back, resting it against Lars's chest. A deep vibration started behind me, and it took me a moment to understand what it was—Lars was purring. The sound melted all my tension and turned me to putty.

His hands followed the trail of Easton's kisses, cupping and squeezing. "I love this," he moaned, hand on my stomach. I squirmed a bit, but he just held me tighter. "You are a fucking goddess." He kissed the spot behind my ear, and I squirmed again, but not out of self-consciousness this time.

Easton moved until his face was level with my pussy. He paused for a moment, spreading my lips with his fingers and just *looked*.

"Easton," I whined.

"I want to memorize everything about you. I want to know the shape of you, the feel of you. You are my obsession, Olive." Before I could respond, he dove in, licking a long line up my pussy before taking my clit into his mouth and sucking. Lars pulled my leg over his, opening me up more for Easton.

"Good girl," Lars murmured. "Just relax and let Easton make you feel good." His tight grip pinned me in place, making movement impossible. A cool breeze kissed my feverish skin, and the salt in the air joined the alphas' scents in an intoxicating blend of earth and sweetness.

Easton continued eating me, circling my clit with his tongue, as he reached up a hand and played with my nipples. My orgasm built, and I was grinding back on Lars. His hard cock slipped between my thighs. My core clenched, feeling way too empty and desperate to be filled. I mumbled something incoherent as I reached back and tried to grab Lars's cock.

"Needy little omega," he said. "You need me to fill you up? To stretch that sweet little pussy and fill you with my cum?"

I nodded, but any words were cut off as Easton pinched my nipple and sucked hard on my clit at the same time, making me come with a rush of slick. I was jelly, completely spent but greedy for more.

Lars groaned. "You're so beautiful when you come. Fuck." The head of his cock pressed against my entrance. He nuzzled the side of my face, his beard rough against my skin. "You sure, sweetheart? We can stop."

I let out a snarl. My cheeks instantly heated. I had never made a sound like that before.

"I think she's telling you she's not done," Easton said. He moved back up my body and cupped my face. "Isn't that right, baby? You need to be filled by your alphas?"

"Yes. *Please.*"

"Don't make her beg, brother," Easton said. "Unless you're into that sort of thing."

I giggled, Lars groaned, and then he was pressing inside me. My eyes widened. His cock was so large it felt like it was splitting me apart. For a moment I wondered if I could do this, take all of him, and then Easton's fingers were on my clit.

"Just relax, baby. You can take him. You were made for us."

I took a deep breath and relaxed, surrendering to them. With another thrust, Lars was seated fully. His cock hit a spot deep inside me that caused me to cry out. Sparks of electric pleasure shot through me, making me tremble. I pressed my ass against the alpha, feeling the swell of his knot against my butt cheeks.

"Is this okay, sweetheart?"

I smiled at the question, feeling so safe with these two alphas. I knew the second I said stop, they would do it, no question. "Yes," I gasped. I tried to thrust back into Lars, but I was pinned too tightly between the two of them.

"What a good girl. Such a fucking good girl," Lars said. "Your tight little pussy is gripping me so hard." Then he froze. "Shit. Condom?"

"IUD," I choked out with a gasp.

A feral growl filled his chest. Without warning, he pulled out almost all the way and then slammed back into me, hard. I was pushed against Easton, who twisted his fingers in my hair and pulled me in for a bruising kiss. Lars continued thrusting in and out, molding my pussy to the shape of his large cock and sending more shocks of pleasure through me until I was on the verge of coming again. Easton's cock leaked precum on my stomach, and it was enough to make me feral. I managed to snake my hand down so I could grip his cock with my hand. He swore, hips thrusting into my hand.

"You want both of us, baby?"

I squeezed his cock tighter, words escaping me. And then I was being moved again, this time onto my hands and knees. Lars somehow stayed inside me the whole time. He thrust inside me again, and my arms almost buckled. He was so much deeper in this position. I cried out and panted and whined, and then Easton was kneeling in front of me, his cock level with my mouth.

His hand came to my jaw and squeezed. "Our little omega, being so good for us. Open up for me, baby."

I took the tip of his cock in my mouth eagerly, sucking his sweet precum. Lars thrust again, pushing me further onto Easton's cock. My eyes watered, but the next thrust I was ready for him, taking a deep breath before he pressed to the back of my throat.

Both alphas swore and picked up the pace, and I loved knowing that *I* was doing that, *I* was the one making them lose control.

Lars bent over my back and cupped my breasts. "Are you going to come for us, sweetheart? I want to feel you strangling my cock."

My body trembled with the stimulation and pleasure and all of it. I was so close to coming, my orgasm hovering just out of reach. And then Lars's fingers were on my clit, and it was enough to push me over the edge. My arms collapsed, and Easton's cock slipped out of my mouth as I rode the waves of my orgasm.

"Fuck, I want to come inside you," Easton said. Lars pulled me up so I was sitting back on his thick thighs, his cock still buried inside me.

"Come inside me," I moaned. "Both of you."

Both alphas cursed. My mind was hazy with pleasure, the world around me taking on an almost unreal quality as the head of Easton's cock pressed inside my pussy, fighting for space alongside Lars's. The pressure was enormous and there was a sting as he continued pressing in, but I welcomed it. I wanted to be sore, to feel the evidence that this wasn't all in my imagination.

Lars collared my throat, keeping me upright. "I'm going to come." His chest rumbled with a growl as he thrust inside me. *Once. Twice.* And then the two alphas came at the same time, their hot cum filling me.

We stayed there, kneeling on the blanket outside the lighthouse, breathing hard.

"Holy shit." Easton finally broke the silence. "Did that just happen?"

Lars chuckled, kissing the side of my face before pulling out of me. Easton followed, and my omega whined as cum dripped down my thighs. She didn't want to lose any of it.

Easton pressed two fingers inside me, plugging me. "Is that what you need, baby?"

I made a satisfied noise as I sucked a patch of skin on his neck. I kept my eyes closed as the alphas arranged me so I was lying down again. Lars pulled me on top of his chest, holding tight. Easton lay beside us, keeping his fingers in my pussy.

Lars stroked his hands up and down my spine. "Are you okay, Olive?"

I nodded and pressed my face to his throat, soaking in his scent.

"Mmm, not feeling very verbal, sweetheart?" he asked.

I shook my head and pressed myself tighter against his chest, breathing in lungfuls of earthy pine and sea. I shivered when the wind picked up, goosebumps rising on my skin.

"Come here, baby," Easton said. I kept my eyes closed as he slipped a warm sweater over me. It smelled like chocolate and hazelnuts and warm pastries and everything good. I made a happy little sound, wiggling so I was pressed tight between them. My last thought before I drifted to sleep was that I never wanted to leave this spot.

17

LARS

OLIVE WAS TUCKED UP AGAINST MY CHEST, COMPLETELY naked under the sweater Easton had pulled over her head. My hand palmed her ass as Easton kept her pussy plugged with our cum.

Olive Olive Olive.

I dipped my head down to her neck and scent-marked her. Intellectually, I knew she was already covered in my scent, but I wanted the entire world to know that Olive was mine. *Ours.* There was nothing that could make me leave this spot, to release her from my arms.

A gust of wind blew off the water, fluttering up the corners of our picnic blanket and making Olive shiver.

Fuck.

Nothing would make me leave this spot except for my omega being cold.

She protested as I moved to a seated position, clinging to me and keeping her face buried in my chest. My alpha fucking *preened*. He wanted her just as addicted to me as I was to her.

"Come on, sweetheart. It's too cold out here for you." Her thighs might be thick and luscious, her body curvy, but she was still so damn small compared to me. I signaled to Easton, but he was already on it. He helped me get up so I didn't have to release the sweet, sleepy omega before shaking out the blanket and wrapping it around her.

I turned to the lighthouse and hesitated. Olive seemed hesitant to have us inside the cottage. I knew from growing up in a pack that omegas could be very protective over their space. I hoped one day she would feel safe enough to let us inside, but for now, I headed to the lighthouse door, moving my hand under her ass to support her as I climbed the winding stairs to the service room. It was warm in here, although I still wished I had a comfortable bed to lay her down on. She deserved all things soft.

I carefully sat on the floor, my back to the wall. Olive was still clinging to me, her arms and legs wrapped around me and her face pressed to my neck. My alpha did a fist bump knowing she was scent-marking me, even as she slept.

I eyed Easton's sweater and frowned. My alpha was a petulant two-year-old whining because he wanted to see her in *my* clothes.

Footsteps echoed on the stairs as Easton popped into the room. He'd gotten dressed and was holding up a large cooler. "I hid this so Felix wouldn't get it this time, but I've got lunch for all of us."

Olive snorted out a laugh, and I looked down to see that her eyes were open.

"Oh, you thought that was funny, did you?" Easton asked.

She sat up more fully, and I had to stop myself from pulling her flush against me. Instead, I helped her maneuver so her back was to my chest, making sure she was still covered by the blanket.

"Felix was doing me a favor."

Easton raised an eyebrow as he pulled out sandwiches, chips, and cookies with Rosie's Cafe printed on the wrappers.

"Felix must like you then." He handed Olive a sandwich. "I got extra pickles on the side, should you want some."

Olive blushed, and I couldn't stop myself from running my finger down her cheek.

"Wait," Easton said, pausing with his sandwich halfway to his mouth. "Has Felix been with you all this time? Everyone's been wondering where he's been." He made a little noise as half his sandwich ingredients fell out from the bottom.

"Oh," Olive said, her brow furrowing. "Did I do something wrong? He was here when I moved in and just kind of stuck around. Although he hasn't been here as often recently."

I squeezed her close. "You did nothing wrong. No one controls Felix."

The three of us fell into a comfortable silence as we ate our lunch, the hum of the lighthouse machinery our gentle soundtrack. Olive ate half her sandwich and then folded it back up and placed it in her lap. Had she eaten enough? Maybe I could coax her to eat a few more chips, or maybe a cookie...

"So..." she said, interrupting my thoughts. "Did we really just do DVP outside?"

I choked on my bite of sandwich, and Easton burst out laughing.

"Fuck, Olive. I wasn't expecting that," I said, letting out a strangled gasp.

She grinned, twisting so she could pat me on the back. "I mean, neither was I," she said dryly.

Easton moved closer and kissed Olive on the cheek. "I'm still not completely convinced that wasn't one of my dreams. Did you like it?"

"Yes," she responded primly.

I jiggled her on my lap, and she laughed. Fuck, I loved it when she was all prim and proper, especially after what we'd just done.

"What are the odds of a repeat performance?" Easton asked.

My heart pounded, waiting for her answer. "Quite good," she said, a mischievous little smile on her face.

Easton relaxed against the wall, nuzzling the side of her face. "Glad Lars's monster cock didn't scare you off."

I reached out to smack him on the head, but he dodged me.

"Mmm, not at all." Olive froze before twisting to face me. "Wait, are you still naked?"

I grunted. "I had a very tired omega who wouldn't let me put her down."

She let out a little squeak and moved to get off my lap. I tightened my hold on her. "Where do you think you're going?"

"I want to see," she said, shocking me even further.

"What?" I spluttered.

"I didn't get to see before," she whined, her omega coming to the fore. "You were behind me." Her eyes were fixed on my blanket-covered crotch like she was hoping to develop x-ray vision.

"Yeah, Lars." Easton leaned back against the wall with a shit-eating grin. "Give us a little show."

I flipped him off, but then I met Olive's eager gaze, and my alpha urged me to show off for her.

"You're trouble," I said, gripping her by the waist and lifting her off my lap.

I stood. My cock was rock-hard again, and I was hit with a sudden wave of nervousness. Would Olive like what she saw? I flexed my arms.

"Woah."

I looked down to see my omega staring at my cock, lips parted. I groaned at the image of her taking my cock into her sweet little mouth, those pink lips stretched around me.

"That's... wow. That was inside me?" Her sweet perfume filled the room, and my chest rumbled.

Easton scoffed. "I mean, he's *okay* if you like monster cocks. But size isn't everything." He hopped up and started stripping.

I groaned, scrubbing my hand down my face. How the fuck did we get in this situation?

Easton stood beside me and fisted his cock. "Pretty impressive, right?"

Olive's eyes flitted between our two cocks, her breathing rapid. A little whine slipped through her lips, and she crawled closer on her hands and knees.

Easton swore and tilted his head to stare at the ceiling. I knew how he was feeling. My jaw was clenched so hard I was convinced my teeth would crack from trying not to come, especially when Olive's sweater shifted, revealing her sweet little ass.

"Can I?" Her sweet voice cut through my haze of arousal.

"You want to take us in your mouth, baby?" Easton asked.

Thank god one of us was still capable of speech. Words had left me. My entire world had shrunk down to the gorgeous, curvy omega in front of me, staring at my cock and licking her lips.

Olive nodded. "But you might have to tell me what to do. What you like."

Easton and I groaned at the same time.

"Open up, sunshine."

I watched as Olive took Easton in her mouth. She took him deep, eyes drifting closed as she sucked hard. He wrapped his hand in her hair. "Fuck," he hissed. "I'm not going to last long." With a groan, he pulled Olive off his cock and guided her to mine.

Olive whimpered as she tried to stretch her lips around me. I found my voice as I collared her throat with my hand. "Relax that jaw, sweetheart. You can take me."

She took a deep breath and tried again, this time opening wide enough to take my tip into her mouth. I lightly squeezed the sides of her throat. "Fuck, sweetheart, you're doing so well. So hot and tight."

She let out a little disgruntled sound and tried to take more of my cock. Her eyes watered, tears streaming down her face as she choked on me. My breaths came in ragged gasps. I pulled her off me, clenching my jaw in an effort to stop myself from coming, and pushed her back on Easton.

"You're being such a good girl," he said, taking over as he thrust into her mouth. "So good for both of your alphas. The perfect little omega." Olive let out a moan of pleasure, and Easton swore. "I'm going to come, baby. Be a good girl and swallow every drop I give you."

I stroked Olive's hair as Easton came. There was something so *hot* about watching her take my packmate.

"You did so well, baby," he murmured as Olive pulled off his cock. "So, so well. Now, are you going to finish Lars off like a good girl?"

She nodded and let him push her onto my cock. I stroked her cheek as she took me a little deeper. Pleasure shot through my body, tingling the base of my spine. "I'm coming," I grunted, giving her the slightest warning before I came down her throat. A few drops of cum escaped, dripping down her chin, and I gathered it up, pressing my fingers into her mouth so she could suck it up.

"Are you okay, sweetheart?" I asked, crouching down beside her.

"Yeah," she said dreamily. Her eyelids were heavy, and she reached her arms out to me. I gathered her to my chest and the three of us ended up in a tangle of limbs on the floor, with Olive on top of us.

My eyes drifted closed and I must have fallen asleep, only jolting awake when I felt lips sucking on my neck.

"Mmm, what are you doing?" I ran my hand down Olive's back until I cupped her ass and gave it a hard squeeze. She let out a little squeak and nipped my neck. I groaned as the desire for her to bite me surged through me. My mouth watered as I imagined sinking my teeth into her, marking her as *mine* and bonding her forever.

"You know, I like my job, but this is definitely the best way I've ever spent my workday," Easton mumbled. Olive was half lying on top of him, his hand firmly gripping her thigh.

She hummed. "I'm not sure this is what the NHLRGHLEC had in mind."

My chest shook with laughter. Fuck, she was funny.

She gave a little sniff. "I get my work done early in the morning."

I chuckled. "What a good girl." She made a happy noise and snuggled closer to me. "What do you have to do?"

"I do daily checks to make sure all the equipment is running. I clean the lantern and viewing room, check the weather reports for storms. Those sorts of things."

"You're so smart. So beautiful. So smart," Easton murmured, his words slurring as he fought sleep.

"Mmm, I guess I tired you out." She trailed her fingers down Easton's jaw. "So... are you guys a *thing*?"

There was a beat of silence, and then Easton and I realized what she was asking. "No," we both said in unison.

She pressed a kiss to my chest. "You seem very familiar with each other's cocks."

I snorted and my hand came down on her ass. "Behave yourself."

Easton's eyes opened and he smiled. "We just spent one too many summers swimming in the ocean. Lars likes to swim commando. Show off that monster of his."

"Swedes aren't as fussed about nudity as you Americans," I huffed.

"Well, that's fine by me," she said.

18

OLIVE

I was sitting on the rolling chair in the watch room with a cup of hot tea. I'd run back into the house to get cleaned up and dressed, keeping Easton's sweater on, and brought back some tea and cookies for all of us.

My body was loose and relaxed, the ache in my pussy a delicious reminder of what had just happened, although I was still in a bit of shock. What did it mean? They had called me their omega, but that had been in the heat of the moment. Was this just a casual thing for them while they were working on the lighthouse? And how did Finn fit into all of this?

The warmth I'd felt since I'd laid eyes on Lars this morning seeped out of me, replaced by insecurity. If I got too close to people, they would see the real me. My moods, my medical issues... it was too much for anyone to put up with.

Easton came up behind me as if summoned by my dark emotions. "How're you doing, sunshine?" He brushed my hair to the side and kissed me on the neck.

I leaned back into him. "Good," I lied. I loved hearing him call me sunshine, but I didn't deserve the nickname. I was the least sunshiny person in the world.

He straightened up but kept his hands on my shoulders, tracing his fingers across my skin. "What got you interested in being a lighthouse keeper?"

I looked at him over my shoulder. His expression was so open and genuine, like he really wanted to know me. "I hadn't considered it until I saw the listing online. I'd been working from home, doing data entry, but I was ready for something different." I didn't know what had brought on my desire to change my life, but one day, I woke up, and my tiny studio apartment and dirt-boring work-from-home job were suddenly unbearable. "I grew up on the water," I continued. "My parents were lobstermen, and I was on the boat really since I was a baby."

"Really?" Lars joined us, standing by my side. The measuring tape he'd been using to take some measurements Finn needed was clipped to his belt. He curled a lock of my hair around his finger and my omega sighed happily. I'd been touch-starved for years. If these alphas kept it up, I would grow too addicted to their casual touches, the way they kept me in their orbit like they didn't want me more than an arm's length away.

"Yeah. I thought I'd be a lobsterwoman, but it didn't work out."

"Why not?" Easton crouched down so we were closer to being at eye level, but I kept my eyes fixed on the horizon.

"My parents died and it was hard to go out on the boat without them. Maybe I should have tried harder, hired people to help me, but I just couldn't pull myself together fast enough before I ran out of money. I had to sell the boat." I shrugged like it wasn't a big deal, like I hadn't cried for days until my eyelids were so puffy I could barely see.

"Baby," Easton said, his voice so tender.

I gave him a quick smile. "It's okay. It was years ago. But I'm trained in ocean rescue and I always read the meteorological reports for my dad, and I don't mind being alone. This was a good fit for me."

Lars's hand rested gently on my shoulder. "I'm glad you're here, sweetheart."

I leaned against his arm, and some warmth returned to me. Even if this was just temporary, I could let myself enjoy this moment.

"How did you all get into restoration stuff?" I asked, pushing my chair so it spun to face them.

"It was really Finn's idea," Easton said, plopping down on the floor and pulling my socked feet into his lap to massage them. My little omega heart soaked up his attention. "We obviously have no shortage of historic buildings up and down the coast. Fredrik, Finn's grandpa, had these big coffee table books about architecture and they always fascinated Finn. He decided he wanted to get his degree in architecture, and the two of us followed him to school."

Lars sat down next to Easton and placed his hand on my thigh, gripping tight. I now had two massive alphas sitting at my feet, and I couldn't stop myself from perfuming. My pumpkin spice scent filled the air, and I blushed.

"Do you also have architecture degrees?" I asked quickly to distract from my scent.

"Nah," Lars said. "I knew college wasn't for me, so I went to trade school for electrical work." There was a tightness in his eyes, but then he smiled and jerked his head at Easton. "He did a wood-working apprenticeship and the two of us supported Finn until he finished his master's degree and apprenticeship."

"We like to remind him of that since he's the one who pulls in all the high-paying jobs now. Keeps him humble," Easton said. He shifted closer to me and laid his head on my lap. The move was so familiar and intimate it made my breath catch. I switched my mug to my other hand and ran my fingers through Easton's curls.

Hearing them talk about Finn made my heart pound. It was clear to see how much they loved their packmate. Would Finn be upset that the three of us had been together? Would he turn them against me? I shifted in my chair, my stress rising again. This was a bad idea. I should do something to create distance from us so I didn't get hurt.

"I don't want to leave," Lars said with a sigh.

"Do you have to?" The words were out of my mouth before I could stop them. I wanted to roll my eyes. Apparently, my resolve lasted all of half a second.

Lars captured my hand and kissed my palm and wrist. "We have a weekly dinner with my family. Do you want to come? We'd love to have you there, and my moms would love to meet you."

"Oh, I—"

"Please come, Olive," Easton begged, his arms encircling my waist with his head still in my lap.

The desperation in his voice brought a smile to my lips. Lars rolled his eyes and mouthed "drama," which made me snort a laugh. For the briefest moment, I imagined what it would be like to go to dinner with them. What it would be like to be a part of a family again, even for just an evening.

"I'm going to stay here, but thank you," I said softly.

Easton clutched at me tighter, but Lars gave me an understanding smile.

"We'll be back tomorrow," he said.

I nodded. Finn would also be here. Would they pretend nothing happened today?

Lars finally convinced Easton to let me go, and I walked with them down to the bottom of the lighthouse.

Easton pulled me into his arms, his large body surrounding mine as he pressed his face to the top of my hair. His rich chocolate scent drenched my skin and clothes, and I couldn't wait to sleep surrounded by it. "Just in case this wasn't clear, we're courting you, baby."

I froze.

"Fuck," Lars said, pressing his body to my back. "It wasn't clear."

"But... What..." My words wouldn't come out.

Easton pulled away enough to cup my face and force me to meet his gaze. "We're in this, Olive. We want you, and not just for one perfect afternoon. For every afternoon. And morning. And evening—"

"Yes, all day long," Lars said with a snort.

"What about Finn?" I whispered.

"He wants to court you, too," Easton said.

I scrunched my nose in disbelief. Nothing about Finn's behavior said *open to courting*. And it wasn't like I wanted him, anyway.

Liar liar.

"We'll prove it to you," Easton said. "We'll be so good to you, sunshine. We'll show you that we'll be the best alphas for you."

My heart was in my throat as he squeezed me into another hug and then reluctantly released me. I went to take off his sweater to return it, but he stopped me with a wink. "Keep it. It looks better on you, anyway." He turned to Lars. "I'll gather up our stuff outside." With one final kiss, he slipped away.

Before my brain could catch up to what was happening, Lars pressed my back to the wall, blocking my view of the room with his broad chest. His hand collared my throat, squeezing just slightly enough for me to let out a whimper.

"I need you to tell me what happened between you and Finn." His voice was deep and commanding. Not quite a bark, but enough to make my omega want to *obey.*

But I locked my legs and stayed strong. "Nope."

Lars let out a little growl. "He's my brother, and I love him. I don't think he's capable of hurting someone intentionally, but he can be careless, especially with what he's been going through lately. It's not okay if he did something to hurt you."

I blinked. It was clear to see how much these alphas loved each other, but here Lars was, defending *me.*

He ran his thumb across my lower lip. "Tell me."

I let out a shuddering sigh, completely hypnotized by his body, his scent, everything about this alpha.

"He just hurt my feelings," I said. "That's all."

Lars scowled. "That's not okay. No one gets to do that."

God, he was so fierce, so protective. My omega fully approved.

"I've got it under control."

"What do you mean?" His nose skated down the side of my face until he was pressed against my neck, scent-marking me. "Does this have anything to do with pickles?"

I wrapped my arms around his neck, pulling him close. "Maybe. My plan for revenge."

He pressed me even harder against the wall. It was hard to take a breath, but I didn't mind. I would be happy to be crushed by Lars's body any time of day.

"If you need more ideas for your revenge scheme, let me know. I've lived with Finn for many years. But sweetheart, please give him a chance. Give *us* a chance."

I ran my fingers through his beard. "Please don't break my heart," I whispered.

"Your heart is safe with me. I promise."

He pressed a hard kiss on my mouth, and I parted my lips, letting him in. Right now, with his arms around me, his lips against mine, I believed his words.

We were both breathless when he pulled away. I clung to him, not wanting this to end.

"I have to go."

He looked so furious about it I had to laugh. "Grumpy alpha."

"I haven't even fucking *tasted* you yet." His hands ran down the front of my body and cupped my pussy through my leggings. A look of determination crossed his face. "I can't leave without tasting you, sweetheart."

I whimpered as slick burst in my panties. Lars's hand slipped under my clothes until his fingers were pressed against my slit, moving back and forth. "Fuck, *fuck*. You're so wet. God, sweetheart, is this for me?"

"All for you," I whined, arching into his touch.

A thick finger slipped inside me as his palm pressed against my clit.

"Maybe I should leave you like this, whimpering and wanting. That way, you'll be desperate to see me again, desperate and begging your alpha for relief."

I shook my head, clutching his arm to keep his hand in place. "Don't make me create another revenge plan."

I could feel his laugh vibrate against my skin, into my very soul.

"Very well." He thrust another finger inside me, and it was so thick I moaned at the delicious stretch. "Be a good girl now and come for me."

I was already so on edge it barely took any time for my orgasm to break over me. I threw my head back, but somehow, Lars's hand was there, cupping the back of my head to stop me from knocking it against the wall.

"So beautiful, so gorgeous. Fuck, I'm so damn lucky."

I was a boneless heap, my limbs weak from pleasure.

Lars pulled out of me, his eyes fixed on mine as he brought his fingers to his lips and sucked them into his mouth. A fresh burst of slick drenched my underwear at the look of pleasure on his face.

"Be a good girl tonight." He patted my pussy. "And no touching yourself until we're back."

I took a sharp breath. "What?"

"This pussy is just for us to play with." He gave me a stern look and kissed my forehead. "Now, get inside, sweetheart. Do you have food for dinner?"

I nodded, still a bit stunned.

"What a good girl. Make sure you eat a nice big meal. You worked hard today."

He gave me one more kiss and waited for me to open the door to the cottage. I gave him one last look before closing it behind me. I leaned against it, heart racing.

"I'll see you tomorrow, Olive." His growl reached me through the wooden door, making me shiver.

19

FINN

I'D SPENT THE DAY ALONE, DRIVING SEVERAL HOURS TO speak to all the suppliers we would need for the lighthouse restoration.

It'd given me time to think, and my path forward had become clear.

I needed to apologize to Olive and come clean to my brothers.

I rehearsed what I would say as I pulled up to Lars's family home. I would tell my packmates that if they wanted to court Olive, I wouldn't stand in their way. I just wouldn't join them. We would finish the project, and I would move out.

I swallowed hard as I parked the car and pulled the key out of the ignition. The Andersson-Spring home was beautiful—an old ocean-blue Victorian with copper trim. We'd spent so many days here when we were young, pretending we were explorers, going through the attic and turrets. Would I ever get to come back here for family dinner after this? After they made their own family without me?

I got out of the car and saw Lars and Easton walking down the street towards the house. I steeled myself. I could do this.

"Hey! How did everything go today?" Lars asked.

"Good, I got most everything ordered—" I stopped talking when the overwhelming scent of pumpkin spice washed over me. My alpha snarled. My packmates were grinning, oblivious to the storm of emotions inside me. "I see you've had a productive workday," I choked out. I tried to keep my resentment and jealousy out of my voice, but based on the way Easton's face fell, I wasn't successful.

"Are you upset?" he asked.

I couldn't respond. Had no idea what would come out of my mouth.

He sighed. "Okay, you're upset. Look, I'm really sorry. This wasn't planned, but we shouldn't have done anything without talking about it as a pack. I wasn't thinking very clearly, and I wasn't sure where you're at with her right now."

"Since no one will tell us what happened between you two," Lars grumbled.

"But you do want to be with her, right? You can take her on a date, get to know her." Easton looked so fucking hopeful, and I didn't want to ruin it. Outsiders would never guess at Easton's dark past with how happy he seemed all the time, but I knew. Right now, my brother was radiating real happiness.

"Yeah," I choked out. Fuck. *FUCK*.

"Great, that's great. Just make it clear to her that you're courting her. She's going to love you, Finn."

I nodded my head, but the movement felt strange and robotic.

Why couldn't I just fucking get it together and *tell them?* I was a coward. Pathetic and afraid of their rejection and disappointment.

But there was also a part of me, a version of myself I thought had disappeared, who smiled. This part of me, the Finn from *before*, was already consumed with thoughts of Olive and what our life together could be. Taking her to jobs with me. Getting her opinion on how to approach a restoration. Spoiling her in the small everyday things—a new jacket, fancy coffee drinks, her favorite breakfast pastry. That part of me sighed with fucking hearts in his eyes, wondering if we should leave her love notes around the lighthouse.

Absurd.

Ridiculous.

Foolish.

That Finn was a fucking idiot.

Easton squeezed my shoulder and bounded up the walkway to the house. I turned to follow him, but Lars caught me by the shoulder.

"Are you okay?" He eyed me carefully, seeing more than I wanted him to. "You're not, are you?" When I said nothing, he sighed. "Is it Olive? Do you not want her? Or is it just too soon?"

I shrugged, miserable. I was used to being the in-charge, confident project manager, but I couldn't seem to get my life under control. "What if this doesn't work?" I finally managed to get out.

Lars's eyes softened. "I really think it will, and if it doesn't, we still have each other. We're family." He pulled me into a hug, which only caused Olive's scent to wash over me stronger, and then he urged me inside the house.

I WAS SULLEN THROUGH DINNER. Isla, Lars's omega mom, and Lucy tried to engage me in conversation, but eventually left me alone with my bitter thoughts.

Scenting Olive on my brothers filled me with furious jealousy... but there was also a part of me that recognized it felt *right*. I wanted them to be marked by her. Maybe the thing that felt wrong was that *I* didn't carry her scent. No one knew she was mine because I was resisting this. Resisting her.

Everything had seemed so clear an hour ago in the car. I had everything planned out—my safe, boring, risk-free future alone— but now I was all jumbled up inside. Could I really leave my brothers? Could I leave Olive? How had she already wormed her way inside my heart?

I barely noticed as dinner ended and everyone moved out to the backyard. I sat on the back porch in the dark, stirring only when Frida, one of Lars's moms, sat down beside me. The alpha patted my hand.

"You're doing a great job with this whole tortured-soul thing."

I glanced over at her. Her eyes were soft and so was her smile.

"Sorry," I mumbled.

"What's going on? I mean, it's obvious this is about an omega, with Easton and Lars showing up smelling like *that*." She snorted. "Nothing else can rock an alpha to their core."

I picked at a thread on my shirt. "Olive." Just speaking her name did something to me—lit up my chest with emotion.

"So, what's the problem?" Frida had always been a no-nonsense alpha. She was the head of her pack and had always been assertive, a real leader. There was something about her energy that made it impossible to lie. With just a single look, she'd gotten us to confess to so much mischief as kids.

"I can't..." I cleared my throat before continuing. "They want us to be a pack." I gestured to where Lars and Easton were hanging out with everyone else in the backyard.

"And why can't you?"

"Do you know the research says there's up to a twenty-five percent chance that an alpha will die if their bonded omega dies?" I asked. That figure had been rolling around in my head since I read a recent article in the Journal of Designation Sciences.

"Huh," Frida said. "I would've thought it was higher."

I whipped my head to face her. "What?" I spluttered. "How are you so calm about that?"

She sighed and took my hand in hers, giving it a squeeze. "I know you're in pain, Finn. We loved Carina and Fredrik. It's been hard without them. But you were with Fredrik those last few weeks—he *wanted* to be with his omega, Finn. He couldn't stand a life without her."

She was right, but her words filled me with anger. "But isn't that wrong? Toxic? To give so much of yourself to another person like that?"

"I think the word you're looking for is *terrifying*. I met Isla and Harper my first week in college, and my alpha knew they were mine right away. I was so scared. I'd just ended a shitty high school relationship. With a man."

I snorted at that. "Are you serious?"

"Unfortunately," she responded dryly. "I was so ready to go to college and just be free—free to make my own choices and hook up with whoever I wanted. And there I was, a few days in with an alpha and omega I wanted to claim."

"Did you resist it?"

Now it was Frida's turn to scoff. "I think I lasted a couple of days before I moved in. Isla brought Jo home a few days later after they'd met in class and announced we were all a pack. Sometimes, the universe has other plans for us."

"You make it sound like it's destiny. Inevitable, or something."

She shrugged. "Maybe it is. I know there's all this research on scent compatibility, but it sounds so clinical. All I know is that these three women are mine, my world. And I wouldn't want to live without them."

I pulled my hand out of hers, my anger re-awakened. "You would leave your kids all alone just because your bonded died?" I snarled.

Frida wasn't put off by my anger. She moved closer and cupped my face. "Finn, honey, Fredrik didn't leave you. He died. He had lived a long, full life, and his body gave out."

"But he knew it was coming," I spit out. "You just said he could sense it."

"He probably could. But honey, he didn't leave you alone. He left you with your *family*. Those two over there are your family. You're not alone. Not if you don't want to be." She patted my cheek and stood up. "Grief can make us hide within ourselves, but Fredrik was never one to run away from suffering or pain or *love*."

She headed into the backyard. The string lights illuminated the way her omega reached out her arms to her alpha.

20

OLIVE

THE GUYS WERE WORKING INSIDE THE LIGHTHOUSE, AND I was hiding away in my nest.

I'd peeked out my window this morning to see the three of them arrive. They were so unfairly hot in their work clothes. My mind wandered to how strong and calloused Lars and Easton's hands had felt against my skin.

I fidgeted with my sweater—Easton's sweater—feeling self-conscious. What did they really see in me? They could have any omega they wanted.

And then there was Finn.

He was back today—wearing a black long-sleeved shirt and low-slung work pants that made me feel the same squirmy, needy feeling I'd had in the movie theater. I wished I could forget the way his thick fingers felt inside me, the sound he'd made when he came. I cupped my burning cheeks with my hands. The two of us needed to talk. Lars and Easton were convinced Finn wanted to court me, but I had my doubts and refused to come between them.

Neither Easton nor Lars had knocked on my door this morning. I tried and failed not to overanalyze it. Was it because Finn was with them? Or had they changed their minds about me?

I took a fortifying breath and did one last check in the mirror. Today was my lunch with Lucy, Summer, and Ivy. It was a brisk day, the cold seeping into my old house, but my anxiety meant I was already sweating. My omega wanted—*I* wanted—to run to the lighthouse and get reassurance from my alphas. I wanted them to wrap me in their arms and tell me I could totally do this—be *normal* and make friends —but I didn't want to come off as too needy. So I quietly slipped out my front door and headed around the side of the house to get my bike.

And came to a sudden stop.

Where the old, rusted bike usually sat, there was a gorgeous, brand new dark red bicycle. It was beautiful and shiny and had the cutest basket attached to the front. A basket Felix was currently sitting in.

My heart pounded, and I looked over my shoulder to see if the gift-giver was there, but there was no one.

Meow.

Well, no one besides Felix.

I reached out to scratch him on the chin. "Did you get this for me?"

Felix cocked his head as if saying *I am, in fact, a cat.*

I grinned. Easton or Lars must have gotten it for me, and that made me want to break out in a dance because this had to be a courting gift. Right? It *had* to be.

I ran my fingers down the beautiful, glossy paint and then got on, wiggling my butt when I realized the seat was the perfect height for me. Felix meowed sternly, batting his paw at the brand-new helmet hanging from one of the handles.

I frowned. "Felix, that will absolutely *ruin* my hair." But he wouldn't budge. I put the helmet on with a huff, buckling the strap under my chin. "Happy now?"

He curled up in the basket, the satisfied look on his face remaining our entire trip into town.

I parked outside Rosie's Cafe, and Felix stretched before jumping out of the basket. "You're welcome for the ride," I called out after him as he strutted away.

I turned to face the restaurant and then screamed when Stanley appeared in front of me.

"Good afternoon, Ms. Harvest," he exclaimed. He was wearing a knitted gray vest, and his white hair was combed back and gelled.

I clutched at my chest, heart pounding. "Umm, hi."

"I'm so glad I ran into you. I've been meaning to talk to you about your role in the upcoming Harvest Festival."

My anxiety was making it hard to track what he was saying. "My... role?"

"Yes, indeed. We pride ourselves on our festivals here in Starlight Grove, and our Harvest Festival is one of our top ten most important festivals of the year! Town member participation is essential."

"Oh, I don't think—"

"And I think with a name like yours, this is destiny. Can I put you down to run a craft booth? You do know a craft, right? And, of course, there's the crowning of the Harvest Queen. It's the most important part of the festival, and again, with a name like yours—"

"Ahh, Stanley! You're not cornering our sweet Olive, are you?" I jolted as Summer appeared at my side. Our only in-person interaction had been when I rudely shut my door on her, but it didn't seem like she held it against me when she looped her arm with mine.

Stanley looked perturbed at the interruption to his monologue. "We were just talking about the Harvest—"

"Harvest Festival," Summer said, cutting him off. "Yes, yes, very important." She cleared her throat. "Must get all omegas to make feminine crafts." Summer spoke the words in a robotic tone that made me laugh. "But we really must be going." She pulled me away from a protesting Stanley and didn't release me until we were safely inside the diner.

"Stanley and his festivals," Summer said, rolling her eyes and guiding me to a large table. "Char! We're grabbing the window table."

"Like I care!" a woman shouted back.

I raised my eyebrows, but Summer looked completely unbothered as she sat down.

"Now, the trick is to always check your surroundings before you come to a stop anywhere in town because Stanley is always waiting to pounce. And then, if he does track you down, you just need to run away as fast as you can."

My lips parted, and I was at a loss for what to say. This town was so much stranger than anything I'd imagined. Summer seemed to read my thoughts in my expression because she just smiled and patted my hand. "You'll get used to it."

"Get used to what?" A tall, blonde woman approached our table with glasses of water, and I realized she was an alpha. I'd only met a few female alphas. My parents' best friends had been a lobstering family consisting of a male and female alpha—Gunnar and Anna—and their omega, Sarah.

"She'll get used to Stanley and this crazy town," Summer said.

"Not sure that's possible." Char turned her gaze on me, her expression kind but assessing. "You're our new lighthouse keeper?"

I nodded.

"Good. We need more omegas in this town." She arched her eyebrow at my sweater. "Those boys work fast." She turned on her heel and headed back to her counter, leaving me with burning cheeks.

The door opened, and Lucy and Ivy entered. Lucy was wearing another pretty floral dress with an embroidered headband, and I anxiously fiddled with my too-long sleeves. Maybe I should have worn something cuter, but my omega had been very upset with the idea of taking off Easton's sweater.

"Oli!" Lucy exclaimed, once again using the nickname she'd bestowed upon me. She pulled me into a hug before she sat down beside me. "I would ask you how things are going, but I feel like that sweater says it all." I shifted in my seat, embarrassed, but Lucy's smile was teasing, not cruel.

"It's nice to see you," Ivy said. Her short hair was sticking up a bit on the side, but it looked really cute. "Do you prefer Olive or Oli?"

"Lucy's decided I'm an Oli," I said, secretly pleased. Nicknames were a thing *friends* gave to each other. "Either is good with me."

"I was so excited when I heard the new lighthouse keeper was an omega. I've never heard of an omega doing a job like that," Ivy said.

I smiled and took a sip of water, doing my best to ignore the uncomfortable feeling curling in my stomach as my thoughts flitted to the lie I'd put on my job application. Everything would be fine. I had a plan to manage everything.

Char came by to take our orders. I hardly ever ate out because of my finances, but I'd made sure I could squeeze this into my budget and was looking forward to it.

I was handing Char my menu when Lucy gasped, making all of us jump in our seats.

"It's Ella and Lincoln!" She excitedly pointed out the window.

"Shit, Luce, give us a warning next time," Summer said.

Two teenagers were crossing the street, and I realized the girl—Ella—was the barista I met in Beans 'n Bliss with Lucy the other day. The guy next to her was broad, dark-haired, and absolutely *fixated* on Ella. He couldn't keep his eyes off her as she chatted brightly away.

"When will they realize they're in love?" Lucy asked with a sigh as the couple turned the corner and slipped out of sight. "They're so cute together."

"I don't know, but this should cheer you up," Summer said. "Some eye candy is walking in right now."

The bell above the door rang as a dark-haired, brown-skinned, handsome alpha entered and headed to the counter to order.

"Okay, he is a cutie," Lucy said, fanning herself.

Ivy pursed her lips, but when she caught me looking at her, she blinked and transformed her expression into a smile.

We all looked on as Char got the alpha two coffees and two donuts to go. He was very attractive, but I could hear my omega go *meh, he's not as good as our alphas.* As he turned to leave, he caught Ivy's eye, and his face lit up. For a second, it looked like he was going to come over, but then he saw all of us sitting there, staring, and changed his mind. He gave her a sort of awkward half-wave with his full hands. Ivy's cheeks turned bright red and she waved back, letting out a little sigh when he left.

"Excuuuuuuse me. Who was that?" Summer asked, eyes wide.

Ivy took a slow sip of hot chocolate before primly putting down the mug. "He's a new teacher. He moved here with his partner at the start of the school year."

"An omega partner?" Summer asked.

Ivy picked at her napkin, cheeks flaming red. "Not that I know of."

"We can work with that," Summer said, grinning.

Ivy shifted in her seat, looking uncomfortable at having the attention on her.

"You're a teacher," I blurted out. Now the eyes turned on me, and I sat back in my chair. *Yes, excellent. Why ask an intelligent question when I could instead loudly declare Ivy's profession?*

A little smile twisted Ivy's lips and she gave me a wink. "Yeah, I teach fifth grade."

"She's an amazing teacher," Lucy gushed. "All her kids adore her. It makes it almost impossible to walk around town with her—it's always Ms. Winter *this*, Ms. Winter *that*."

"Lucy's exaggerating," Ivy said, but she was smiling fully now and it was obvious how much her friend's words meant to her.

"I think that's amazing," I said. "I was homeschooled, which was my decision. I preferred to spend my days out on the boat with my parents." At their confused expressions, I clarified. "My dad was a lobsterman. His family was for generations. And my mom and I helped him on the boat."

"That's so cool," Summer said. Then she dropped her voice. "But don't let Stanley know or he'll recruit you for our annual Jumpin' July Rockin' Lobster Roll Competition. Which, if the name didn't tip you off, is a three-part competition where you have to jump rope, play a rock song, and then present a lobster roll for judging."

My jaw dropped. "Um, how many festivals do you have?"

"The limit doesn't exist," Lucy said. "Stanley invents new ones each year."

Char and another woman came to drop off our food.

"I'm not sure you're doing a good job convincing the girl we're normal," Char said. She put my burger and fries in front of me. It looked and smelled *amazing*.

"Well, that was always going to be an impossible task," the woman beside her said. "I'm Rosie, this one's omega." She nodded her head at Char. "She named the cafe after me and now thinks she can put me to work whenever she wants." She let out a little squeal when Char pinched her butt.

"Omegas," the alpha said, rolling her eyes. Then she leaned down and kissed Rosie on the forehead. "Stay and chat if you want, darling. Gavin will be here soon."

Rosie pulled up an extra chair. "You don't mind me crashing the party?"

"Oh my gosh, you don't have to ask. Sit down," Lucy said. "We really need a name for our little posse."

Ivy held up her hand. "If you suggest the Omega Overlords one more time..."

Lucy turned her bright eyes on me. "What do you think, Olive? Want to be part of the Omega Overlords?"

I covered my laugh with a cough, but the other omegas' expressions told me I wasn't very convincing. "I'm not sure I'm the overlord type."

Lucy huffed and sat back in her seat. "Well, since you all turned down Omega Otters and the Official Omega Squad, I don't know what you want from me."

Summer held a hand up to her ear and looked around. "Oh, yep, that's right. No one is demanding a group name except *you*."

Rosie grinned. "Is this the relaxed lunch you were expecting, Olive?"

"I'm quite sure I did not promise a relaxing lunch," Lucy sniffed. "Just a fun one."

"Well, it's definitely that," I said, digging into my burger and curly fries. It was the best meal I'd had since the pho Summer included in the welcome basket. Although it wasn't difficult to impress me, the person who subsisted on microwave meals and ramen.

"Pass me the ketchup?" Summer asked, grabbing it from Ivy.

"Oh, Stanley cornered Oli when she got here, talking about the Harvest Festival."

"Oh god," Rosie said while Lucy gave a loud, exasperated sigh, and Ivy lightly rubbed her forehead.

"Look," Lucy said, waving her french fry in the air, "I enjoy all our festivals, but no one loves a festival like Stanley. And he always wants us to do some sort of girly craft."

"Lucy, you're the craftiest person I know," Rosie said with a grin.

Summer's fist came down and hit the table. "It's the *principle* of the thing. Just because we're omegas doesn't mean we like to do feminine crafts or spend time with children. Even though Lucy does tons of girly crafts and Ivy loves children."

"It's the principle," Ivy said.

"The *principle*," Lucy repeated. "Which is why we always put together crafts that Stanley will hate. Last year, I led a cross stitch class."

I raised an eyebrow.

"She taught everyone how to cross-stitch their favorite curse words onto pillows," Ivy clarified, her lips twisting in a smile.

"And I made balloon animals for the children," Summer said, an evil smile on her face. "It's not my fault they were all snakes because I don't know shit about balloon animals."

"And then all the children used their balloons like swords and attacked Stanley with them," Rosie said.

"Tell us, Olive, what horrible talents can you show off?" Lucy asked.

The iron fist of anxiety squeezed my chest at the thought of having to run a booth at a festival. "Nothing," I said, shaking my head. "I have no talents."

"Excellent," Lucy said. "That is *exactly* the energy we need."

I choked on my drink.

"You don't have to participate," Ivy said warmly. "I've decided this year, I'm going to have the kids paint rocks. It will be fun."

"Rocks?" Summer rubbed her hands together. "That sounds exceptionally dull. It's perfect."

"While this is a thrilling conversation, I want to know about

Olive's sweater," Rosie said, a mischievous glint in her eye. "Because I can smell Easton on it from across the table."

My cheeks burned so hot I was on the verge of bursting into flames, but my omega was a snarling, furious mess that another omega knew what *my* alpha smelled like.

The girls must have seen something in my expression because Summer leaned forwards and squeezed my arm. "We've all grown up with Easton, but it's never been romantic."

"Oh, I'm sorry, Olive," Rosie said, looking truly contrite. "I shouldn't have said that."

I shook my head. "It's totally fine."

"I remember those early days, especially before I bonded with Gavin and Char. I hated the idea of any omega being within a hundred feet of them... or maybe a thousand. It's normal to feel possessive of what's yours."

I twisted my fingers in the sweater. "They're not mine," I mumbled.

Summer nudged me with her elbow. "I think they are."

"And they better act right," Lucy sniffed. "I've been wanting a sister ever since Lars pushed me at the playground when I was five."

"He pushed you?" I asked.

"Well, maybe not on purpose," she said, and Summer rolled her eyes. "But brothers are just so *ughhh*. Big and annoying and bossy. Sisters are way better, and I can't wait for you all to make it official."

I swirled my straw in my drink. Along with that anxious fist in my chest was a warm, syrupy feeling. At Lucy's acceptance of me dating her brother. At the fact that all the omegas at the table thought the guys wanted me.

Rosie reached across the table and patted my hand. "My best advice is to make them work for it. Alphas need a challenge, so make it hard for them. You're the prize here. And even once you've bonded, keep them on their toes."

"Aren't you—" I swallowed my words, fighting the voice in my head that told me to just nod and stay quiet. But this might be my only chance to talk to a bonded omega. I looked around, making sure Char was still at the cash register, and lowered my voice. "Aren't you worried they'll get tired of you? That they'll think it's all too much work?"

"Olive," Rosie said, her eyes soft. "When you find the right alphas, they'll never make you feel like you're too much because you won't be. You'll be just enough for each other. If they think you're too much work, they're not the right alphas for you."

I gave her a tight smile, trying to let her words sink in. The alpha from the *incident* years ago obviously wasn't the right one for me, but there was no escaping the reality that I was an exhausting person, prone to pushing people away with my less-than-sparkling personality and multitude of issues.

The rest of lunch rushed by way too quickly, ending with Summer presenting us with cookies—a new recipe, she said. She wanted to start a bakery and was testing what should be on the menu. Char grumbled about outside food, but ate two of them.

The omegas sent me home with a package of cookies, lots of hugs, and promises to get together soon.

By the time I got home, my cheeks hurt from smiling.

21

EASTON

I perked up when I heard Olive's bike coming down the path, the dirt and gravel crunching under the wheels. I threw down what I was working on and sprinted out of the lighthouse. By the time I rounded the cottage, Olive was unlocking the front door. I snatched her up around the waist, and she squealed in surprise as I spun her in the air.

"Easton," she cried out, laughing.

"You've been hiding from me, Olive." My voice was a low growl as I pressed my face into her beautiful hair. She was wearing *my* sweater and it was almost too much for my heart to handle. That anxious voice in the back of my head kept warning me that I was going to scare her away with my intensity, but the fact that she was wearing my clothes, covered in my scent? It seemed her omega liked my possessiveness.

Her breaths came fast as she clutched at me. "No, I haven't."

"Little liar." I put her down on the ground but didn't let go. My omega liked to run and hide, but she needed to know I would catch her every time.

"I had lunch with Lucy and her friends." She said it quietly, like she was shy about it. My chest almost exploded with happiness at knowing everyone in town had seen her in my sweater.

I caressed her face. "They're your friends now, sunshine."

Olive bit her lip, not quite meeting my gaze, but then she said, "Yeah, I guess they are."

I smiled and pressed a kiss against her lips. Her beautiful, soft, pink lips that I couldn't get enough of, that had been stretched around my cock just yesterday. *Not now not now*, I chanted at the image, pushing it from my mind. I needed to be focused.

"I'm so glad you're making friends, baby, but I hope you haven't made any plans for tonight."

She tilted her head up, rubbing her cheek against mine, and I couldn't stop my purr. It rumbled through my chest, the sound tailor-made to soothe my omega. Olive gasped, and I clutched her tighter to my chest in case she was freaked out enough to pull away. But she melted against me, rubbing her cheek against my t-shirt, getting her scent all over it. It wasn't very strong—she must be wearing some of that horrible deodorant—but it was enough that I knew I'd go to sleep tonight with my shirt tucked under my pillow.

"Why is that?" she asked.

"Because I'm taking you out."

"Oh."

I waited for her to say something else, but she stayed silent. I pulled back enough to see her face. Did she not want to go out with me?

"Are you sure?" she asked, chewing her lip. "Are you sure you want... *me*?"

"What kind of question is that?" I searched her face, waiting for her to shout, *Just kidding!* I understood why Olive might doubt me. She didn't know me well yet, didn't understand how serious I was about this, but how could she doubt her own perfection?

"You didn't knock on the door this morning." Her eyes were on the ground, her voice unsure.

My heart seized in my chest. I'd wanted to take her out for breakfast this morning so I could show everyone around town that she was *mine*. And then after, she could come watch me work in the lighthouse. I'd practiced flexing in the mirror to make sure I looked impressive—like a good, strong alpha who could provide for her. But

Lars said we shouldn't pressure her and to let her come to us. *Well, just goes to show how much Lars knows.* The more space we gave Olive, the more she doubted us.

No more space.

I picked her up, my hands cupping her gorgeous ass. The press of her luscious body against mine made my cock harden, straining to be inside her again.

Her arms and legs wrapped tight around me. "What are you doing?"

"This is your punishment for doubting that I want to take you out."

I carried her around the side of the house, heading to the lighthouse door. She ran her nose down the side of my neck and pressed the whisper of a kiss against my skin. "I'm not sure this is punishment."

A low groan slipped through my lips, and I was tempted to fuck her against the exterior of the lighthouse, but I didn't want Olive to think this was all just about sex for me. Besides, Finn would be pissed about me disturbing the "fragile exterior" of the historic structure.

I juggled her so my arm was under her ass, leaving my other hand free to open the lighthouse door. "You're going to be a good girl, stay where I put you, and watch your alphas work."

There was a sharp inhale of breath. Olive wriggled against me, her sweet pussy pressing against my cock. "Easton, you can't carry me up all the stairs."

"That's funny because I'm pretty sure I am." I wasn't sure why I was being so grouchy—that was usually Finn's territory—but it had been excruciating to leave Olive yesterday. I wanted to sleep in her bed, carry her around so her feet never had to touch the ground, and make sure she ate and got as many orgasms as she needed. Now that she was back in my arms, I didn't think I had the strength to let her go.

"Bossy Easton." Her breath lightly skated across my skin.

"That's right." I opened the door, and Finn and Lars turned towards us. Lars grinned and Finn shifted, looking uncomfortable. I needed Finn to get on board with all of this. He and Olive had so much in common—both were prickly and reserved and completely *mine*.

My brother, my omega, my family.

I sat Olive down on a chair and caged her in with my arms. "Now, are you going to be a very good girl and stay put?"

She gave a little shrug. The slight furrow in her brow smoothed out, and her mouth turned up in the barest hint of a smile. "Guess we'll have to see."

Excitement shot through me at her teasing, the reappearance of her sass. I craved it, *needed* it. I leaned in close, brushing my lips against the shell of her ear. "Just remember, I'll have all evening to deal with my naughty girl."

22

FINN

OLIVE. OLIVE. OLIVE.

She was here.

Mere feet away.

The service room in the lighthouse was cramped, but it wasn't like I would be able to ignore her presence, no matter the size of the room.

Easton was chatting away, telling Olive all about our plans for the restoration. While his back was turned, Lars crowded the chair she was sitting on and pulled off the sweater she was wearing—one of Easton's. Then he pulled one of his sweaters out of a tote bag he'd brought this morning. Olive's cheeks were bright red when her head emerged from Lars's sweater. It was swimming on her and she looked so fucking cozy. A rumble started in my chest, my alpha wanting her in *my* clothes, but luckily the sound was covered by Easton's outraged shout when he saw Olive wasn't wearing his sweater anymore.

The rest of the afternoon passed too fast and too slow. Easton and Lars peppered Olive with questions, throwing me exasperated looks when I stayed quiet. I kept my hands busy, but I hung on every single word.

She was smart and sassy, and underneath it all, there was a tender vulnerability that I couldn't help but recognize.

Occasionally, I felt her eyes on me, whereas my eyes were strained from staring unseeingly at blueprints I'd already memorized.

I'd thought being back at the lighthouse would feel like descending into a dark valley of ghosts—horrible and oppressive. That was how it felt the last time I was in the cottage, packing up boxes of my grandparents' things. But now, there was a lightness in this space, like all the ghosts had turned friendly as they welcomed me back home.

And I knew the reason was Olive.

She wasn't a ghost, but she was haunting my every thought.

I wanted to know everything about her. What her favorite ice cream flavor was. If she was a morning person or night owl. How she'd learned to ride a bike. Did her father run alongside her and cheer her on, comforting her when she skinned a knee?

Did she have any idea what her scent did to me? How it was everything calm and cozy, the reminder of the transition of the seasons, heading into the quiet of winter? How it centered me, making me feel like I was coming back to myself after a long journey away?

Easton was right when he called Olive *sunshine*. There was a brightness in her, bright precisely because it had been hard won. And I wondered for the millionth time if I was being the biggest fool, trying to stay away. Maybe the reason I hadn't been able to be honest with my brothers was because I wasn't being honest with myself.

I wanted Olive.

I swallowed hard.

But I couldn't have her.

I jolted at the sound of a door shutting and looked up from the papers, realizing that Easton and Lars had left. I'd been zoned out and had no idea where they went, but now there was no avoiding the cute omega.

"Finn?" Her voice was so gentle. She was back in Easton's sweater—he'd managed to switch them while Lars did some electrical work. "Do you want me to leave? I don't... don't want to make you uncomfortable."

"No," I blurted out before I could think. I told myself it was because my brothers would be upset if she left, upset at *me* for asking her to go, but the excuse was so fucking feeble it didn't come close to being convincing. I took a deep breath, taking off my reading glasses. "Olive, about the other night..."

I was cut off when the door opened and Lars re-entered, holding up his smaller toolkit he'd left downstairs. He stopped abruptly and looked between Olive and me, clearly reading the tension in the room. "Should I leave? Easton's grabbing coffee for us, but I can distract him if you want some time together?"

Olive looked at me, but I was at a loss for words. I needed to apologize, but my apology would lead to an explanation of why I did what I did, which would then lead to me having to tell her I wouldn't be courting her. The idea of hurting her feelings killed me.

When I stayed silent, she turned back to Lars. "No, come in." She held her arms out to him and he quickly squeezed her to his chest. "I want to see your *special* toolbox," she said with a wink when he pulled away.

Lars snorted a laugh at the terrible innuendo, but I saw the heat in his eyes as he pressed his fingers into her curvy hips.

I wished they were my hands.

He pulled Easton's sweater off and replaced it with his own, Olive's hair sticking up with static when she emerged laughing.

I turned around before my jealousy ate me alive.

23

EASTON

I FIDGETED WITH THE BUTTONS ON MY SHIRT AS I WAITED for Olive to open the door. I rarely dressed up, so I kept tugging at my suit jacket. Lucy had tailored it for me so it fit, but I still felt a little awkward in it. Would Olive like it?

The door opened, and there she was. My omega. She was wearing those fucking fishnet tights again, this time with thigh-high boots, a short black skirt, and a cream sweater. My mouth gaped like a fish as I tried to come up with something to say, any words to describe how fucking sexy she was. I wanted to bury myself between those thick thighs again, dig my fingers into her every dip and curve.

"Am I dressed okay?" she asked, her words hesitant. "I can change."

"No," I almost shouted. I pulled her out of the house by her waist, shutting the door behind her. "Don't you fucking dare."

"Oh." Her lips parted and I captured them with my own, my fingers twisting in her hair, my other hand gripping her hip tightly. She wrapped her arms around me, pressing her soft breasts against my chest.

"My Olive," I murmured against her lips. "I can't think clearly around you." I palmed her ass and she let out a moan, which went straight to my cock. I stepped forward until her back was against the door. "Fuck, your body is perfect. So fucking soft. You fit against me like you were made for me."

"You like my outfit, then?" she asked as I kissed my way down her throat.

"Like is an understatement, little siren. I would wreck my boat at sea just to get close to you."

Her fingers ran through my hair. "That is the weirdest compliment I've ever gotten."

I reluctantly pulled away, cupping her cheek. "Get used to it."

I took her hand and we headed up the pathway to town. People peered out of shop windows at us, and I tugged Olive closer to me, trying to distract her. I loved showing her off, wanted to run around town shouting that she was mine, but I didn't want her to feel self-conscious.

"Do you like Chinese?" I asked as we neared the restaurant. Shit, what if she didn't? She ate a lot of instant noodles, but that didn't mean...

"Yes, I love it."

Her smile was radiant as she looked up at me.

"Good, because here we are."

I stopped us in front of the Red Lantern. "This restaurant actually belongs to Summer's parents."

She cocked her head. "Isn't Summer Vietnamese?"

"Yep."

She laughed. "Well, okay then."

Olive was quiet when we first sat down, but I didn't mind. I could talk enough for both of us. And slowly, over General Tso's and Kung Pow Chicken, she opened up. Told me about her family, about pranks she pulled on her dad while they were out lobstering. With every word, I fell more and more in love with her.

Our server brought the bill—which I grabbed before her hand could so much as twitch towards it—and fortune cookies to our table.

She squirmed a little in her seat. "Are you sure?" She gestured at the bill.

I handed her a fortune cookie. "Absolutely. Now, read your fortune. They're always a bit unique."

Olive pursed her lips but did what she was told, cracking open the cookie. "Never give up on your dreams. Unless they're unrealistic. Then yeah, give up on those." She scrunched her nose adorably.

I broke apart my cookie and flattened the fortune. "Mine just says, 'For rectal use only.'"

Olive had just taken a sip of her drink and spat it all over the table. "It does *not*."

I held up the paper slip as she wiped down the table.

"Oh my god, it does."

"So, you know, a little preview of what's to come." I gave her a wink.

Without missing a beat, she asked, "Oh, you're into pegging?"

Now it was my turn to choke on my drink. "No, nope, absolutely not."

Olive just smiled.

Cheeky omega.

I pulled out my phone to check the time. "Oh, shit. We're running late. It's time for phase two of our date." I put some cash down on the table and reached for Olive's hand.

"Phase two? Lead the way."

"Phase two is dancing?" Olive asked, staring at the sign outside the Starlight Grove Community Center.

"Marisol and Carmen are teaching a class. I thought it could be fun."

Olive chewed her lip. "I don't know. I can't dance."

"Neither can I. That's why we're taking the class."

A wisp of bitter scent came off her, and I wrapped my arms around her. "We don't have to go if you don't want to, baby." Had I gone too far? I thought this would be a fun way for her to become a part of the town, but maybe it was too much too soon.

She took a deep breath. "It's okay. We can give it a try. Just don't make fun of my terrible skills."

"I would never." I tilted her chin so I could press a gentle kiss to her lips. "My brave girl. Let's go make fools of ourselves."

We slipped into the back of the large community room, already filled with pairs of dance partners.

"We'll stay back here," I said, tucking a strand of Olive's hair behind her ear. She nodded and clung to my arm a little tighter.

"Welcome, everyone!" Marisol said, clapping her hands. "It's so exciting to see everyone here." Her eyes zeroed in on the two of us, and her smile widened.

"Tonight, we will learn the basics of Bachata, a very sensual dance." Carmen drew out the word *sensual*, staring directly at Olive and me while she said it.

They grabbed a couple of hot, young male volunteers and showed us the basic steps. Olive and I fumbled through them, but the more we danced, the more she loosened up.

"Bachata is about feeling the music," Carmen said. "Olive, loosen your hips. I want to see them swaying side to side with each step."

Olive gave a little frustrated huff as we fumbled through the next series of steps.

"You're supposed to loosen your hips," I tease.

"Well, *you're* supposed to be leading me," she snapped back, her voice all frosty. I grinned. I loved snippy Olive.

I moved my hand down from her waist until I was palming her ass cheek and pulled her tight against me. "There, now I can help you with your hip movements," I murmured.

"This was not part of the instructions," she hissed. But she didn't try to move away. With every step and swing of her hips, her hot little pussy ground against me.

"I'm not sure what that is. It's not Bachata, but it *is* sensual."

Olive jolted and we both turned to find Carmen and Marisol a few feet away, looking fucking gleeful.

I cleared my throat and looked back at Olive. "You know, I think we've mastered this dancing thing. Do you want to head out?"

Her cheeks were flaming red, and she couldn't quite look anyone in the eye. "Yep, yep. No one has the moves like us."

I chuckled, gave the sisters a wave, and led my omega out of the community center.

"I'm never going to be able to show my face in town," Olive groaned once we got outside. The night air was cool, and I tugged her flush against my body to make sure she stayed warm.

"Nah, it will be fine. And if they make a big deal about it, I'll egg Stanley's car. Give the town something else to talk about."

She pursed her lips, but I knew she was fighting a smile. Relief flooded me that she wasn't too upset. I couldn't stand the idea of hurting Olive in any way.

"Should we walk back?"

She stood on her tiptoes and gave me a kiss, running her fingers down the stubble on my jaw. "Yes, please."

24

OLIVE

I paused at my front door, Easton beside me. I'd been so anxious about this date, but everything with Easton was just... *fun*. Easy.

The date could end here, and I knew Easton would accept it. Wouldn't be mad at me for it.

But I didn't want the date to be over.

"Do you want to come inside?" Ugh. My question came out so unsure and pathetic. I cleared my throat, gearing up to sound more confident.

Easton blinked, his lips parted. "Really?" Now it was his turn to clear his throat. "You don't have to," he rushed to say.

For as persistent as Easton could be, he had never pushed this, never even asked why I didn't want them inside.

"How do you *know*?" I asked. This time, exasperation tinged my tone.

He furrowed his brow and took a step closer, his hand cupping my elbow, his thumb massaging my arm. "What do you mean?"

"How do you know I'm nervous about having people in my space? I swear you understand me better than I understand myself sometimes."

A self-satisfied grin spreads across his face. "Because I see you,

Olive. I've known you were meant to be mine since the moment I first spotted you." He twisted a piece of my hair around his fingers. "And I've been watching you."

"Watching me?" I asked, sounding breathless.

"Just when you would come into town, not like setting up cameras inside your home. Because that would be inappropriate." He nodded a little too aggressively, as if he was proud of himself for knowing that would be wrong. "I was just... observing you, sunshine."

"Observing," I said slowly, running my hands down his chest. "Is that what we're calling stalking these days?"

Easton huffed and pulled me into his tight embrace. "I don't fucking care, Olive. You can be mad at me all you want, but I can't stop."

"I mean, I did suspect something was going on when you were always at the market with me." A smile tugged at my lips. I couldn't even pretend to be mad at him. My Easton. My stalker. "But... I don't want you to just watch me. I want you here." I took a deep breath. "Here, with me, inside my home."

He squeezed me even tighter. I was crushed against his chest. Not a whisper of space between us.

"I know you're a private person. You're shy and prickly and so adorably snarky. You need time to trust people, and that's something I understand."

I didn't move, barely breathed, too afraid to break the spell. I could tell by the way Easton's body trembled, the way his scent turned bitter, that whatever he was thinking about was painful. My arms flexed around him, as if they were powerful enough to stop the bad memories.

"Do you want to tell me about it?"

He buried his face in my hair, breathing in deeply, and it made me wish I hadn't worn deodorant today. I always wore it while going out so I didn't irritate anyone else with my scent. But I wanted to give Easton my scent now.

"My mom wasn't a good mom," he started, his words slightly muffled against my hair. "There were always men in and out of our house, and they were always more important than me. I never invited anyone over because I was ashamed. I didn't want them to see how I was living—the trash and cigarette butts everywhere." His hands twisted into my hair, and he pressed my face tighter to that spot where his neck and shoulders met. "I didn't want them to see how she treated me... how she hit me and yelled when she was angry. By the time I was a teenager, I stopped coming home. I started by camping out—first in the woods, but it freaked me the fuck out. Then on the beach. Carina found me one night and demanded I come inside, and I ended up living here, in this house, for a lot of high school."

The image of a young Easton, bright and sweet and *good*, being abused destroyed me. We stood there in silence, clinging to each other. Finally, the lump in my throat eased enough so I could speak without bursting into tears.

"You didn't deserve that." I pressed my lips against his skin.

I felt him shrug. "I was an obnoxious kid."

I sucked in an angry breath and pulled away just enough to see his face. "No," I said fiercely. "You never deserved that. No child does."

He took a deep, shuddering breath, and the tension in his face eased. "My fierce Olive. I was lucky. I had Lars and Finn and this whole community to care for me."

"That's good," I whispered. I hated that I hadn't been there for him. It didn't make sense—we hadn't lived in the same town, and our seven-year age gap meant we wouldn't have spent time together as kids anyway. But I wished it all the same—that I could have loved young Easton.

I would just have to love him now.

My heart skipped a beat. Did I love Easton? I wasn't sure, but the lightness filling my chest felt a lot like it.

I pulled away and took him by the hand. "Come inside."

Easton's grip tightened as he interlocked our fingers. "This is your safe space, baby. I might not be the most patient or laid-back guy in the world"—I snorted, and he gave my ass a smack—"but I would never push you into something you're not ready for. We're going to have forever together, so I can wait until you're ready."

Forever.

I fiddled with the collar of his button-down, keeping my eyes fixed on his throat. "Easton, you can't be sure about me."

"But I am."

I had to resist stomping my foot. "But you can't be. You barely know me—"

He cupped the side of my face, and I couldn't stop myself from leaning into his palm. It was rough from his work and so warm against my cold cheeks. "I thought we'd determined that I know you better than you know yourself."

"But—"

"And if that's the case, then it makes perfect sense that I know we're made for each other."

His words were so sincere, so *sure*.

He pressed a soft kiss to my forehead. "We need to get you warm, baby."

I reached into my bag, pulled out my keys, and unlocked the front door. Easton hung back as I took a step inside. I didn't give him a chance to doubt himself again and pulled him inside.

The smile he gave me was so bright and brilliant it would be burned in my mind forever. His warm hands grasped my cold one, and he followed me in.

25

EASTON

I'D DONE IT—TOLD OLIVE ABOUT MY PAST.

Even after all this time and years of therapy, I still got that cold pit of shame in my stomach when I thought about it. I knew my mom abusing me wasn't my fault, but sometimes I still felt like I must have done something to cause it.

I shook the dark thoughts from my mind as Olive pulled me into her home—what had been my home, for a short time at least. But I came to an abrupt stop when I saw that it was empty.

Completely empty.

The entire time I'd known this house, the living room had been filled with an eclectic assortment of comfortable couches and armchairs. Now, there was a single basket with a blanket in it next to a tired-looking lawn chair. There were no decorations on the walls. I caught the corner of something wooden in the kitchen.

I knew what it was—a small, beat-up table.

I knew because it was one of the few things we'd decided to leave in the house when the three of us packed up all of Carina and Fredrick's furniture and put it in storage.

"I know it's, well, kind of awful right now, but I'm going to fix it up," Olive said, her scent growing bitter with embarrassment. "There must have been some mix-up because I was told it would come furnished, but it didn't, and I haven't had the mon—I mean, time—to buy stuff. But I will, promise." Her tone grew more high-pitched and frantic as she spoke. She could obviously read the growing horror on my face and thought it was aimed at her when she wasn't to blame.

We were the ones to blame. Lars, Finn, and me.

The stuff that had been in here belonged to Finn's grandparents. We'd all decided to move it to storage until we bought a home and had more space for it. But Stanley and Carmen must have thought those things belonged to the lighthouse. I mean, fuck if I knew who it actually belonged to—Fredrik and Carina had lived here for about a million years, so maybe some of their things had come with the lighthouse.

My alpha was urging me to throw Olive over my shoulder and drive however long it took to find a 24/7 furniture store and fix this. Or I'd take her to my wood shop and fucking *make* her furniture tonight.

I also hadn't missed that she'd been about to say she hadn't had the *money* for furniture. Hmm. That would be tricky. How was I going to convince my Olive to let me furnish her house?

It took every therapy coping skill I'd ever learned to help me stay calm, shake out my shoulders, and turn to her with a smile. Fuck. She looked so tense and sad right now, all curled up on herself. I ran my hand down her arm. "I see you're embracing minimalism. I watched a documentary about that once."

Her startled eyes met mine. "How was it?"

"Couldn't tell you. I fell asleep a few minutes in. Must be why Finn always yells at me for being messy. It's not my fault he doesn't pay attention to where he's going. You leave your backpack at the top of the stairs *one time* and never hear the end of it."

The corner of Olive's lips twitched, and it eased the horrible sinking sensation in my stomach. "I might have to agree with Finn on that one. Bit of a tripping hazard."

"Yeah, I figured that one out when he fell down the stairs."

Olive blinked up at me before giving me a shove. "Easton! That's terrible."

I shrugged. "He was *fiiiine*." After wearing a brace on his wrist for a month, but I didn't think Olive needed to hear that part of the story. I'd felt guilty as fuck and had been much more careful of where I put my things... mostly. "Shoes on or off?"

Her head tilted to the side.

"In the house," I clarified. "Do you wear shoes inside?"

Olive swallowed hard and there was the slightest tremble in her lip. "You still want to come in?"

My heart thumped. I could bear a lot in the world, but seeing Olive sad or ashamed wasn't one of them. I took her hand, interlacing her fingers with mine. "I'm a big, strong alpha. It takes more than a radical commitment to minimalism to scare me away."

She ducked her head, but not before I saw her pleased expression. "Shoes off, please."

"Lars will love that," I said, toeing off my shoes as Olive did the same. "Those Swedes hate shoes in the house."

"I think there might be some Swedish ancestry on my mom's side," she mused. Then she fell silent and was looking everywhere except at me.

If it were anyone else, I would think she wanted me to go, but I knew Olive. She was just feeling shy.

"Why don't you show me around, baby?"

She nodded. "Right, yes. Although... you probably know the house better than I do."

"Show me anyway." I leaned down and kissed her forehead.

I followed Olive around the house. She scowled at each room, was flustered as she offered some tea (I declined) and a homemade cookie, Summer's latest experiment (which I accepted). Finally, we were standing in front of a closed door. "This is where I sleep." She was staring at the door, anxiety radiating off her, and I'd had enough. I picked her up in my arms so her front was pressed against my chest.

"Olive, baby, if you're not comfortable inviting me in, that is absolutely fine. We can go to my house or"—and I spoke these words through gritted teeth—"end the night here."

A startled laugh burst from Olive, and it was the best fucking sound.

"You sound so angry at the idea of ending the night."

"Yeah, well, I'm greedy with you. I want all your time—every single second of it."

She ran her fingers through my hair. "My stalker."

"Yours, baby."

She clutched one arm around my neck before leaning to the side and opening the door with another.

"Want to come into my nest, alpha?"

"Fuck yes, sunshine."

I TURNED on the floor lamp, and it cast a glow across Olive's nest. It was precious—a mattress on the floor layered with colorful blankets and, to my absolute thrill, a couple sweaters I recognized as mine and Lars's.

"I love your nest, baby." I pressed hot kisses down the side of her face and neck. "It's so perfect. You're perfect."

I lowered us down to the mattress.

"Oh wait—"

I let out a strangled, surprised noise as the bed moved violently below us.

"It's an air mattress," she finished.

I let out a burst of laughter as I hit the edge and tumbled to the floor.

"Sorry, sorry," she said, her hands trying to pull me back onto the bed.

I rolled both of us to the center to avoid falling off again. "We might need to upgrade the mattress, sunshine. Not sure air mattresses are rated for this much sexiness."

"Yeah... it's amazing it's held me this long," she said.

It took me a minute to process her words, but then I started laughing harder. I tugged at her sweater, pushing it above her breasts. She was wearing a black lacy bra and I groaned, capturing her nipple with my lips. She let out a little moan, and I sucked the opposite one. "I need to see you, baby. All of you."

I stripped off her sweater. While I took my shirt off, hands shaking as I worked on the buttons, she got her bra and skirt off. Then she was lying there naked except for those fishnet stockings and a tiny thong. She covered her stomach a bit as if feeling self-conscious, and I pushed them aside, kissing a line down her soft stomach. "Don't hide from me, baby. I love all of you." I ran my hands down her legs, squeezing hard. "Including these fucking tights. God, can't get enough."

I spread her legs wide, savoring how her breath caught, and ran my nose up her slit. "I fucking hate your deodorant. I want your scent on me all the time. I want you to come over and roll around on all my clothes. I want to start every day with the taste of your sweet pussy on my lips."

She choked out a laugh. "Oh my god, Easton. You're ridiculous."

But her fingers twisted in my hair, keeping me in place.

As if I would pull away.

I licked the slick off her inner thighs, groaning at her sweetness. I needed more. I tugged her g-string out of the way and licked her sweet pussy with a groan. I would get her completely naked soon, but I wanted this memory burned in her mind so she would think about it every time she put on these tights. I licked and sucked, getting lost in the taste of her.

Olive let out a shriek. "Right there, right there, fuck, *Easton.*"

"That's right, baby, give it all to me. What a good girl."

I pressed two fingers inside her, her wet heat sucking me in. I was seconds away from humping this horrible air mattress to get relief for my rock-hard cock.

I sucked her clit into my mouth, and that did it. Olive fell apart with a loud cry, and I licked up the slick that gushed from her as she shook and whimpered.

"Oh my god," she gasped.

I grinned and moved up her body so I could hold her in my arms. "You're so fucking sexy."

She nuzzled into my neck, scent-marking me, and I kissed her forehead.

"I love forehead kisses," she murmured, clutching at me tighter and perfuming when I gave her another kiss on her cheek and forehead.

"Mmm, I've never had one," I mused. "But you can have as many as you want."

Olive shifted so she could cup my face. "You've never had a forehead kiss? You need forehead kisses, too." She wrapped her hand around the back of my neck and tugged me down so she could press a gentle kiss to my forehead.

A warmth spread inside me at the gentleness of it. How special it made me feel.

"Thank you, baby." My chest felt tight with all the love I had for her. I wanted to tell her... but would it be too much for my skittish Olive? Instead, I poured all my love for her into a kiss. My hands cradled her face as the kiss deepened. I carefully rolled us so I was on top of her, the mattress shifting precariously under us.

"What are the odds we break this?"

"I don't know, alpha. Do you have plans for more rigorous activity?"

"Mmm, so rigorous." I pulled back slightly. "You want that, baby?"

"I want to feel all of you."

We engaged in a clumsy dance to strip off the rest of our clothes, and then I was back on top of her.

"I love how you feel against me," she said. I groaned as her fingers surrounded my cock and squeezed. "I need you inside me."

She moved me to her entrance and I pressed inside. I tried to keep it slow in case she needed to adjust, but then her legs were wrapped around me, and she pulled me in all the way. I swore as the heat of her surrounded me, and I had to close my eyes and grit my teeth to keep from coming.

Olive giggled. "You okay, there?"

I opened my eyes and saw my omega's amused expression. "Just trying not to embarrass myself," I choked out.

She ran her fingers through my hair again. "You won't, Easton. You've already made me feel *so* good, and now I need you to move."

I wasn't about to make her beg. I pulled out almost all the way and then thrust inside her, hard. I wanted to record the little noises she made so I could listen to them all day long.

I hitched her thigh up to give me more access as my knot started to swell. I ground forward so my knot hit her clit with every thrust.

"*Ohmygod* I'm going to come again," Olive cried out.

She came with another thrust and I couldn't hold off anymore. With another big thrust, I pressed my knot all the way inside her. I buried my face in her hair as the strongest orgasm I'd ever felt washed over me, stealing my words, stealing my breath. My whole world narrowed down to *her*, my Olive.

Her arms and legs were still wrapped around me when I finally came back to earth.

"Am I crushing you?" I croaked.

She wiggled beneath me. "Maybe a little."

"Hold on tight." I palmed her ass, keeping her pressed to me as I rolled us over so she was on top. She cried out at the movement, her pussy clamping down tight.

"Did you just come again?"

She laughed. "Yeah, I think I did."

I jiggled her, savoring her soft giggle, and pressed my smile to the side of her face. "You're amazing."

"You are." She traced her fingers down my chest. "Thanks for seeing me, Easton. For not letting me push you away."

My heart squeezed at her words. I knew she couldn't move—she was stuck to me until my knot went down—but I still clutched her to my chest, one arm banding around her back and my other hand cupping her inner thigh.

"This is it, Olive. You gave me a chase, but I caught you. I hope you don't think I'm going to let you go."

She didn't respond and I thought she'd fallen asleep, but then her words came, so quiet and vulnerable they made my heart ache. "I hope you don't."

26

OLIVE

EASTON MIGHT HAVE AN OBSESSION WITH STAYING inside me.

I woke with the sunrise like I always did, and Easton's knot was still locked inside me. We'd fucked *several times* in the night, my sleepy memories covered in an orgasm haze, and he'd knotted me every time. I loved having him inside me, feeling the stretch and ache and fullness, but now I had to get up.

I shifted, and his knot slipped out with a gush of fluid. I wrinkled my nose. I'd have to do laundry later.

I tried to move off him, but his arms banded around me like steel.

"Where are you going?" His voice was muffled in my hair.

"You are not knotting me for like the fifth time." I laughed. "Go back to sleep. I'm going for a quick swim and then to do my daily lighthouse checks. I'll be back in a minute."

His hold didn't loosen.

"Eastonnnn."

"Oliveeeeee."

I laughed as I pushed off of him. "I'll be right back."

Easton sat up, his curls sticking up every which way and his eyes bleary. "Did you say *swim*?"

"Yeah." I pulled on Easton's sweater and a pair of leggings, quickly taking my pill before he noticed. "I go every morning."

Easton grumbled as he got up and pulled on his pants—no underwear. "That sounds dangerous."

I wrapped my arms around him. "Come on, grumpy alpha. You'll love it. Nothing like a sunrise dip."

"I only want sunrise dip if I can eat it with chips."

I laughed as I dragged him out of the house and down to the beach where Felix was sitting on my rock.

"See, Felix knows this is the hot place to be." I scratched him under the chin. "Are you going to come in with us?"

Felix flopped down on his side and meowed.

I stripped off my clothes and heard Easton's sharp inhale. "Sunrise swimming is naked? You should have led with that."

In an instant, Easton's clothes were off and he'd picked me up bridal style. I shrieked, self-conscious of how on-display my fat rolls were in this position, but Easton didn't care. His hot gaze ran down my body, and then he jogged towards the water.

"Fuck, fuck!" He swore as the cold waves hit his legs.

I shifted out of his arms and laughed as I ran further into the water.

"You're not normal!" Easton shouted at me. His arms were crossed as he shivered.

"Normal is overrated," I shouted back, and then instantly, a lump formed in my throat because it's what my dad always used to say. I leaned back in the water, floating on my back as the waves rocked me back and forth.

Then a hand encircled my arm. "Alright, baby, that's enough of that." I clung to Easton's arm as he pulled me out of the water. His teeth were chattering as we made our way up the beach to the rock... the rock Felix was currently jumping off of, Easton's pants in his mouth.

"No, Felix!" Easton ran after the cat, buck naked, and I bent over with laughter.

27

LARS

I walked into the bookstore over my lunch break, feeling self-conscious. When I'd left the lighthouse, Olive was curled up on Easton's lap as he fed her lunch, and Finn had been pretending to be engrossed in work.

Fuck. The three of us needed to have a real conversation about our pack and what we were doing. Easton had his date with Olive last night and had slept over. Petulant jealousy seeped through my veins. I wanted to spend every night with Olive.

But today was the day. My turn to take her out on a date, and I would start things off by giving her a gift.

I'd never stepped foot in the bookstore before, but I would do it for Olive. I'd learned so much about her yesterday when she'd kept us company in the service room—while wearing *my* sweater—including that she loved romance books. She'd blushed so prettily when she said it, which made me want to howl at how cute she was, and it had given me the perfect idea for a courting gift.

I did my best to squeeze my massive form through the tight bookstore aisles without knocking everything over. I tried to figure out the different sections, but soon, I was sweating at all the swirling letters. I shut my eyes against the overwhelm and took a breath. I should have asked Lucy for recommendations, but my alpha had been too proud to ask for help. He wanted us to provide for our omega, but the longer I was here, the stupider the idea felt. I hadn't read a fucking book in *years* and had cried my way through the last few I was forced to read in school. All the tutoring and extra help in the world wasn't going to fix my fucked-up brain.

I turned to leave, determined to drag Lucy out of her shop so she could help me pick out books, when Hank appeared, a fierce scowl on his face.

Apparently he hadn't forgiven me for ding-dong ditching a couple decades ago.

"What do you want, boy?"

I fought to keep the smile off my face. My brothers and I were destined to always be kids to some Starlight Grove townspeople, even now in our thirties.

"I'm looking for romance books," I said.

Hank scoffed. "Romance? Waste of time."

I shrugged. "If you don't have any, that's fine. I'll just head over to the bookstore in Briar's Landing."

Hank spluttered his outrage. "Come with me," he practically snarled, leading me through the narrow aisles as he muttered insults about the neighboring town's bookstore. I dared to grin now that his back was turned to me. God, I loved this town. I hoped Olive loved it as much as I did.

"Here you go," Hank said, thrusting a stack of heavy books in my arms. "Those are our best romance sellers."

I looked down at the top one, not recognizing the title. There was a naked man on it, which seemed to be correct... although he was all gold and clutching his head. It didn't look particularly romantic, but what did I know?

I paid for them and Hank thrust them in a paper bag. "Don't come again," he shouted at me as I exited the shop.

I rolled my eyes at his rudeness, but that was just Hank. He was all bark, no bite.

Main Street looked particularly cheerful on this sunny day. Shop owners had put up their elaborate Harvest Festival displays, all vying for first place in the shop display contest. Hints of pumpkin spice reached me from Beans 'n Bliss, and I couldn't stop myself. I'd never been into sugary coffee drinks, but now I couldn't go a day without my pumpkin spice latte.

A few minutes later, I exited the shop with a latte in hand and a bag of pastries for Olive. I passed Lucy's shop and found her in the window, working on her decorations. She waved, her eyes widening when she saw the bookstore bag in my hand. She rushed out the door.

"Are those for Olive?" she asked, pink-cheeked and breathless.

"Well, they're definitely not for me." I looked down at the bag, and suddenly, it seemed so small and... not enough. My omega deserved something better, fancier.

"She's going to love them," Lucy said, beaming. "She's been so sad because her e-reader broke, and she hasn't had anything else to read. I loaned her a couple of my favorites, but she's going to be so happy."

"E-reader?"

"Yeah, like to read books electronically."

Shit. Maybe that was a better gift. "Should I get her a new one?"

"Yes," Lucy said. "Absolutely. I'll send you the link."

The tension in my chest settled. Good. This was good. I would give her the books but let her know another present was coming. And then another one after that. As many as she wanted, whatever she wanted. My Olive deserved it all.

Lucy squeezed me in a quick hug. "I'm so happy for you. I just think this is really good."

I ruffled her hair which earned me a quick scowl as she carded her fingers through her blonde strands. "I think so, too."

I quickly headed back to the lighthouse. It already felt like I was attached to my omega by a golden thread. I couldn't wait to bond her... if she wanted that. I breathed through my anxiety. While I was with her, everything felt perfect. I didn't want to overwhelm her... I just wished she needed me as much as I needed her.

I headed around the back of the cottage and found Olive and Easton lying down on a blanket, limbs tangled with each other. Before jealousy could take hold, Olive's head popped up as she spotted me, and her smile was enough to wash away every doubt. Easton caught my eye, and he gave me a wink before kissing Olive on the forehead and getting up.

"I think Finn's head will explode if I don't get back to work. Something about us being off the timeline," he said before heading inside.

Olive held her arms out to me. "Want to join me? Or do you have to get back to work?"

I lowered myself to the blanket, pulling Olive to sit between my legs. "I'm not afraid of Finn's wrath."

Olive smiled, but it was strained. I stroked her hair, a light purr rolling through me to comfort my omega. She clung to me harder, pressing her cheek to my chest.

"This is all going to work out, sweetheart," I murmured.

"You really think so?"

"Yeah, I do." I cleared my throat and pushed the two bags towards her.

Olive perked up. "For me?"

Damn. She was so cute.

"It's nothing big, and it's fine if you don't like them. Just a small courting gift..." I trailed off when Olive fixed me with a sweet smile before opening the coffee shop bag.

"I love chocolate croissants, thank you." Her lips parted as she opened up the second bag. "Books." She smiled at me.

"In case you need some romance to read," I mumbled.

"That's so sweet. Thank you."

I sat up a little straighter, my chest puffing up. "Are you free to come out tonight? On a date with me?"

Olive ran her fingers through my hair. It was half-up today, and I felt like a goddamn cat at her touch.

"Are you nervous?" she asked. "Because you don't have to be. I always want to see you, Lars." Her cheeks turned bright pink at her admission, and I wrapped my arms around her, jiggling her on my lap.

"You've done it now, little omega. You'll never get rid of me."

Her giggle was the best sound in the world. I replayed the sound of it and the feel of her as I returned to work.

"Shit." My heart pounded as I tried to decipher the text message. My panic made it hard to concentrate, and I needed to make sure I understood every word correctly.

"What's wrong?" Finn asked, the wind stealing bits of his words. We were up on the walkway, checking the glass around the lighthouse lantern.

"Mom just texted, and they had a small fire." I rubbed my hand over my chest. The thought of my moms being in danger was enough to make me feel like I was having a heart attack.

"What? Where are they? Are they okay?" Panic filled Easton's voice as he looked over my shoulder. He had to steady the phone in my shaking hand.

"They're okay," he confirmed. "The fire is out—it was just in the laundry room. The fire department is there, but they're asking if Lars can come over and check it out."

"Do you want us to come, too?" Finn clasped me on the shoulder. "Just tell us what you need."

Fuck, I was so grateful I had them. Finn was a stickler for keeping all our projects on schedule, but family was still the most important thing for all of us.

"Let me check it out first, and I'll let you know if we need more help," I said.

"Of course, just keep us posted," Easton said, giving my shoulder one more squeeze before I headed out.

I sprinted down the stairs and rounded the front of the cottage. I glanced around for Olive, but she must have gone inside. Should I knock on the door to explain where I was going? The panicked pounding of my heart urged me to keep running to my moms' house. I would call Olive later and let her know what was going on once I knew more.

28

OLIVE

I smiled as I folded the picnic blanket, took my gifts from Lars, and headed into the cottage. I'd been so embarrassed for Easton to see my empty house and patched-together air mattress nest, but he'd been so kind about it. He hadn't judged my omega for not providing a better nest for him, and it just made me more motivated to create something better for him... for all of them.

I started munching on the chocolate croissant and eagerly opened the paper bag from the Grove Bookstore. I'd been too distracted by Lars's scent and presence and *everything* to notice what the books were, but as I pulled out each one, I grew more and more confused. Finally, they were all laid out in front of me on the kitchen counter.

"What the fuck?"

I needed backup to make sense of this. I ran to my nest to grab my phone and opened our group text message, now sporting the name *Omega Overlords Live Again*.

OLIVE

Code red alert!

IVY

What's wrong??

OLIVE

Lars just gave me some books as a courting present

SUMMER

That's...good? You like to read

LUCY

I saw him after he left the bookstore!

OLIVE

He said he got them for me in case I wanted to read some romance

SUMMER

Ok?? Still not seeing a problem

I sent them a picture of the stack of books, which included *Atlas Shrugged, Dune, 1984,* and *The Catcher in the Rye.*

LUCY

Oh my god LARS NO

IVY

Well...that's not great

SUMMER

That's what Lars reads?? Those are the biggest red flag books I've ever seen. Did he google "most obnoxious bro books of all time?"

OLIVE

I just don't understand why he thinks these books are romantic!!

LUCY

Noooooooooo

I can't believe this

Now I'll never get to have a sister-in-law!!

IVY

They're not going to break up over this

SUMMER

I mean…that is a terrible selection of books

LUCY

This has Hank written all over it! Lars doesn't really read, so I'm guessing Hank recommended those

I grimaced as I remembered my run-in with Hank. The man didn't seem to be a big romantic.

OLIVE

What do I do? He's going to ask if I've read them!!

IVY

I think you just gently tell him the truth, that the books aren't quite right for you

I squirmed uncomfortably at the suggestion. I didn't want to upset Lars or make him think I was too high-maintenance.

LUCY

Don't worry. I will handle this.

OLIVE

Wait, Lucy, what are you going to do?

It's fine, I'll just read them.

Maybe they'll be good

SUMMER

Eww Olive no. Don't do that just for a MAN

IVY

Just be honest with him. Lars is a sweet guy.

How's it going with all the guys? If you want to tell us

SUMMER

TELL US

I smiled, my fingers hesitating before I typed out my answer.

OLIVE

Good…I think. Easton and I went on a date last night and it was really nice

LUCY

Marisol and Carmen already gave us the play by play!

SUMMER

Lucy, Olive might not want to feel like everyone is watching her

Oh god. I could only imagine what people were saying about my terrible dancing skills.

SUMMER

They said you two looked adorable together, by the way.

OLIVE

I'm sure that's not the only thing they said, but thank you. Lars is taking me out tonight

LUCY

I will be screening his date plans, don't worry!!!! Operation Obtain Sister is underway!!

I snorted and worked on making a cup of coffee to go with what remained of my chocolate croissant. I was excited to get some alone time with Lars, but there was still the question of Finn. He'd been on edge the whole time I'd been in the service room yesterday, even though he'd said he didn't want me to leave. I had forgiven him for the movie theater situation and his pretending not to know me the next day... mostly. But the main issue now was that I wasn't convinced he wanted to court me. It was so obvious these three were a pack. I was the outsider, the one who would be abandoned if Finn decided he didn't want me.

I boosted myself up on the counter, leaning my back against the cabinets as I sipped my coffee, wishing it was one of those fancy coffee shop lattes. One day, I would have the money to buy one as often as I wanted.

My phone vibrated.

LUCY

Ahhhhh there was a small electrical fire at my moms' house!

SUMMER

What??? Is everyone ok?

LUCY

Yeah, it's contained and Lars is over there now to look at the electrical.

IVY

Oh no, that's so scary. You ok?

LUCY

Yeah. I have appointments coming up in the shop but as soon as those are done, I'm going to head over. I guess Isla was in the laundry room when it started and she's pretty shaken.

My heart lurched. I hated this for Lars—he was so close to his family. I chewed my lip and wished there was something useful I could do. A very small part of me was sad Lars had left without saying goodbye, but that was such a stupid, needy thought. I was better than that. I was from a fishing family. We were strong, resilient, and got shit done, especially when someone was in need.

I PULLED the cookies out of the oven. Last time I'd been in Mariposa Market, I'd splurged on some half-priced slice-and-bake cookie dough. I was a horrendous cook and baker, but these seemed pretty foolproof.

I poked one. How did I know it was done?

I stared at them while waiting for them to cool before putting them in a small tupperware I'd found in the cabinet. I wondered if I should tell Easton and Finn that I was leaving, but if I didn't go now, I would give into my anxiety and chicken out. I headed outside to my bike, where Felix was once more curled up in the basket.

"I'm going to need that." I held up the cookies as if he would understand what I was saying.

Felix stretched and hopped out of the basket, rubbing himself against my legs.

I crouched down, petting his ears. "Is this stupid?" I asked, my voice a low whisper. "Is it going to be creepy if I just show up at his family's home?" I'd gotten the address from Lucy when I'd still felt confident about this idea. "He's probably busy. I'll just be in the way."

Felix batted at my leg, pushing me towards the bike.

"Okay, okay. I guess I've already made the cookies. I wouldn't want them to go to waste. I can just drop them at the door and run away." I nodded to myself as I put the cookies in the basket and got on the bike. "Yep, that's what I'll do."

I rested my phone in the basket, the maps app open to help me navigate. Lars's family home wasn't far—nothing was *far* in Starlight Grove—but it was off Main Street in a neighborhood I hadn't explored yet.

My jaw dropped when I pulled up to the house. It was a stunning Victorian with gorgeous mature trees in the front yard. I could imagine a young Lars growing up here, climbing trees with Easton and Finn and getting into trouble.

I was too distracted by the house to notice a tall, blonde woman walking towards me. Her expression was assessing as she ran her eyes over me, but then she broke out in a smile.

"Are you Olive?"

"Um, yes." My voice was all weird and croaky.

"I'm Frida, one of Lars's moms. It's so nice to meet you."

She was right in front of my bike as if subtly blocking me from riding away. Why had I done this? I should have just stayed home. I was going to make a fool of myself in front of this alpha, and then Lars would realize I wasn't good enough for him.

"I made cookies." I thrust the tupperware at her. "They're probably not very good. And, um, sorry about the fire."

Frida's mouth twitched as she took the container. "Why don't you come inside? Lars is busy tearing open all our walls to check the wiring, but we can keep you company. And now we'll have cookies."

"I don't want to intrude." *Please, please don't make me.*

But then, somehow, Frida was guiding me off the bike, putting down the kickstand, and gently nudging me across the front yard until we were inside the front door. Oh god, I wasn't even dressed up. I was in leggings and an oversized sweater, and I still had my helmet on.

"I think everyone is in the library right now," Frida said as she unbuckled my helmet and put it down by the door. She seemed to understand I was too dazed to do anything right now, or maybe it was just her alpha instincts taking over.

"Isla, our omega, is a big reader, so we made her this library," she said as she led me into a dark green room with built-in shelves lined with books. "Hey, everyone, this is Olive."

Three women were curled up on a plush green velvet couch.

"*The* Olive?" The smallest of the women jumped off the couch and pulled me into her arms. She had white-blonde hair and blue eyes. "I'm Isla. I'm so excited to meet you." Her scent was woodsy and floral, reminding me of both Lars's and Lucy's scents, and I wondered if she was their biological mom.

"Olive baked us cookies." Frida pressed a kiss to the side of her omega's face.

"Oh, that's so sweet."

The other two women introduced themselves as Jo, a tall alpha with broad shoulders and a dark pixie cut, and Harper, a bubbly alpha with curly, jet-black hair, and before I knew it, I was sandwiched between them on the couch.

Frida put the cookies on the coffee table in front of us and everyone grabbed one, thanking me.

"They're probably not good," I muttered, but they completely ignored me.

"I love chocolate chip," Jo said, sighing happily. "We should probably save one for Lars, or he'll throw a fit."

"Olive, you're sooo pretty," Harper said. "You better make sure Lars puts in the work to earn you."

I didn't know what to say. It was the same thing Rosie said in the diner, but in my experience, *I* was the one who had to earn an alpha's approval. I took a bite of the cookie Isla pressed into my hand and was pleasantly surprised that it wasn't terrible. Slice-and-bake for the win.

Lars's moms carried the conversation, occasionally pulling me in, and I slowly settled deeper into the couch, the tension from my shoulders easing.

"Here he is," Isla said, smiling at Lars, who came to an abrupt stop in the doorway to the library, eyes wide as he took me in.

"Olive."

Oh god. Did he not want me here?

Before I could spiral, he was across the room, pulling me off the couch and into his arms. His hold was crushing, and I melted into him.

"Are you okay, sweetheart? Why did no one tell me you were here?" His tone was accusing as he looked around at his moms.

"You were busy," Harper said, waving away her son's concerns. "And we needed a chance to get to know your omega."

"Mom," Lars said with a growl.

"Don't talk to your mama that way," Frida said.

Lars cursed under his breath, and it made me smile to see the big alpha being scolded.

He pulled back and cupped my face with both hands. "I was just going to call you." His fingers ran across my cheeks, and I wanted more of his touch. "I need to finish up some stuff here and it might take a while. Can we move our date to tomorrow? I'm so sorry."

"You don't have to apologize. Of course, we can move it." What I wanted to say was that I'd be happy to sit with him while he worked. I just wanted to be near him. But that was weird, needy behavior, so I kept my mouth shut.

"I'll make it up to you, I promise," he murmured. His eyes flicked over my head like he just remembered we had an audience.

His lips brushed against my ear. "Do you need me to extricate you from the moms?"

"We heard that," Jo shouted.

I chewed my lip and realized I maybe wanted to stay. His moms were treating me like I was already part of the family, and I wanted to soak up all their care and attention. The scared part of me shouted that enjoying this now would make it hurt all the more when it was ripped away, but it was hard to pay attention to that voice with Lars's scent surrounding me.

"Oohhh, what's going on here?"

I pulled away from Lars at the sound of Lucy's voice. Her hair was piled on top of her head, and she was wearing a pretty, pale blue dress with voluminous sleeves.

"I'm so glad you're here." She pulled me out of her brother's arms and gave me a hug, ignoring the low rumble in his chest. "Alphas," she said with an eye roll.

"It's just the male ones that are obnoxious," Harper shouted from the couch.

Lars scrubbed his hand down his face. "I'm literally here fixing your wiring for free."

"As you should," Jo said.

"Be nice," Isla said, scolding her alphas. "We appreciate you so much, Lars. You're an angel. Now, go on and get back to work so we can hang out with Olive."

Lars couldn't keep a smile off his face. He snagged me back from Lucy and I couldn't quite understand how I was here, with multiple people fighting over spending time with me. Lars pulled me out of the room, ignoring everyone's indignant shouts. He stopped when we were in the kitchen. He picked me up and put me on the counter and I perfumed, my scent breaking through my deodorant. My cheeks burned as I realized he would know how much I loved him moving me around and putting me where he wanted me.

His hands were on my thighs, spreading them wide so he could step in closer between them. I let out a low whimper as slick drenched my underwear.

"Fuck, I want you," he murmured. "I'm so sorry about tonight. I promise it's not that I don't think you're important or that I won't prioritize you..."

I scented the anxiety rolling off him, and I wrapped my arms around him as far as they would go. "I know that. Preventing your moms' house from burning down is more important than a date."

He ran his fingers through my hair, his touch so gentle it made me want to purr.

"I need you to know you are my priority, sweetheart. Not a minute of the day goes by that I'm not thinking of you."

He looked so vulnerable, like he was worried I would reject him. I furrowed my brow, moving one hand to run it through his beard. "I feel the same," I whispered.

Lars let out a shuddering sigh, banding his arms around me and crushing me to his chest. "I've never felt this way before."

I rubbed my cheek against his neck, wishing I wasn't wearing deodorant so I could leave a stronger scent on him.

He chuckled, the sound rumbling through his chest. "You feeling a little possessive, sweetheart?"

I nipped his neck. "Maybe."

"Good." And then he captured my lips in a kiss, his tongue pressing against mine. His lips were so soft in contrast to the slightly scratchy texture of his beard. I wanted to feel him all over my skin.

The sound of a throat clearing made us break apart.

"I was sent to stop you from fucking in the kitchen," Lucy said.

Lars groaned, giving me one last squeeze before lifting me off the counter. Lucy's smile was radiant.

"Can you stay for dinner, Olive?"

I glanced up at Lars. "I have to go get more supplies, so I won't be here," he said. "But you should stay if you want to, sweetheart."

"You're sure it's okay?" I asked Lucy.

"We want you here! It's settled." She took me by the hand and started pulling me out of the room. "Bye, Lars! Have fun with your electrical wire!"

I giggled and glanced over my shoulder in time to catch Lars's wink.

29

OLIVE

I biked my way down Main Street. The gas lights were on, and twinkle lights illuminated the shops. Lars's moms had tried to get me to let them drive me home, but it wasn't a long bike ride, and I was scared they would ask to see my house. One day, I would have a home I was proud to show off... and less anxiety so I could trust more people to come inside.

"Ms. Harvest!"

I slowed down, trying to figure out who was shouting, and saw Stanley jogging down the street towards me, holding a clipboard aloft.

Shoot. Should I do what Summer said and just ride away?

I groaned. I couldn't do it. I slowed to a stop and moments later, a panting Stanley stood before me.

"Ms. Harvest, I really must get details on your Autumn Harvest craft booth."

"Look, I'm really not good at crafts."

Stanley waved his hand, dismissing my answer. "I'll put you down for knitted goods. I'm sure you can pick that up in no time."

"No, that's not—"

"Thank you!" he shouted as he quickly made his way back up the street, the shadows swallowing him up.

I turned back around and let out a scream when I saw Felix sitting in my bike basket. "Oh my god, announce yourself next time."

Felix fixed his gaze on me like he was staring deep into my soul. I huffed. "Stanley wants me to learn to knit."

Felix stayed silent.

"Okaaaay. You want a ride back to the lighthouse, then? Looks like I'm on my own for tonight."

That got a reaction from Sir Cat. He sat up straight and cocked his head.

"Lars had to cancel our date," I said, my voice a little too frosty. I didn't want to go back to a cold, dark house. I hadn't figured out the fireplace yet, and the evenings were getting cold. "Why am I explaining this to you? You're a cat."

Felix leaned forward and batted my arm before leaping out of the basket.

"No, come back," I called after him. "I didn't mean it."

But Felix was gone, and I was furious with myself for chasing away the only person who wanted to hang out with me this evening.

I resumed pedaling. As I approached the path to the lighthouse, I cursed when I realized I'd forgotten my flashlight. I hadn't expected to be out for so long. The thought of trying to navigate the rocky path in the dark made me feel even more pity for myself. I fumbled with my phone—the light wouldn't do a whole lot to illuminate the way, but it might be better than nothing.

I made the final turn to the path and saw all my worries were for nothing. Short lights had been inserted into the ground, illuminating the entire way to my cottage.

"Oh my god."

Tears sprung to my eyes. Had Easton done this for me this afternoon? I squeezed the handles of my new bike, the one I kept forgetting to thank the guys for. As I made my way to my home, the soft lights cutting through the darkness, I felt cared for in a way I hadn't since my parents died.

30

FINN

EASTON HAD ASKED IF I WANTED TO GRAB DINNER WITH him, but I'd refused. I had my secret project to complete, plus my mind was too jumbled to be around anyone.

Once I finished up, I headed into town. The streetlights flickered on as the sun set, and I wandered aimlessly until I found myself in front of the Starlight Grove cemetery. I hadn't been here since the day we buried my grandparents. I barely remembered that day. Just the smell of the wet earth, the feel of the sun shining down, and Lars and Easton refusing to leave my side.

I opened the metal gate now and wound through the gravestones until I found the one I was looking for.

Fredrik and Carina West.

They were buried together. They'd barely spent a day apart when they were alive.

Beloved grandparents and parents.

The grave was bare, and I hated that. I should have brought them flowers. I would tomorrow.

My eyes trailed down to the poem they'd included on the stone, one by Federico García Lorca.

Ay, the pain it costs me
to love you as I love you!

For love of you, the air, it hurts,
and my heart,
and my hat, they hurt me.

Who would buy it from me,
this ribbon I am holding,
and this sadness of cotton,
white, for making handkerchiefs with?

Ay, the pain it costs me
to love you as I love you!

I hadn't understood it when my grandpa had chosen it after my grandma died, but reading the poem now, I thought I understood. My grandparents had experienced a lot of loss in love, but they had chosen it anyway.

They knew it would hurt, and they chose it anyway.

I leaned against the headstone and cried.

31

FINN

I walked the path from the lighthouse down to the beach, hoping I would find Olive there. Lars texted us earlier that she was eating dinner at his house before heading back home. I'd knocked on the cottage door, but she hadn't answered.

My feet hit the sand, and there she was, sitting on a large, flat rock.

Anxiety surged through every part of my body as I approached her. She glanced up at me and then looked back at the horizon.

"Can I join you?" My voice was like gravel.

"Oh, you're talking to me now?"

My chest tightened with shame. No matter how confusing my mixed-up feelings were, there was no excuse for how I'd treated Olive the past few days.

I stopped a few feet away from her, scuffing the packed sand with the toe of my boot. "I'm sorry. For all of it. How I treated you in the movie theater." My throat was so tight it was painful. "You didn't deserve that. I should have held you close and made sure you were okay, then cleaned you up and walked you home. I panicked, but it had nothing to do with you. And I'm so sorry for ignoring you afterwards." My words felt so small and inadequate.

The faint moonlight highlighted her figure enough for me to see her shrug. "It's fine."

Her voice was quiet, monotone. Nothing like the lively omega I'd spent the evening with at the movies, or the one who laughed and talked with my brothers.

"No, Olive, it's not. I've been all messed up inside, but it's no excuse for how I've acted."

She didn't say anything, but she scooted over a tiny bit on the rock, leaving me space to sit down. My heart leapt, and I quickly sat before she changed her mind. The rock was icy, even through my jeans.

"Are you cold?" My eyes had adjusted enough to the light to see that Olive was bundled up in an oversized sweater that I recognized as one of Lars's. My alpha rumbled as I was struck by the over-whelming urge to see her in my clothing.

"I'm fine." Her eyes were fixed on the waves. I wanted to lecture her for being out here alone in the dark, but I understood the draw of the quiet beach. How many nights had I sat in this same spot as my grandma grew sicker inside the house?

"It's hard for me to be at the lighthouse," I blurted out. All the warning systems that told me to keep everything locked up neat and tight, to never let my vulnerability spill over, were blaring. But no matter how much I tried to deny it, Olive mattered to me. The idea that she thought I disliked her or didn't want to be near her? I couldn't stand it.

She turned towards me, her head tilted. "What do you mean?"

I took a deep breath. I wasn't used to expressing myself... of doing anything that made me vulnerable. But in this moment, with Olive's sweet scent mixing with the salty air, I thought it was time to be brave.

"I grew up here. In that house. My mom was a single mom. She'd gotten pregnant during a one-night stand and never found the guy again. I don't have many memories of her because she died in a car crash when I was two. My grandpa was the lighthouse keeper, and he and my grandma raised me. I grew up in that lighthouse, spent my childhood on this very beach." My eyes burned with memories. The ghost of my grandpa chasing me in the waves. My grandma teaching me how to swim. Sitting at the top of the lighthouse, watching storms roll in with a cup of hot chocolate and my grandpa's deep voice explaining weather patterns and the coastal rescue system for lost boats.

Now, it was my turn to keep my eyes on the waves as I did my best to keep my voice from shaking. "I met Easton and Lars in elementary school and we just fit together. Our childhoods were spent here and at Lars's home. We were inseparable, spending our days and most of our nights together—usually causing chaos." I snorted, remembering all the trouble we got into. "We were little shits. But we loved each other and loved this town. We all revealed as alphas around the same time. I'm not sure we even had a conversation about becoming a pack—we already were. We were all excited to find an omega to complete our pack, but then I went to college, and we started our company, and things just got so busy." I didn't tell her that Lars had become obsessed with a no-longer-mysterious omega years ago—that was his story to tell.

"And then, about a year ago, my grandmother got sick—cancer. The first two chemos they tried didn't work, and she kept getting sicker. She decided to stop treatment." My throat was so tight, each word like a razor forcing its way through. And then Olive's hand surrounded mine, anchoring me. I interlaced my fingers with hers, and the tightness in my throat and chest eased.

"I stayed with them those last few weeks. My grandma and grandpa spent every minute *remembering*. They told story after story of their early courtship days, memories of my mom, some I'd never heard before. One of the last things my grandma said to me was that losing her daughter was the greatest tragedy of her life, and there were days she hadn't known how to keep living under the grief of it. But *I* had become her reason for living. She said raising me had been the greatest gift of her life."

Tears rolled down my cheek and I quickly wiped them off, embarrassed. Olive leaned into my side. Her scent swirled around me, settling into my very skin and bones like it was always meant to be there.

"My parents died on the same day," Olive said softly. "I had to go back to our house all alone. I lasted a couple of months before I moved. Maybe I shouldn't have. Sometimes, I wish I could go back there, but I just couldn't stand being there without them. So I get it, the not wanting to remember."

I tightened my hold on Olive's hand as my grief expanded to include her loss. My Olive. Alone in the world.

"When did they die?"

"Five years ago," she said. "I've had a long time to figure out how to live in the world without them. Sometimes it's still hard." She hesitated for a moment. "Why did you take on this project, knowing you'd have to be back here?"

A small smile tugged at my lips. "Easton applied without telling Lars or me." I found I couldn't summon any of that anger I'd had at his actions with this sweet omega pressed to my side.

"Well, that makes a lot more sense," Olive said. "I was wondering why you were..."

"An asshole?" I supplied.

Olive turned to me and grinned. "Maybe."

"Easton shouldn't have done it, but he knew I would have refused to apply for the grant. I also think he knew that, ultimately, I would have been devastated if anyone else did this work. I also think he was eager to do some matchmaking."

I wished it was lighter out so I could read Olive's face. There was a burst of sweetness in her scent, but she didn't meet my gaze.

"He can be very insistent," she finally said. "But..." She sighed deeply, chewing her lip. "I don't know that pack life is for me. My parents ruined me for love." Her voice was a low whisper.

I shifted on the rock and wrapped my arms around her shoulder. For a second, her body was stiff and I thought she'd pull away, but then she softened into me.

"What do you mean?" I kept my eyes on the distant horizon, the velvet blue sky speckled with bright stars. I wanted to look at her, hold her face in my hands, but I kept still, unwilling to disrupt the moment.

"My dad was an alpha and my mom a beta. One time, when I

was ten, I asked my dad if he ever wanted a bigger pack or more kids. He stopped everything he was doing on the boat and cupped my face. He said, 'Why would I ever want more when I have perfection in front of me?'" Olive sniffed and wiped a tear off her cheek. I held her closer, pressing my face to the top of her head. "He never treated me differently when I revealed as an omega. Never made me feel like there were things I couldn't do." She cleared her throat, as if speaking this aloud was painful, and I knew how that felt.

"When I started having some, um, medical issues, it was right in the middle of the busy season. I felt like I was losing my mind. I couldn't be on the boat. My mom stayed home with me, making sure I was never alone. I felt so bad that I wasn't working. My dad had to hire extra guys to help him, which was money we didn't have. The next time I had an episode, my dad stayed home with me."

She was crying steadily now, her voice hitching on each word. Panic filled my chest at the mention of health issues. I fought the urge to ask her for more information, to set her up with the best doctors, but she was already working so hard to be honest with me now, I didn't want to push for more yet.

I awkwardly shifted so I could get a wad of napkins out of my pocket left over from lunch. She took them, but it wasn't enough. Before I could overthink it, I pulled her onto my lap. Surrounded her with my arms. Curled my body around hers. Wishing it was enough to shield her from her grief.

Olive didn't push me away. She pressed her face into the side of my neck and breathed deeply.

"I was so upset that he stayed with me that day. I kept yelling at him to leave, that he had more important things to do. But he didn't leave my side. He said—" Her breath hitched, and it was a moment before she could speak again. "He said he was right where he needed to be. The boat could wait. The lobster could wait. Everything could wait, because the most important job in the world was being my dad."

My heart clenched at the pain in her voice, but there was gratitude there, too. Gratitude that Olive had grown up with parents who loved her, gratitude for my grandparents doing the same for me.

"So you see, they ruined me. How am I supposed to go on living knowing there's love like that out there? How can I settle for anything less?"

"You don't," I said fiercely. "You don't ever settle. One day, you will feel love like that again, and then you'll know."

Olive wrapped her arms around me tighter, and we fell quiet as we listened to the crashing waves and our heartbeats.

"What about you?" she asked, her voice soft as she trailed her fingers along my jaw.

My jaw automatically clenched as if trying to stop the words from getting out. What I hadn't admitted to anyone. But here, cloaked in darkness, maybe it was safe enough to release them.

"I always wanted a relationship like my grandparents had. They were high school sweethearts. My grandpa started courting my grandma when they were fourteen. She died right before their seventieth anniversary of becoming girlfriend and boyfriend. My grandpa lived another month after she passed, but he wasn't really there. Looking back, he was preparing for the end, and he didn't seem remotely upset by the idea. His life wasn't worth living without his bonded, and that fucking terrifies me. To give another person that amount of power over you that the grief of them takes you under? Is that really the best way to live?"

Olive hummed as she traced her fingers down my chest. "I used to think grief was the worst thing in the world. And it is, at least in the beginning. But now, five years out, I've befriended my grief. It connects me to the two people I loved most in the world. It's all the memories I had with them, how they made me feel so *important*, even as a little kid. Grief is the price we pay for love, and at some point along the way, it started feeling beautiful instead of ugly, like there's something sacred in the midst of the agonizing pain."

Tears streamed down my face. Could my grief for my grandparents become something beautiful? Maybe love wasn't the thing that killed my grandpa. Maybe it was what gave him peace to face the end.

"I think you know Lars and Easton are courting me, but I would never come between them and you. You're brothers. You've lived so much life together. I don't ever want to ruin that."

"Sweet girl, you could never ruin anything." I pressed a kiss to her forehead and breathed her in fully.

She clutched at me, her fingers twisting in my shirt. "I'm just saying, if you're not ready, Finn—if you don't want this, or at least not right now, that's okay."

My heart melted. "It's hard to believe you're real, darling. I don't know that I'll ever be ready." She stiffened in my arms, so I quickly continued. "But maybe that's the point. We won't ever feel quite ready to risk ourselves for love, and we should do it, anyway."

32

OLIVE

Finn stayed close to my back as I climbed the stairs to the top of the lighthouse. It was a calm night—the wind and waves almost silent, as if holding their breath in anticipation of this moment. My heart was aching, my chest flayed open with our hushed beach confessions.

Finn's arms surrounded me from behind, his face buried in my hair. There was still an edge of anxiety to his sweet maple scent, and I was sure mine was the same. This moment felt momentous, make or break.

"I used to come up here most nights as a kid, at least in the summer," he said, the heat of his body against my back keeping me warm.

"I come up here most nights, too."

He pressed his lips to the side of my face, turning me so I was facing him. "Is it safe for you to be up here all by yourself? The wind might take you." He gripped my jaw tight, his hold possessive.

I grinned. "Are you fussing over me, alpha?"

He palmed my ass, pulling me tight against his hard cock. "I'll fuss over you as much as I want, omega."

I fidgeted with the collar of his sweater and took a deep breath as my heart pounded. "Are we really trying this? A relationship?" My voice wasn't more than a whisper. I couldn't handle rejection again from this alpha.

His fingers dug into my hair. "Yes. *Yes*, Olive. Would you do me the absolute honor of letting me court you? I'll be so good to you. I promise."

The hard press of his body, the grip of his fingers, his sweet words healed the little sad part of my heart that had been hurting since the movie theater.

"Yes," I said. I wrapped my hand around the back of his neck and pulled him in for a kiss, which Finn instantly deepened. One of his hands gripped my jaw, holding me in place as he plunged into my mouth.

"You're so good, sweetness. I don't deserve you."

I rubbed myself against him like a kitten, craving all of him. His scent swirled around me, deepening until it was pure maple. It was the scent of home, of New England autumns and crisp days eating maple candies.

I ran my hands under his sweater, pressing my hands against his bare chest.

Finn groaned, dragging his hand beneath my sweater, the calluses of his fingers rough against my back. "We don't have to go any further, pretty girl. But I promise if you trust me with *you*, I'll make it so good for you."

Now my heart was pounding from anticipation. "Touch me, Finn."

He groaned and flipped us so the lighthouse was against my back. He was so tall and broad, blocking out the rest of the world.

"Is my omega going to be a good girl for me?"

I nodded.

"Mmm, that's right. She's going to let her alpha make her feel so good."

I'd gotten a hint of dominant Finn in the movie theater, but fuck did I want more. I arched into him, trying to get more of his touch. His hand cupped my pussy, applying firm pressure to my clit. It felt so good, I whimpered.

"That's it, my needy omega." He peeled off my leggings and

underwear and then his fingers were there, playing with my swollen clit. "You're going to come for me over and over until all you can feel is pleasure, and the only word you can form is my name."

I wanted to say something snarky, to tell him off for having such a big ego, but then his fingers were inside me, curving to hit that spot that made my legs weak. I clutched his shoulders, using the leverage to ride his hand, his murmured praise in my ear.

All too quickly, I came with a moan, the pleasure stealing my breath.

"That's good. You're doing so fucking well for me." But his touch didn't ease. He kept working me, adding a third finger as he pressed inside me. "Now you'll come again."

He swallowed my whimpers as he hitched my leg around his, opening me up more to him as he forced another orgasm from me. I shook with pleasure as I came, his grip on me the only thing keeping me from falling to the ground.

"I can't," I whined as he kept working me. Slick drenched my inner thighs and his hand, the sound obscene.

"You can." He circled my clit. "All of this beautiful slick is for me. Your body knows to obey its alpha and *come*." His voice was a growl with the slightest hint of a bark, and my omega was putty in his hands. I screamed his name as I came a third time.

He handled my limp body with his strong arms, arranging us until he was sitting down with my legs straddling him. I leaned into him, my face pressed against his neck. I nipped at his skin, wishing I could put my mark on him.

His strong hands ran up and down my back, soothing me. "That's it, pretty girl. You were absolutely perfect."

I felt empty without his fingers inside me. I rocked my pussy against him. I knew I was soaking his pants, but I didn't care. I wanted him inside me, needed him to fill me.

I told him so and he swore, his fingers digging into my ass cheeks. "You need more, sweet girl?" He huffed a laugh when I unzipped his pants and pulled out his cock. It was warm and thick in my hand. Some precum leaked onto my fingers, and I sucked them into my mouth. "I guess that answers that," he teased.

I let out a whine as he lifted me so I was hovering above his cock, the tip of him teasing my entrance. He moved me around with ease, and I loved it.

"Finn, alpha, please," I begged when he didn't lower me down on his cock. "I'm so empty."

"What a good omega, begging for your alpha's cock." And then he finally, *finally* lowered me down. He was so thick I whimpered at the stretch of him. "You can take me. Yes, good girl. Look at that, your sweet little cunt stretching around me. That's it, all the way down."

I was flush with his lap, impaled on his cock. I fidgeted, rocking back and forth and trying to get some friction. And then Finn took over, his fingers digging into my hips as he set a quick pace, thrusting his hips up as he pulled me down.

"You feel..." I trailed off, my words stolen. "*Finn.*"

"That's right, scream my name, sweet thing." His voice was strained, like he was barely keeping it together, and it sent a thrill through me. I wanted to be the one who made this alpha lose control.

His knot pressed against my entrance, teasing me with every thrust. I gripped his shoulders tightly, and the next time he thrust his hips towards me, I pressed down all the way, taking his knot inside me. The swell of him was enough to push me over into another orgasm. I trembled against his chest as he came, too, his hot cum pouring inside me, sealed in by his knot. I whined as it swelled even larger, locking us together.

"Fuck," Finn gasped. His arms banded tightly around me, hugging me to his chest, shielding me. "My naughty girl, being all greedy and taking your alpha's knot."

"Mine," I said, scent-marking his neck.

Finn's laugh vibrated against my cheek. "That's right, sweet girl. All yours."

33

OLIVE

I GROANED AS THE MATTRESS DIPPED AND SOMEONE slipped into the bed behind me. In my sleepy haze, I forgot to be panicked. And then I was surrounded by Lars's scent.

"What?" was the only word I could mumble.

"Fucking Finn didn't come home. No way am I going to be the last one to spend the night with you."

That was absurdly sweet.

"Where's—" Before I could find the energy to form a full question, the mattress dipped again, but this time, a body was trying to squeeze between Finn and me from the bottom of the bed.

Finn tightened his hold on me. "Easton, get off me," he groaned.

Easton stopped when his face was level with my pussy. He wrapped his arms around my legs. "This is the perfect sleeping position for me."

"That can't possibly be comfortable." My voice was soft as sleep clawed at me again.

A tender kiss pressed to the back of my neck. "Just go to sleep, sweetheart, with your whole pack around you." Lars's words were so precious, I collected them up and held them close to my heart.

IT WOULD TAKE a while for me to get used to waking up in a tangle of limbs.

I couldn't believe Lars and Easton snuck into bed with us. Maybe I should be upset with them for breaking into my home and coming into my nest uninvited, but my omega was too busy basking in the glory of having her alphas around her to muster up any irritation. Besides, Easton had been honest about his stalking tendencies.

My alphas.

My chest clenched at the thought. Were they really mine?

For the first time, I let myself imagine what life with the three of them could be like. Waking up like this every morning, spending time with Lars's family, going into town because it wasn't so scary when they were with me... Maybe even going through a heat together.

A thread of anxiety worked through me, wrapping itself tightly around my heart. The voices of those other alphas filtered in.

Too needy.

Too loud.

Too whiny.

Not enough. Not enough. Not enough.

My guys wouldn't be like those alphas during my heat. They wouldn't speak to me like that, wouldn't treat me how *he* did, but that didn't mean they wouldn't think the same things. And regret being with me.

I scrubbed my eyes with my hands. It was too early in the morning to dwell on something that was still weeks away.

I was tempted to stay all tucked in with their warm bodies against mine, but the ocean was calling me. I was already feeling a little off-balance and needed my morning routine to get me back on track. I started my slow wiggle to escape the guys' holds. I didn't want to wake them, but they had me trapped. I'd almost managed a full extraction when a large hand grasped my ankle.

"Where do you think you're going?" Lars's deep growl sent a shiver through me.

"Just out for a quick swim," I whispered. "Go back to sleep. I'll be back in a few minutes."

Easton let out a groan. "Baby, please, *no*. This is an *every morning* thing? Must put a stop to it. The morning is for sleeping and cuddling, not freezing cold water."

I grinned at how grumpy he sounded. "You don't have to come. I promise I'll be right back."

But Easton rolled off the air mattress, hitting the floor with a loud thud. He pushed up with a groan, his eyes still half-closed. "Naked," was the only word he spoke.

"What's he going on about?" Finn asked, finally stirring.

"Only good part of this morning routine," Easton muttered. "Although you could just stay in bed, naked."

He held his arms out to me for what I thought was a hug, but then he picked me up and started walking to the front door.

"We have to put on clothes." I laughed as I clutched my half-asleep alpha as he stumbled to the door, my two other bewildered alphas following us.

"Felix," was all he said, and that was fair. It had taken him ages to get his pants back from Sir Cat last time.

"Sweetheart, what is it we're doing at *six-thirty in the morning*?" Lars asked as we headed out the door.

"I start my mornings with a swim in the ocean. It's part of my routine."

"Some people drink coffee and have breakfast in bed for their morning routine," Finn muttered.

We made our way down to the beach, the early morning air crisp and cold. I pushed at Easton's arms and he carefully set me down. The sand was icy under my feet.

My three guys stood side by side. Naked and shivering.

The absurdity of it all filled my chest with giddy happiness. How was it that I had three guys who would follow me outside, even though it was too early and too cold for them? It made me feel powerful.

And loved.

I swallowed the lump in my throat and headed towards the water, lifting my arms and spinning in the air. "I thought you were big, strong alphas," I taunted.

"This is unnatural," Finn shouted back.

"Lars, you're Swedish." I squealed as the first wave hit my skin.

His grumbled response was lost in the wind as I ran further into the water. The water was so cold it hurt, but I loved it because it made me feel grounded and *alive*.

I turned around to see my alphas still on shore but inching closer to the water.

"I don't think this is safe," Finn said. "Come back here, Olive. You'll get sick." He injected his voice with that stern tone that made slick pour down my thigh, but I just fell back in the water on my back, the waves cooling my overheated skin.

"I guess no one wants a blow job!" I called out.

"Wait, what?" Easton took a few clumsy steps into the water, swearing copiously as a wave snuck up on him and drenched his side.

"First alpha to come here gets a blow job."

I'd never seen anyone move faster. Lars, Finn, and Easton ran into the waves. Lars shoved Finn, who fell back and started shouting about a red card, and Easton seemed to fall over his own feet and crash into the water. Tears streamed down my face from laughter, and then Lars's strong arms were around me, picking me up.

"I see we're going to have to keep a very close eye on you, naughty girl." He started carrying me towards shore. I snuggled into his chest, my arms and legs wrapped around him as I soaked in his warmth.

"Does that mean you don't want a blow job?" I nibbled on his throat, his skin salty.

He cleared his throat. "Didn't say that."

I pressed my laugh to his chest as the other guys joined us.

They all pressed in around me; the loneliness I'd felt for so long washed out to sea.

EASTON STARED AT MY FRIDGE, grumbling at the lack of food.

"I didn't know I was going to be hosting," I said, my heels hitting the cabinets as I swung my legs. After I did my daily lighthouse checks and got dressed (in Finn's sweater, no pants), he'd placed me on the kitchen counter and told me to "stay there like a good girl" while they made breakfast.

Yes sir.

I hadn't put on my No-NonScent Deodorant this morning, so they could all scent me as I perfumed at his words.

"Forget about hosting. This isn't enough food for *you*." Easton shut the fridge angrily. He moved to stand between my spread legs, and I wrapped my arms around him.

"I'll buy more, okay?" I said. Easton's scent told me he was really agitated.

"*I'll* buy it for you." His voice was pure grumpiness as he rubbed his cheek against mine, scent-marking me.

I would have protested to him spending money on me, but this seemed really important to him. Had Easton experienced food insecurity growing up? The thought made me hug him tighter.

"I'm assuming you want this creamer in your coffee, sweet girl?"

My cheeks heated as Finn held up the pumpkin spice-flavored creamer I'd splurged on. "Umm, yep."

"Excellent," Lars said, rubbing his hands together. "My favorite flavor." He raised a suggestive eyebrow as he whisked something in a bowl, and I squirmed on the counter.

"What are you making?" I asked.

"Swedish pancakes. A staple in my home growing up."

"That sounds so good. Thanks for doing that." That stupid lump was back in my throat at how my alphas were taking care of me.

Finn nudged Easton out of the way and handed me my coffee. I looked down at it and bit my lip.

"What's wrong?" he asked.

"Nothing," I said quickly. Too quickly, judging by his stern expression. Why did Finn scolding me get me so hot? "I want more creamer," I whispered.

He grinned. "I should have known." He poured more in until the coffee was a pale tan color. "That better, pretty girl?"

I took a sip. "Perfect."

He grinned and ran his hands up my bare thighs. "I like you like this," he murmured in my ear. "Sitting so sweetly for us." His heated gaze ran down my legs, but his expression quickly turned to anger as his hand froze on my leg. "Why the fuck are you covered in bruises?" He ran his hands down my calf. "Did—" He cleared his throat. "Did *I* do this?"

The very air in the room transformed as all three alphas closed in on me.

"Huh?" I looked down at my leg and saw a series of small bruises. "Oh. No, I don't think you did that. It doesn't matter, anyway. I just bruise easily."

Now Lars's hands were on my other leg, his fingers carefully tracing the line of bruises I had no memory of getting. "Olive, if you're lying right now—"

"No, I'm not, I swear." I caught Lars's wrist and ran my thumb over his pulse. Fuck, I had to tell them. "I'm on blood thinners, and it means I bruise easily. I never even remember how I get them. They just seem to show up. I know they're not very attractive."

Easton huffed and shoved Lars out of the way, pushing so he was between my spread legs. "As if we fucking care about that. Why are you on blood thinners?"

I chewed my lip. This was the moment I'd been dreading—the first obstacle in our new romance that might just be enough to make them run.

Finn shoved Easton back so he and Lars had a little more space to crowd in around me. The cottage had a good-sized kitchen, but it seemed miniscule with these alphas in it.

"You said last night you have health issues," Finn said softly. "Will you tell us about them?"

I nodded, fixing my eyes on a frayed spot on my sweater—Finn's sweater.

"I have a genetic hormonal condition that affects the omega hormone omestrogen, and also increases risks for blood clots." There. Simple. Easy.

Finn cupped my face, and his touch was so gentle I had to swallow back my tears. "I'm sorry, angel. Do you have a doctor? I'm sure we can find someone for you."

I shrugged. "I just check in with my hematologist once a year and they renew my prescription. The condition doesn't really require monitoring."

"And are you okay as long as you take the medication?" he asked.

Ughh. Damn them for having follow-up questions.

"Pretty much." My voice came out in the most unconvincing high-pitched squeak I'd ever heard. There was silence in the kitchen, and then all of us burst out laughing.

Lars put his arm around me, tucking me into his side. "At least we know you're a shit liar."

I pressed my hesitant smile into his chest and breathed him in. There was a salty tinge to his earthy scent this morning.

"It might affect a few more things," I said with a sigh. "Like my mood." I squeezed my eyes shut. I didn't want to see it—the way they would awkwardly shift their weight and tell me it wasn't a big deal when we all knew it was. "I call them my dark days. There doesn't seem to be any rhyme or reason to the timing—they come up out of the blue, sometimes lasting for a day or two, and other times up to a week."

Someone's hand gently squeezed my leg, but I kept my eyes closed. "I can feel it coming on. It's like... it's like being out in the middle of a still ocean and then, out of nowhere, a wave starts to build. There's nothing you can do, no place you can go to hide. All you can do is brace yourself as it crashes down. The sadness is so overwhelming it's like I'm drenched and gasping for air. No matter what I do, how hard I try, I can't get dry or warm. Even though I know this has happened before, and all those times I somehow made it out of the storm, in that moment, it feels like forever."

"Baby." Easton's voice was devastatingly tender. There was a shuffle of movement, and then he was in front of me again, pressing a kiss to my forehead. I allowed myself to melt into his chest. "That day I came with the welcoming committee?" he asked softly.

I nodded. Of course, he put it together, my awful behavior that day. I couldn't hide anything from him. Would he still want me now that he knew I wasn't his sunshine?

"Eventually, it passes," I continued. "And you should be happy, and to some degree, you are. But then you walk through your house and see the mess you've made and the bridges you've burned in your relationships, and it convinces you that this is all your life will ever be. You're too much of a burden to those around you, and you wouldn't want to subject them to the darkness anyway."

Easton picked me up off the counter, my arms and legs wrapped around him. He moved me so Lars and Finn could surround me. Their large bodies caged me in, shielding me, protecting me.

"It's a good thing I'm not afraid of the dark," Easton said.

Just tell them all of it, the voice in my head said. But maybe it was better to space it out. Knowing their omega was a moody, irritable mess was enough information for the day.

"What helps when you're feeling that way?" Finn asked, his voice rough. "You said your parents would sit with you?"

"Yeah, they did. But there's no medication or anything that will fix it."

"I get that, sweet girl. But we want to help you when you feel like that."

"It's not just depression, though," I said. "I'm irritable and just awful to be around. The next time it happens, I can let you all know and you can keep your distance until it's over."

"Huh," Easton said, jiggling me in his arms. "Did you two know our omega was such a comedian?"

"I certainly didn't," Lars said, stroking his hand down my hair.

Finn gripped my chin, forcing me to look at him. "You will tell us the next time you feel it coming on, and we will do whatever the fuck we can to make it easier for you, except for leaving you alone."

"You say that now..."

"Yeah, I do." His gaze was firm, unwavering, and it made me want to submit to him.

I wrinkled my nose as I caught the scent of something burning, and it broke the tension in the kitchen. Lars cursed as he removed the smoking pan off the stove, Finn muttered something about me needing a spanking, and Easton set me back on the counter, his body still pressed against mine.

"We're here for you, baby," he said. "And we're not leaving."

I believed that he believed his words, but things could change. My omega was *a lot* to handle, and not in a good way. But as Lars handed me a plate with rolled-up cinnamon sugar Swedish pancakes, I decided I would let myself enjoy this. Even if it didn't last, nothing could take away this slice of happiness right now.

34

EASTON

NONE OF US WANTED TO LEAVE OLIVE, BUT WE HAD TO go back to the house to grab our work gear and supplies for the day.

Even Finn, who was a stickler for sticking to our job timelines, had been slow to get going. Especially after what Olive told us about her health. Even now, it took everything in me not to sprint back to the cottage. What if she needed me in the fifteen minutes we were gone?

Last night, when Lars returned from helping his moms with the house repairs, he'd found me sitting on the front porch, waiting for Finn to return. He'd taken one look at me and announced we were going to the cottage. I was glad he suggested it so I didn't have to. Give him a chance to be the stalker for once.

Finn's shoulders were tense and bunched as I followed him up the path to our house. I had so many questions for him—like how the fuck he went from acting terrified of our omega to being in her bed—but I held my tongue until we were inside. Olive was a private person, and I didn't want our nosy neighbors to overhear us. Even now, Mrs. Cassini was casting us curious looks as she pretended to weed her already pristine flower bed.

The front door closed behind me. Finn turned to face us, eyes a little wild and his hair sticking up in the back. "She has no furniture," he blurted out.

Huh. Not what I expected him to lead off with, but okay.

"Yeah, I know," I said. "I just spent half the night on the floor because of a slowly leaking air mattress."

Finn growled as he looked between me and a quiet Lars. "How are you not more upset about this? She has *no furniture*." He swallowed hard, looking anguished. "And it's my fault."

Lars crossed his arms. "So you care about Olive now?"

That pulled Finn up short. "I... yeah. I want to court her."

"You said that before, but it feels like you didn't mean it," Lars said. "What changed?"

"I wasn't sure before." Finn looked down at the ground. "Actually, that's a lie. I was sure. I was sure I wasn't going to court her. I was going to leave the pack."

My chest squeezed, and the room spun around me. Finn wanted to leave us? The room darkened, and it felt like I was breathing through a straw.

"Easton, hey. Just breathe." Arms guided me down to the couch as blackness encroached on my vision. Then those arms surrounded me in a hug. "I'm not leaving. I'm sorry. I'm so sorry. I love you."

I clung to him, unable to speak. Everyone in my early life had left me—my father, who didn't even stick around to see me turn one, and my mother, who chose abusive men over her son. Fredrick and Carina had been surrogate parents, and now they were gone. The only constants in my life were Lars and Finn. I couldn't do this without them. I didn't want to. We were meant to be a pack, a *family*.

"Are you unhappy with us?" My voice was hoarse, words barely intelligible.

The couch shifted as Lars sat on my other side, his arm slung around me.

"No. *No.* You're my brothers, the very best part of my life. I would never choose to leave you."

My breathing steadied a bit. "But?"

"But seeing how my grandma's passing affected my grandpa

really shook me. He just gave up at the end because he couldn't live without her, and it scared the shit out of me. And, if I'm honest with myself, it made me angry. Why wouldn't he stay around for me? Why give your bonded that kind of power over you? So I decided I wasn't going to bond with an omega. I just didn't expect you to find someone so fast... and I knew you would choose her over me."

"What the fuck?" Lars asked, anger in his voice. "You thought we would reject *you*?"

"You're telling me you would choose me over Olive? She's your *omega*."

"She's your omega, too," I choked out.

Finn gave me another squeeze. "I know that now. I don't want to let my grief and my fear dictate my life decisions, but I think I understand more now. My grandparents' love for each other is what gave them peace at the end."

We sat in silence, and I sifted through his words. I realized how thoughtless I'd been. I hadn't recognized how much Finn was hurting. "I didn't realize getting the grant would be so hard for you. I just got fixated on this image of our future and wasn't thinking. I'm sorry."

He huffed a laugh. "Fuck, I was angry with you. But I was partially angry with you because you were right to apply for the grant. Don't let it go to your head, though." Finn winked, and the tightness in my chest loosened.

"You talked to Olive about all of this?" Lars asked. "She knows you're courting her?"

"Yeah. We talked last night."

"And what was going on with you two that first day? She wouldn't tell us anything."

Finn cleared his throat and he was fucking *blushing* as he told us about meeting Olive at the Hollywood Theater.

I was ready to hit him. He had treated my Olive like that? But Lars choked out a laugh. "You deserved way worse than a pickle sandwich."

"Yeah, I know."

I punched Finn in the arm. "Don't do that shit again."

"I won't," he said seriously. "Olive's forgiven me, and I don't take that lightly."

Lars stood and stretched. "For the record, I'm taking her out tomorrow."

I guessed that was fair. He hadn't had a date with Olive yet. But why did he get to take her out on a Saturday? Bastard was obviously going to drag it out all day.

"I'm going to get changed, and then I'm going to get a pumpkin spice latte." He took a few steps towards the stairs before clarifying, "*Lattes*. Multiple. For anyone who wants one. Not just for me."

Uh huh. As if I hadn't seen the empty cups in the trash.

"And Finn?" he said. "We never would have kicked you out of the pack. You're ours, and we would have figured something out."

Finn slumped back on the couch as Lars headed upstairs. "I'm really sorry I freaked you out," he said.

"You've always gotten lost in your head."

"Yeah." He put his arm back around me. "I don't know how you do it, East. How you stay so positive with all the shit you've been through."

I shifted on the couch so I was leaning up against him. "It's because I have you and Lars. You brought lightness into my world."

"Well fuck," Finn choked out, swiping at his eyes.

"And now we have Olive." I wanted to bring all the light into her world. She deserved it, since she was the pure sunshine in mine.

"Yeah, we do. And she needs some fucking furniture."

I grinned. We were finally working together as a pack, and we were going to sweep our omega off her feet.

35

LARS

"WHAT ARE YOUR FAVORITE BOOKS?"

Olive's sweet voice reached me from where she was curled up in the passenger seat, facing me. She'd already been all smiles when she walked out of the house this morning, ready for our date, but when I told her we were road-tripping to different romance bookstores? She'd let out a shriek, jumped in my arms, and pulled me in for a deep kiss I could still feel against my lips.

She was so fucking easy to please, and it made me want to do everything I could to make her happy.

Olive seemed to think that she was a difficult omega... that her medical issue would scare us away. It was the biggest load of bullshit. I hadn't seen her on one of her dark days yet, but there was nothing that would put me off, and I would do whatever I could to prove I wasn't going anywhere.

I glanced over at her. Fuck, she was so pretty. She was wearing some sort of plaid long-sleeved dress today and knitted tights, and I wished I could pull her into my lap. I turned my eyes back on the road and placed my hand on her thigh. She immediately surrounded it with hers, clinging to my wrist like maybe she wanted my touch as much as I craved hers.

"So... do you have one?" she asked.

My brain whirred, trying to remember the question.

Fuck, she was asking me about *books*.

I knew this would come up today. How could it not, when our date was literally all about books? My chest swirled with that familiar shame, and my throat was tight as I tried to clear it. Why did it feel like such a big deal to tell her? Olive wouldn't judge me. I *knew* that, but fuck, I couldn't stop the squeezing feeling in my chest.

"I don't really read," I hedged.

"Yeah?" She traced her fingers up and down my forearm, and I tightened my hold on her leg, digging my fingers into her lush thigh. "No favorites from what you have read?"

I stayed quiet as I changed lanes, passing a slow tractor. "I'm dyslexic," I finally said when the silence stretched on too long. "I had to read books in school, but I hated it. It always felt impossible."

My huge size had stopped me from getting bullied about not being able to read in school, but my omega loved books. Would she see me differently knowing we could never share this hobby?

Her hold on me tightened. "Did you not get any help or support?"

"My moms advocated for me." Understatement of the century. They'd been in and out of the school constantly to make sure my teachers were following my education plan. "But none of the tutoring worked." And that was the real issue, wasn't it? No matter how many specialists they hired, I couldn't figure it out. I wasn't smart enough.

Olive squeezed my hand. "That sounds so hard. I'm sorry."

I kept my eyes on the road. I couldn't look over at her, didn't want to see the pity in her eyes.

"Wait," she said, sitting up straighter. "So you don't know anything about the books you gave me?"

I furrowed my brow, unsure why she was asking. "No?"

"Oh thank God," she breathed out with a laugh. "I was really worried there for a second."

I braved a glance at her. She was smiling. "What do you mean?"

"I *love* that you gave me a courting gift," she said quickly.

Uh huh. "But?"

"But those were the biggest bunch of red-flag bro books I've ever seen." She giggled and tightened her hold on my hand as if I were going to pull it away. "I'm relieved you didn't know. But I really, *really* appreciate you getting them for me."

I couldn't believe I had an omega this sweet—thanking me multiple times for my apparently shitty courting gift. I captured her hand and brought it to my mouth, kissing it. "Fucking Hank," I muttered. "I don't really know what a bro book is, but I promise I'll get you better ones today." Lucy had given me a list of bookstores in nearby towns that catered to romance, so I wouldn't fuck this up.

Olive let go of my hand, and my chest tightened at the loss of contact. My anxiety turned to anger when I heard the click of the seat-belt and saw her *unbuckled*, leaning over the center console towards me. I swore, tightening my grip on the wheel. "What are you doing? Get your ass buckled." I couldn't stop the bark in my voice, my heart pounding at the idea of crashing with her unprotected. Olive wavered, briefly sitting down in her seat, but then she moved back over the console.

I was getting ready to fucking pull over when she planted a kiss on my cheek. "Thanks for telling me about your dyslexia." Her words were soft and sweet, and I couldn't help but fucking melt, my alpha instantly soothed by our omega.

I cleared my throat. "Get buckled. It's not safe." My words came out gentler this time.

Olive gave me one more kiss on the cheek before doing what I said. "Yes, alpha."

I put my hand back on her leg, this time higher up, so my pinky was dangerously close to brushing her sweet pussy. "I should punish you for that, naughty girl. Car safety is very important."

I grinned as I caught a bit of her sweet perfume. She'd worn scent-canceling deodorant today, and while I wished she hadn't, I understood it. Lucy always wore it, too. Said it made her feel less exposed in public.

"I take it you're not a fan of road head, then?" she asked.

My brain stuttered. Stopped. Was probably melting out of the bottom of my fucking skull as my cock hardened. A low growl rumbled through my chest as images of her pouty lips wrapped around my cock as I drove—my hand on top of her head, pushing her down to take me more—flashed through my mind.

"That would be unsafe." My voice was strangled.

She just hummed.

The steady sound of the blinker filled the truck as I turned into the first bookstore parking lot.

"Will you park there?" She pointed at a shady spot in an empty area at the very back of the parking lot.

"You sure? There are spots closer."

"Yeah, I'm sure."

I turned left to get to the back of the lot. Today was her day. Whatever my omega wanted, she got.

I put the truck in park and took a deep breath, willing my hard-on to go away. An impossible ask, really, since I was always hard around Olive. I would just have to do my best. Limit my walking. Keep Olive in front of me.

"You ready, sweetheart?" I asked, giving her leg one last squeeze before reaching for the door.

"Wait." She was leaning over the middle console again, a mischievous look in her eye. "You won something yesterday." Her hand trailed down my chest. *Down down down* until she was cupping my aching cock through my pants. "My alpha also said he needs to punish me." Her voice was a sultry whisper. "But I'm a good girl. I don't think I deserve to be punished."

Her ass was in the air as she leaned over, and I couldn't stop myself from palming it, squeezing hard. "Naughty little omegas don't get to decide when they get punished. That's why you need an alpha to keep you in line."

Her pupils were wide, her chest rising and falling rapidly as she lowered herself and kissed my cock through my clothes.

"You're going to give me a fucking heart attack one of these days, sweetheart," I said with a groan. "Take out my cock."

A smile tugged at her lips as she did what I commanded. Because she really was a good girl. *My* good girl.

But if she wanted to be my naughty girl right now? Who was I to refuse?

Her small hand fisted the base of my cock.

"That's it," I said through gritted teeth. I wrapped her hair around my hand and guided her down. Her ass tipped higher in the air as she balanced herself over the console and took the tip of my cock in her mouth.

I tightened my grip on her hair. "You want this rough, sweetheart? Want your alpha to take control?"

Her moaned "yes" sent vibrations through me, making my hips jerk. Fuck, I wasn't going to last long.

I pushed down on her head, forcing her to take me deeper. "Relax that throat for me." Her mouth was so wet and warm. The best thing I'd ever felt. She choked a bit and I pulled her back. "Take a breath. That's it. You're doing so well." Then I pushed her back down. "Relax again for me. There you go."

The tip of my cock forced its way into her tight little throat. Tears streamed down her face, but she stayed where she was, swallowing me down. I swore and pulled her off me. "Take a breath." As soon as she had, I forced her back down again, thrusting up in her throat. I would have been worried about hurting her, about being too rough, but her scent filled the truck, thick with arousal, and her moans of pleasure just spurred me on.

"Get ready to swallow." I barely managed to get out the words of warning before I came hard and fast down her throat. My hold on her immediately eased, and I gently stroked her hair as she caught her breath and lapped up any spilled cum.

After a few minutes, she slowly moved until she was sitting on her heels in the passenger seat. "Did I do good?" she asked, bouncing slightly.

I snorted. As if she fucking didn't know she'd just ripped my soul out of my body. "Look at you, sitting there so proud." I gripped her chin. "You did so well, little omega."

"I've been practicing," she said, cheeks flushed.

My heart sped up. "Practicing?" I growled.

"With a dildo," she clarified.

The growl in my chest intensified. "Stay right there."

I got out of the truck and checked our surroundings. Our area of the parking lot was still empty, and my body would shield anyone's view of my omega.

Being away from her for the few seconds it took for me to get to her door was too long. Possessiveness surged through me as I flung the passenger door open.

Big brown eyes met mine. I leaned down and collared her throat with my hand.

"You need a cock to practice on, you come get me, sweetheart. Understand?"

Her lips parted, and I pressed my thumb inside her mouth. She immediately started sucking on it as she nodded her head.

"Good. Now, we need to deal with you being naughty."

An indignant look crossed her face, and I pressed my finger deeper into her mouth before she could say anything.

"No arguing. You gave me a blow job like a very good girl, but we still have to deal with you unbuckling your seatbelt in a moving car. We'll take care of this quickly, and then we can go inside the bookstore and I'll buy you whatever you want. Okay, sweetheart?"

I pulled my thumb from her mouth. There was still a pout on her lip, but she didn't argue.

"Spin around and face the middle console."

She did what I asked, showing me her delicious ass. Part of me wished we had stayed at home today so I could fuck her all day long, but she deserved to be taken out on dates and spoiled.

I just needed her to know who she belonged to before we went inside.

I flipped the skirt of her dress up and quickly pulled down her tights. My heart stuttered. "You're not wearing fucking panties?" I squeezed her ass cheeks in both hands, my cock fucking growing hard again as I took in how she filled my palms, how beautiful her curves were.

She wiggled her ass. "I just didn't feel like it today."

"Uh huh. I think you wanted to tease your alpha."

My hand came down on her ass cheek, which turned pink and

jiggled under my hand. I gave a matching smack on her other cheek. She tried to crawl away, but I secured her with a hand on her hip. "You can stop this anytime, sweetheart."

"Don't stop." Her voice was a full omega whine.

"Fuck, you're perfect for me."

I spanked her again, harder this time until her cheeks were bright red, my rhythm broken only by thrusting my fingers inside her dripping cunt. I groaned as I brought my fingers to my lips.

"You taste so fucking good."

"Alpha, please," she begged.

I smacked her ass again and then rubbed in the sting. "What do you need?"

She peered back over her shoulder. "I need to come."

I cupped her pussy. "Such a greedy girl. You're dripping for me." She rocked back into me to gain friction, but I quickly pulled away and moved her tights back in place. "Naughty girls don't get to come. But if you're a very good girl today, maybe your alpha will let you come this evening."

Olive turned around and fixed me with a look so fierce it would have struck fear into my heart if she didn't look as adorable and harmless as a kitten.

"You can't leave me like this," she whimpered.

I lifted her out of the truck, making sure her body was pressed against mine. "I can." I fisted her hair, tilting her head back. "I want you to be reminded with every step that your pussy is all pink and puffy and dripping because of me."

My chest rumbled, and Olive whined.

I gently patted her ass. "Come on, sweetheart. Let's get some books."

36

LARS

OLIVE POUTED FOR ABOUT ONE MINUTE AFTER WE entered the bookstore, and then the allure of the books overpowered her frustration at her denied orgasm. We were in a massive warehouse for used books. Olive bounced happily over to the carts and grabbed one, but I nudged her aside and took it from her.

"You just focus on the books, sweetheart."

She grinned, standing on her tiptoes to give me a kiss.

I followed her through the aisles until we got to the romance section. My eyes kept moving down to her ass, and my alpha rumbled in satisfaction. I forced my gaze back to her face as she started pulling books off the shelf. With each one she grabbed, she took the time to read me the title and description.

My throat was tight at how easily she accommodated me. I pulled her into my chest and pressed a kiss to her forehead. "You're getting so many orgasms tonight."

Her cheeks flushed with pleasure. We locked eyes, and I knew for a moment that both of us were thinking of skipping out on the rest of this date. But I wasn't going to let that happen. I gave her ass a squeeze. "Keep shopping, sweetheart. You've got lots of shelves to fill."

The cottage had large built-in bookcases on either side of the fireplace that were now sitting empty, and I couldn't wait to see them full of all the books I'd buy her.

"I can't get that many books," she mumbled.

"Challenge accepted," I said with another kiss.

AFTER THE USED BOOKSTORE, we got lunch at a small lobster shack Summer had recommended. The menu was simple, but Olive had read it out loud as she decided, making it easy for me to know the options. It brought a lump to my throat.

"This is a pretty good lobster roll," Olive said. "And I'm a lobster expert, so I know."

I grinned. "That's right. Did you eat a lot growing up?"

"Actually, not really," she said, taking a sip of her soda. "Money was always tight, especially as new fishing regulations rolled in. They're to preserve the environment, but make it hard to earn a living. Eating a lot of lobster would cut into profits." She shrugged. "But my dad always organized a big summer potluck and people would bring lobster rolls and sides and all that."

There was a wistful smile on her face.

"Did it stop after he died?"

She fidgeted with her napkin, ripping it into even slices. "No. One of my dad's closest friends, Gunnar, took over organizing it. Actually, he hired me to work on his boat after they passed, which he definitely didn't have to do. He's also the one who bought my dad's boat when I realized I had to sell it."

She looked out the window. The sky was growing dark and a few drops of rain landed on the glass. "It hurt to be out on the water without my parents. To check buoys that weren't our colors." At my questioning expression, she added, "Everyone had buoys in certain colors attached to lobster traps. My family's buoys have a red, light blue, and dark blue stripe. The colors have been the same for generations."

I reached out and squeezed her hand, reminded of how privileged I was to have my family, to never have worried about money.

"Anyway," Olive said, shaking off her sadness. "After that one season with Gunnar, I took an online data entry job and pulled away from the community. It felt safer to just be on my own."

I dragged her chair over to mine, the loud scrape causing a few people to look our way, and lifted her onto my lap.

"Lars," she hissed. "We're going to break the chair."

I grunted. She might have a point. These chairs were flimsy, but I needed her in my arms. "You're not alone anymore, sweetheart. Never will be again, okay?"

"I mean, I might need alone time at some point," she mumbled.

I pressed my smile against her hair. "I'm sure that can be arranged. Maybe."

She huffed, but her body relaxed against mine.

"Ready for more book shopping?"

She perked up at that and wiggled in my lap. "Yes."

SOMETHING WAS WRONG WITH OLIVE. We were in a new bookstore—a smaller one this time with new books and fancy displays—but Olive had only picked out two books. I gently pried them from her hand so I could hold them for her.

"Does this store not have a good selection, sweetheart?"

She turned to look at me, her eyes wide as if she'd forgotten I was there. "What?"

"We've been in here a while, and you haven't picked out that many books."

She fidgeted and looked down at the floor. "Am I being too slow?"

I frowned. "Not at all. This is your day."

"But it's not fun for you. Do you want to do something else?"

She was shifting around like she was restless or uncomfortable. I crouched down a bit so I wasn't looming over her. "What's wrong, sweetheart? I'm not bored. I love seeing you excited about books."

She chewed her lip. "But these are a lot more expensive."

I cupped her face. "That doesn't matter. Get what you want."

Olive turned back to the shelves and half-heartedly looked at a few more books before putting them back on the shelves. She'd put up a fight when I'd paid for the used books and for lunch, but I wondered if something more was going on. She'd been so happy earlier and now she seemed... *shit*. Was this one of Olive's dark moods? Or had I done something to upset her?

I trailed her through the store a bit longer until I caught a hint of her bitter scent breaking through her deodorant. That was it. I couldn't stand for her to walk around upset.

I put my hand on her lower back, gently rubbing. "Are you okay?"

"I think I want to go home."

"Okay, sweetheart." I pulled her into a hug. "We'll come back when you're feeling up to it."

"Yeah? I didn't ruin it?" Her whispered question broke my heart.

"You could never ruin anything. We can go back home and have some good cuddles, okay?"

She didn't quite meet my gaze but nodded. She stayed quiet while I paid for her books.

I grimaced as I looked outside at the pouring rain. "You hold on to these." I handed her the bag of books. "And I'll pull the truck around."

The rain soaked my sweatshirt by the time I got to the truck, but I didn't care. All I cared about was my Olive and making her feel better.

37

LARS

THE WIND SHOOK THE LIGHTHOUSE COTTAGE, AND THE mood inside matched the weather. Tension filled the kitchen, sharp enough to cut through. Olive had been bright and sunshiny all day, but her dark mood seemed to roll in with the arrival of the storm. Or maybe the weather was just as obsessed with Olive as I was and changed itself to match her mood.

Her deodorant must have worn off because her scent was all burnt coffee—bitter and acidic—and her usual sweetness was absent. The cabinet doors slammed shut as she worked her way around the kitchen, followed by her little sounds of frustration. And it fucking broke my heart. To think she'd been alone all these years, managing all of this on her own. The way her body turned her mind against her at the drop of a hat. I couldn't imagine how fucking disorienting that must be.

"Come here, sweetheart," I said when I couldn't take it anymore.

Olive turned to me, her eyes dull and her expression pinched. "What?"

I crooked my finger. "Come here for a minute."

"But I need to make us tea."

I arched my eyebrow, barely keeping my alpha contained. I wanted to close the space between us and pull her into my arms. But my omega was skittish, and I wanted her to know that I was the one she should always run to.

Olive looked back at the mug she'd pulled out from the cupboard and then at me. Painfully slowly, she shuffled towards me, my thick woolen socks on her feet dampening the sounds of her steps. She stopped about a foot away, looking down at the floor. I cupped her chin with my hand and lifted her face to find her lip trembling and her eyes glassy.

I couldn't wait any longer. I pulled her against my chest, folding myself around her. Her breaths came quickly as she wrapped her arms around me, holding tight.

I rubbed my hand down her back. "You having a hard time, sweetheart?"

The only sound I got back was a tiny little sob.

"That's okay. I've got you."

"I'm ruining everything." Her words were muffled against my t-shirt.

"How could you possibly be ruining anything?"

"It was such a good day," she sobbed. "Why do I feel like this now?"

I rubbed my cheek against hers, scent-marking her. "I don't know," I murmured. "But it's not your fault, and it's not ruining anything."

She needed the comfort of her nest, so I palmed her ass and lifted her. She wrapped her legs around my waist as I headed down the hallway. I paused outside the door. "Will you invite me inside, little omega?"

"Don't leave," was her response.

I pushed inside and settled her down on the bed, the air mattress shifting underneath her. Then I had an idea. "I'll be right back."

She clutched at my arm with a whine. "Sorry," she whispered, curling in on herself.

I leaned down to kiss her forehead. "I'll be back in thirty seconds. You can time me."

I ran back to the living room and grabbed the books we'd gotten today. Olive was completely hidden under a blanket when I returned.

"I got your books if you want to read something."

Her head poked out from under the blanket. She sniffed, scrubbed a tear from her cheek, and pulled a book out of the bag.

"You don't have to stay," she said, turning away from me.

I huffed and lay down behind her, pulling her close to my chest.

"Stop worrying," I murmured, my face pressed into her hair so I could breathe in her scent, which had turned the slightest bit sweet. "I'm not bored. You don't have to entertain me. Just relax."

Olive made a disgruntled little noise, and I grinned. My girl liked to pretend she didn't like being told what to do, but the tension in her body finally drained away as she settled fully against me. I wrapped an arm around her waist and pressed a leg between hers. She shifted, her curvy ass nestling against my rapidly hardening cock. I angled my hips away from her, not wanting her to think I was pushing for sex, but she moved right back.

I grinned. Alright then.

I didn't see which book she'd chosen, but it made my alpha ridiculously proud that I had provided it. I propped myself up on my elbow so I could read over her shoulder, but the words swam and she flipped the page way too quickly for me to keep up.

"What are you reading?" I should probably stay quiet, was probably testing my luck, but I wanted to know everything about Olive, including what she liked to read.

"It's a Mafia romance."

I let out a bark of laughter but quickly sobered when I realized Olive was serious. "What is a Mafia romance?" My only frame of reference for the Mafia was watching *The Godfather*, but I didn't think that's what Olive had in mind.

"The main characters are part of rival mafias and get married for an alliance."

"And... you like this?"

"If you want to judge me, you can just get out," Olive snapped. She tried to disentangle herself, but I held on tighter.

"You're not going anywhere, kitten. I'm not judging, just curious. Want to read it out loud to me?"

That made her stop squirming. "You are *not* calling me kitten."

I hummed, running my hand down her side. "You're cute and small, with the occasional claws. Seems to fit."

"I'm not small," she grumbled.

I flipped her onto her stomach and laid my full weight on top of her.

"Oh my god!" Olive squealed, trying to buck me off.

I laughed and quickly rolled off of her before I actually crushed her. Her cheeks were flushed, and her hair was flying everywhere. "You seem pretty small to me," I said with a wink.

"Not all of us can be big Viking alphas." She pushed her hair out of her face.

"No, some of us have to be perfect, precious omegas." I ran my hand down her side and squeezed her hip. There was so much more of her I wanted to squeeze, but I wouldn't push it right now. I ran my nose down the side of her face, my lips skimming her soft skin. "In case there was any confusion, I love every part of your body."

She blushed and couldn't quite meet my gaze. I rubbed my beard against her cheek until she laughed and pushed me away.

I flopped onto my back with a smile. "Now that we've determined my nickname for you is perfect and you love it, read me your book."

Before she could protest, I arranged Olive so we were spooning again, moving her limbs until she was right where I wanted her.

"You're not always going to get what you want," she huffed.

I stroked my hand through her hair, smoothing it down. "Noted."

OLIVE'S BOOKS WERE *DIRTY*.

Holy shit.

And hearing her read it? It made me so fucking hard. She was so prim and prissy, all blushes as she read out the explicit scene, and it was so cute I could howl.

The Mafia guy in the book was using rope to tie up his wife.

My cock twitched against her ass.

My omega was growing squirmy.

Her breathing heavy with each new sentence.

Her thick perfume filling the room.

I tightened my hold on her and pressed my knee tighter against her pussy. "Is my girl feeling needy?" I murmured as I planted kisses down the side of her face. "Does she want her alpha to tie her up?"

She closed the book with a huff. "You're assuming you're the one who gets to tie me up? Maybe you don't get to be in charge all the time. Maybe *I* want to be in charge." I rolled her onto her back so I could see her face. She scowled and crossed her arms.

I bit the inside of my cheeks to stop from grinning. I decided I loved prickly, grumpy Olive. As if there had ever been any doubt.

I loved Olive.

I loved Olive.

The realization washed over me like a sweet, warm latte.

I pressed a kiss to her scowling forehead and sat up, leaning against the wall. "Alright, kitten. You're in charge."

She blinked. "What?" She was so shocked she forgot to scowl.

I grinned. "If that's what you want. Have your way with me."

Olive chewed her lip as if wondering if this was a trap. "What if I want to tie you up?"

"Mmm, I bet my girl knows how to tie a good knot. Seems like a skill for a lobsterwoman." I waggled my eyebrows and she huffed, but she couldn't hide her *almost* smile.

She moved into a kneeling position, a bundle of blankets still surrounding her. "Okay. Then... then you should take off your clothes."

Her expression was pure challenge, as if she thought this was when I was going to tap out. Adorable.

I quickly stripped out of my clothes, throwing them over the side of the mattress. Olive's heated gaze ran down my body, stopping when she got to my cock that was so hard it was almost standing up.

"Strip for me, kitten. Show me all those beautiful curves."

"I'm in charge," she muttered, but she did as I said, throwing her clothes to the ground in a huff. I held myself back when all I wanted was to lunge at her, to pull her sweet, dripping pussy down on my cock.

"Stay here," she said with a point of her finger before leaving the room.

I wanted to chase. Images of me hunting her in the dark, creeping up on her, flitted through my mind.

Fuck. I didn't know chasing was one of my fantasies, but it definitely was now.

Olive quickly returned with a length of rope, and a spurt of precum hit my stomach. I groaned, leaning my head back against the wall. "Are you going to tie me up, kitten? Have me completely at your mercy?"

She crawled onto the bed, confidently holding my gaze. Her breasts swung with her movements, and I was mesmerized by her pretty pink nipples.

Olive took hold of my arms, encircling my wrists with her small hands. "Are you really okay with this?" she whispered.

"Yes, sweetheart. More than okay. Don't overthink it, okay?"

"You'll tell me if I do something you don't like?"

"Of course." She'd have to try very hard to do something I didn't like.

She straddled me, and her slick dripped onto my cock. I cursed, but stayed still as she tied a loop around my wrist.

"I don't have anything to attach this to," she said with a frown. I made a note that we needed to make sure the bed we got her had a frame or slats or some shit. Because this was *not* going to be the last time we had rope in her nest. "Can I tie your hands behind your back?"

I cradled her head in my hands, bringing her lips a whisper away from mine. "I told you to have your way with me, omega." My voice was low and gravelly, my alpha coming to the surface. "And I meant it."

Her pupils dilated, and she let out a little whimper as she arched against me. My cock was weeping, desperate to be inside her hot little pussy.

Olive quickly moved my hands behind me and secured them. I tugged against the rope, but they didn't budge.

"What a good job you did, kitten. You'll have to teach me how to do that." I leaned forward and nipped the skin between her neck and shoulder. The skin I wanted to sink my teeth into. "Keep going," I encouraged.

A look of determination crossed Olive's face as she ran her hands down the planes of my chest. She wiggled a bit, nestling my cock in between her pussy lips and soaking me in her slick. Then she took it in her hand, giving it a squeeze that made me let out an undignified shout, which made her giggle.

She notched it at her entrance but looked a little hesitant. Did she have much experience being on top? My alpha growled, hating the idea of anyone else touching her, seeing all of *this*.

I swallowed down my possessiveness and focused on my omega. "You're doing so well, kitten. That's it, just lower yourself down."

Her breath came in pants as she took more of me.

"You feel so good," I groaned. "Your little pussy is working so hard to take me."

She moaned as she let herself sink all the way down, her slick drenching my balls.

"Good girl." I barely choked out the words with the way she was strangling my cock. "Such a good fucking girl."

She wrapped her arms around my neck, pressing her breasts against my chest.

"Are you supposed to be talking this much?" she asked, breathless.

I nuzzled her neck. "Do you not want me to talk?"

She shifted, whimpering as her clit brushed against me. "No... I guess it's fine."

I hid my smile, wondering how far I could push me taking charge. I tugged against the ropes, wishing I could touch her. There was something sexy about being at her mercy, but not being able to touch her was torture.

She tentatively raised up and then slammed back down, taking my cock all the way to my knot. My eyes widened. *Fuck*, I wanted Olive on top all the time. With each thrust, her breasts swung and her stomach jiggled and I wanted it all. Her fingers dug into my shoulders as she used me for leverage, her eyes closed, head thrown back.

She was perfect.

I planted my heels on the mattress and thrust up, helping set the rhythm she needed. "That's it, kitten. Take what you need from me."

"I want your knot," she said. "I need it, alpha."

Her scent was thick and I could feel myself being pulled ever so slightly to a rut. If I were ever lucky enough to spend a heat with Olive, there was no doubt I would go absolutely feral.

"Take it, omega," I barked. She moaned lightly and crushed her lips to mine, running her hands through my hair and *tugging*. The sting just made me thrust harder.

And then my knot was partially inside her. For a moment, it seemed like she was going to pull back. "No, kitten, keep going. I know you can be such a good girl and take all of me. Just relax that sweet little pussy. There you go. So perfect."

I lost my ability to speak when she took the rest of my knot, her heat surrounding me fully. Her pussy fluttered around me, whimpers slipping through her lips, swollen from kisses, as she came. I groaned, struggling against the rope as my orgasm ripped through me. I filled her with my cum and tried to push deeper inside her. I wanted to be locked so tight she could never leave.

"Untie my hands, kitten," I murmured, brushing my lips against her hair. She was exhausted, and I wanted to make sure I could take care of her the way she needed.

She managed to reach around me and undo them. My arms were immediately around her, holding her tight to my chest.

"You did so well." Her skin was so soft as I ran my hands up and down her back, my chest rattling with a purr. Her eyes fluttered closed, and she relaxed fully. The tension I'd been carrying since Olive's mood went south eased. It was like my body had been waiting for this, the moment when our omega was safe and secure. I shifted on the bed, getting in a more comfortable position as my omega slept against my chest while her pussy was stuffed with my knot and cum.

It took about thirty minutes for my knot to go down. Olive shifted as it did, her eyes blinking open.

"I fell asleep," she said, looking around, a little confused.

"You worked very hard," I murmured, placing a kiss on the side of her face.

She sat up and grabbed my arms so she could inspect my wrists. I realized a beat too late that she was looking to see if the rope left any marks. Then she shifted off me, letting out a gush of fluid, and got up off the bed.

"Where are you going?" My voice was a low growl, my alpha telling me to grab her. Keep our omega close. It took all my self-control to stop myself from barking at her to cuddle with me.

She didn't go far, though. Just to the edge of the nest to grab her water, an extra blanket, and a bottle of lotion. What was she doing? If she needed something, *I* would get it for her. She got back on the bed, but instead of curling up in my arms again, she *tucked the blanket around me*. What was happening? She held a straw up to my lips. My brow furrowed as I took a few sips of water. Then she gently took my wrist, freed it from my blanket, and rubbed lotion into my skin.

It clicked.

My lips twitched.

"You giving me aftercare, kitten?"

"Yes," she said, still focused on my wrists, which weren't one bit sore after her expert tying. She met my gaze. "Do you want a snack, too?"

She looked so serious, so fucking sweet, that I didn't have the heart to tell her I'd been topping her all along. I snagged her around the waist, pulling her tight to my chest.

"I love you fussing over me."

I carefully leaned forward and snagged another blanket, wrapping it around her. I held the straw up to her lips for her to take a drink. Her eyes drifted closed, and I gently rubbed my hand up and down her back, savoring these quiet moments with my omega. I knew I needed to get up soon, feed her dinner, but I didn't want to break this perfect moment.

"Lars?" Her voice was sleepy and muffled from how she was pressed against my chest.

"Yes, kitten?"

"I don't think I want to be in charge again."

She couldn't see me, so I felt safe smiling. "That's okay. You don't have to be."

She wrapped her arms around me even tighter and dozed off.

38

LARS

I STRETCHED WITH A QUIET GROAN AS I WOKE. MY BACK was fucking killing me. Our plans to transform Olive's nest couldn't happen soon enough.

I blinked my eyes open and was met with big brown eyes. Big, brown, *exhausted* eyes that looked so fucking sad.

"Morning, sweetheart." My voice was hoarse with sleep, and I wondered if my omega had slept at all. Last night after dinner, we'd gone up to the top of the lighthouse for a while and just sat together before heading to bed early. I'd fallen asleep instantly, and now I wished I'd forced myself to stay awake so Olive wouldn't be alone in the night.

She didn't say anything.

I shifted so I could tug her closer to my chest and run my hand through her hair. "Is it still a dark day?" The sky outside was dim and gray, the stormy weather persisting.

Olive nodded against my chest. I brushed my cheek against hers, hoping my scent provided her some comfort. What could I do to support her? I wished I could take all the darkness away.

A purr started up in my chest and Olive let out a little sigh, her breath a puff against my bare skin. I stroked my hand up and down her back. I could get her breakfast. A pumpkin spice latte. Cuddles. And then it hit me—Olive craved routine.

"Do you want to go out to the water?" My voice was a whisper against her hair.

"Oh." She trailed her fingers against my skin, and I forced myself to be patient and wait for her to say more. "I don't know if I have the energy."

"It's a good thing you have me, then." I glanced back out the window. It was sprinkling and looked cold. I grabbed one of the fluffy blankets from Olive's bed and wrapped it around her until she was completely bundled up. I located my clothes on the floor and threw them on before picking her up.

"My little omega burrito," I said as I carried her out of the room. I stopped by the front door to shove my feet into my boots and then headed outside. I winced as icy air hit us, and I held Olive tighter. "You okay, kitten?"

"Yeah."

I pressed a kiss to her forehead and quickly headed down to the beach. The waves were rough and choppy, crashing on the shore in a way that made me distinctly nervous. "Do you want to get in the water?" *Please say no.* Because if she said yes, I would be the one carrying her in.

She freed her hand from the blanket burrito and ran her fingers through my beard. Now *I* felt like a fucking kitten, purring as she pet my face. The corner of her lips twitched like she was tempted to smile.

"Can we just sit and watch the waves for a few minutes?"

"We can do whatever the fuck you want, sweetheart."

I walked us over to the large flat rock and arranged her on my lap so she was facing the waves, my arms like iron bands around her as I tried to use my body to shield her from the drizzling rain and bitter wind. Even with the stormy weather, I had to admit there was something peaceful about being out here, with just the wind and waves keeping us company.

Olive shifted on my lap so she could run her nose down the

column of my throat, followed by a gentle kiss. "I'm sorry I'm like this."

I scowled and threaded my fingers in her hair, tugging her head back roughly so she was forced to meet my gaze. "If you apologize again, I'm spanking your ass until you can't sit for a week. Understand?"

Her lip jutted out in a pout and, *fuck*, she could never find out how much power that little lip had over me. "Don't you wish I was different?"

"I wish you didn't have to experience this pain, but I don't wish *you* were different. You're my Olive, my kitten."

"Still not sure about that name."

I grinned and pressed a tender kiss to the tip of her adorable nose. "Nah, you're definitely sure about it." I tucked her to my chest and stood. "Now, let's get back inside and ask the guys to bring us breakfast and pumpkin spice lattes."

She nuzzled into my neck. "I think you just might be addicted."

I inhaled deeply, catching her scent mixed with the salt in the wind. "No fucking doubt about that."

39

EASTON

"Why are you crying, baby?"

I held Olive close as tears streamed down her face. She was on my lap and we had just finished lunch, but she was still having a hard time. Lars had filled us in on what happened on their date, and Finn and I had rushed over.

I hated seeing her like this, especially because the issue was hormonal and there was nothing I could do to fix it, except be here with her.

It didn't feel like enough.

Maybe I wasn't enough.

My mother's angry voice echoed in my head, telling me how useless I was. I closed my eyes and took a deep breath against the fear that I was failing Olive, that she would leave me.

My mom's words weren't true. I had a place here. With my brothers. By Olive's side.

"I don't know," she blubbered. "I'm just sad. And my hair looks awful." She started crying harder.

"Your hair looks beautiful, sweet girl," Finn said, leaning forward to run his fingers through her waves, which maybe looked just a *little* unkempt and frizzy. Not that it mattered, but Olive cared about her appearance.

"Why don't we take a bath together?" I suggested. "It will be nice and relaxing, and we'll wash your hair."

"But then I'll have to dry my hair," she sobbed.

I caught the briefest flash of a smile on Lars's lips before he schooled his expression. Our omega's distress wasn't funny, but her dramatics were cute and in such contrast to how reserved she usually was.

Lars leaned in and kissed her on the forehead. "Come here, sweetheart. I'll dry your hair afterwards, okay? You won't have to do anything."

"Really?" she asked, eyes wide and glassy, as if there were any doubt we would do anything for her.

Lars just nodded and picked her up, carrying her to the bathroom. It was a cramped room with a small tub, and I had visions of replacing it with something large enough for all of us. On second thought, that might just be the size of a pool. Okay, a bathtub at least big enough for *two* of us.

Finn started the bath, and I looked through the cabinets for bath oils. I frowned when I saw they were practically empty. We needed to get her bath bombs or something. She deserved to feel special.

Lars put Olive down on the bath rug, and the two of us gently stripped off her sweater (mine) and got her in the bath.

Her scent turned sweeter once she was in the water, the tension draining from her shoulders. But then a little frown marred her face. "Why am I the only one naked?"

The three of us were off the floor and stripping immediately. I hesitated before pulling off my boxers. I was half-hard and didn't want her to think I expected anything. My cock only saw a gorgeous naked goddess in the tub. He really didn't have a sense of occasion. But if she wanted us naked, who was I to argue?

I sat down on top of my sweater so my ass wasn't against the freezing floor. Lars massaged the shampoo into her hair, and her eyes drifted closed.

I leaned forward, my lips brushing against her ear. "Look at you, doing whatever you can to get your alphas naked."

The tiniest smile tugged at her lips as she brushed her cheek against mine, scent-marking me. The gesture soothed the part of me terrified of abandonment. *I* had been the one to make her smile because I knew Olive. I had peered into the deepest parts of her soul, just as she had done to me.

She entwined her fingers with mine. "I would never be that diabolical."

"Sure, sunshine. Whatever you say."

Night had fallen and the four of us were in the lighthouse control room, bundled up again in thick sweaters, empty pizza boxes stacked to the side. Olive sat in the main chair, looking out of the large windows at the storm. The static of the radio and intermittent announcements cut through the heavy patter of rain and thunder.

"It's been a while since we got a storm like this," I said. "Remember that one a few years ago that damaged the market?"

"Cut the power to half the town, too," Finn said. "What a mess."

Lars stood behind Olive, running his fingers through her dry hair. "Want me to give you a couple of French braids?"

Olive blinked up at him. "You can braid?"

"Lucy trained me well."

"Okay," she whispered.

Her blanket had slipped down her shoulder, and I adjusted it. It was cold in this room.

"We should get some space heaters up here, especially with winter coming." The idea of my Olive being cold was unbearable. I didn't want her to live alone in the lighthouse cottage this winter or any other time. How long did we have to court her before we moved in? I needed to see what the internet had to say about it.

Lars started working on Olive's braids. She leaned into his touch as he tenderly parted her hair, moving with her when she leaned forward to adjust some controls.

"What is it you're doing?" I asked. The three of us had spent plenty of storms up here with Fredrik when we were teenagers, but we'd never paid much attention to what he was doing. We would bring up pillows and card games and music to keep Fredrik company during long nights, and he'd seemed to love it. He and Carina had always seemed to love spending time with us. It had made me feel so fucking special.

"In bad storms like this, I'm in touch with the Ocean Rescue to ensure everyone in the water stays safe. Starlight Grove's marina is small, so the rescue boats don't usually launch from here, but they can if it's the most proximate location. I also keep track of communications with ships in the water, adjusting the flash sequence of the lantern, using the foghorn, and sometimes even Morse Code messages through the light and radio so they can orient themselves."

Lars pulled a small hair tie from his pocket and tied off Olive's first braid. "Where did you learn all of this?"

"I trained in open ocean rescue once I turned eighteen, and I always read the meteorological reports for the lobster boat." She shrugged as if it was nothing, as if she wasn't incredibly impressive. "But the lighthouse stuff, I learned from that." She pointed at a large binder on the desk in front of her.

Finn flipped it open and swallowed hard. "My grandpa wrote this."

"Yeah. Fredrik. I feel like I've gotten to know him as I've read through it all. It's pretty funny, too. He put lots of little commentary notes throughout the manual."

"I wish I had paid more attention to all this growing up," Finn said, his voice thick.

Olive reached out to grab his hand and squeezed. We lapsed into a comfortable silence, squeezing close to our omega as we watched the storm roll over us.

40

OLIVE

"I don't understand this Mafia guy at all. He makes Finn seem downright chipper."

Easton's hand ran up and down my side as I read my new book to him. I was sitting between his legs, curled up against his bare chest and breathing in his rich chocolate scent. It anchored me. The deep pit of despair I was so familiar with was still there, and I was still in it, but I hadn't entirely vanished into the darkness like usual. My guys wouldn't let me. And somehow, they weren't upset when I lashed out or pushed them away. In fact, they just smiled, gave me a kiss, and forced more cuddles.

I couldn't quite wrap my head around it all.

All weekend, they'd made sure one of them was always in my nest with me. I told them it was unnecessary, that they probably had better things to do, and was promptly ignored. I could just imagine Finn creating some sort of rotation schedule. Today was Sunday, so the guys weren't working, but Lars and Finn had left the house mid-morning and told me to stay in my nest with Easton. Of course, that made me want to defy them and see what was responsible for the loud noises I kept hearing in the rest of the house. But Easton was an unwavering jailer, trapping me with cuddles and giving me smug little smirks.

Asshole.

Sorta.

Not really.

When my guys were in my nest, they'd all demanded I read my Mafia romance out loud to them and were getting *very* invested.

"I do like the whole necklace tracker situation. I should definitely get you one of those," Easton said.

"You should not," I grumbled.

"I think I should. That way, I can chase you down whenever I want." His voice was low and sent a shiver through me as I imagined being hunted by my alphas. How adrenaline would surge through me as I tried to get away, the thrill of being caught and thrown to the ground.

I'd had my fair share of hookups throughout the years, but I'd never trusted anyone enough to really embrace my kinks. But with my guys? I wanted it all.

"Maybe that would be okay," I mumbled.

Easton groaned. His hard-on rubbed against my ass as he shifted to brush his cheek against the top of my head, scent-marking me. I hadn't put on any deodorant this weekend, and my guys couldn't keep their hands off me, even more than usual.

My reading was interrupted when the door to my room creaked open. Lars and Finn entered, looking excited.

"Everything ready?" Easton asked.

"What is everything? What have you been doing?" I huffed.

Lars chuckled and plucked me from Easton's arms into his own, holding me bridal style. "You've been such a good, patient girl—"

Easton snorted. "Who are you talking about?"

"And now we can show you your surprise," Lars continued, ignoring Easton.

I crossed my arms. "Fine."

God, I could hear myself being a bitch, but I couldn't stop the words coming out of my mouth. Unreasonable irritation clawed at my chest that Lars and Finn had left my nest this morning, even though I told them I was fine on my own. I wasn't in the mood for surprises right now. I just wanted to be in a bad mood and they weren't letting me.

My alpha just smiled and brushed his hand over the French braids that were still in my hair. He'd ended up braiding his own hair to match, and somehow it totally fit his whole fierce Viking vibe.

"Ready?" he asked before carrying me out of the room. The first thing I noticed was a massive mattress leaning against the wall.

"This is for your nest," Finn explained. "Unless you're particularly attached to the air mattress."

I blinked. The air mattress made for a somewhat miserable sleeping experience when all of us were on it, and I honestly didn't know how much time we had before it just popped under our weight.

"And once you're feeling up to it, we're going to go to Nest Wonderland to buy you whatever you want for your nest. It's supposed to be the best store for omega stuff," Easton said, rubbing his hands together.

My insides were a swirl of emotion. Did they not think I'd done a good job with my nest? And how could they possibly want to buy me stuff when I was so awful to them?

Finn moved close and cupped my face. "Come see the rest, sweet girl."

Lars moved out to the living room, and my jaw dropped. It was fully furnished. A deep green velvet sectional filled the room, along with two floral armchairs, a large walnut coffee table, and a plush rug. Books filled the built-in shelves on either side of the fireplace— some old and sea-related, but also tons of my favorite romance books. My eyes flitted to the dining room, where a beautiful wooden table sat. Copper pots and pans hung from the ceiling rack in the kitchen. It looked like something out of a magazine.

I blinked. "What? How?"

Finn ran his hand through his hair, looking anxious. "When my grandparents died, we moved their things into storage. I had no idea this place was advertised as being furnished, and I'm so fucking sorry you've had to live for over a month without anything." He looked truly devastated. "So we wanted to move their things back for you. They really belong here, anyway."

A lump filled my throat, and I reached out my arms to him. Finn gathered me to his chest and sat down with me on the couch. I knew how personal these things were, how tied up in grief they could be, and it meant the world that he wanted them to be in my space.

"Are you sure?" I whispered. "It's okay if you want to keep them for yourself."

"I'm sure," Finn murmured. "My grandma would smack me on the head for keeping her stuff in storage when a beautiful omega could enjoy them." He swallowed hard. "She would have loved you. My grandpa, too."

I thought about these two kind people who had taken in Finn and, later, Easton. Looking around the cottage now, how warm and cozy it felt, I could only imagine what it would have been like when it was filled with teenage boys and laughter.

"I wish I could have known them."

He squeezed me tight to his side. "Me, too."

Easton and Lars sat down beside us, the sectional easily big enough to hold all of us.

"So none of this is stuff you bought for me, right?" I asked. "Because you shouldn't spend your money—"

Easton placed his finger over my lips. "We will buy you whatever we want." His expression was pure challenge, and I frowned. He traced his finger across the bow of my lip. "And we want to help you financially, too, if you need it."

I met his gaze, and it felt like he was staring straight into my soul. I squirmed, feeling uncomfortable. Inadequate.

"I know what it's like to not have money," he continued. "It's nothing to be ashamed about. Would you hold it against me, against us, if we were struggling?"

I took a deep breath. Of course I wouldn't. But that deep-seated independent streak I'd been raised with was hard to shake. "I'm okay, really. I ended up with some credit card debt because of my medical bills, and I've been slow to pay it off. But I'm almost done."

"Give us the information and we'll take care of it," Lars said quickly.

I shook my head. "No, I'm honestly really close. I should be able to pay it off next month." I'd been counting down the days on my calendar. After three years of payments, I was almost there.

Lars frowned, but he didn't push it.

"Fine," Finn said after a beat of silence, his sharp jaw tense as if the word cost him something to speak. "But you *will* let us spoil you, omega. I'm afraid you have no choice."

I looked around at the gorgeous room. "But this is too much."

"We didn't buy new things. This is just the stuff from storage." He wasn't quite meeting my gaze, and I cocked an eyebrow, feeling suspicious.

"Let's go check out the rest," Lars said, getting up and pulling me up off the couch as if trying to distract me. "See if you want to change anything."

I walked through the rest of the cottage in a trance-like state, struggling to believe this was truly my space. As the guys eagerly showed everything off, a tremendous sense of *home* washed over me. It had nothing to do with the things and everything to do with what they represented—the tremendous love and care I felt from these three alphas.

I ran my fingers along the smooth top of the dining room table. It was a rich, dark brown with organic edges, like it was made of driftwood. The more I looked at it, the more I noticed how the knots and waves in the wood made it feel alive.

"I've never seen a table like this," I said.

I glanced up and saw Easton looking off to the side, cheeks red. I blinked as a slow realization washed over me.

"Easton?" I stepped towards him until I was almost touching his chest. "Did you... did you make this?"

He cleared his throat. "Might have had the wood in the shop, and I just, you know"—He waved his hand in the air—"put it together."

My perfume filled the room, bright and happy. "You made me a table."

Easton finally turned to meet my gaze and gave me the slightest nod. My chest ballooned with happiness and tender affection for this exuberant alpha, who still had his anxieties about being good enough. I cupped his face, my thumb rubbing along the stubble on his jaw.

"You're incredible," I murmured. "I can't believe you did this for me."

"Anything for you."

I swallowed the lump in my throat and pressed my face to his chest, inhaling his sweet pastry scent and wishing I could dig my teeth into his skin and make him mine forever.

41

OLIVE

I TILTED MY HEAD AS A WEIRD SCRATCHING SOUNDED AT the door. I was alone for the first time in days. My guys had reluctantly returned to work this Monday morning. There was some complicated thing that needed to happen at this stage in the restoration that required all of them to tackle it.

I begrudgingly got off the couch—still cocooned in my large blanket—and shuffled to the door to see what was making the noise. I was unsurprised when I opened it to find Felix, who meowed loudly and head-butted the door so it opened wider.

"Sure, make yourself at home," I said, trying to sound annoyed but secretly pleased to see my buddy again. I crouched down to scratch his head. "Where have you been lately?"

I didn't get an answer, but I did lose my balance, falling back on my butt as Felix tried to get on my lap.

"Thanks for that." I scratched him under his chin as I leaned my head back on the doorframe. We should move inside instead of sitting here with the door open, letting all the cold air in, but my energy was zapped.

Felix fussed when I stopped petting him, but I was distracted by the two figures heading down the path towards me. As they grew closer, I realized it was Lucy and Summer. I froze before glaring down at Felix. "You knew they were coming, didn't you?"

Felix just rubbed himself against me.

Great. Just great. At least my hair still looked okay after sleeping on my French braids, but I was dressed in an assortment of the guys' clothes and was swaddled in a blanket.

Lucy gave me a wave when she spotted me. She was wearing a green peacoat with gorgeous floral embroidery on the lapels, and I wondered if she had done it herself. Summer looked great in a mustard yellow jacket and a pink striped scarf. Both omegas had big reusable grocery bags on their arms.

"Hey, Oli," Lucy said, stopping a good six feet away from me. "We were just coming to drop off some lunch and goodies for you. Lars mentioned you were feeling a little down."

"We're not here to intrude or anything," Summer said, pushing her hair out of her face as the wind whipped around us. "But those boys are terrible cooks, and we didn't want you to starve."

I swallowed hard. I couldn't believe they were here. The first time they'd come with the welcome basket, I'd been so rude. And here they were, trying again.

Felix head-butted my chin, and I got the hint.

"That's really nice of you," I said, my voice coming out too quiet. I cleared my throat and asked more loudly, "Would you like to come inside?"

Lucy smiled. "Oh, are you sure?"

No, not really. I still wasn't feeling quite myself, and was afraid I'd say something to drive my new friends away. But after all the care from my guys, and the passage of time, the most brutal part of my storm seemed to pass. Figuratively and literally—it was still overcast today, but the rain had stopped this morning.

Felix hopped off my lap and strutted inside the house like he owned it, and I clumsily got to my feet.

"Yeah, of course. Please come in." I gestured for them to go ahead of me.

"Oh, it looks so good in here, Oli!" Lucy said. "Oh my gosh, I love this new sectional." She ran her hand along the back of the sofa. "Green velvet? So fancy."

I furrowed my brow. *New sectional?*

"I love this armchair and the new dining table," Summer said. "It's a great mix of the vintage furniture and these new pieces. You've got a real eye for interior design."

"No, I don't," I blurted out. The two of them looked at me, confused. I pursed my lips and looked down the hall at the lighthouse door. I couldn't believe my alphas. "I was told the cottage would be furnished, but when I got here, it was empty," I explained. "The guys were upset when they found out. Apparently, they'd put Finn's grand-parents' things in storage before I moved in, so yesterday, they moved the furniture back. I told them not to buy me anything new, and they *insisted* none of this was new. Besides the table, which Easton made." I puffed up a little at that, feeling so ridiculously proud to have such a talented alpha.

Summer snorted out a laugh and put her bag down on the kitchen counter. "What liars. Those alphas are obsessed with you. Let them spoil you. That's what they're good for."

I stared at the couch—the soft, cozy couch that was exactly what I would have picked out. I didn't know if I wanted to tell off my alphas for lying to me or kiss them for finding a way to sneak me new furniture without me feeling guilty.

"Nope," Lucy said, nudging my side. "I know that expression. You have that omega look in your eyes that says you're about to run after your alphas. This is a girls-only lunch." Then her eyes softened. "Unless you need them?"

The realization that neither of them would judge me if I did need my alphas hit me right in the chest. They were really just here because they *cared*.

I shook my head. "They can wait." I blinked quickly to stop from crying. I was always extra tearful during my dark days, but I was tired of it.

"I brought roasted pork banh mi," Summer said, cutting through the emotional tension as she pulled out a large stack of the Vietnamese sandwiches wrapped in brown paper. "I'm trying to perfect my recipe, so I expect honest critique and abundant praise. I've also brought brownies for dessert. With sprinkles because... why not?" She set a ziplock bag of slightly smooshed brownies beside the sandwiches.

Felix had been curled up on the basket bed I made for him, but at Summer's words, he ran over and rubbed himself against her legs. Summer rolled her eyes but lowered the almost empty bag to the floor. "We had a banh mi casualty. One of them got unwrapped, so I guess you can have that." He scampered back to his basket, dragging his prize behind him.

What a little freeloader.

My stomach rumbled, and I covered it with my hand. I hadn't had much of an appetite the past few days, but suddenly I was starving. "That sounds amazing."

"And I brought you a blanket," Lucy said. She pulled a white fluffy blanket out of her bag. "Freshly laundered, too, so it shouldn't have other scents on it."

This was too much. I didn't have anything to give them in return. I should've refused their gifts, told them it wasn't necessary, but my omega urged me forward until the blanket was in my arms.

"I love it," I breathed. "Thank you." I looked down at the blanket. "I'm sorry I don't have anything to give you."

Summer made a dismissive noise. "That's not how friendship works."

I swallowed hard and nodded. Maybe that was true. I didn't have much experience with friends, and I still wasn't quite sure why these omegas wanted to spend time with *me*.

"Where's Ivy?" I asked.

"At work," Lucy said, taking a plate from Summer and handing it to me.

"Oh, right." My cheeks heated. "I forgot it was a school day." Without the rhythm of my dull nine-to-five data entry job, it was hard to keep track.

"Time is a construct." Summer shrugged. "I should be at work, too, but Harry didn't have enough for me to do this week."

I cocked my head. I hadn't heard Summer talk about a job, just about the bakery she wanted to open.

"I help Harry, Stanley's husband, with accounting work. But it's hourly, and there aren't quite enough hours. I also help in my parents' restaurant. I just need to save enough for a commercial bakery space."

"You'll sell out of everything the moment you open," I said. Everything Summer had made me so far had been incredible.

She smiled at me. "Should we be monsters and eat on the fancy couch or civilized and sit at the table? You choose, Oli. It's your home."

I bit my lip. I didn't want to mess up the sectional, but I was itching to curl up under my new blanket. "Couch."

"Monsters it is," Summer said.

Lucy grabbed some paper towels, and we all settled down with our food. Lucy and I were on the couch, and Summer was in the armchair. I spread my new blanket over me and balanced my plate on my lap before taking a bite of the banh mi. The pork had a sticky sweet sauce with it, and the veggies were fresh and crunchy. "Oh my god. Summer, this is one of the best things I've ever eaten."

"Yeah, this is definitely the best one yet. This one has more of a kick than the ones last week," Lucy said.

"Not too spicy, though," I said.

Summer beamed. "Excellent. I'm playing with the amount of chili peppers, so I'll mark this as a success."

"Definitely," I said around a mouth full of food.

Lucy and Summer started talking about potential locations for the bakery, and I was content to just listen. I curled up further under my blanket as I ate, a wave of fatigue washing over me. This was the thing about my dark days—I was left exhausted even once the fog lifted.

The thudding of steps in the back of the cottage let me know the guys were on their way down. Finn was the first through the door and headed straight to me, leaning down over the back of the couch to give me a kiss. "Hey, pretty girl. How're you doing?"

"Good. Summer brought lunch."

"For Olive," Summer said. "Not for the boys."

"You wouldn't deprive us like that, would you, Summer?" Easton asked as he squeezed in next to me. His hand moved towards my plate and I frowned, pulling it close to me. I only had a few bites of sandwich left and they were *mine*.

"Ohh, that was cold," he said, but his smile told me he wasn't actually upset.

"You can't steal food from your omega," Lucy said, outraged.

Lars joined Finn at the back of the sofa, leaning down to kiss my cheek. "That's right, Easton. We can't have our omega going hungry."

Easton reached back to smack Lars on the side of the face.

Summer rolled her eyes. "I brought plenty for everyone. Not that you deserve it."

"You're an angel," Easton said. He pulled me in for a kiss and then bounced to the kitchen.

Finn took the spot beside me, and I snuggled into his side. "I missed you," he murmured. "Do you need anything? Are you warm enough?" He eyed my blanket. "I can get a fire going."

I eyed the wood stove with longing. A fire sounded so cozy, but I was scared of messing something up and burning down the cottage. "If it's not too much work?" I whispered.

Finn fixed me with a stern expression that said he was holding back from scolding me. He tucked my hair behind my ear and brushed his cheek against mine before getting up to start the fire.

I'd grown up with a wood-burning stove, but my dad had always been the one to keep it going. And now, watching Finn gather wood from the stack by the fireplace, I was struck by how happy he would be that I was taken care of.

Now it was Lars's turn to squeeze in on the sectional beside me, a plate of food in his hand.

"Did you get enough to eat, sweetheart?"

I nodded, but the whole time, I was eyeing the brownie on his plate. I'd already finished mine and it was *so* good. Lars chuckled and moved his brownie onto my plate, brushing his lips against my cheek. His beard tickled my skin, and I leaned further into his side.

"You sure? You don't have to." I said, but the brownie was already in my hands. Lars's chest shook with laughter.

I shouldn't get used to being spoiled like this. I was a self-sufficient, independent omega who had made it these five long years alone. But... maybe I didn't want that anymore. I wanted to be spoiled. Craved it.

Easton sat on the floor in front of me, his head brushing against my legs. I stuffed the rest of the brownie in my mouth so I could run my fingers through his curls. The room was filled with bright conversation, the girls and guys teasing each other like only people who grew up together could do. No one pressured me to join in or asked why I was quiet. Their easy acceptance of me challenged how I'd seen myself these past years. In my own mind, I'd been cold and prickly and annoying and *too much*. But maybe that had been wrong all along.

I was halfway asleep when Finn sat down on my other side. I blinked sleepily and realized Lucy was helping Summer pick things up in the kitchen.

"Is my girl tired?" he asked.

"Just a little."

Finn hesitated before speaking. "One of the panes of glass around the lantern needs to be replaced, and our supplier just let us know that it's ready. The issue is, they're going to be closed the rest of the week because he's going out of town, so we have to pick it up today."

I frowned. Finn's shoulders were all bunched, and he was speaking carefully. "Okay?" I looked over at Lars. "Why is that a big deal?"

Lars played with the ends of my hair. "It means we have to drive an hour away to pick it up, and because it's so large, the three of us need to go."

"You can come with us," Easton said, turning around on his spot on the floor to face me. "I'll even let you choose the car playlist."

Hmm. I didn't like the idea of being separated from my guys for hours... but I also didn't want to leave my spot on the couch and the cozy fire.

"I think I'll be okay here," I finally said.

The guys' scents turned slightly bitter, and prickly defensiveness rose in me, ruffling my imaginary feathers. "I've lived alone for years."

All my guys squeezed in closer until I could barely breathe. "It's not that we don't think you can take care of yourself," Finn soothed. "But you've had a hard few days and we want to take care of you."

"I can just stay here," Easton said. "I won't be helpful in carrying the glass. I'm not very strong." His eyes widened when he realized what he'd just said. "I mean, no, I *am* strong. *So* strong. The strongest. Just not when it comes to lifting panes of glass."

Lars snorted before gripping my chin and turning me to face him. "If you want to stay here, that's okay. You'll need to check in with us regularly." When I opened my mouth to argue, he slipped his thumb in. I scowled but didn't pull away. "Do this for us, kitten. We're big, overbearing alphas who need to take care of our precious omega."

"He's got that right," Lucy shouted.

Oh god, I'd forgotten they were here. My cheeks burned as I pulled away, Lars's finger slipping from my mouth. He didn't look one bit embarrassed with that little smirk on his lips.

"Yes, fine, okay. I'll check in," I huffed.

Lars pressed his lips to my forehead and then kissed his way down the slope of my nose to my lips. "Good girl."

Well, that just made my cheeks heat more. I squirmed in my seat.

"We can always stay if you need company, Oli," Lucy said as she plopped down on the armchair. "I don't have any tailoring appointments for the rest of the day."

"We could even try to convince Ivy to join us if she doesn't stay super late at school again," Summer said.

Were they just saying that out of obligation? Or did they actually want to stay? Why couldn't social situations come with a manual? I cursed myself for being an anxious overthinker.

"You good with that, baby?" Easton asked. I nodded. "Glad we got that settled. We can bring back pizza for dinner."

"Yes, please," Summer said.

The guys very slowly packed up their stuff and lingered by the door. I couldn't even make fun of their slow departure because I was right there with them, snuggling up to their sides.

"You know I'm strong, right?" Easton said for the third time, flexing his arms as he ran his fingers through his hair. "See, I can pick you up." His hands cupped my butt and lifted me against his chest. Then his face transformed again. "Not that it takes a lot of strength to lift you! Not at all." He bounced me in his arms, anxiety pouring from him.

"It's like watching a train crash," Summer said from her spot on the couch.

I grinned and pressed a kiss to his forehead. "You're very strong, alpha."

Lars crossed his arms. "I'm strong, too."

"Oh my god, don't you have places to be? Go!" Lucy shouted from the couch.

All my guys grumbled, but Easton finally lowered me to the floor. After final hugs and kisses, my guys headed out the front door.

"Ivyyy, stop stressing," Summer whined.

"Sorry, sorry," Ivy said, hands fluttering as she adjusted a throw pillow. Felix had gone to fetch her thirty minutes ago after Summer threatened to show up at the school and drag her away. "I just keep remembering things I need to get done. I was going to cut out paper leaves so the students could write what they're thankful for on them and use them to decorate the classroom."

I recognized a bit of myself in Ivy—her deep care for her work mixed with her inability to ask for help.

"Do you have the paper with you?" I asked.

Ivy blinked, her expression a little confused and owlish. "Umm, yeah, in my bag."

"We can help you, then, while we watch a movie."

"Great idea," Lucy said.

"Oh no, that's not—"

Lucy pulled the construction paper out of Ivy's oversized bag.

She passed out stacks of colorful paper to each of us and fished a pair of scissors out of her bag.

"I've got two pairs of scissors in the kitchen," I said.

"This is really not necessary," Ivy said, her cheeks heating as she took all three of us in with stacks of construction paper, leaf templates, and scissors.

Summer ignored her protests. "What movie should we watch?"

"Something chill." Lucy's eyes flitted to me, and I wondered how much Lars had told her about my mental health the past few days.

"*Pride and Prejudice*," Summer and Ivy said at the same time.

"Precisely," Lucy said, turning the TV on. "Are you a fan, Olive?"

"I've never seen it," I confessed.

Their jaws all dropped.

"This is an emergency!" Lucy shouted as she logged into a streaming service and pulled up the movie. "Your life is about to change."

"Isn't this the movie you said Finn hates?" I asked.

"Oh yeah, he totally hates it," Lucy said. "Maybe because I would always make the guys watch it when it was my turn to choose the movie for family movie night."

"Not everyone understands the brilliance," Summer sniffed.

I snuggled under my blanket, the soft sounds of a piano washing over me as the movie started, my hands staying busy cutting out colorful paper leaves.

"I don't know why Finn doesn't like this," I said as I watched Elizabeth run away from Mr. Darcy in the rain. "He has a lot in common with Mr. Darcy."

"That's what I'm always saying," Summer almost shouted. "He's grumpy and a bit pretentious. It's like that Spider-Man meme where they're pointing at each other."

I grinned as an idea started to form. "Do you guys know the owners of the Hollywood theater?"

"Missy and Herbert? Yeah, we know them pretty well. We grew up going to the theater, and I tailor Missy's dresses," Lucy said. "They're such a sweet older couple."

"Well... do you think there's any chance they might help me get some revenge on Finn?"

"Has he done something again?" Ivy asked, eyes wide.

"No, no, this is still from the first thing. I made him eat a pickle sandwich."

"Oh, that's excellent. But you think it's not enough?" Summer asked.

I shrugged. "Maybe."

"You can love someone and still plot revenge against them," Lucy said, nodding sagely. "And the movie theater was the original scene of the crime, right? I like it." She tapped the end of her scissors against her lips in a way that made me concerned she would cut herself. "They've never shown a Hollywood movie... but I bet I could convince Missy to arrange some sort of secret showing for the sake of revenge."

"Missy's a girl's girl," Summer said. "We'll get it set up, don't you worry."

The plan took hold in my mind, and a delightful sense of evil anticipation filled me.

I'd forgiven Finn for that night at the theater. I understood now why he'd behaved the way he did, and we *had* just been two strangers hooking up in a dark room. He hadn't really owed me anything, and I was sure the reason I'd reacted so strongly to him leaving me was because my omega knew before I did that we belonged together.

My mom and dad had always called each other soulmates, even though they couldn't be properly scent-matched since she was a beta. Designations didn't matter to dad, and he didn't act like your typical alpha, except for the protectiveness. He'd had that in spades.

So while I wasn't angry with Finn anymore, just eating a pickle sandwich seemed to be getting off too easily.

I paused cutting out leaves as Mr. Darcy walked towards Elizabeth in a field. All four of us sighed.

"I hate the mornings, but I would stand in a field at dawn if a man like that was walking towards me," Lucy said with a sigh.

My guys didn't like mornings either, but they went out to the beach with me. I swallowed hard as my chest filled with that sensation again, the one that was suspiciously close to love.

The rest of the evening flew by—my guys returning with stacks of pizzas, Summer putting on Spider-Man, Finn tending to the fire so the cottage stayed warm and cozy, and Easton carrying me into my nest at the end of the night, all of us piling onto the brand new mattress.

42

FINN

NEST WONDERLAND WAS AN OVERWHELMING EXPLOSION of all things omega. Large swaths of fabric hung from the walls, stacks of blankets and pillows filled rows and rows of shelves, and in the back was a full sex shop with toys, bondage tools, spanking implements, positioning wedges, and lingerie.

Images of all the things I wanted to do with my omega flooded my mind and hardened my cock. I subtly adjusted myself as I glanced over my shoulder to where Olive and Easton were occupied inspecting pillows. I grabbed a bag and started to fill it. Soft leather handcuffs. A small paddle. A set of butt plugs. A variety of vibrators.

"Find something good?"

I jumped as Lars appeared beside me, and he snorted at my reaction.

"Just getting a variety," I mumbled. "I don't know what she likes."

Lars grabbed another bag and put in a bundle of soft rope and nipple clamps.

"I have a feeling she'll be just fine with all of this," he said. "I'll bring all this to the front." He grabbed my bag and took it to the check-out.

I headed back to Olive, noticing how empty her cart was. We'd tried to get her to tell us about her dream nest on the hour-and-a-half drive to get here—pumpkin spice lattes and pastries in hand, courtesy of Lars—but she was tight-lipped. I'd gathered that she hadn't grown up with a lot of money, and certainly hadn't had much since her parents died. My alpha was agitated that she resisted us spoiling her, but the reasonable side of me understood it would take a while for her to get used to it.

Good thing I was persistent and wouldn't stop until she had everything she ever wanted.

I came up behind her, wrapping my arms around her waist. She melted back into me, all softness. Easton gave me a wink before he slipped away, and I was sure he was about to fill a cart for our omega.

"I don't see you picking out nearly enough things, pretty girl." I buried my face in the crook of her neck and breathed in deeply.

She shrugged. "I don't really need more things, Finn."

I grasped her hips and turned her around to face me. "But I know you *want* them. Your omega craves being spoiled. Why are you resisting?"

"It's just a lot. I don't deserve—" At my furious expression, she cleared her throat and changed course. "My nest is fine. You should spend your money on something else."

Before she could get herself into even more trouble, I took her by the waist, tipped her over my knee, and smacked her ass several times *hard*.

She squawked and squirmed and tried to get away, but my arms were iron. She gasped as I flipped her so she was upright again, now plastered to my chest.

"What was that for?" Her eyes blazed with fury and arousal, her tone indignant.

I gripped her jaw tight, preventing her from looking away.

"That was just a taste of the punishment you're getting later for questioning our buying things for you. We might not be millionaires, but we have money, Olive, and the only words I want to hear when we spoil you is, 'Thank you, alpha.' Anything other than that, you'll be over my knee again, and I don't fucking care who's around." Her eyes were wide and glassy as I ran my lips down the side of her face.

"Believe me, it will be no hardship for me to have you writhing over my lap as I redden that sweet ass until you're sore for days."

Her perfume was sweet and heady around us, and the only sound that slipped from her plush pink lips was a whine.

"You want that, sweet girl?"

She nodded. But then she bit her lip, looking unsure.

"What is it, darling?"

She shifted her weight, her eyes fixed on my chin. I tipped her face so I could take in her gorgeous brown eyes.

"Do you think my current nest is bad?" she whispered. "Because I tried to do a good job."

My chest tightened so much it was hard to breathe. Olive was so often fierce and snarky it could be easy to forget how tender and vulnerable she was underneath it all. Something we both had in common.

I caressed her face, loving how she softened into my touch. "Your nest is wonderful, just as it is. You've done such a good job with it. The *perfect* job. This is about my alpha wanting to provide for you." I hesitated for a moment before pushing on ahead. "And it's a symbol of us building something together as a pack."

Her lips parted and then they were against mine, all desire and passion. I palmed her ass as her arms went around my neck, each of us pulling the other closer until there was no space between us. We were both breathing heavily when we pulled apart.

Olive's cheeks flushed beautifully pink as she peered around my shoulder. "I guess we shouldn't do that in the store."

I chuckled. "I'm sure this store, in particular, has seen it all." I patted her ass. "Now, we're buying at least three new blankets and a shit-ton of pillows before we leave, so you better start picking your favorites."

I could see it warring inside her—the desire to snark, to misbehave, with the desire to obey.

"Thank you, alpha," she finally responded.

I smiled, pressing a firm kiss to her lips. "Good girl."

OLIVE DISAPPEARED into her nest with all her new supplies the moment we got home. Apparently, we weren't allowed in until she felt it was complete, so the three of us were sitting side by side on the sectional, completely at a loss for what to do without our omega.

"We should take her out to a nice dinner," Easton said, glancing back down the hallway for the millionth time.

Irritation flashed through me. "I still haven't gotten a solo date with her."

"Pretty sure that's your fault," Easton grumbled.

"Okay, settle down," Lars said. "Finn can have his date with Olive first, but I agree, we need to take her out together. Make her feel special and show her we're serious about being a pack. About bonding her."

He cocked his eyebrow at us as if waiting to see if we would put up some sort of argument, but he got none from us. My heart beat faster at the thought of bonding her. The fear of losing her, of suffering through grief again, was still there, but it wasn't enough to tamp down my overwhelming desire to make her fully mine. *Ours.*

"I would have bitten her the first day I saw her," Easton grumbled.

I nudged him in the ribs. "What's got you so cranky?"

"I just don't understand what's taking her so long."

I grabbed my packmate's hand and squeezed it. Easton struggled with separation in general, but I knew his alpha was riding him hard to be with our omega, just like mine was.

The sound of a door opening had the three of us turning around. Olive skipped out to us, looking bright and happy.

"Did you finish, baby?" Easton asked, his shoulders instantly relaxing.

"Almost," she said. "I need help hanging the canopy, but other than that, it's all set."

"Should we go see?" Lars asked, moving to get off the couch.

"Hold on," I said, cocking an eyebrow. "Our omega is owed a punishment." I'd filled the guys in on my promise to Olive in the store. They might not be as into impact play as I was, but they had certainly been on board to watch. "I think we should get it taken care of here. We don't want your first memory of your new nest to be a punishment."

Olive crossed her arms and huffed. "Yes, very considerate." She spat out the words, but we all knew it was for show. Olive's scent was filling the room, thick with arousal, and her cheeks were flushed. If she didn't want this, she could stop it in an instant, but my little omega liked the idea of punishment.

I leaned back on the couch, spreading my legs wide. "Strip, omega." I injected my words with the slightest bark, just enough to send that shiver down her spine but not enough to actually force her to act.

Her eyes flicked to Lars and Easton. Easton looked ready to leap out of his seat and tackle Olive, but he was letting me have this moment, and I was grateful.

Slowly, ever so fucking slowly, Olive started peeling off her clothes. First her skirt, leaving her in just those fucking fishnet tights. Then her sweater. The tank top underneath the sweater.

A growl rumbled through my chest. I needed to see all of her *now,* but she was taking her time, tormenting me. She smirked, not dropping eye contact as she peeled off her panties and bra. My defiant girl.

She didn't cover herself, just stood before us, fierce and completely unashamed.

My heart was pounding so loudly I was sure she could hear it, but I maintained my stern exterior as I crooked my finger. A tiny huff escaped her, but she walked towards me until she was standing between my spread legs.

"You're so fucking sexy," I murmured, running my hands up her sides. Squeezing. Kneading. I traced the blush on her cheeks. "Now, lay down over my lap. If you take your spanking like a good girl, I might even let you come. If not..." I let the threat of leaving her needy and wanting hang in the air. She let out an adorable squeak and quickly lay on my lap.

I ran my hand down her back, stroking her until the tension left her body. "That's it, darling. What do you say if it's too much?"

"Red," she responded.

"Good girl."

She tensed again when I cupped her butt cheeks, squeezing them hard enough to make her whine. She no longer had the deodorant on, allowing me to monitor her by her scent. There was a hint of anxiety mixed in with her sweetness, but no acidic fear. Good. It was fine for her to be a bit on edge—it could even heighten the sensation —but I never wanted her to be afraid of me.

"Do you need me to restrain your hands, or can you keep them out of the way?"

She took a moment to think and then moved so her hands were at the small of her back. I nodded to Lars, who grabbed the leather cuffs I'd picked up in the store and passed them to me. I wrapped them around her wrists, making sure they were firm but not too tight, and connected them together by the short chain.

A gush of slick rushed out of her, soaking my pants. I wanted her to drench all my clothes so everyone would know who I belonged to.

I ran my fingers through her pussy, gathering her sweet slick on my fingers, and wiping them on her ass cheeks. "What a naughty girl, being aroused by your punishment. This puffy pink pussy is so fucking desperate to be touched."

She arched against my lap, grinding against my hard-on. And then my hand came down on her ass in a loud smack. A startled gasp slipped through her lips, making me grin. I rubbed the reddened spot and then spanked her again, creating a rapid rhythm as I warmed her skin.

Lars groaned as our omega's thick, heady scent filled the air, the whole room filling with the most delicious pumpkin spice. His hand grasped her legs, pulling them onto his lap while Easton stroked her hair.

She attempted to buck off my lap as my hand came down with a smack hard enough to draw a cry from her, but the three of us kept her pinned. I followed it with another and another, savoring her whines.

We were all breathing hard when I paused, rubbing in the heat on her bright red ass. "How are you doing, sweet girl?"

She wriggled on top of me and nodded.

"Words," I commanded.

"I'm good, alpha."

"Yes, yes, you are. You're doing so well for me. Taking your punishment like such a fucking good girl."

I kept rubbing her cheeks, lulling her until she was fully relaxed against me. And then I came down in a hard flurry, giving her a dozen more smacks, harder than any she'd taken. By the end, she broke out in a sob.

I stopped, unchaining the wrist cuffs, and arranged her so I could hold her in my arms. Easton grabbed one of the new blankets and wrapped her in it. All of us pressed tight around her, murmuring praise.

She pressed her face to my neck, breathing in deeply. A sense of calm washed over me as I brushed a tear from her cheek. I loved this part—aftercare—holding her when she was all soft and snuggly.

"You okay, pretty girl?" I asked.

Olive kept her eyes closed and nodded.

Lars ran his fingers through her hair. "Sometimes our omega goes a little nonverbal, doesn't she? And that's okay, because we're here to take care of her."

Easton reached over to grab a bottle of water and held it up to her lips. She drank a few sips and then pulled back, shaking her head. She leaned into my neck, sucking on a patch of skin, as she whimpered and squirmed.

My chest rumbled with a growl, and I wrapped my hand in her hair, tugging hard. "Does our girl need to come?"

She nodded—at least, she moved her head as much as she could with how I was gripping her.

I grinned. "You've earned it. Will you invite us into your nest, omega?"

She nodded, scrambled off my lap, and scampered off to her nest. She didn't look back to see if we were following her because, of course, we were. My eyes were fixed on her red, plump ass as it jiggled with every step. My mouth watered, and I wanted to bite both cheeks.

She paused in front of her door and took a deep breath, some tension coming back in her shoulders. "It's not totally done, so don't judge it too harshly."

"Hey," Easton said, wrapping his arms around Olive and placing his chin on the top of her head. "You don't have to worry about that. In case you haven't noticed, we're a little obsessed with you."

Olive snorted and leaned back into him, but she still seemed tense as she opened the door. I needed to talk to the guys about how to convince her that we were serious about her and weren't going to leave. She deserved a grand gesture, something that would remove any doubts.

I did a double-take as I stepped into her bedroom, which was completely transformed. The massive mattress we'd purchased took up most of the floor, and it was now covered with plush layers of bedding and a perimeter of pillows. In between the layers of cream blankets, I caught sight of some familiar articles of clothing.

"I was wondering where that sweater went," Easton said.

Olive crossed her arms, pushing up her soft tits. "You left it behind. It's not like I stole it."

The three of us had to hide our smiles because our omega was such a little thief. We'd taken to leaving our sweaters and sweatshirts around the lighthouse while we worked because, inevitably, they wouldn't be there when we went to retrieve them.

I was down to my last sweatshirt, and I already had plans to buy more because over my dead body would my omega return any of my clothing.

"Kitten," Lars said, leaning down and cupping her face. "You did such a good job. I can't believe we're so lucky to have such a talented, perfect omega."

Olive preened, a beautiful smile on her face as she melted into his arms. "You really like it?"

Easton and I crowded around, making sure not to step onto the mattress without her explicit invitation.

"We love it," I reassured her, squeezing her hip. "And if you want anything else, we'll get it for you." Her perfume blossomed, growing even thicker around her, and it was hard to keep my train of thought.

She melted into my chest and I growled, causing another burst of slick to run down her inner thighs.

"There is something I need." Her voice was breathy, and her eyes were taking on a glazed quality.

"Mmm, what's that?" I teased.

Olive pulled away from me, a fierce pout on her lip.

"The answer is orgasms," Easton said, stripping off his clothes. "And I'll give you as many as you want because I'm your favorite alpha."

Now it was mine and Lars's turn to pout as we stripped off our clothes.

"Fuck that," he grunted.

We might be good at sharing, but we were all a bit competitive with our omega's attention.

Olive flopped back on the bed, lying there like a fucking goddess, while the three of us stood along the perimeter of the mattress. My mouth watered as her hands went to her breasts. She squeezed her thick thighs together, hiding her pretty pink pussy, and I wanted to pry them apart.

"Will you let us in your nest, omega?" I asked.

She eyed me skeptically. "Will you give me orgasms?"

A slow grin spread across my face. "Are we in a negotiation? How about this, pretty girl—let me in your nest, and I'll eat that sweet pussy until you come so many times you forget your own name."

"Okay, okay, get in here," she gestured at us and we piled onto the mattress.

I wasted no time pulling her thighs apart so I could bury my face in her black curls.

"Fuck, your scent." I swore as I took my first lick, her sweetness bursting on my tongue. I got lost in sucking, licking, curling my fingers inside her. A muffled cry from Olive had me looking up to see Lars feeding her his cock while Easton sucked her nipples.

I redoubled my efforts, circling her clit with my tongue as I pressed three thick fingers inside her. My cock was dripping precum on the sheets, and my alpha snarled in satisfaction that my scent would be even more entwined with hers in her nest.

My fingers dug into her lush thigh as I forced her to stay open for me as she came, her pussy fluttering around my fingers. Even Lars's cock couldn't completely muffle her moans as she fell apart.

"Oh, god, Finn." Her shout spurred me on and I returned to her pussy, drinking up her slick.

"Fuck, kitten," Lars said with a grunt as he came across her chest.

"More," she cried. "I need more." Her hand cupped her breasts as she writhed in her nest. "Easton, fuck my tits."

"What? I—" Easton's eyes were wide as he fumbled to sit up. I kept my fingers inside her as he moved to straddle her stomach.

Olive pressed her tits together, big and round and soft and *everything*. Easton shifted forward, his cock brushing against her skin.

And then he came all over her chest.

All of us froze, staring at a horrified Easton.

"Huh," Olive said, running her finger through the cum. "Not quite what I was expecting."

"That doesn't count," he blurted out as Lars and I fell back on the mattress, laughing loudly. "You took me off guard! You can't just say something like *fuck my tits* and think I can hold myself back!"

Olive's bright giggle filled the nest as she pushed herself up to a seated position. She moved onto Easton's lap, straddling him, and kissed her way up his jaw.

"I take it as a compliment," she murmured.

"Good thing you have two alphas who aren't as quick on the draw," Lars snorted.

Easton flipped him off as Olive just laughed.

43

OLIVE

SUMMER

Operation Darcy is underway

Missy's agreed to show Pride and Prejudice as long as you never tell a soul they showed a Hollywood movie

OLIVE

Omg really? You're amazing

SUMMER

Why yes I am

It's a private showing. 10pm tomorrow night

LUCY

I wish I could be there to see Finn's reaction!

IVY

We'll probably hear his cries for help across town

44

FINN

THE SMELL OF BUTTERED POPCORN HUNG IN THE AIR AS I balanced our snacks and drinks and followed Olive into the movie theater where we first met. She threw me a smile over her shoulder, several small boxes of candy in her hand, as she held the theater door open for me.

I'd been surprised when Olive said she wanted to plan our date. Her chosen location of the Hollywood Theater had been even more unexpected. My alpha was disgruntled—he wanted to plan something more extravagant—but if this was what she wanted, I was determined to redeem our first movie-watching experience if it was the last thing I did.

We settled in the same seats as before, and Olive wasted no time tearing into her Junior Mints and offering me some. I popped one in my mouth, but it was nothing compared to the sweet pumpkin spice flavor I constantly craved these days.

"I wonder if anyone else will show up," I mused as I popped a couple more candies in my mouth. These late-night showings were usually pretty empty, and I was greedy and wanted Olive all to myself.

"Oh, this is just for us," she said, eyes flashing full of mischief. "I spoke to Missy and she agreed to make this a private showing."

The way she said *private showing* made me grow hard. I grunted and shifted in my seat, the popcorn placed strategically over my erection. Missy and Herbert might kill us if we hooked up in the theater *again*, but it would be worth their wrath.

I lifted the armrest separating us so I could tuck her against my side. "What are we seeing, then?"

Olive gave me the sweetest smile and laid her head on my shoulder. "I'm not sure. It didn't say on the board."

"Maybe more aliens, if we're lucky."

"Only if they have choreographed dance numbers."

I grinned and rubbed my cheek on the top of her head. "Thanks for giving me another chance, darling. I promise I'll be good to you forever."

"I know," she murmured. She reached across me to grab a handful of popcorn, munching on it slowly. Her scent didn't indicate stress, but I could feel a question brewing. "Is it still feeling scary?" she finally asked. "For us to be together?"

My heart lurched and I squeezed her shoulder, spilling some popcorn in the process. "I'm still scared of losing you. Always will be, I'm sure." I swallowed hard against the emotions in my throat. "It just means I need to treasure it all, treasure *you*. And I will, I promise."

Her fingers trailed against my jaw. "I trust you, Finn." She leaned in, pressing her lips against mine, and the taste was just as sweet as her words.

The lights in the theater dimmed, and I settled in to watch whatever absurd indie movie Missy and Herbert had chosen. The gentle sound of chirping birds and piano music filtered through the speakers, and I froze.

No.

Fuck *no*.

My heart pounded in my chest, and then the title card confirmed my nightmare: *Pride and Prejudice*.

I kept my arm around my omega, my mind whirring. How did this happen? This was a fucking *popular* movie. This had to be a setup. Lucy knew I hated this movie—had forced me to watch it approximately one million times growing up until my hatred for it settled deep in my bones. And now my little omega was getting her revenge on me by forcing me to sit through the movie from hell.

Olive said nothing, but she shifted so she was halfway in my lap as though keeping me pinned to the seat when I really wanted to drag her far, far away.

I took a deep breath. If this was my penance for my bad behavior, I would suffer it for her.

The minutes ticked by excruciatingly slowly. I attempted to distract myself by digging into the popcorn and playing with the ends of Olive's hair, but I couldn't hold in my scoff at a particularly annoying part of the film.

Olive finally broke out in a laugh. "How're you doing over there?" she asked, patting my chest.

I groaned. "Just trying to figure out how I landed such a naughty, evil omega."

Her self-satisfied giggle brought a smile to my lips. I put the popcorn safely to the side and pulled her fully onto my lap.

"You think torturing your alpha is funny?"

The light from the screen was strong enough to illuminate the wide smile on her face. "Hilarious."

I palmed her ass, squeezing hard, and she let out a delicious little whimper. She quickly moved so she was straddling me, her pussy hot even through her clothes.

"Is this worse than the pickle sandwich?" she asked.

I threw my head back against the seat with a laugh. "Fuck, that was awful, but this movie lasts longer, so it's probably the worse punishment."

"Poor alpha, being punished by his omega." Her lips ghosted against mine. Surely, my heart was pounding loud enough for her to hear, even over the dramatic period piece music. "I wonder what I could do to make it better?"

I swore as her hand went to the zipper of my pants, effortlessly freeing my cock and squeezing it in her small hand. My hands immediately went under her skirt, my fingers digging into her skin, only to find her tights were *crotchless*. And she wasn't wearing any underwear.

My brain short-circuited, but my hands moved on their own accord—pulling her ass cheeks apart, spreading her wide so I could press my fingers into her dripping pussy.

"Oh, pretty girl," I murmured as I thrust my fingers inside her. "Have you been sitting here dripping for your alpha this whole time? You should have said. It's not good for little omegas to be so needy."

A smile tugged at her lips, and I could practically feel her resist the urge to roll her eyes. "Well then, you better fix it."

The two of us moved as one—her hands gripped my cock as she sank down in one slow movement, mine pinched her nipples through her pretty little top. Urgency underlined our movements as we thrust and squeezed and moaned. I made sure to grind her cute little clit against my knot every time she sank down on me. Her ragged moans, her gasping breaths, were perfection. I pressed my thumb against her clit, circling it as she worked herself closer to an orgasm. She was wet and warm and slippery. The biggest temptation of my life.

Her little gasps turned into whimpers as she threw her head back and took her own release, her tight little cunt clamping down on me with her orgasm. For the briefest moment, she stopped moving, slumping down against my chest as she caught her breath. I dug my fingers into her lush hips. I was so close, *so fucking close* to coming, but I wouldn't rush her.

But then she suddenly climbed off my lap. My cock slipped from her pussy, rock-hard and weeping, and Olive gave me a devious smile. I stared up at her, stunned, but she offered no explanation. She simply braced her hands on my shoulders, kissed me on the lips, and sauntered away.

Out of the theater.

My limbs were lead, unable to move from the shock of my interrupted orgasm.

A ragged chuckle burst from my chest as the theater room door shut with a bang. This was everything I deserved after I'd left her in this very theater our first time meeting, but if my omega thought I was going to sit back and let her get away, she had another thing coming.

I zipped up my pants, groaning at the strain of my hard cock against my zipper, and prowled out of the room. Olive's scent called to me—rich from her recent orgasm, the one she *stole* from me—and I tracked it through the dark lobby. Wild urges I'd never felt before rose in me as I hunted my little prey to a back hallway. I wanted to chase, to fuck, to *rut* until the only thing she could scream was my name.

I wanted to own her like she already owned me.

The hallway was silent except for the steady hum of the HVAC, but my heightened senses caught on to the little gasp that reached me from the dark corners of the wall. A feral smile spread across my face. There she was, tucked behind a free-standing vintage movie poster.

Mine.

I lunged towards her and she shrieked as she took off running, but her short legs were no match for mine. I snagged her around the waist, my other hand moving between her legs and lifting her by her cunt. She soaked my hand with her sweet slick and a loud snarl roared through my chest. I pressed her against the wall, her plush ass rubbing against my cock as I thrust against her through our clothes.

"My little omega thought she could escape from me. Now I have you all alone, tucked back here in the dark. What should I do with you?"

"Who says you get to do anything to me?" she snapped back. She wriggled against me, but all that did was grind her cunt harder against my hand.

"You can fight me all you want, but your drenched pussy says otherwise. Making such a fucking mess." I kissed her cheek before checking in. "You good, darling?"

She nodded quickly. "Don't stop."

A growl roared through my chest. "I should rip this dress off you and these fucking tights. God, these fucking *tights*." My fingers moved without my meaning to as I tore through the delicate fishnet webbing that had tempted me from the first time I saw her wearing them.

She let out an outraged cry of protest and my hand came down on her ass cheek, the sound like a gunshot in the hallway. "Look at your perfect ass bouncing against me." She moaned as she arched back towards me, offering me *more*. "You belong to me, little omega. Mine forever. To fuck, rut, fill whenever I want."

Olive just scoffed and struggled harder against my hold, but I had her pinned.

"Let me go, brute," she snarled.

I chuckled in her ear. Her scent was bright with arousal, all happiness without fear. I ran my nose down the side of her neck, breathing her in.

"I'm not letting you go until I take exactly what I want from you... and maybe not even then."

In one swift movement, I was poised at her entrance and thrusting into her. Her toes barely touched the ground, her weight forcing her fully down on my cock. We both cried out at the intensity of it. I gripped her inner thighs to give me leverage to move her up and down my cock as her fingers scrabbled against the wall, fighting for purchase.

"Oh god, Finn," she cried out. "That feels—" Her words were cut off with a loud cry as she shattered around me.

This time, I fucked her through her orgasm. My knot teased her entrance every time she fell back down on my cock. With one more burst of slick from her perfect cunt, my knot slipped in, locking us together. The tight squeeze of her was overwhelming as my orgasm tore through me like fire. I bit down on her shoulder as I came—not hard enough to break the skin, but *fuck* did I want to. My alpha urged me on—*bite her, claim her*—but I was just lucid enough to hold back. But only *just* as her loud moan filled the air as she came again, clenching harder on my knot than anything I'd felt before.

I sucked the tender patch of skin as we both came down from our orgasms, from our game.

I wrapped my arms around Olive, gently pulling her back against my chest. Satisfaction filled me as she relaxed against me, all limp and sated.

"I really hope there aren't cameras back here," she said, breaking the silence.

A startled laugh rumbled through my chest. "I'll make sure Missy erases any footage without watching it." I tried to move us into a more comfortable position, but I couldn't fully stand without her being lifted off the floor.

"Knotting me in this hallway was certainly a choice," she said.

I smacked the side of her thigh. "Like you weren't begging for it." But I kissed her cheek in apology, anyway. I hadn't meant to knot her, but holding my alpha instincts back when my omega was crying out my name had been too much for me.

I hitched her up higher—my palm still holding her by the pussy —and clumsily maneuvered us down to the floor until she was curled up in a little ball of omega in my lap.

She swore as my knot shifted inside her, her fingers digging into my arm. "I didn't know how this date would go exactly," she mused. "But this definitely exceeded expectations. And now I know my alpha likes to chase me."

My chest rumbled with a purr. "We've never talked about doing anything like that." A thread of anxiety worked through me. I knew Olive had been into what we'd just done—her cries of pleasure, her thick scent had urged me on—but maybe it had been too much for her. Would she regret it now, without the adrenaline? Had I taken things too far?

"That's right," she mused. "Easton and I were alone when we talked about chasing."

My heart stuttered in my chest, and I was only capable of making a strangled sound.

She tipped her gorgeous face up to me, a smile playing on her lips. "Feel free to chase me anytime, alpha. Just don't expect me to make it easy on you."

Now a growl ripped through my chest. "If you keep looking at me like that, my knot will never go down."

The breath of her laugh tickled my chest as she settled against me. I wished I had a blanket or somewhere else soft and warm to settle her while we stayed knotted.

Next time.

We stayed perfectly still and relaxed, distracting ourselves by chatting about anything and nothing, until my knot loosened enough to slip out of her. I ran to grab napkins from concessions to clean her up, and did my best to right her clothes. The tights were a lost cause and I slipped them into my pocket as a little trophy.

We gathered up all our things and headed out the front door, only to find Lars and Easton sitting by the curb in a golf cart.

"Finn! You're alive. We weren't sure how far our omega would take her little revenge scheme," Easton said. "Figured Olive might need some help dragging the body back."

Lars cocked an eyebrow as he got out of the cart, clearly taking in our disheveled appearances. "I thought you were going to punish him, sweetheart." His hands moved to Olive's waist and for the flash of a second, I wanted to shove him away so I could keep her all to myself. But as quickly as it came, the urge vanished and gratitude filled me instead. This was what it meant to be a pack—to know that our omega wouldn't have to walk all the way home after being fucked within an inch of her life in a dark, dusty movie theater hallway.

"I did," she said primly. "And then he punished me back."

Easton snorted, but his expression was all lightness. He pulled Olive into a big hug and whispered something in her ear that made her laugh. I stole her back to my side and the two of us slid into the back of the golf cart. I tucked her head under my chin and ran my fingers through her hair, unable to stop from touching her.

"Where did you even get this?" Olive asked, gesturing at the cart.

"Stole it from Stanley," Easton said easily. "Although, is it really stealing when he left the keys in the ignition?"

"Yes," Olive and I said at the same time, putting a grin on my face.

"Huh," Easton said as if this was brand new information for him. "Well... any complaints?"

"Nope," Olive responded. "I rather like this—riding in style." Then she gasped and sat up straighter. "Oh my god! I never thanked you all for my new bike. It just totally left my mind, but I appreciate it so much. I can't believe you did that."

Lars twisted to face the back. "What new bike?"

My cheeks heated. I hadn't told the guys how I'd slipped away one day and purchased Olive a new bike. She had been using my ancient one from when I was a kid, and it wasn't nearly good enough for her.

Olive blinked slowly and turned to me. "Finn?"

I rubbed the back of my neck and shrugged. "Yeah, well, you couldn't keep riding the other one. It was all rusted."

"But that was when you weren't even talking to me," she whispered, her brow furrowed, lips parted. "You didn't even *like* me."

I wrapped her hair around my fingers, holding tight. "That's where you're wrong, pretty girl. You consumed me from that very first moment."

There was a slight jolt in the golf cart as Easton maneuvered us onto the rugged path to the lighthouse. The path that was now lit with the solar lights I'd installed, the ones Olive was now staring at.

She turned back to me and put her hand around the back of my neck. "Thank you." She whispered the words against my lips before pulling me into a deep kiss.

45

OLIVE

I RAN MY FINGERS ALONG THE CLOTHING RACK AS I walked down the aisle, my chest tightening with every step.

I'd been inside Star Styles—Starlight Grove's only clothing store —for an excruciating twenty minutes. I'd circled the same racks over and over, as if what I needed would magically pop into existence if I made enough rotations. The guys surprised me this morning by saying they wanted to take me out on a date. A *fancy* date, according to Easton. Which meant I needed fancy clothes.

"Can I help you?"

I let out a startled yelp and whirled around to find the shop assistant right behind me. She was a young beta dressed in an adorable cream sweater dress and a name tag that identified her as Emma.

"Oh, I'm sorry," she said with a laugh. "I didn't mean to scare you. I just wanted to see if I can help you find something."

"I'm just browsing," I said, cursing myself for not escaping the store sooner.

"You're Olive, right? The new lighthouse keeper?"

I nodded, still not used to how small this town was. The arrival of one new person was a whole event.

"Are you looking for anything specific?"

Oh god, why does she have to be so helpful? Please just leave me alone to my suffering.

"It's okay, really. I'm fine."

How could I escape now? Maybe she would go back to the front of the store and then I could run away.

"That one is super pretty," Emma said, leaning in a bit to see the dress I'd been looking at. It was black and sparkly, with a high slit on the skirt. The exact type of dress I'd love to wear. "Want to try it on?"

I took a slow, deep breath before speaking. "There aren't any in my size. In fact, I don't think you offer anything in my size in the entire store. So no, I think I'm just going to head out."

Emma's face fell, and I saw her eyes move down my body.

Yes, that's it, really take in each of these rolls.

"Really? I'm so sorry. What size are you? I just started working here, but maybe—"

"Look, it's fine. I'll figure something out." I cringed at my harsh tone. This wasn't Emma's fault, but fuck, it was embarrassing to be in a huge store that didn't have a single thing that fit me. And now Emma was practically tearing up beside me and I would have to awkwardly comfort her. I should have just stayed home. Told the guys I didn't want to go out.

Before she could say anything else, my feet were already carrying me to the exit. "Don't worry about it!" I called over my shoulder. "Nice to meet you!"

A burst of crisp fall air hit me as I launched myself out of the store. A few stray tears ran down my cheeks and I wiped them away quickly, my anger rising. I loved my body, loved my curves, and I hated that a stupid clothing store could make me feel like this.

What would I tell the guys?

I crossed my arms and headed down the street. I was so lost in my own head that I almost ran straight into Lucy.

"Hey! I just saw you out of the window of my shop..." She trailed off as she caught my expression. I quickly tried to force a smile on my face, but the swirling mix of humiliation, anxiety, and rage in my stomach made it almost impossible.

She reached out and grabbed my arm, squeezing it gently. "What's wrong? What happened?"

I cleared my throat, but my voice still sounded thick when I spoke. "It's nothing."

Lucy fixed me with a fierce expression that was so unexpected for the sweet omega that it jolted me into telling the truth.

"The guys want to take me out to a fancy dinner and I have nothing to wear."

Lucy's face softened. "Oh, clothes are my thing! Let me help you, please!"

"That's so sweet, but I don't think—"

She was now pulling me back the direction I'd come. "Star Styles is a bit limited in their selection, but I can tailor just about anything."

I dug my heels in and we came to a stop. "I don't think that's going to help, Lucy. They don't have anything big enough for me."

She blinked and I braced myself for her pity, for that expression that said, *Oh right, I forgot you're fat.* But instead, her eyes narrowed.

"Are you actually kidding me right now? That is so wrong! I make most of my own clothes so I don't shop there, but how could they not be size-inclusive? I will be bringing this up at the next town meeting."

"Umm, I don't think—"

"Inclusive sizing is a social justice issue," Lucy said firmly. "But in the meantime, we can go to this boutique I love in Briar's Landing. Or I could make you something!"

Lucy's enthusiasm was a lot to take in, but her strong reaction eased some of my embarrassment. She was right. It wasn't my fault the store didn't carry inclusive sizing.

I chewed my lip. "The guys are supposed to pick me up in like an hour."

"Drat. Okay, let me think." Lucy tapped her foot against the sidewalk. "I have this cape I'm working on that could look really cool."

"It's really fine, Lucy. I just want to head back home. But I appreciate you wanting to help."

I felt bad at her crestfallen expression, but this whole outing had been a lot on my frayed nerves, and I just wanted to get back home.

"Are you sure?"

"Totally sure. I need to get going, but I'll see you later. We're doing lunch Sunday, right?"

"Yes, I'll see you then."

I gave Lucy an awkward wave as I headed down Main Street, holding myself back from breaking out into a full-on sprint. I rounded the corner to head to my cottage, and a loud *meow* was the only warning I got before Felix launched himself into my arms. The startled scream that left my lips sounded something like *aarrglblerg* as I caught him and pulled him close to my chest.

"You almost lost one of your nine lives," I gasped.

Felix just purred and rubbed his head under my chin.

"That's right, you probably have infinity lives, you magical little creature."

I hitched him up so I was holding him more securely and headed down the lighthouse path.

"Do you ever have trouble shopping for clothes? You are a bit of a chunk." I pet his fluffy belly. "An adorable little chunk," I quickly clarified.

His purr intensified.

"Maybe the two of us could stay in tonight. Would you like that? We could watch a movie or something."

I swore Felix practically rolled his eyes.

"There's nothing wrong with staying in," I snapped. My trip into town had been quite enough social activity for the day, thank you very much.

Felix refused to allow me to put him down when I got home, so I awkwardly juggled him to one arm and unlocked the door with the other. I flopped down on the couch and Felix settled on top of me.

"I'll just ask the guys if we can cancel. Hopefully they're not too disappointed in me."

I swallowed hard at the realization that I still carried around the fear that they would leave me. I needed to trust them—they had earned my trust. I hadn't told them about my upcoming heat... and all that came with it, but time was quickly running out. Maybe I could take tonight to myself and work up my courage to tell them tomorrow. I could make them dinner to make up for canceling and then break the news.

I pulled out my phone and agonized over the wording of my text to the guys for way too long.

OLIVE

> Hey! I'm sorry about this, but I don't think I'm up for anything fancy tonight. Could we maybe cancel our date? I could cook for you tomorrow instead.

I held the phone up to Felix.

"What do you think?"

Felix batted the phone straight out of my hand.

"Oh my god, Felix!"

My shout was drowned out by a knock at the door. I scowled at him as I went to answer, picking my phone up off the floor on my way.

My mouth went dry at the view that greeted me when I opened the door—Easton, Finn, and Lars were standing side by side in suits.

Fuck, the way the jackets stretched across their broad shoulders was everything. My omega wanted to pull them inside and get those suits all messy. Lars's hair was tied up in a topknot, and I wanted to take it down and run my fingers through it.

He caught my eyes and winked. "Hey, kitten. I missed you today." He went to pull me into his arms, but I took a little step back.

"You're early."

Easton grinned. He wasn't wearing a tie, and his shirt was unbuttoned enough to show off a bit of his golden skin. I wanted to lean forward and lick it. "Couldn't stay away. But there's no rush if you still need time to get ready."

I fidgeted, shifting my weight from one hip to the other. "I was just going to text you to ask if we can cancel tonight. I'm just not feeling up for it."

They looked immediately concerned.

"Are you having a dark day?" Finn asked. "What do you need, pretty girl?"

Why were they so sweet? It was so much more than I deserved. "No, I just... I don't want to go." My tone was all ice as I resorted to my tried-and-true standoffishness that had driven so many people away.

"Uh huh," Easton said, obviously not buying it.

"Why don't you guys still go out? You're already dressed for it. You can have a nice dinner together."

Finn scoffed and crossed his muscular arms that looked ready to burst out of his jacket. "You really think we're going to leave you here alone and go out to a fancy dinner just the three of us?"

"I'm not alone," I mumbled. "Felix is here."

I turned around to gesture at the cat, but he had apparently vanished into thin air. Sneaky little traitor.

"Alright, so now she's seeing things," Easton said as he shoved his way into the living room. He gripped my chin and forced me to meet his gaze. "Tell me what's actually going on."

His heady chocolate hazelnut scent washed over me and I melted against him, my defenses completely destroyed. "I don't have anything to wear," I finally whispered.

Easton frowned. "What are you talking about? You always look cute."

The front door clicked shut and then Lars's arms were around me, pulling me back into his chest. He pressed his face to the top of my head, and a purr started up in his chest. "You smell stressed, sweetheart."

"I don't have anything *fancy* to wear, okay? Nothing that would be appropriate for a nice restaurant, and I didn't have time to get anything today. So you guys just go, and we can see each other tomorrow."

"Okay," Easton said.

An inexplicable lump formed in my throat at his easy agreement. I was the one telling them to go away, but now that they were here, the thought of them leaving sent a pang of sadness through me.

"Okay. So I'll see you tomorrow?"

Finn snorted, doing something on his phone. "No. *Okay,* we'll change our plans. If you don't feel comfortable going to a fancy restaurant, even though you'd be the hottest fucking person there, we'll just change our plans."

"No, that's not what I—"

"Come on," Easton said, grabbing my hand and pulling me to my room. He went straight to the closet where my clothes were folded in cheap plastic drawers and started pulling things out.

"What are you doing? That's my underwear drawer."

He turned to look at me over his shoulder with a cheeky grin. "Did you want to skip the underwear tonight, sunshine? Because I'm down for that."

I turned to Lars and Finn, who had followed us in, and gestured at Easton. "What is happening?"

Finn removed his suit jacket and rolled up the sleeves of his button-down, revealing thick forearms. My brain stuttered. What had I been saying? Now all I wanted were his arms around me.

"It sounds like Easton is picking out an outfit for you before we go out." Finn flopped down on the bed, his casual pose a complete contrast to his tailored black suit and tie. "You did a great job with this, Lars," he said, running his hand along the gauzy canopy Lars hung last night.

"Thanks," Lars responded. He sat down next to his pack mate and then snagged me by the waist, pulling me down onto his lap. I should tell them off for entering my nest without permission. Actually, I should be upset with all of them for not listening to my request for space, even though it wasn't what I actually wanted.

Lars's hand cradled the back of my head, authority radiating from him, and I automatically leaned in to breathe in his scent. "Was there another reason you didn't want to go to dinner, or just the outfit?" His chest rumbled, sending vibrations through my body.

"Outfit," I whispered.

Lars nodded. "You look amazing in everything you wear, kitten." Before I could argue, he cocked an eyebrow. "We will choose an outfit for you and you'll be a good girl and put it on for us. Then we are going out together so your pack can prove that we're worthy of your omega by spoiling you."

Part of me wanted to push back. I was still a bit shaken and raw from my trip to the store earlier. I wanted to curl up alone so I could avoid being perceived. But another part of me just wanted to do whatever I could to be Lars's good girl.

"Well, well, what do we have here?" Easton said. He turned around and held up a corset lingerie top made completely with sheer black lace. I'd found the piece on sale online about a year ago and had splurged on it but had never worn it.

Lars cleared his throat and shifted, his erection obvious against my ass. "Be a good girl and put it on for us." He lifted me by the hips until I was standing on the mattress.

I took the corset from Easton with a huff. "Fine." I stripped off my clothes and put on the corset and matching thong, turning around so Easton could do up the back. And then I remembered why I'd never worn it. I loved how it lifted my boobs and cinched in my waist, but the front perfectly framed my stomach rolls and seemed to push them out even further. I grimaced and was ready to take it off when Finn swore.

"You're right, we should skip going out." He stared up at me from his spot on the bed, eyes wide. "My god, Olive. I have no fucking idea how the three of us landed a literal goddess."

Lars cupped his cock through his pants with a groan. "Fuck, kitten. *Fuck.*"

Standing before them, their jaws dropped and gazes transfixed on my body, made me feel powerful. But old insecurities still rose to the surface. I cupped my belly, cringing a bit at how it spilled over the skimpy thong. "You don't think this is... unattractive?"

Lars and Finn were on their feet, their chests vibrating with growls as they crowded Easton and me.

"I'm sorry. What did you just say?" Lars asked, voice low and dangerous.

Finn gripped my chin, forcing me to meet his gaze with my burning cheeks. "There is no part of you that could ever be *unattractive.*" He spit the word out like it had personally offended him.

Easton's hand collared my throat from behind, adding the slightest bit of pressure, while the other dragged down my side until it cupped my stomach. It took everything in me not to move away.

"Can't you see what you do to us?" His erection pressed firmly against my back. "Don't doubt yourself, baby."

He didn't move his hand, and I slowly relaxed into his touch, letting my belly go. "Good girl," he murmured. "Such a fucking good girl for us."

I shivered as he moved my hair to the side and kissed me, starting at my shoulder and working his way up my neck until his lips pressed against a sensitive spot behind my ear. "Maybe we should stay in so we can prove to you how sexy you are."

I whimpered as he squeezed my pussy, causing slick to drench my underwear.

Lars snarled a growl and then pulled me out of Easton's arms. "No. We are going to prove to you that we are good alphas who can provide for you, and not just in your nest."

I jutted my lip out in a pout, but Lars firmed his jaw. "That is not going to work. We are going to go out and spoil you, kitten, and nothing you say is going to dissuade us."

"Fine, but only if you agree to keep the suits on."

A satisfied grin spread across Lars's face. "Oh, you like us dressed up for you, omega?"

I shrugged. "You might look nice."

My alpha chuckled as he palmed my ass. "What our omega wants, she gets."

46

OLIVE

WE PILED INTO LARS'S LIGHT BLUE VINTAGE VOLVO truck, my face briefly heating at the memories of what had happened the last time I was in here.

Easton gave me a boost before crowding in the back with me, his massive frame taking up most of the space. He leaned over and did up my seatbelt before wrapping his arms around me, his fingers absentmindedly playing with my hair and brushing against my skin as we headed to the restaurant.

"I missed you today," he murmured.

I rested my head on his chest. "I missed you, too."

My social interactions over the past few years consisted of my monthly trips to the pharmacy, greeting the grocery clerk when the self-checkout was closed, and the occasional dating app hookup. I'd started to believe I wasn't made to have friends or a pack or any kind of life.

And now I had people who *missed* me after just hours apart.

A loud crunching sound filled the air, and I jolted at the sound. Easton's arms tightened around me.

"For fuck's sake, Lars," Finn said. "You said you'd fixed this."

"I did," he protested. "Gavin looked at her last week and said she was running great."

"What were his *exact* words?"

Lars cleared his throat. "Look, here we are."

"Lars!" Finn shouted as the alpha put the truck in park and quickly got out.

"Such drama," Easton said with a chuckle as we watched Finn chase after Lars. "You ready, baby?"

"Where are we?" I scooted out of the truck and gasped when I saw the sign at the entrance: Applecloud Farm. Underneath the name was a list of offerings, including apple picking, a corn maze, hay bale rides, and fresh apple cider donuts.

"Welcome to your autumn paradise, Ms. Harvest," Easton said.

I snorted. "Maybe I should have let you change out of your suits." The guys had ditched their ties and jackets but were still wearing their dress pants and button-downs. They'd dressed me in a long-sleeved plaid dress with tights—the corset and thong underneath. With every step, I was reminded of what I was wearing, and it sent little jolts of arousal through me.

"Nah," Easton said with a stretch. "Now we look like your bodyguards."

I laughed and grabbed his hand as we headed over to where Finn and Lars were having a heated argument about the drivability of the truck.

I wrapped my arms around Finn and gave him a tight squeeze. "Don't stress. We got here just fine." He grumbled something under his breath but returned my embrace.

I winked at Lars, who rolled his eyes and grabbed my hand.

My steps were bouncy as we headed to the entrance. This was going to be a good night. A *great* night. I thoroughly ignored the itch under my slightly too-warm skin and how my extra-sweet scent kept breaking through the double layer of No-NonScent Deodorant. Tonight, I would show my guys that I could be fun and easy-going, and tomorrow, I would tell them everything.

We approached a wooden stand to get baskets for apple picking. A pretty omega with long black hair, bright red lips, and a cute flannel tied in the front was there to greet us.

"Welcome to Applecloud Farm. You're all dressed for a party!" Then her smile faltered as she did a double take. "Oh, hi."

My nose wrinkled as my alphas' scents turned slightly bitter.

After a silence that was a beat too long, Lars spoke. "Aurora." He lifted his chin. "Didn't know you worked here."

She cleared her throat. "Just for the season. My aunt actually owns it and she needed some extra help. How're you doing?" Her eyes flicked to my face before she quickly looked away.

Tension clawed at my chest. Had the guys been involved with this omega? They clearly knew each other. Easton's hand closed around the back of my neck, squeezing lightly.

"We're doing well," Finn said as he inched closer to me. "We need baskets for apple picking."

"Oh, of course," she said. "It's nice to see you again."

I kept a blank expression even as my omega was having a meltdown. My body vibrated with the effort of resisting the urge to scent mark my guys in front of Aurora, to prove to her and everyone that they were *mine*.

But this was exactly the issue—my omega was too feral, too needy. If I wanted to keep my guys, I couldn't give in to my instincts. I forced a deep breath, trying to let my alphas' scents ground me.

I could do this. Be cool, calm, and collected.

Nonchalant.

The omega's fingers brushed against Lars's as she handed him the baskets. I swallowed down a snarl, feeling very fucking *chalant*.

I was so on edge I barely noticed anything around me as we headed into the orchard. We stopped at the beginning of a row of apple trees.

"Baby?" Easton's voice was hesitant as he ran his hand down his arm. "Are you okay?"

I blinked and took a deep breath before forcing a bright smile. "Yeah, of course. Let's pick some apples."

The guys looked at each other.

"If you're wondering about..." Finn trailed off, rubbing the back of his neck.

"We went on a couple of dates with Aurora last year," Lars said, saving Finn from trying to complete his sentence. "But that's it. It didn't work out. We don't want her. We only want you."

I nodded, hoping the movement looked more natural than it felt. "Makes sense. I mean, it's a small town, so this was bound to happen eventually, right? It's not like I've never dated anyone." Well, I didn't know if I could call my hookups *dating*. Some of the guys I'd hooked up with several times, though, so... close enough.

A loud growl burst from all three of my alphas' chests, and I frowned. "Really? *You're* going to be possessive?"

Easton tugged me to his side. "Won't apologize for feeling possessive of you when you're my everything, baby."

I swallowed hard, a bit of warmth seeping into my chest. "I guess it's fine if we're possessive of each other," I said.

Finn's fingers twisted in my hair as he pulled my head back and kissed me. "Good, because it's impossible to not be possessive about our omega."

I whimpered at his tight hold. Some slick trickled into my tiny thong that would do nothing to mask my scent. My guys' scents deepened in response.

Lars's hands landed on my hips from behind and squeezed. "Should we do some apple picking?"

"Fiiiiine," I said with more than a little bit of sass. "But I better be fucked within an inch of my life by the end of tonight."

Easton groaned, Finn's hold on me tightened, and Lars purred against my back. I grinned, loving the power I had over them.

I turned around and grabbed the baskets, handing them out to Easton and Finn before I took Lars's hand.

The hand that brushed against the other omega.

I may have clenched it a bit too tight, but Lars just squeezed me back and tugged me close to his side as we headed down the tree-lined aisle.

I LAUGHED as Easton picked me up by the hips so I could reach a higher apple. Once it was in my hand, he dropped me back to the ground but didn't let go.

"Thanks for the boost," I said, turning my head to look at him. His fingers dug into my hips, and I pressed my ass back against him.

"What are the odds—"

I didn't get to hear the rest of his sentence because a woman's voice cut through the air.

"Oh my god, Finn!"

I turned to see a small group of beta women—all gorgeous and perfectly styled like they were out of a fall catalog—walking towards us.

"I thought that was you," a brunette at the front of the group said, her eyes fixed on Finn. "I didn't take you for the apple-picking type."

The woman went in for a hug and my vision turned red. Finn managed to shift it into an awkward side hug, but my skin flushed and I was teetering right over the abyss of turning feral.

"Sarah," Finn said as he disentangled himself. "Let me introduce you to my omega, Olive." His words were pointed, and Sarah's expression fell.

She recovered quickly and smiled at me. "It's nice to meet you. You're very lucky to have this one."

Finn put his arm around my shoulders. For the briefest flash of a second, I had the urge to shove it off. But I didn't, like the very reasonable omega I was. Although, when I scented Finn's stress, the petty part of me was filled with a tiny bit of satisfaction. Why shouldn't he be stressed when I had to meet another one of their fucking exes?

"I am," I said with a smile that was only a little forced. Sarah seemed perfectly nice. It wasn't her fault my omega was a possessive little creature who wanted to hoard her alphas away like a dragon.

"Do you live in Starlight Grove?" she asked.

"I just moved here a couple of months ago to be the lighthouse keeper."

Sarah's eyes widened as she looked between Finn and me, clearly understanding the significance. "Oh, that's so lovely." There was a beat of awkward silence. "Well, it was nice running into you, Finn. I'm glad you're doing well. And maybe I'll see you around town, Olive."

I gave her an awkward wave as Sarah and her friends headed away down another row in the orchard.

Finn tugged me to the side so we were out of the way of the other apple pickers. "I'm so sorry, sweetness."

I let out a forced laugh. "I guess everyone decided tonight's the night for apple picking." I kept my tone light but couldn't quite meet his gaze. It was taking all my effort to stop myself from rubbing my body against his to remove any trace of Sarah's scent.

His arms enveloped me, pulling me into his broad chest so I was surrounded by warmth and maple sweetness. A purr rumbled through him, and his lips brushed my ear. "Yours are the only arms I want around me. The only scent I crave."

He cradled my head as he pressed furious little kisses all over my face until I laughed. I pursed my lips, fighting a smile. I guess he was forgiven.

"I can't wait to get you back home tonight. Strip you down." He kissed my nose. "Eat that pretty little pussy of yours." He kissed my cheek. "And then watch it stretch around my knot as you cry out your orgasm." He kissed my forehead.

My knees weakened, my mind hazy with arousal. His tight hold around my waist was the only thing keeping me upright, the only thing keeping me tethered to the earth.

I let out a moan, and he swallowed it up when he finally kissed my lips.

I would be counting down the minutes until we got back to my nest.

EASTON NUDGED ME. "It looks like those three are on a super awkward first date."

"Where?" I asked under my breath.

"Those chairs diagonal to us."

We'd finished our apple picking and eaten dinner—hot dogs and tons of apple cider donuts—and were now cozy around the bonfire. Finn and Lars had gone to the snack hut to get us supplies for s'mores.

I tried to be discreet as I peered at the three chairs close to us. Two large alphas—one blond and one with black hair—were sitting with a petite red-headed omega. I snuggled in closer to Easton so we could inconspicuously lean in to listen to their conversation.

The blond-haired alpha was loudly explaining cryptocurrency to the omega, who wore a blank expression.

"Wow, that's interesting," she said, looking away as she spoke. She glanced over at us, and Easton and I quickly pretended to be absorbed in our apple cider.

"You think *that's* interesting? We haven't even gotten to NFTs," the alpha continued, oblivious to the wilting omega in front of him.

"Do we stage a rescue?" Easton asked out of the side of his mouth.

"We need something dramatic to distract the alphas."

"Oh, I've got it. Once Lars and Finn get back, we put a ton of marshmallows on the skewers and set them on fire. Then Finn makes a move on you, and I have to take up my flaming sword to defend my omega."

Easton's excited voice faded into the background as the black-haired alpha looked up from his phone, and I caught a glimpse of his face. A shudder went down my spine, but I didn't know why. There was something familiar about him, something that made uneasiness rise in me. Then his eyes met mine, and my body turned cold.

He was the alpha who had walked out on me during my last heat. Rick. Or Rick the Dick as I'd named him afterwards.

The one that said I was too needy, too feral, *too much.*

I quickly looked away, hoping he didn't recognize me. It was several years ago. He'd probably serviced a ton of omegas through that agency.

"Olive?"

I jolted as I realized Easton had been trying to get my attention. His hand was rubbing up and down my back.

"Was juggling the flaming skewers too much?"

I scrunched my nose. "You know how to juggle?"

"Nope," he said, grinning.

I snorted. "Yeah, maybe that's too much. But actually, I'm feeling really full. Maybe we should skip s'mores and just get Finn and Lars and go home."

Easton's brow furrowed, and he scooted his chair closer to me. I was sure my scent was giving away everything I was feeling.

"Yeah, baby, we can go home. Are you feeling okay?"

I nodded, working hard to keep myself from looking back at Rick as I went to stand, but then Lars and Finn approached with a tray of s'mores supplies.

"We come bearing treats," Lars said. "And they had pumpkin spice marshmallows. Did you know that existed?"

Finn rolled his eyes, but his lips twitched. "We had to get more after Lars ate the entire bowl before we'd even finished paying."

My mouth watered. I couldn't decide if pumpkin spice marshmallows sounded disgusting or amazing, but I wanted to try them. Maybe everything would be fine if we stayed for a bit. I braved another glance over at Rick, only to find his eyes fixed on me.

And then he opened his mouth.

"Oh my god, it's *you!*"

The sound of his voice made me want to vomit. It had taken me years to undo the insecurities he'd given me, and my lingering anxiety about asking my alphas to be with me during my heat told me I wasn't fully over it.

I squeezed my eyes shut. *Someone rescue me from this nightmare, please.*

"Yes, it *is* you. What's your name again—Carrot? Peach?"

My alphas turned to look at him while I prayed for the orchard to be hit by a meteorite. Or better yet, a black hole could open up underneath just me and take me out. No need for others to be harmed in the process.

"What's going on?" Lars set the tray on the empty chair before crossing his arms as he looked at Rick.

Rick's face broke out in a condescending smirk. "Oh, don't tell me you're courting her." He let out a cruel laugh. "All I can say is good luck, man. You're better off test-driving someone else."

Easton stood, his chair falling back to the ground as a growl ripped through his chest. "What the fuck did you just say?"

"Do you know him?" Finn asked, resting his hands on my shoulder. "Fuck, you're shaking."

I looked down. My hands were trembling and that pissed me off. I hated that this horrible alpha could still make me feel small and useless.

"Sort of." My voice was barely louder than a whisper. Easton was growling, the sound startling coming from my sweet, playful alpha. I reached up to grab his wrist, giving it a tug. "Let's just go."

"I'm not letting some fucker say shit about you," he snarled.

I stood, tightening my hold on him as if I could hold him back. "It's okay. It doesn't matter." When that didn't work, I added, "He's a lawyer. Don't start anything."

"He's the one starting things by insulting my omega." Oh fuck, Easton's scent was thick in the air and his chest was puffed up.

Rick stood, matching Easton's stance. "Oh, how cute." He sneered, and now I was itching to punch that expression right off his face.

I moved to stand in front of Easton. He immediately tried to push me behind his back, but I stayed put, squaring off fully with Rick.

"It's amazing that it's been, what, four years, and you're still this obsessed with me." I flicked my hair behind my shoulder and crossed my arms. "Ultimately, she's the one I feel sorry for." I gestured at the red-headed omega, who looked confused and uncomfortable. At least finance bro alpha had finally shut up. "She's out with one alpha who's more boring than dirt and another who couldn't find the clit even with GPS assistance."

"How fucking dare you," Rick seethed. He took a step forward, and my guys were immediately in front of me, Easton holding a metal marshmallow skewer.

I shifted to the side so I could see the omega. "If you want to leave, we're happy to walk you out to the parking lot."

She quickly nodded and grabbed her purse.

The two alphas she was with looked like they were about to argue or stop her from leaving, but quickly shut up when Lars took a few steps forward.

My omega preened. That's right. They should be scared of my big, Viking alpha. I was briefly distracted as I ran my eyes down his body—the way his white button-down stretched across his broad back. His hair was half up in a knot at the top of his head and I almost reached up to run my fingers through it, but it wasn't the right time. Probably.

I moved around Lars and waved at the omega to come with me.

"Are you okay?" I asked.

"Yeah. I know I shouldn't say this, but I'm kind of glad that happened because I had no idea how to extract myself."

"I totally get it. Did you come with them? Do you need a ride?"

"No, I drove separately. My only smart decision tonight." She glanced over her shoulder at my three alphas who were following close behind, forming a protective wall around us. The omega sighed. "How did you land those three? Dating is such a nightmare."

"Umm, well, there was some light stalking, and then this cat matchmaker..." I cleared my throat. "I just got really lucky." I thought of everything I'd done to push my guys away and how they inexplicably kept coming back.

The omega gave me a sweet smile as we came to a stop in front of her car. "Seems like you did. Well, thanks for coming to my rescue tonight."

"Anytime," I said. "And remember to invest in cryptocurrency."

She snorted a laugh before getting in her car, giving us a little wave as she drove away.

I turned to face my alphas, who were still radiating rage.

"Who was that asshole?" Lars asked.

I wilted, feeling completely drained of energy. "I don't want to talk about it right now. It was so many years ago, it doesn't matter."

"I don't like it," Finn said, crossing his arms.

"Yeah, well, I didn't like meeting two of your exes today either, so tough stuff," I snapped. I was being rude. Unreasonable. But I couldn't stop myself. I was a horrible mix of jealous and insecure, and it was pushing my omega instincts hard.

"Let's wait to have this conversation when we get home," Easton said, pulling my stiff body into his arms. I relaxed a bit at his touch and nodded.

My guys kept their hands on me until we got to Lars's truck and all piled in. He turned the key in the ignition, and there was a dull *click*. He swore and tried again.

"Oh, what were you saying about your truck? Its unbreakable Swedish craftsmanship? It will never die?" Finn asked.

Lars rested his head on his steering wheel like he was trying to gain his composure.

The whole scene would have been funny, except I think I'd reached my limit on *fun* tonight.

Easton sighed. "I'll call Gavin's shop."

Finn helped me hop out of the truck. Easton quickly followed, keeping his hand on the back of my neck while he made the call, as if worried I would run away.

Lars pulled the tailgate down and lifted me up so I could have a place to sit.

"I'm sorry, sweetheart," he said.

I rested my head on his chest. "It's okay."

"Gavin's sending a tow truck for us," Easton said. "Should only be about ten minutes."

"You warm enough?" Lars asked.

Before I could answer, Finn draped a blanket over my lap, although I didn't really need it. The night air was cold now that we were away from the fire, but my skin was flushed. My guys hadn't noticed yet, so that was good. Obviously, we had a lot to talk about, and my body certainly wasn't going to let me forget my upcoming heat, which was not so much inching as stampeding towards me. But the parking lot of Applecloud Farm really didn't feel like the right place for this conversation, and my omega was fixated on all the promises Finn had made earlier. I just wanted to forget all the tension of today and lose myself in my alphas.

My omega had her priorities, and who was I to question them?

47

EASTON

THE TOW TRUCK PULLED INTO THE ORCHARD PARKING
lot, and I helped Olive hop down off the tailgate.

It parked in front of us, and the driver got out.

"You've got to be kidding me," I muttered under my breath.

The universe was playing a joke on me. Or we were all trapped in
some sort of horrific reality TV show.

Because I knew the name of the tow truck driver before she
introduced herself.

Georgia.

I stood in frozen disbelief as the beta I'd briefly dated last year
walked closer.

Fuck my life.

"What?" Olive asked, looking between us. "You're acting like..."
The realization dawned on her, and her scent turned burnt and
acidic. "You're kidding me."

"Baby, it's not—"

Olive let out a shriek. "It's not *what?* I didn't realize you'd gone
out with every single person in Starlight Grove. My mistake!"

"Olive, sweetheart—" Lars started, hands out in front of him.

Finn lurched towards her, trying to pull her into his arms.

But Olive was already pulling away, her pupils wide and eyes glazed. Before we could make her listen, reassure her, *anything*, she turned around and ran away, back into the now-dark farm.

"Shit!" Finn said.

"Here are my keys," Lars said, tossing them to a bewildered-looking Georgia. "Just drop it at Gavin's."

And then the three of us were running after our omega.

48

OLIVE

My heart pounded in time with my rapid footsteps as I ran. I had no idea where I was going or what I was doing, just that my instincts had taken over.

I hated that my hormones had turned me into everything Rick said I was—needy and territorial and too fucking much. But I couldn't stop myself. I'd been pushed to the limit tonight and couldn't handle it anymore.

My guys obviously had many choices of who they could date. When they inevitably grew bored of me, they would have a line of women to choose from. To upgrade to. Because I was sure those women were perfectly lovely and happy, not prickly and possessive like me. Women who would stick around and have a calm conversation when confronted with her alphas' exes, not run away like an idiot.

But I didn't slow down. My omega was driving me forward through the dark rows of the empty orchard until we came to the mouth of the corn maze.

I should stop. Turn back around.

But my omega was determined and in full control. I ran into the maze without so much as a backward glance.

The tall corn was ominous, looming above me as the moon cast shadows onto the ground. I quickly grew disoriented and my feet slowed, my heavy breaths the only sound breaking the silence. Fear crept into my chest, pushing out some of my jealous rage, and I spun around, trying to orient myself.

But then I heard it. Footsteps coming towards me.

I started running again, hitting dead end after dead end. I turned to double back and let out a piercing scream as hard arms closed around me from behind.

Finn's maple scent wrapped around me and his lips dipped to my ear. "Say red if you want to stop this at any time."

I nodded, and he tightened his hold on me.

"I need words. What do you say if you get scared or want to stop for any reason?"

"Red," I whispered.

"Good girl. Otherwise, we're going to do what we want with you, even if you fight back. Is that okay?"

"Yes," I gasped.

I hadn't realized my omega was baiting my alphas—daring them to prove their dominance over me—but if this was the outcome? I certainly wasn't going to complain.

"I've got her," Finn shouted.

My panting alphas rounded the corner, their eyes burning as they locked on me. A snarl rose in my throat when I spotted Easton. He had been with someone else and it electrified me with rage. I needed to mark, bite, do whatever I could to ensure everyone else in the world knew all of them belonged to *me*.

"You're mine," I said, struggling against Finn's hold. He released me and I jumped at Easton. He caught me easily, one hand supporting my ass and the other gripping the back of my neck.

"Yours," he said. "Only yours."

I dug my hands into his back, wishing my nails were strong enough to tear through his shirt and mark his skin.

"That's a good girl, claiming your alpha. Showing everyone I belong to you."

My skin felt like it was on fire, and my core was horribly empty. I whined as I tried to unzip Easton's pants.

"Fuck. Baby, are you sure? We can call a cab and wait until we get—"

I finally got what I wanted—his hot, heavy cock in my hand. My omega purred happily at the precum already leaking out.

My thoughts grew hazy as his mouth-watering chocolate hazelnut scent overwhelmed me. The next few minutes were a blur of hands—fabric ripping, Lars's lips at my throat, Easton pushing inside me, Finn palming my ass. I closed my eyes, my body floating as my alphas took full control.

Easton's next thrust hit that electric spot inside me, and a hand covered my mouth.

"Shh, our omega's cries are just for us." Finn's voice was low as he slipped two thick fingers into my mouth. I sucked on them as my orgasm built, my whimpers muffled in the night air.

"My baby, my sunshine, fuck. I want this forever. I want you forever." Easton tightened his hold on my ass, his knot grinding against my clit.

"Yes, alpha," I said around Finn's fingers.

My orgasm crashed over me so suddenly it took my breath away. My entire world narrowed until it was just waves of pleasure, and I was only vaguely aware of Finn's fingers leaving my mouth and collaring my throat.

I was jolted from my reverie by Lars's harsh voice. I whined. I didn't want my alphas to be upset.

"You can't knot her here."

Easton swore and increased his pace until he came with a gasp. I whined, trying to push myself down on his knot. I wanted it. Needed it so I could keep this alpha with me forever.

"I'll give you my knot when we get back home," Easton murmured, his breaths as heavy as mine. "I'll keep you locked to me all fucking night long, so you'll never doubt who you belong to."

I rested my head on his shoulder, my body loose and relaxed as I came down from my high. I was vaguely aware of a cool breeze brushing my bare ass.

"How's our girl feeling?" Finn asked.

"Good," I murmured.

"Mmm, that's good." He rubbed his cheek against mine. "Because now it's time for your punishment."

I blinked as I tried to clear the haze around me. "What?" Before I could get my bearings, Lars grabbed my hands and I was tipped over Easton's knee.

"Our omega needs to learn that she doesn't run away from us, even when she's upset, and she certainly doesn't risk her safety by running into a dark maze," Finn said.

I twisted around until I met his smug gaze with a glare so intense I was surprised fire wasn't shooting out of my eyes. I had only run away because they had dated half the town, but he was undeterred. His rough fingers gripped my face, squeezing just hard enough for me to feel his complete control.

"I understand you're upset, but that is not an excuse for putting yourself in danger."

I pulled back, trying to escape his hold, but it was futile. My alphas held me fast—my ass was in the air, my toes barely touching the ground. Finn flipped my skirt up and rubbed his hand up and down my ass cheeks, which were bare now that my thong and tights had been ripped. I clawed and snarled and shouted, but it didn't matter.

Lars's hand twisted in my hair, and he forced my head back. "Do you think she needs something to keep her quiet for us?"

"Oh, I definitely think she needs some help," Easton said. *Traitor.*

Lars unzipped his pants and his huge cock sprang out, hard and dripping. "Open your mouth, kitten. My cock will keep you nice and quiet as you take your punishment."

The head of his cock pressed against my lips and I opened automatically, my jaw stretching around him. Lars's hand kept me still as he forced more of his cock into my mouth. I was so distracted that Finn's hand coming down hard on my ass made me cry out in shock. Lars's cock muffled the sound and he grunted as he thrust inside more, his cock hitting the back of my throat. I choked a bit and then Finn's hand crashed down again, reddening my ass cheeks as I let out another startled cry.

Each smack on my ass sparked more and more pleasure in me until my slick ran down my thighs.

Finn groaned and his fingers dipped into my sex. "Fuck, you're soaked. So needy for us."

With each firm touch and growled command, my omega felt more and more secure in my place with them. It didn't make sense that a fast fucking and fierce spanking would make me feel like I belonged at their side, but somehow it did. Their behavior showed me that they were willing to fight for me...that I was worth being chased after.

Finn hit an especially tender spot, and the pain went straight to my clit. My orgasm took me by surprise and I cried out. Lars swore and wrapped my hair around his fingers, holding me in place. "You're going to fucking swallow me down," he growled seconds before he spilled down my throat. He held me fast, and I swallowed him down as I rode the waves of my own orgasm.

And then Easton's arms were around me again as I curled up against his chest. My eyes were so heavy they drifted closed.

"That's it, sunshine. Just rest. We've got you."

49

FINN

"Something's off," Easton hissed. The two of us were in the kitchen, unpacking the Red Lantern takeout I'd picked up for dinner.

I nodded. My alpha was on edge, pushing me to fix whatever was going on with our omega. If only I knew how. "It has to just be because of last night, right?"

What were the fucking odds all our exes decided to go apple-picking at the same time? It was exceptionally rare for me to miss living in a larger city like I had in college—pretty much only when I wanted takeout at midnight, and when I wanted to take my omega out without running into *everyone we'd ever dated.*

Easton scrubbed his hand down his face, his shoulders bunched and tense. "I just want her to know we're all in on this. I hate the idea that she could be doubting us."

I nodded, dishing up some orange chicken into a bowl. I wanted that, too. I also wanted to end that fucking alpha from the apple orchard. Olive had given us some vague non-answer when we asked how she knew him. A growl rose in my chest. My alpha wanted to push her to tell us everything. *Get her locked on our knot and spank the truth out of her.* Fuck. I couldn't listen to my alpha. I needed to be reasonable.

Right?

I glanced over to where Olive was curled up on Lars's lap. The fire was going in the woodstove and an old season of some reality show was playing on the TV. Not that any of us were really paying attention.

It had been a quiet Saturday. After the maze, we'd returned home and fucked most of the night—showering our omega with praise and reassurances of how much we wanted her. We'd slept in—even Olive, which was practically a miracle, although she still dragged us out to the beach when she got up.

Even though we'd talked through everything that happened at the apple orchard and she said everything was fine, her scent was unusually strong with an edge of bitter anxiety that flared anytime we left her side. She kept swallowing whines and moving from one of our laps to the other. There had been moments where it seemed like she wanted to say something, but when we pressed her, she changed the subject.

The only thing I could think to make sense of her behavior was that she must still be unsettled after running into our exes. Hopefully our plan would unfold as I imagined, and it would be exactly what she needed to feel secure in our relationship.

"I'm waiting for Gunnar to call," I said quietly.

"Good," Easton said. "It's going to work." He shook out his shoulders, grabbed several containers, and headed into the living room.

I was about to follow when my phone vibrated. My heart leapt and I snuck out the back door through the lighthouse so Olive wouldn't overhear the conversation.

By the time I hung up, the tension had eased from my shoulders.

Everything was coming together for our grand gesture. The guys and I had started planning this after our trip to Nest Wonderland. Olive needed to know we were all in, and we wanted to do something big for her before asking if she wanted to bond.

If she wasn't ready, that was totally fine. We would never pressure her. But she needed to be clear on what we wanted, how sure we felt about her, and by tomorrow, she would.

50

OLIVE

I braced myself against the wind as I headed to Rosie's, trying to keep my bike straight on the path. It was already sprinkling, and the forecast said there was a big storm front rolling in. I needed to get back to the lighthouse before it hit so I could monitor the radio, but I didn't want to cancel this lunch. Especially because my guys had left the cottage early this morning with a vague excuse about having to pick something up for the lighthouse.

Even though it was Sunday.

And they wouldn't tell me what they were getting, just that they would be gone for the entire day.

Maybe I had just imagined how shifty they'd been, how they couldn't quite meet my gaze. Because it was fine that they were doing something without me. Absolutely *fine*. My omega definitely wasn't clawing in my chest, telling me to hunt them down.

I took a deep breath as I parked my bike outside Rosie's—this time making sure I looked both ways before stopping to avoid Stanley—and adjusted the hood of my rain jacket to protect myself from the increasingly heavy downpour.

I knew why I was feeling so upset about my guys leaving me alone, and it had everything to do with my upcoming heat. All the signs were there—I'd barely felt the cold of the ocean this morning, my skin felt sensitive and uncomfortable, and I'd had to bite my cheek to stop myself from bursting into tears when the guys told me they were leaving. It didn't help that I was still a little raw from seeing their exes. What if they went to pick up this thing and ran into another omega? A less prickly one? A prettier one?

Okay, get a grip, Olive. You can survive a day without them.

I steeled myself as I entered the diner, the bell above the door and the chatter of townsfolk greeting me as I slipped inside. Lucy, Ivy, and Summer were already at the corner table, smiling and waving me over.

My tension eased at seeing them, and I couldn't stop my matching smile. Hormones were such a bitch because, truly, how was this my life? I had amazing alphas, friends, a home I loved... it was a dream come true, and I wouldn't let my body ruin this for me.

Lucy waggled her eyebrows. "I would ask why you're running late, but I don't want to know."

I rolled my eyes but couldn't stop my cheeks from heating. I was late because of the rain, but she wasn't far off. Before heading out the door this morning, Easton had insisted on giving me one more orgasm. He'd pressed me against the wall and knelt down to eat my pussy.

"Bike trouble," I responded, flipping my hair over my shoulder as I took a seat.

"Is that what we're calling being fucked within an inch of your life?" Summer quipped.

I huffed. "It's nice to see you, *Ivy*," I said pointedly.

Ivy grinned. "It's nice to see you can still walk." She lifted her mug of hot chocolate and took a prim little sip while Lucy and Summer screamed out with laughter.

"That was cold," I said, but I couldn't hide my smile. "But not wrong."

That spurred on more peals of laughter from the table.

"Did things work out the other night?" Lucy asked.

"Yeah, it did. We went apple-picking instead." I hesitated for a moment. Should I tell them about the disastrous ex encounters? Part of me wanted to, but my guys had reassured me all day *and* night that they only wanted me. And I had more pressing things I needed to talk to my friends about.

"Good," Lucy said, reaching out to squeeze my hand. I smiled, lightness filling my chest. These girls really had accepted me into their group, and it made me feel brave enough to ask them for their opinion on the question that had been plaguing me.

I leaned forward and lowered my voice. It would be just my luck if the two old men at the table next to ours overheard this conversation. "Actually, I have a question, um, about heats."

"Ooh, are you considering having a heat with the guys?" Summer asked, leaning forward as well.

"Sort of," I hedged. I knew my alphas had picked up that something was going on with me yesterday, but I had been too afraid to tell them about my heat. *Again.* "Are you all on suppressants?"

Most omegas took suppressants these days so they didn't have heats, but they could intentionally go off them if they wanted to experience a heat with their pack.

"I am," Ivy said.

Summer and Lucy nodded.

I realized I was shredding my paper napkin, and I hurriedly dropped the pieces on the table.

"So... I'm not." I kept my eye on the table so I didn't chicken out. "I have a blood clotting disorder and it means I can't take suppressants."

"Oh," Ivy said, brow furrowed. "So you've had heats before?"

"My first one was when I was twenty," I said. "None of you have had one?"

"I almost did," Lucy said, her voice low. "I was dating a pack, and I thought... well, I thought they were the ones. I was planning to go off my suppressants so we could go through a heat together and bond, but luckily, they showed their true colors before that happened."

Now it was my turn to squeeze her hand. Lucy was amazing and deserved better.

"How do you handle your heats?" Summer asked.

"The first two, I used a heat service, and it just didn't go well at all. So the doctor prescribed me sedatives and pain medication so I can get through them alone."

Three horrified faces stared at me across the table.

"Alone? Oh, Olive," Ivy said. "That sounds so hard and scary."

"Is that even safe?" Summer asked.

I shrugged. "I mean, the doctor gave me the medication, so I assume so?"

Lucy scowled. "Yeah, except doctors don't know anything about omega medicine."

Well, that was true. Omegas had been excluded from drug trials and research until just a few years ago.

"But now that you have your pack, you don't have to do that anymore," Summer said.

I chewed my lip. "My heat is actually coming up. Like super soon. But... I don't know. Isn't it a lot to ask for them to take care of me through my heat? We haven't been together very long..."

"You say that like it would be a burden to them," Lucy said, brow furrowed.

I shrugged. "The alphas hired through the heat service said it was, or I guess that I was just a lot more work than they signed on for."

"Excuse me?" Ivy said, her voice low and cold. "They said that to you?"

I clenched my jaw to keep the wave of emotion at bay. I'd shoved those memories to the far recesses of my mind, but seeing Rick the other night brought it all back and shook me. What if my alphas reacted the same way he did? Even if they didn't abandon me during the heat, maybe they would decide I was too much work afterward and end things.

"Olive," Summer said, her voice uncharacteristically soft. "I'm sure they would be incredibly excited to spend your heat with you. They should be bowing at your feet for the honor of even being considered."

The sound of a throat clearing over my shoulder had me jumping.

"Ladies," Char said. "Do you know what you want to order?"

Lucy's eyes flicked between the alpha and me. "Do you want to ask Char's opinion?"

My cheeks grew hot with embarrassment, but maybe it was a good idea to get an alpha's perspective.

"My opinion on what?" Char asked. "If it's about what to order, I highly recommend the home fry scramble, and I'm not just saying that because I over-ordered potatoes and have run out of storage space."

"That sounds good. I'll have that," I said.

Ivy, Summer, and Lucy all gave me an exasperated look.

"Ugh, fine. Char, what's it like for alphas to handle an omega during heat?"

Char blinked. "I better sit down for this." The alpha pulled a chair over from a neighboring table.

"Oh no, that's really not necessary. You're working." My cheeks felt like they were on fire.

Char ignored me and sat down with a satisfied sigh. "I'm tired of working, anyway. You're curious about heats?"

"Just what it's like for alphas," I mumbled.

"Well, I can certainly tell you my goal isn't to *handle* my omega during a heat. It's to take care of her."

I pursed my lips. That sounded like semantics.

"Olive thinks that heats are a big burden on alphas," Summer said.

I threw her a dirty look, but she was unrepentant.

A flash of shock crossed Char's face. "Where on earth did you get that impression? Heats are so fucking fun. The sex is amazing, obviously, but having my omega trust me to care for her when she's vulnerable? There's nothing like it. We alphas get off on being needed."

I was back to shredding napkins in my lap. "Is it different for male alphas? Because that's just... not my experience."

Char fixed me with her intense gaze until I was forced to look away.

"I'm not one to turn down the chance to insult male alphas, but it sounds like you might have found some particularly shit ones in the past. Don't your three guys know how to take care of you?"

I immediately bristled at her insulting *my* alphas. "They know exactly how to take care of me," I snapped without thinking. My hand flew to my mouth in horror. "I'm sorry. I didn't mean—"

Char just tipped her head back and laughed. "Omegas are so fucking cute. Tell your alphas what you need from them, and they'll fall over their feet to make it happen. It's obvious to see how obsessed they are with you. I'm pretty sure Lars is keeping Beans 'n Bliss in business with the amount of pumpkin spice lattes he's consumed since you came into town."

I wrestled with her words, and she stood up and took the others' orders.

"How're you feeling about everything now, Olive?" Ivy asked gently once Char headed back to the counter.

"Better, I think." Char was right. My guys did know how to take care of me. They'd been with me through my dark days and hadn't been scared away. Maybe I could trust them to stick with me through a heat... to not reject me.

I took a deep breath. "I'll ask them tonight."

Lucy clapped with excitement. "Yay! I'm going to ignore that one of your alphas is my brother and say I hope you have the most fun time!"

Our food arrived quickly and the breakfast scramble I got looked amazing. We all tucked in, but a loud alarm on my phone interrupted our conversation. I fumbled as I pulled it out of my bag. "Storm alert." I chewed my lip as I looked at the dark red and orange blotches on the weather radar. "I need to eat and get back quickly."

"You should have the guys pick you up and drive you back to the lighthouse," Summer said. "It's really starting to come down." She had to raise her voice to be heard over the loud pounding of the rain.

"They're out." I drummed my fingers against my phone screen before sending a message to my group text with the guys.

OLIVE

There's a storm warning. Are you driving? Please stay safe.

"Out wh—" Ivy started to speak but abruptly cut off and whispered *oh no* under her breath. It was obvious to see why—Stanley had just entered the diner and was making a bee-line for our table.

"I'm glad I found you here," he said, sounding out of breath. His white hair was damp with rain, and he had a slightly wild look in his eye. "The Autumn Harvest Festival is less than a week away."

"Oh my goodness! We had no idea!" Summer exclaimed, her tone laced with sarcasm. It was impossible to forget the festival with posters around every corner and Stanley tracking us down any chance he got, but I still found myself surprised that it was so soon.

Which meant my birthday was soon.

I hadn't told anyone it was the same day as the festival. It felt strange to just mention it out of the blue—almost like I expected people to celebrate me. I'd barely acknowledged my birthday over the past five years, and my celebrations with my parents had never been extravagant. My mom would bake me a yellow cake with chocolate frosting, and they would take me out to an early dinner after we finished up on the boat for the day. Money had always been tight, so I'd never expected big gifts. Since they'd passed, birthdays had been quiet days for me, but I always allowed myself to splurge on one new outfit.

I was fine with my twenty-fifth birthday passing me by. I already had more than I could ask for, anyway.

Stanley ignored Summer and kept going. "I need final confirmation on all your booths. You will need to set up on Friday." He turned to Ivy as if knowing she was the easiest victim. "Ivy? Your booth this year?"

"Well, you see, it's been really busy with the start of the school year..." Ivy trailed off at Stanley's expectant expression.

"We'll let you know later today what we're doing," Lucy cut in.

Stanley let out an aggrieved sigh. "Where is the enthusiasm, the passion, the town pride?"

"We will make sure to bring all our enthusiasm and passion on Saturday," Lucy said sweetly.

Stanley grumbled before heading to the counter. Char saw him coming and turned around, heading back to the kitchen even though she had been in the middle of taking a customer's order.

"I guess we should decide on our booths," Lucy said. "We give Stanley shit, but the festivals really are so fun. They're actually one of my favorite things about living here, and Stanley is great at managing everything."

"Manager, dictator, who can say?" Summer said.

I was about to tell them I had absolutely no ideas for a craft booth when my phone went off again.

"Okay, I really need to go." I quickly shoved the last few bites of lunch into my mouth. "It looks like this is going to be a really bad storm so you all might want to get home, too."

The girls all hugged me goodbye and I headed to the counter to pay. I pulled out my wallet and hesitated. Finn had given me their pack credit card last night and *very sternly* told me to use it or there would be consequences. The threat of punishment wasn't quite the deterrent he thought it was, but I handed Char his credit card all the same.

A wave of fatigue washed over me as I pulled up my hood. This was going to be a long night and I needed something to keep me up. As I headed out of the diner, the rain pelting me hard, I turned to Beans 'n Bliss instead of going back to my bike. I needed a hit of caffeine to keep myself going... and I might have been craving a pumpkin spice latte.

51

OLIVE

Marisol and Carmen were ahead of me in line at Beans 'n Bliss and immediately pulled me into their conversation. The sisters were wearing matching cherry-red rain jackets and glittery eyeshadow.

"Olive! It's so good to see you, cariño. We're hosting another dance night soon. You should bring all those hunky men of yours," Carmen said with a wink.

"You and Easton were the stars of the evening," Marisol added.

My cheeks heated at the reminder of what terrible dancers we were. "Um, thank you."

Marisol leaned in and lowered her voice, although for her that just brought it down to a normal volume. "How is it going with them?"

I clutched my phone as if I could will them to respond to my message. "It's good. They're wonderful."

Carmen nodded. "They've always been good boys. Poor Easton with that horrible mother of his. I think the whole town celebrated once she finally moved away."

"And losing Carina and Fredrik was awful. The whole town attended their funeral," Marisol said.

"I cried for days." Carmen dabbed her eyes. "And I'm so glad Lars has finally gotten over that other omega."

I froze as her words echoed in my head like some sort of horror movie soundtrack.

"Other omega?" I asked, keeping my tone as nonchalant as possible.

Marisol gasped. "Oh, I had completely forgotten about that. Years ago, Lars scented an omega and became absolutely obsessed with her. It's one of the reasons he's barely dated—he was waiting for her."

"It was quite romantic," Carmen said with a sigh. "But also unhealthy, I think, to be so fixated on someone. It's much better he's with you now."

The line moved and it was Carmen and Marisol's turn to order, saving me from answering. Not that I would have been able to form words right now. My heart was pounding, sweat was pouring down my armpits, and the room spun around me.

Lars had wanted another omega for *years*?

He'd been *obsessed* with her?

And he'd never said anything, even after we talked about exes the other night?

I ordered my latte and stepped to the side as I waited for it to be ready. My chest was tight and I was on the verge of hyperventilating. I squeezed my hands into fists as I tried to keep my breathing even, but it felt hopeless—my omega was equally devastated and filled with rage.

The barista called out my name. My hands shook as I put a lid on my drink.

"Olive?"

I held in a frustrated scream. I didn't want to talk to anyone now. All I wanted was to be home, in my nest, alone.

I turned around and saw Frida, Lars's mom, sitting at a corner table. I slightly softened seeing her and forced a smile on my face.

"Hi."

She looked around for a minute. "Are you here alone?"

I nodded. "The guys left earlier to get something for the restoration. I just wanted some coffee, but I do have to head back to the lighthouse to monitor the storm."

There was a loud crack of thunder, and Frida's brow furrowed. "How're you getting home?"

"I have my bike." I wasn't looking forward to riding it back. It might be a better idea to walk it back. The path to the lighthouse was probably muddy.

"Absolutely not," Frida said with a frown. "I'll drive you." She immediately started packing up her things—a laptop, a small notepad, and a pen.

"Oh, you don't have to do that. You should stay."

"Nonsense. I'm done with my work, and it's probably best for all of us to be home before this gets worse."

I should have protested more, but the truth was I was too intimidated to argue with this alpha.

"That's a nice rain jacket," she said as we headed to the door, throwing out her empty coffee cup. "I always say there's no such thing as bad weather, just bad clothing."

A pang of longing went through me. Just then, Frida had sounded so much like my dad. I wished more than anything I lived in an alternate timeline where my parents could come with me to a family dinner at the Andersson-Spring house.

I pulled up my hood and braced myself for the cold wind and rain. Luckily, Frida was parked right in front of Beans 'n Bliss. I opened the passenger side door and got in, but right before I closed it, Felix leapt inside. He was absolutely drenched.

"Oh my goodness," I gasped, pulling the door shut. "Did you get caught in the storm?"

Felix meowed pitifully. I put my coffee in the drink holder and unzipped my jacket so he could crawl inside.

Frida shut the driver's side door behind her and pulled down her drenched hood. "Felix, what on earth? I have never seen him act like that. He's usually quite reserved."

Reserved was the absolute last word I would use to describe Felix. Diabolical mastermind, meddling matchmaker, and mystical otherworldly creature felt more accurate.

"He seems to like the lighthouse cottage, so we've spent a lot of time together."

Frida pulled away from the curb and headed to the access road that allowed cars to drive up to the back of the lighthouse. "I don't think it's the cottage he loves. Lars said he's been staying at your house pretty much since you moved in. Felix usually picks a new home every night to sleep in, so this is unusual behavior for him."

The idea that Felix had specifically chosen to spend time with me made me tear up and hold him tighter.

I sent another text to my guys and stared at my phone screen, desperately wishing they would respond. My heart felt raw and exposed, like I was teetering on the edge of a gaping hole of loneliness and rejection. Why had they abandoned me? What if something happened to them? What if they were hurt?

I wouldn't be able to handle it. They were mine.

Except for Lars, the traitor.

And then I burst into tears.

"Oh dear," Frida said. "Olive, honey, are you okay?"

"The guys aren't responding to me," I choked out as I tried to hold in my sobs.

"Reception around here is absolutely terrible with storms," the alpha said, speaking in a low, soothing tone. "I'm sure they're absolutely fine. I'm sure they're not ignoring you."

Her words just made me cry even harder. Great, now she would definitely regret offering me a ride home.

The car came to a stop and I squinted through the window, realizing we were already at the lighthouse. The rain was coming down so hard I could barely see the back entrance.

"I know this is a delicate question," Frida said slowly. "But are you close to your heat, honey? Your scent is quite strong."

"Oh no," I said, covering my face with my hands. "I'm so sorry." Now her car would smell like me, and I'm sure that would upset her omega. "I'll just go."

"Stop." A gentle hand encircled my wrist. "Your scent doesn't bother me, and it certainly won't bother my pack. What I need now is to know my son's omega is taken care of."

Her son, who was apparently *settling* by being with me when he'd spent years dreaming of someone else.

But that wasn't a conversation I could handle right now, so I needed to pull my shit together.

I took a deep, shuddering breath. "I'll be fine, I promise." I curved my lips into a watery smile, but the expression felt foreign. "I'm sure they'll be back this evening. This is just hormones." I waved at my tears. "And I have Felix to keep me company."

The cat chose that moment to poke his head out from his cozy spot under my jacket. He locked eyes with Frida and meowed.

Frida didn't look convinced, but she sighed. "At least let me give you my phone number. If you need anything, please reach out. You won't be any bother."

She needed to stop being so nice to me or I would never stop crying. We exchanged numbers, and the whole time I wished my mom was here.

"Thank you," I said. "For the ride and... just thank you."

Frida gave my hand a gentle squeeze, and then I was out of the car and clumsily running to the door, making sure Felix was securely tucked into my jacket.

TEN MINUTES LATER, I had changed into dry clothes, wrapped a blanket around Felix, and made a cup of hot chocolate. After all that drama, I'd forgotten my latte in Frida's car.

I perched on my chair in the lighthouse observation room, a dry Felix curled up on my lap. I had the radar pulled up and the radio on to catch any ship or Ocean Rescue transmissions.

The radio crackled with static. "Attention: Ocean Rescue is needed for a fishing boat that's run into rocks. Starlight Grove is the nearest marina."

I sat up straighter. Ocean Rescue generally didn't leave from Starlight Grove since Briar's Landing had the larger port.

"Ocean Rescue responding." A female voice crackled through

the radio. "We have a team dispatched to Starlight Grove Marina that is set to arrive in ten minutes."

"Copy that, Ocean Rescue." The man reported the details of the ship's location. "There are three people on board and no injuries are reported. The name of the boat is *My Sweet Olive*."

I froze. My knuckles turned white from how hard I was gripping the table. Did he just say what I thought he said? I fumbled with the radio until I hit the correct button.

"This is Starlight Grove's Lighthouse Keeper. Did you say the boat is *My Sweet Olive*?"

"Affirmative."

The room spun around me and the edges of my vision grew black. I pulled myself together enough to adjust the lighthouse settings before picking up the radio again.

"The Starlight Grove Lighthouse is now unmanned. The beacon's storm pattern is lit."

If there was a response, I didn't hear it. I was already sprinting down the stairs, grabbing my rain jacket and boots as I went. Felix chased after me and batted at my leg.

"It's them, Felix," I shouted, almost falling on my ass as I pulled on my boot. "That's why they're not responding. They're on the fucking boat."

Because there was only one fishing boat with that name.

And only one reason it would be on its way to Starlight Grove.

52

EASTON

"ARE YOU SURE YOU KNOW HOW TO PILOT THE BOAT?" THE massive, gruff alpha crossed his arms as he stared us down, skepticism heavy in his expression.

We were on the boat dock in Echo Bay, about an hour north of Starlight Grove. The air was filled with salt and the smell of fish.

Finn had looked up the public sales records of boats in Echo Bay and found that Gunnar Christensen had purchased the fishing boat *My Sweet Olive* four and a half years ago.

He'd tracked down his phone number and called him last week to see if he would be willing to sell. Olive had had to sell her family's boat because she needed the money, but that boat held memories of her parents. We hoped this gesture would show her how serious we were about her.

Olive deserved it. She clearly hadn't grown up with extravagant things, but she's had extravagant love from her parents. We would bring that love back into her life.

"We'll be fine," Lars said with unearned confidence. We knew shit about boats, but we'd watched a few videos on how to pilot a fishing boat and it seemed simple enough, especially since we were just heading a short way down the coast to Starlight Grove's marina.

"This is a very special boat," Gunnar said. "Belongs to a very special girl."

"Yes, sir," I said. "We know she's too good for us, but we're going to do everything we can to give her the best life possible."

Gunnar's expression softened ever so slightly. "Well, you better get going. Storm's going to blow in soon."

The three of us got on the boat and fumbled around a bit before Gunnar rolled his eyes and showed us the basics.

"This is a horrible fucking idea," he muttered under his breath before leaving us to it.

It was a little rocky, but we managed to get the boat out of the harbor. Soon, we would be back in Starlight Grove, this time with a gift that would hopefully prove to our omega how serious we were about her. It was Olive or nothing for me now.

The wind picked up and ruffled my hair, and anticipation filled my chest.

53

OLIVE

I held my boobs as I sprinted to the marina, my hood flying off with the wind. My leggings were quickly soaked and muddy, but I didn't care. All that mattered was getting to my guys.

I blinked the rain out of my eyes as I made my way down the final hill. My heart pounded against my ribs when I spotted the Ocean Rescue boat. Three men were preparing it for launch.

I waved at them and shouted, "Hey! Wait for me!"

Relief washed through me as one of them turned around. My boots thumped loudly against the wooden dock, and I was gasping by the time I came to a stop. I leaned against the boat as I tried to catch my breath.

"I'm coming with you," I wheezed.

"Umm... who are you?" a tall, brown-haired beta standing on the dock asked. The two other men—also betas—were already in the boat.

"Lighthouse keeper," I said, clutching my chest. "I'm authorized." I pulled a card out of my pocket and flashed it at them.

"Is that a library card?" he asked.

"That would be weird," I said as I climbed into the boat. "I'm Olive."

"I'm confused. But also, I'm Ezra," he said as he followed me onto the boat.

"I'm Michael." I shook the hand of a blond beta with a mustache.

The third beta introduced himself as Leo.

"You're rescuing the three alphas on *My Sweet Olive*, right?" I asked.

"That's right, Ms. Lighthouse Keeper Librarian. Do you know anything about boats?" Ezra asked.

"Grew up lobstering and I'm trained in open water rescue. Those three guys also happen to be mine, so let's step on it."

"Oh shit," Leo said, wiping water out of his face. "This just got interesting. I love me some drama."

"I would like our rescue to be drama-free, thank you," Ezra said dryly. "Any chance I can convince you to wait for us here?"

I shook my head.

He sighed deeply. "I figured." Then he mumbled something about alphas and omegas under his breath before continuing. "I'm the captain. You will listen to me and not get in our way."

He gestured for me to take a seat under the hardtop as the three of them worked to get us out on the choppy waves. I held on tight as we were jostled side to side. For all my time on boats growing up, it had been rare for us to get caught in bad weather. At least I didn't get seasick.

I unzipped the top part of my jacket. My skin felt like it was on fire, but I ignored what that meant because my alphas were out here in this, crashed against the rocks. Now that I was forced to stop and think, panic overwhelmed me as I was brought back to that horrible day when I lost my parents. My mom hadn't been feeling well. Dad had tried to convince her to stay home, but she'd insisted she was fine. We were out on the boat when her symptoms worsened. The race to get back to land had been the most agonizing minutes of my life.

By the time we docked and the medics got to her, she was unconscious. My dad and I rode in the ambulance to the hospital, but she was already gone when we got there. They said she'd had a myocardial infarction... a widowmaker.

My dad kept repeating, "But I'm not a widow."

They'd brought us to a small room where we waited for someone to tell us what our next steps were. My dad was having trouble breathing, and then he clutched his chest. I panicked and ran out into the hallway, screaming that my dad was having a heart attack.

I'd watched as a medical team burst into the room. I refused to leave my dad's side as they got him on a gurney. But it turned out it wasn't a heart attack. It was a thoracic aortic aneurysm.

Hours later, I was back in the same fucking room. Except this time, I was alone.

Salty spray from the sea hit my face. I struggled to breathe through the panic. I couldn't lose anyone else. I refused. We would get to them in time.

Once we got out of the harbor, Leo sat down in the seat beside me and shook the water out of his hair. "How did your alphas get themselves into this pickle?"

That was the million-dollar question, but I had a pretty good guess. "I think they're trying to make a grand romantic gesture. The boat they crashed belonged to my parents."

"Weird way to make a gesture, but what do I know?" Leo shrugged. His eyes narrowed as he looked me over. "Are you okay? Because I don't have the greatest sense of smell, but I would swear that the ocean has turned into a pumpkin spice latte."

My cheeks burned even more. "Don't worry about it."

"Yes, absolutely nothing happening here is worrisome," Michael said as he squeezed in beside us.

I clenched my hands. "Have you gotten any more updates? Any injuries reported?"

"No injuries reported," he said, his voice raised in an almost-shout to be heard over the engine and the storm. "Seems they got too close to the coast and ran aground on some rocks. This storm wasn't supposed to hit this hard so early in the day, so I'm sure it took them by surprise."

It wasn't long before Ezra let out a shout. My eyes followed where he was pointing, and there she was—*My Sweet Olive*. I was four years old when my dad brought me down to the marina to show me his new boat. I'd just learned to read my name and had jumped up and down when I recognized it written on the side. Seeing it now, battered against the coast, sent a pang through my heart, but it was nothing compared to how I felt seeing my alphas wave at us. Hot tears streamed down my cheeks, mixing with the rain.

Years ago, I'd been devastated to let this boat go. It felt like my parents were dying all over again. But as I'd waded through my grief, I'd come to understand that my parents were present for me in my memories.

The boat was just a boat, but the men on it? They were my home.

Ezra prepared the dinghy to go get them, staunchly refusing to let me join. So my fingers clenched the metal guard rail as I watched the small boat brave the waves until it got to the lobster boat. I clenched my teeth as my alphas piled in, their massive bodies looking way too big for the dinghy. But then they were on their way back. The tension in my chest eased, and so did the storm—the waves growing quiet as my guys crossed them until they were finally back safe with me.

Easton was the first one off the dinghy. He tripped and almost fell, but managed to right himself in time to crash into me. His arms pulled me into a tight hug, enveloping me in his chocolate hazelnut scent. I breathed him in as I clutched at his soaked clothes.

More arms surrounded me as Lars and Finn joined our group hug.

They're here. They're safe.

They're here. They're safe.

I grew dizzy with relief as I slumped against them.

"Surprise! We got you a boat," Easton said, his voice muffled in my drenched hair.

My laugh was watery as our hug pile broke apart, my alphas still keeping their hands on me.

"You're idiots," I choked out.

Finn turned me to face him, a stern expression on his face. "You shouldn't be here," he growled, leaning down so we were eye-to-eye. "What were you thinking, putting yourself in danger like this?"

I sputtered, momentarily at a loss for words. "What was *I* thinking? What were *you* thinking? I'm not the one who needed to be rescued!"

"She's got a point," Leo said.

"That she does," Lars responded with a smile. "Our omega isn't one to sit by quietly." He tried to pull me into a hug, but then I remembered I was angry with him. The rage and jealousy and devastation I'd felt in the coffee shop all flooded back to me and I moved back, giving Lars my shoulder.

A flash of hurt crossed his face, and I almost crumbled. Luckily, my omega was better at holding on to grudges.

"Sweetheart? What's wrong?"

"Oh, what's wrong?" I snapped, tapping my chin. "Let me think, let me think. What could it be? Oh! I know! Maybe it's because I just found out the guy who said he was *my* alpha is actually pining after another omega!" My voice was a shrill scream above the crashing waves.

"Oh shit," Michael said behind me.

Lars's jaw dropped, and it made me even more furious. Easton's hands settled on my shoulders and gave me a squeeze. "Baby, I think—"

I turned my dagger-filled expression on him, and he stopped talking immediately. But he didn't step away from me, which I was glad for. I needed my guys' touches to convince me they were really safe.

"Sweetheart. Olive," Lars said, holding his hands up as he took a step towards me. "Can you explain what you're talking about?"

Raindrops dripped down the front of his face, soaking his hair and beard.

"I heard you scented an omega years ago and have wanted her ever since. But *thank god* you're *settling* with me."

"Damn," Leo said. "This is better than that reality show, *Go Scent Yourself.*"

"I'm more of a *Rut Island* kind of guy," Michael responded.

I was expecting Lars to stammer out some sort of useless explanation, but instead, a grin spread across his face. Rage flared in me. He thought this was funny? That was it—I had to kill him.

I shrieked and launched myself at him, pounding my fists against his chest. "How dare you fucking smile?"

Lars wrapped his huge arms around me and lifted me off the ground, trapping my fists against his chest.

"You're right, I shouldn't smile." His voice was deep and low, and his chest started vibrating with a purr.

"No, this isn't fair," I muttered as my entire body went lax in his hold. "You can't use your alpha witchcraft on me."

"I'll use whatever tools are available to me if it will make you listen."

"I don't want to listen to you," I snarled. I would stay strong. He wouldn't win me over with his stupid alpha purr. And I was definitely not rubbing my cheek against his neck to scent mark him.

Lars ignored me and kept talking. "Six years ago, I was walking down Main Street when I scented something. It was the best thing I'd ever smelled in my life, and my alpha knew immediately that it was an omega and that she was ours. I'd never put much stock into scent compatibility, but at that moment, it felt like the entire world had shifted."

I closed my eyes tight. It felt like my actual heart was breaking inside my chest. How could I ever compete with this mystery omega?

"I never found her," he said. "I realized she must have just been passing through town. I tried to forget her, tried dating other omegas, but it never felt right. Until a few weeks ago, I scented her again."

My muscles froze.

"Throughout the years, I'd convinced myself that I must have been exaggerating what the scent did to me. But I hadn't because when I scented her again on Main Street, I knew she'd returned to town to be mine. Ours."

I sniffled.

He adjusted his hold so I could wrap my arms and legs around him.

"Olive, my soul has known you were mine for six years, and when I finally laid my eyes on you that day on the beach, I knew I would love you for the rest of my life."

I inhaled sharply. "You love me?"

Lars tightened his hold on me. "How is that even a question? Of fucking course I love you."

I sniffled again as happy tears fell down my cheeks. "I love you, too."

One of his hands cradled the back of my head as he pulled me in for a kiss. I immediately deepened it, needing to taste him, needing to merge my body completely with his.

"I'm sorry I didn't tell you sooner," Lars said against my lips.

He slowly set me down on the deck, and Finn and Easton crowded around us.

"Just so you know, I loved you from the first moment I saw you in the market," Easton said. "I just didn't say it because I didn't want to freak you out."

My lips quirked at how put-out Easton sounded. I wrapped my arms around him, pressing my smile into his throat as I scent-marked him. "Are you upset you didn't get to say it first?"

"Yes."

I cupped his face and ran my thumb along his pouty lips. "I love you, Easton. Thanks for seeing me."

His expression transformed into a smile. "I love you, sunshine. This is forever, baby. I hope you're okay with that."

"Yeah, I'm okay with that."

And then I was in Finn's arms.

"Sorry for lecturing you." His hands were running up and down my body as if he were trying to make sure I was unharmed under my soaked clothes.

"You wouldn't be you if you didn't lecture me."

He broke out into a smile so beautiful it made my breath hitch.

He cupped my face with both hands, his thumbs running up and down my cheeks. "My omega, my sweet girl. I love you."

"My Finn. I love you, too."

He tipped my head back and then his lips were on mine, hungry and desperate. A moan slipped through my lips, and he pressed his tongue inside my mouth. He was all sweet maple and salty ocean air.

Loud clapping filled the air and broke us apart with a start. I turned to see Leo and Michael cheering us on.

"Fuck, that was even better than the *Rut Island* finale," Michael said.

Ezra rolled his eyes, but he was smiling. "Anyone mind if we actually complete this rescue and head on back?"

"I guess that's acceptable," I said. "What will happen to the boat?" I pointed at *My Sweet Olive*, hating the idea of just leaving her here. She hadn't tipped over, but the bow was wedged between rocks.

"Once this storm fully passes, you'll have to get someone to tow it out," Ezra said.

"We'll get her fixed up, pretty girl," Finn said, rubbing his hand up and down my back a little too fast to be soothing. "We wanted to do a grand gesture so you would know how serious we are about you, but we fucked it all up. We just want you to know we're not a pack without you." His typically sweet maple scent had twisted with his embarrassment.

I leaned into his side. Finn, my sweet, sensitive alpha who was still working through his fresh grief, had done this to help me with mine. And that meant everything.

"We'll figure out the rest, as long as we're all together."

"Alright, let's get going," Ezra said, looking at his phone. "This storm is supposed to pick up again soon and I'd like to be on land when that happens."

There wasn't enough room for all of us under the hardtop, but the guys ushered me in and insisted I take a seat. The wind picked up as Ezra drove us back to Starlight Grove's marina. I grabbed my hair to keep it from blowing in every direction. It was a lost cause, though.

"Are you cold, kitten?" Lars asked, crouching down in front of me. He put his hands on my cheek, and his brow furrowed when he felt how hot I was.

I started shaking my head when a cramp rippled through my core. I whimpered and clutched my stomach.

"What's wrong?" Lars's voice was sharp with panic.

I closed my eyes. This was not how I wanted to ask them if they wanted to see me through my heat. I'd planned to cook them dinner tonight and explain everything. This was what I got for pushing it off.

Another horrible cramp rocked through my core, and I bit my lip to stop from crying out. Fuck, I already felt so empty. My skin was crawling and I just wanted to dive into my alphas' arms.

"Olive." Lars's sharp tone forced my eyes open. Easton and Finn were crowded around me now.

"Baby, your scent is really strong," Easton said slowly. "Are you..."

"You're in heat," Lars finished.

I hesitated before nodding my head.

Immediately, I was gathered up in Lars's arms. His wet, prickly beard rubbed against my skin as he scent-marked me. Easton and Finn quickly did the same, and some of my discomfort settled.

"Oh my god," Leo said in a hushed voice that was still loud enough for us to hear. "Remember how this happened in season two of *Go Scent Yourself*? She had a breakthrough heat after meeting her pack."

Except, this wasn't a breakthrough heat, which could sometimes happen when an omega on suppressants spent time with scent-compatible alphas. Those heats were typically short and less intense. My body was barreling full speed ahead to a real heat, one that would last for days and bring out my feral omega instincts.

"I've got you, sweetheart," Lars murmured, his beard brushing against my face. "We'll be back in your nest soon."

54

EASTON

I CARRIED A WHIMPERING OLIVE OFF THE BOAT. Thankfully, Finn's car was in the lot from where we'd parked it this morning. I clutched my omega tight to my chest as we piled in and drove the few minutes back to the lighthouse.

"We're almost there, sunshine," I murmured. "Almost to your nest, and then we'll take such good care of you."

She was soaking wet, but she was a little furnace in my arms.

"Easton," she whimpered.

"I'm here, baby."

"Please don't hate me. I can't stand it if you leave."

I held her tighter as Finn slammed on the brakes and threw the car in park outside the lighthouse.

"Never. Never ever, baby," I said fiercely.

Lars opened the car door for me, and we ran inside.

"Should we shower first?" Finn asked, eyes looking a little wild. "Olive, sweet girl, what do you need?"

She blinked and looked around as if only just now realizing we were in her living room.

"Put me down," she mumbled.

I wanted to argue, wanted to hold her longer, but she was already pushing out of my hold.

She stood in the middle of the living room with the three of us around her, looking devastatingly unsure of herself.

"I need to tell you something. And I know I should have told you earlier. I was going to yesterday, but then I was so tired and scared, so I pushed it to today. Obviously, that didn't go according to plan, and I'm just really sorry."

Her eyes welled up, and my chest felt like it was splitting apart watching her.

"Sweetheart, whatever this is, it can wait. You're in pain and—" Lars started, but Olive cut him off.

"No, please, we have to do it now."

Lars looked like he wanted to argue, but instead, he picked Olive up and settled her on his lap on the couch. Finn and I quickly joined him, sitting on either side. I stroked my hand down her back.

"What's going on, sunshine?"

Olive looked miserable and her lower lip trembled. Fucking *trembled*.

"I'm not on suppressants," she blurted out. "I went on them before my first heat, but that's when I developed the blood clot. The doctors said it's not safe for me to ever take them again."

My hand froze on Olive's back. She wasn't on suppressants? That meant this wasn't a breakthrough heat caused by being around our scents. This was a real heat. Fuck, she must be in so much pain right now.

"But... what have you done for your heats?" Lars spluttered. Of all of us, he was the most familiar with omegas since he grew up in a pack.

"I signed up for a heat service."

I scowled. Unbonded omegas used services where screened alphas would take care of them just for their heats. The thought of other hands on Olive, other alphas even having their eyes on her... no, I didn't fucking like that at all.

"The first time didn't go so well." Her voice was a hoarse whisper now, and I didn't miss how she flinched with pain at what I was assuming was another cramp. I resisted the urge to steal her onto my lap and do whatever I could to take the pain away.

"What happened?" Finn asked. His tone was even, but the look in his eyes was deadly.

"There were two alphas, and afterward, they said I was just... a lot."

"A lot?" Lars asked.

Olive's eyes were fixed on her hands. "My omega was too much for them. They said I was demanding and whiny and that I made the heat really difficult for them."

"Difficult for *them*?" Finn gritted out.

Olive nodded. "And then the second time, they could only find one alpha on short notice, which was my fault. I'd been nervous to call the agency and tell them I was going into heat after my first experience, so I left it too long. That alpha said the same thing about my omega... when he left halfway through."

No. No. No.

He left Olive? My Olive? All alone? I was going to end him.

Finn was clearly on the same wavelength because he was off the couch and pacing, hands formed into tight fists. "The bastard fucking left?" he shouted. "I'm going to fucking kill him!"

Something clicked in my mind. "The alpha at the apple orchard? Is he the one who left you?"

Olive nodded miserably. "He's an asshole for sure, but it's not really his fault. I think there's something wrong with my omega. When I go into heat, I just turn kind of"—She waved her hands around like she was trying to catch the right word in the air—"*feral*. It's too much for anyone to handle. So after that second failed attempt with the heat services, the doctor there gave me sedatives to take during my future heats."

"Sedatives?" Finn hissed. "They gave you fucking sedatives so you can, what, be unconscious for *days*?"

Olive whimpered and tilted her head to show Finn her neck. His face immediately softened and he crashed back onto the couch, pulling Olive onto his lap. "Shit, I'm sorry, sweet girl. I'm not mad at you."

"Baby, please, we can help—" I started, but Olive cut me off.

"I'm not totally unconscious. The sedatives keep the edge off when the pain gets to be too much." She chewed on her lip, and I leaned over to free it with my thumb. "But I lied about it when I took this job."

Now her tears were falling steadily, her shoulders shaking with silent sobs. Finn cursed and tightened his hold on her, a purr starting up in his chest.

"I said I didn't have any issues that would prevent me from being on call for storms and stuff, but that's not true. I thought I could maybe make a nest in the watch room and take less medication than usual so I'd be more alert. But that's so irresponsible. Although, I'm sure I'm going to be fired anyway because I left the lighthouse unmanned during this storm. And I have no savings and can't afford to live here without having this housing, so I'll have to move away and then we'll never see each other again."

"Oh, darling." Finn arranged her so she was pressed to his chest, her head resting on his shoulder. "We'll make sure you don't lose your job. It was our fault, anyway." When Olive opened her mouth to argue, I placed my finger over her lips.

"No," I said, my voice low and stern. "Listen to us. You are not moving away. You are *ours*."

"But I lied to you," she sobbed. "How can you still want me?"

I looked at my brothers, and they wore bewildered expressions that met my own. I understood intellectually why she'd be scared to tell us about her heats, but how could she think we would be anything but fucking thrilled to see her through them?

Before I could figure out what to say, Olive continued.

"You shouldn't have to deal with me during this heat. I have my medications with me and then once it's over, I'll talk to Stanley and tell him I'm not fit to be the lighthouse keeper."

I saw the moment Finn snapped. A growl ripped through his chest, and he gripped Olive's chin. "The only reason you're not over my lap right now getting spanked is because I know you're not thinking clearly with your heat starting. We are your fucking pack and it's our responsibility to see you through heats." He tightened his grip on Olive's jaw when she tried to respond. "You are *not* too much. Those alphas were wimpy motherfuckers who probably signed up for that service because they wanted to fuck an omega and had no idea how to actually alpha-up and take care of you the way you deserve. You are not drugging yourself with sedatives. I'm not sure that's even legal for a doctor to prescribe. We're going to stick with you for however many days this lasts and fucking take care of you. Because you're ours and we want to."

Olive blinked, looking stunned.

"How could you think we would leave you, baby?" I asked. "We also had plans to talk to you today." I glanced over at my brothers and they nodded. This wasn't how we'd planned to tell her, but she needed to know. "We wanted to give you the boat to show you how serious we are about you. We'd do anything for you. And we were planning to tell you we want to bond you."

At that, Olive burst into fresh tears. Finn's purr intensified as he rocked her back and forth. "We don't have to bond!" he almost shouted. "There is no pressure."

"I want to," Olive sobbed, and then she clutched at her stomach, her mouth open in a soundless scream.

"Alright, enough," Lars said, his voice gentle as he rubbed Olive's lower back. "Let's get in the shower, sweetheart. The water will feel good. We'll make some calls to make sure the lighthouse is taken care of, and then we're going to take care of *you*."

Lars gestured for me to take Olive. "I'll call my moms so they can organize shifts for the lighthouse," he said in a low voice.

I nodded and picked her up bridal style. She curled into my chest, arms tight around my neck like she was afraid I would let go.

"Are we really going to do this?" she asked, eyes wide.

"You mean, are we going to fuck you and take care of you through your entire heat and bond each other? Hell yeah."

Her hesitant smile was everything, but by the time we were in the bathroom, she was back to chewing her lip. I carefully set her down and rubbed my thumb along it. It was all red and sore. She reached up and grasped my wrist, holding hard.

"Are you really sure about me? If we're bonded, you'll feel all my bad moods and dark days. I'll make you miserable and you'll finally realize what a horrible person I am."

My chest ached for my Olive. I cradled her face with both hands. I wanted her eyes on me, to see that she was really going to absorb what I was about to say.

"I know what it's like to feel like you're dragging people down. I hid what was going on at home from Lars and Finn for so long because I didn't want to burden them. But eventually, it all came out, and it turned out they weren't burdened by my suffering—they were strong enough to lift it off me. Their families became my family, and suddenly, a dozen people were shouldering my pain. Let us be that for you, baby. Let us help you carry it, because even if you can't see it, you bring sunshine into our lives every moment of every day."

Tears spilled down her cheeks, but she nodded. "I want that."

The bathroom door opened. Finn walked in carrying a large basket, followed by Lars, who shut the door behind him.

Finn quickly put the basket on the floor—it looked like it was filled with bath oils and lotion—and came to Olive's side.

"What's wrong? Are you in pain?"

"Easton's just making me cry." She held her hand out to him and Lars. "I just... are you sure about this? About me? You can't take your bond marks back and I don't want you to regret—"

Finn quieted her with a growl and a kiss. "Yes, we're sure."

I moved out of the way so Lars could get closer. We needed a much bigger bathroom.

He ran his hand through her hair. "So fucking sure, sweetheart. Are you sure about us?"

She nodded quickly.

"Glad we're in agreement." Lars kissed her forehead and then we squeezed into the shower, taking turns being in there with Olive.

By the time the shower was over, she was having a hard time staying upright and was begging for our knots, her heat fully taking over.

55

OLIVE

I DUG MY FINGERNAILS INTO EASTON'S BACK AS HE fucked me.

"Mine," I snarled.

"Yours," he said.

Fuck, my alpha felt so good. His thick cock filled me, his knot hitting my clit with every thrust. The room smelled like a woodland forest bakery filled with chocolate croissants, maple candies, and pumpkin spice lattes. I inhaled deep lungfuls until I was dizzy.

But something was missing.

I clutched at him, whimpering.

"Baby? What's wrong?"

"I need... I need..." I trailed off, frustrated. I needed *something*, but I wasn't sure what. I sniffled, and immediately, Lars and Finn's hands were on me, stroking as much skin as they could touch.

"I need more," I finally choked out. My heat hormones were overwhelming, my emotions forming a tangled ball.

"Do we need to fill all these holes, kitten?" Lars's hands were on my leg, fingers digging into my thigh as he hitched it up so I was even more open to Easton.

I nodded furiously. *Yes yes yes.* My alpha was so smart figuring it out.

"I think we can arrange that," Finn said.

Easton rolled over so I was on top of him. Before I could gain my bearings, Finn's hand collared my throat and lifted me so my back was pressed to his chest. Having him control me like this, knowing he could cut off my air at any moment but trusting he wouldn't, made another gush of slick burst from me. He coated his fingers in my slick and pressed two of them inside my ass. I closed my eyes, throwing my head back against Finn's shoulder, but then let out a startled cry when Lars sucked my nipples.

Easton groaned. "Fuck, she just clenched down so fucking hard when you did that." His movements grew more frantic until he pulled me down hard on his already inflated knot. I screamed at the stretch, panting as my orgasm hit me like lightning.

My alphas didn't let me rest. Lars kept sucking and biting my nipples until I was on the verge of coming again. Then something was in his hand. He lifted it to show me. I squinted, confused, until I realized they were nipple clamps.

"Will you let me clamp these sweet little nipples? With every movement, every shift of your perfect body, you'll remember you belong to us. Every single part of you."

"Yes," I cried out as Finn pressed another finger in my ass.

"Relax, pretty girl," Finn murmured. "Open up for me."

I whimpered as Lars tightened the clamps. It stung more than I thought, but it felt so fucking good.

"That's it, kitten," Lars said. "Breathe through it. You can take it." He stroked my hair until I adjusted to the sensation. "I'll be right back." He moved away from my side, but before I could complain, Easton's hands were cupping my breasts.

"Your nipples look so pretty, baby. We should pierce them so we can play with them all the time."

I didn't know if it was the heat haze, but right now, that sounded like a great fucking idea. He played with the clamps, sending jolts of pain and pleasure straight to my clit until I came again. I clamped down hard on Finn's fingers and he swore.

"Good girl. Such a good omega for us. I can't wait to knot this ass."

"Yes," I gasped. "I need it."

Then Lars was back with a length of soft rope. He bound my hands in front of me while Finn held me by my throat to keep me balanced. But once my hands were tied, Lars took hold of the end of the rope and pulled me forward so I fell forward onto Easton's chest. I cried out as my nipples pressed against his skin. The pain shot straight down to my clit and I came, my slick gushing out around Easton's knot and filling the room with my scent.

"That's our good girl," Finn said, hands squeezing my ass cheeks. "Coming for us so prettily."

The way they were handling me told me they were feeling just as possessive as I was. I was completely under their control as they arranged me exactly how they wanted me.

Lars stroked my hair, murmuring praise, while Finn's cock pressed against my asshole. My body trembled as he thrust in, inch by inch. I was already so filled I couldn't imagine how I could possibly take any more.

"Are you all the way in?" I asked, my words coming out slurred as the heat haze thickened.

Finn chuckled. "Not even close, pretty girl. But you can take me." His hands ran up and down my back until I relaxed enough for him to push in further.

Lars's fingers wrapped in my hair, pulling me up enough so his cock was level with my mouth. Easton pinched my nipple and I gasped, giving Lars the perfect opportunity to thrust into my mouth. Right as he did, Finn pressed in all the way, his fucking knot included.

My scream was muffled around Lars's cock as the strongest orgasm I'd ever felt crashed over me. I had never been this full, and the waves of pleasure were so strong, so overwhelming, tears streamed down my face. My vision went black, and my heat dragged me completely under.

56

FINN

MORNING LIGHT CREPT THROUGH THE WINDOW, FILTERED through the hanging canopy around Olive's bed. We'd gotten her to eat a few bites of breakfast, but now we were locked in a fierce stand-off.

I tightened my grip on her chin.

"You have to take your medicine," I said, injecting my voice with a bark.

But she just clenched her jaw harder, shaking her head as she fought my command.

I had her blood thinner in my hand. It was dangerous for her to skip it, but my omega was not being reasonable right now. She fixed me with an intense glare, truly looking like a fierce little kitten. The corner of my lip twitched, but I fought my smile. She needed to know I was serious.

Olive was a total brat in heat and I fucking loved it. It gave me every excuse to spank her ass when she didn't listen, although with the way she perfumed, it wasn't much of a punishment. But her ass was already rosy pink, and she was still not taking her pill.

My stubborn girl.

Lars and Easton had already tried to sweetly coax her into taking it, but she'd refused. So now it was up to me to get creative.

"Hands and knees, omega."

This command she paid attention to. We'd fucked her non-stop throughout the night, but she was still begging for more.

I pressed the head of my cock against her mouth, smearing precum against her lips. "Open up. I want to hear you choke on me."

Her lips parted and I didn't give her a chance to adjust. I thrust in until I hit the back of her throat. She went to shift back, but my fingers were already woven in her hair, keeping her on my cock.

"Relax that throat. You're going to take all of me."

I held her there until she relaxed enough for me to push further in. Her throat was so fucking tight I had to fight myself not to come right there. She whined as her air was cut off, but I kept her there for a few more seconds before moving back far enough.

"Take a breath."

As soon as she did, I pushed deep into her throat again. I fucked her, controlling every movement, every breath. Her perfume filled the room, overwhelming my senses until I was close to a rut. I gritted my teeth and I fought to maintain control.

"Fuck, look at you, taking your alpha. Letting me fuck your face, use you however I want. Such a good little slut for me."

She moaned and sucked harder.

"One day, I'll press all the way in until you take my knot in that pouty little mouth. Then you'll really be at our mercy."

Her eyes glazed over at my words. I would never knot her mouth, never risk her that way, but fuck, the thought of it, of all her holes filled and knotted, made my balls ache.

I couldn't hold my orgasm off anymore.

"I'm going to come and you are *not* going to swallow," I barked.

I tightened my hold on her. The moment she gave a slight nod of agreement, I came in her mouth. I threw my head back, the pleasure overwhelming. Something about her heat pheromones made my orgasms more intense than any I'd had before. My vision went white as I shattered. I breathed heavily until I was able to speak again.

I pulled out of her mouth. "Open and let me see."

She did as I commanded, her lips parting to show me her sweet mouth filled with my cum.

"What a good fucking girl. Hold it there. You're not allowed to swallow until I say."

She whined, but she stayed still, her mouth open. I gripped her jaw and slipped in her pill.

"Swallow."

She closed her mouth and swallowed. My fingers flexed on her jaw.

"Show me."

Her mouth opened again, and I confirmed she'd swallowed her pill.

My hold on her gentled. "That's my good girl, listening so well to her alpha."

Olive whimpered and she moved forward, wrapping her lips around my half-hard cock. I groaned and ran my fingers through her hair. Her eyes grew heavy, but she continued lightly sucking. I tried to move her back, and she let out an adorable growl.

Okaaay. If this was what she wanted, who was I to refuse?

I was self-sacrificing like that.

"Come on, pretty girl, let's get you more comfortable."

She fought as I pulled her off me, but calmed when she realized I was just arranging her so she was lying on her side. I lay down so my cock was level with her mouth, and she immediately took me into her hot little mouth, content to lightly suck my rapidly hardening cock. I pet her hair gently as she made cute, sleepy noises.

"Fuck, that was hot," Lars choked out, shifting so he was spooning Olive.

"I guess we've got to do that twice a day until her heat is over," I said.

"Like it's such a fucking sacrifice," Easton mumbled, half-asleep.

Lars's moms had sent us a list of heat dos and don'ts, and one of them was that we needed to take turns and sleep as much as possible. But it was hard to sleep when Olive was so fucking captivating.

I grinned. My dick was already raw and sensitive, and we were only getting started. I didn't care. I would do whatever Olive needed and enjoy every fucking moment.

57

LARS

Olive fought me as I grasped her wrists and bound them together with rope.

Our omega was determined to fight us at every turn, like she needed us to prove ourselves.

That was fucking fine with me. I loved her being a brat for us because it meant she trusted us enough to be herself.

"It's my turn to tie you up, kitten."

She struggled against me as I tied the rope to a metal hook on the wall, twisting and working herself into a frenzy on the bed. She was dripping with arousal, her perfume filling the room. When I gripped her ankle, she kicked and twisted and did everything she could to escape my hold.

I just chuckled darkly as I put a leather cuff on both ankles, attached a length of rope to the cuffs, and lifted her legs towards her head. I tied the lengths of rope to additional hooks on the same wall, meaning her legs were spread wide in the air, bent towards her head.

Her ass and pussy were completely open to us, and no matter how hard she fought, she was bound fast.

It took me a second to get myself under control. I ran my hands up and down her legs, squeezing her lush thighs, cupping her sweet cunt. "Fuck, kitten, you're so sexy." I dipped my fingers into her pussy and they came out dripping with her slick. I sucked them into my mouth. "I'll never get enough of your taste."

She arched against me as I sucked her nipples in my mouth, her little whimpers spurring me on. But I was determined to keep my pace slow as I kissed my way up her body until I reached her pouty lips.

"Look at my good girl, submitting to her alpha."

I laughed as she gave me a scathing glare, but I decided to have mercy on her. I returned to her splayed legs, rubbing my face along her sensitive inner thighs before licking her drenched pussy. My hand flew to my cock, gripping it tight as I reveled in her sweetness. I greedily licked her drenched pussy, my alpha roaring in satisfaction as more and more slick spilled from her. Her pheromones overwhelmed me, and I took her clit in my mouth, sucking it hard. She came for me, hips arching off the bed as much as she could as she fell apart. I didn't let her rest as I thrust my fingers inside her and lapped up her slick, pulling orgasm after orgasm from her. By the time I moved away, my cock was rock hard and dripping for her. All for her.

My eyes were locked on her as I pressed inside slowly, savoring how her pussy clenched around my cock. I kissed her, my tongue thrusting into her mouth as I slowly fucked her, pouring all my love into every movement.

Her expression was soft and glazed when we both came.

"You did so well for me, kitten." She practically purred at my praise. "But I think your other alphas need a turn."

I moved to the head of the mattress, cradling her head in my lap as Easton and Finn took turns with her—teasing her, fucking her, playing with her ass—until she was putty in the nest. I stroked her hair, her face, unable to keep my hands off her.

Once she was covered in our cum and limp from orgasms, I freed her from the rope. She curled up against me, her burning hot skin like a brand against my chest as she drifted off to sleep.

58

OLIVE

My alphas weren't paying attention to me.

Easton had gotten up to get snacks—as if I were interested in *food* right now—and Finn and Lars were sound asleep in the nest. Leaving me completely unattended.

They should know better.

I extracted myself from the tangle of limbs and crept out of the room.

I had a vague awareness at the back of my mind that what I was doing was unreasonable and unsafe, but that didn't matter right now.

The front door shut behind me and I headed down the path to the beach. The sun had just sunk over the horizon, bathing the world in dark blue light.

My feet hit the cold, packed sand, and I took off running. The cold air kissed my bare skin, but I couldn't feel it with how over-heated I was. The dark beach stretched in front of me, illuminated by the almost full moon. My feet were silent as I hit the sand. I raised my arms, feeling like a mystical night creature as the salty air from the ocean whipped my hair.

A roar behind me let me know I wasn't alone on the beach. I

grinned, feeling absolutely feral, as I ran faster. Slick drenched my inner thighs and my core tightened with a painful cramp.

Too *empty*.

But I kept going.

A growl close behind me caused me to let out a shocked gasp. I whipped my head around and glimpsed a flash of brown hair. I changed direction, running left towards the water. My heart pounded with fear and excitement. The alpha's hands brushed against my skin, my hair, his dark laugh taunting me as he chased. The beach was too exposed. If only I could make it to the tree line ahead at the base of the mountain...

"Little omega, just *begging* to be caught."

Easton's arm snagged me around the waist and we tumbled to the ground, his body protecting me from the brunt of the fall.

My legs kicked out, my nails scratching until his grip loosened. I wasn't going to make it easy for him. He had to *earn* his prize. I pushed myself to stand on trembling legs, but before I could take a step, an unyielding hand closed around my ankle. I fell to my knees and immediately tried to drag myself through the sand.

But then the alpha was on top of me, the full weight of his body keeping me pinned.

"Mine." His growl vibrated through my body from the top of my head to the tips of my toes, electrifying and visceral.

My hips lifted as I tried to buck him off, but he just snarled as his large hand closed around my wrists. My ragged breaths filled the air and my muscles ached, but I wasn't ready to submit yet. I kicked out again, but my foot hit air.

I heard the loud crack before I felt it—the alpha's hand coming down hard on my ass.

"Submit," Easton barked. His command surged through me and I stilled.

His hand came down on my ass again, the sting of it making me cry out. He paused, rubbing the aching spot. "Are you ready to be a good fucking omega for your alpha?"

I shook my head, and he chuckled darkly. He rained down a

flurry of hard spanks. Before I could adjust to the pain, his thick fingers thrust inside my pussy.

"So fucking wet."

My body was already electrified, so close to coming. I arched against his hand. I just needed a little bit more to go over the edge...

He withdrew his fingers, his hand coming down again on my tender sit spot. I screamed, not from the pain of his hand but from the agony of my ruined orgasm.

"Naughty little omegas don't get to come. They get spanked and fucked over and over, their alpha taking whatever pleasure he wants and giving you none." His threat hung in the air and I whined. *No no no.* I didn't want that.

"Please," I begged. "Please let me come, alpha."

His fingers twisted in my hair and he forced my head back, arching my back. "You beg so prettily. But you're going to have to fucking earn it." He released his hold on my hair and wrists. "Roll over."

Indecision warred within me. I could run again, but I had no doubt my alpha would follow through and fuck me without letting me come.

I rolled over.

In the darkness, Easton looked even larger than usual, making me feel small and weak... like prey. I'd never seen him like this, and I realized he was consumed by rut. His grin was wild as he loomed over me, his eyes taken up by black pupils as he pinned me to the sand by the throat.

Yes. This is what I wanted. My alpha, feral for *me.*

I turned my head as much as I could, giving him my neck in submission. His responding growl caused slick to pour out of me.

"Part your legs."

I did what he asked, but he snarled. "Wider."

I whimpered as I spread my legs as far as they could go, my dripping pussy fully exposed to him.

"This sweet little cunt wants to feel pleasure, doesn't it?"

"Yes," I cried out. Being spread out like this while he just *stared* made my cheeks burn in humiliation.

"Then your cunt will take my punishment. Five spanks to earn an orgasm."

My breath hitched, my heart pounding out a rapid rhythm in my chest.

"But if the little omega can't handle it..."

I snarled at his taunt. "Bring it, alpha."

His hand came down on my pussy without warning, the sting of it taking my breath away.

"One." His gaze met mine, full of challenge. I widened my legs.

His hand came down again and again and again.

I whined and panted, the pain and pleasure almost too much and not enough at the same time.

"Last one."

His hand landed directly on my clit and I screamed at my orgasm. It rocked through my body, so intense it felt like I was unraveling. But then my alpha's body was on top of me, his weight grounding me back to earth.

He cradled the back of my head and his lips crashed against mine. I opened for him, soft and submissive as he dominated the kiss. Licking into my mouth. Nipping my lip.

"If you run, I'll chase you down every fucking time. You're mine. Have been from the first moment I saw you."

I smiled dreamily. "Yours."

He thrust inside my heated pussy, drawing a gasp from me as he seated himself fully. His movements turned gentle as he rubbed his face against mine, marking me with his scent. A gentle kiss brushed against the tip of my nose. "I love you."

I brushed my fingers down his face, my fingers catching on his stubble, which was now a short beard after days of not shaving. "I love you, too."

Then he was moving, filling me fully with each hard thrust. I clutched at his back, my fingers digging in.

I needed to mark, claim, make him mine.

His knot teased my entrance until I was sobbing and begging for it. After what felt like an age, he *finally* sank in all the way. His knot split me open in blinding pleasure as my orgasm shattered me.

And then his teeth were at my neck, biting down hard.

There was an explosion of emotion in my chest. Because Easton was there, crashing in with all his love. The bond was like golden strands sinking deep into my very soul. All his passion and enthusiasm and care for me. Fuck, his love was so *extravagant*.

"Olive. My Olive."

I clutched at his hair, my fingers wrapping in his curls and forcing his head to the side. I sank my teeth into his neck, shuddering with relief as the bond was completed.

My alpha's eyes filled with tears and awe, and I flooded the bond with my love, needing him to know the depth of my feelings. I'd never had anyone see me like Easton. He uncovered all those parts of myself I thought were too ugly and held them like they were precious.

Now neither of us would ever feel unloved again.

59

EASTON

Olive was curled up on my lap, arms and legs around me with my knot deeply seated inside her.

I wasn't ready to let go.

A flood of emotions that didn't belong to me wrapped around my heart. Olive was so convinced she wasn't my sunshine, but here she was, filling my soul with the brightest light. I'd spent my early childhood alone and scared, trying to ride out my mom's abuse until Lars, Finn, and their families changed my life with their love and stability. Now Olive was transforming it again.

I licked and sucked at the bond mark I'd placed on her skin, and she did the same, every brush of her lips a shock of pleasure straight to my cock.

The longer we sat there, the more I came back to myself. When I'd heard the door shut, my alpha had pushed to the surface. My world had narrowed until the only thing I was aware of was the hunt for my omega. I'd never gone into a rut like that.

I gently brushed my hand down her back. Her skin was still hot but not as much as it had been these past days. Now that the chase was over, I was fucking freezing with my bare ass pressed against the cold sand.

I lifted my lips from her skin. "Are you okay, baby? Was I too rough?"

She immediately shook her head, meeting my gaze with a soft smile. "Never." She pressed soft kisses down my jaw. "You're exactly what I need."

I groaned and kissed her, getting lost in the drugging sensation of her taste, her warmth, her everything. The only thing that could get me to break away was my need to take care of her.

"I've got to get you inside and we need a fucking bath."

She looked down at her body as if only now becoming aware of our surroundings. She let out a startled laugh as she found herself covered with sand.

Her hips shifted, pulling on my knot, and she let out a little whimper. "I guess we just have to wait."

"Nah," I said. I clutched her tighter until I got the right leverage to stand up. She squealed and tightened her hold on me. "I'll carry you back."

With every step, my knot shifted inside her. Olive cried out, sucking hard on my bond mark until I was so dizzy with arousal I could barely walk. We were only halfway back up the beach when she clamped down on me so hard it forced another orgasm from me. My legs shook with the effort to stay standing as I spilled inside her again, my cum sealed inside her by my knot.

Olive giggled, the sound like magic. "How're you doing there, alpha?"

I gave her a half-hearted spank and kept walking. "Trouble."

"Your trouble," she said happily, resting her head against my shoulder.

So true.

We managed to make it back to the house, and I walked us straight to the bathroom and turned on the taps. I gently tested my knot and found it had gone down enough to pull out of her. A gush of cum and slick rushed down her thighs, but she wouldn't let go of me.

"Come on, baby. Let's get you in the tub."

Olive made a little sound of protest and clung to me harder. Her eyes were turning glassy again after her moments of lucidity on the beach. My hand supported her ass as I leaned over to shut the water off.

"I'll be right here next to you." I ran my hand up and down her back slowly. We were such a mess—covered in cum and dirt and sand —and I knew her muscles had to be sore. I still couldn't believe my naughty girl had run away, but I couldn't wait to chase her again.

Olive clung to me tighter and shook her head in protest.

"I need you to be a good girl for me. Let go so I can put you in the bath." I tried to make myself sound stern, but who was I kidding? Olive had me completely wrapped around her finger.

She started sucking on my bond mark, and my cock hardened. I honestly didn't know it could still do that after days of marathon sex.

I sighed. I wasn't going to win this argument. I tightened my hold on her and carefully got in the bathtub that was way too fucking small for both of us. I managed to sit my ass down with my legs awkwardly bent in front of me while Olive's wrapped around my waist. It was nowhere near comfortable, but when she sighed happily and relaxed against me, it made it all worth it.

"Okay, baby, we'll make this work. And once your heat is over, we're getting you a bigger tub."

"Thanks, alpha," she whispered.

I ran the washcloth over as much of her skin as I could get to. "How're you feeling? Are you sore? Hungry?"

She didn't respond and I ran my hands down her body, trying my best to massage her muscles.

"I'm happy."

A lump formed in my throat and a purr roared through my chest. My omega was *happy*. I had done that, and it was the best fucking feeling in the entire world.

Her fingers trailed down my chest. "I love feeling you." She cut off with a little sniff, but I knew from the bond it wasn't sadness she was feeling. "Easton, you're...you're *everything*. I love you so much."

My throat was tight, my chest filled with stunned gratitude that this was my life. "My sunshine, my bonded."

We sat there in silence as a whirlwind of emotions played

through the bond. Finally, the water grew cold and my legs cramped from how they were contorted in the tub.

I pressed a gentle kiss to her lips. "We should get out."

A burst of longing and excitement reached me and I smiled, tucking Olive's hair behind her ear. "You want your other alphas, baby?"

She nodded.

"Let's go get them."

60

OLIVE

EASTON CAREFULLY DRIED ME OFF AND I GLIMPSED MYSELF in the mirror. My pupils were huge, my cheeks flushed, and my skin littered with little bruises, which I loved. I furrowed my brow as I touched my hair, which was in two French braids I had no memory of getting. They were slightly worse for the wear, but were still doing their job. My heart ached as I realized Lars must have done them for me. I couldn't remember much of the past few days, but my alphas were present in each fragmented memory, taking care of me.

I leaned back into Easton as he wrapped his arms around me from behind. He pressed hot kisses down my neck and shoulder, but my eyes were fixed on the matching bond marks on our necks. My omega was bursting with pride. Everyone would be able to see my mark on him.

He kept kissing me, and my eyes fluttered closed. My core clenched, wanting to be filled, but the need wasn't as intense as before. My heat wasn't quite over—the world was still covered in a delicious haze of warmth—but I could tell it was coming to a close. And before it did, I had two more alphas to claim.

Finn and Lars were still fast asleep in the nest when we entered. Easton snorted. "Amateurs."

I grinned as I threw myself back down on the nest, landing on top of Lars. He let out a soft *oof* and his eyes opened.

"Kitten." His arms wrapped around me, pulling me tight against his chest in a bear hug. "Do you need my cock?" he mumbled sleepily.

I grinned, feeling strangely proud that I had exhausted my alpha. I ran my hands over his hair, which was in braids matching mine.

I wiggled back until my pussy rubbed against his thick cock. The heat haze grew thicker as pleasure sparked through me. Lars groaned, his fingers digging hard into my hips. I positioned him at my entrance, slick already dripping down on his cock, and took him all at once. My alpha shouted a curse, his hips thrusting as he tried to get deeper. His knot ground against my clit and it was almost enough to distract me from my mission, but my omega and I were united in our goal. I leaned down and stroked my fingers down his face and beard. His blue eyes met mine, and he leaned into my touch.

"I love you," I murmured.

"I love you so much, sweetheart."

I brushed my lips against his skin until I found the perfect spot on his neck and bit down. Lars entered the bond, solid, strong, and sure. He had been my rock, my steady alpha, since we met that day on the beach, but as I felt him through the bond, it was like I was finally tethered after floating alone for so long. I was tied to him and it was like coming home.

He gasped, his hand cradling the back of my head. "Look at you marking me, sweetheart, without any warning. You like giving your alphas heart attacks, don't you?"

I just smiled, my self-satisfaction echoing through the bond as I sucked on the mark I'd left on my alpha's neck.

He gripped me tight and rolled us over so I was on my back. "I waited for you for six years. I would wait a hundred years for you, search every corner of the earth. You're mine, sweetheart. My soulmate, my everything, my Olive." And then his teeth sank into my neck, completing the bond. Love and relief washed away my insecurities about bonding. How could I ever have been scared of this? We were all meant to be together.

Lars swore as he thrust inside me, his arousal amplifying mine. He sucked on my bond mark and I shattered, my orgasm surprising me with its intensity. He let out a shout as he came, flooding me with his cum. He collapsed on top of me and I loved the weight of him crushing me into the mattress. His earthy pine scent surrounded me, and he twitched as I sucked his bond mark.

We lay there for a few long moments, our breaths coming quickly as we came down from the intensity of our orgasm. But I quickly grew restless. My bond marks were incomplete.

Lars must have sensed my distress because he pushed off of me with a smile. "Go get your alpha."

I reached out towards Finn and then he was there, holding my hand, moving on top of me. There was a fierce look in his eyes as he gripped my chin. "Forever?"

"Forever," I responded.

"Good, because you're mine, and I'll be yours for as long as the universe gives us. Because even if I lose you—" His voice hitched and he took a slow, deep breath. "Because even if I lose you, it will have been worth it. Our love is worth it. You are worth it." He caressed my arm until his hand wrapped around mine. His lips brushed my palm and bit down.

Finn entered the bond tentatively, as if he wasn't quite sure he belonged there. I didn't hesitate—I sank my teeth high on his neck and flooded the bond with all my love. Finn and I knew intimately how fragile life was, how loss could devastate you until you no longer recognized yourself. But here we were, both being so fucking brave to embrace living again.

"I need you," he whispered.

"You have me," I responded.

He sank inside me and I arched against him. His cock felt so fucking good, like he was made for me. Everything was soft and hazy —my fingers running through his hair, his lips against my throat, his sweet maple scent flooding my senses.

Finn pushed deeper inside me. There was a slight sting as his knot entered me, locking us together. My orgasm came like gentle waves, washing over me in endless pleasure.

I was vaguely aware of Finn shifting us, so I was lying on top of him. I reached out, needing all my alphas around me. Easton and Lars were there right away, their hands on my skin, their legs thrown over mine.

My eyes grew heavy, and I shivered as my skin cooled. A blanket was immediately tucked around me. My heat had ended and my alphas were still here with me, healing that part of me that always expected to be left.

My omega settled, feeling perfectly content and relaxed.

Mine mine mine.

They belonged to me. My alphas.

The bond was a riot of emotions—love and passion and joy all mixed together like golden threads.

I would never be alone again.

61

OLIVE

I was bundled up on the couch in front of the fire. It was my first time leaving my nest since my heat started... well, besides my beach adventure. My muscles were sore and my emotions were raw as I rode the waves of hormones still surging through me, but I could feel my alphas through the bond, sending pulses of love and care to me. An unshakeable sense of calm filled me from head to toe.

Felix had braved coming back inside and was curled up on my lap while my guys cleaned up the nest and got us food. Lars had gotten my phone for me and I turned it on for the first time in days. I blinked when I saw 142 unread texts. Holy shit. Almost all of them were from the omega group chat. I scrolled back to catch up on everything I missed.

There was a barrage of texts telling me not to worry because they had the lighthouse shifts under control and to have so much fun. Summer had sent a long series of dirty emojis that made me smile. I skimmed through the texts until I got to the ones from today.

LUCY

Did you hear Stanley's announcement? Most of the shops on Main Street don't have power after the storm and it looks like the Harvest Festival will be canceled

SUMMER

Oh no, really? Is your shop ok?

LUCY

Shop's fine. No power but also no damage, so I'm relieved. But I'm so sad about the festival. I know we make fun of Stanley but I actually love it

IVY

Me too. And I already have everything for my booth ready

SUMMER

Don't tell him but yeah, I do too. And I've seen how much work he's put into it from my hours working with Harry

IVY

Are you sure there's nothing we can do? Like an alternate location?

LUCY

It would be a ton of work to move everything but maybe we can make it work. The issue is that we have to have a power source, so the park isn't really an option

"This is sad, Felix. Do you like the festivals?"

Felix meowed.

I chewed my lip and drummed my fingers against my phone screen. If they needed an open area with access to power, there was an obvious solution.

Here. My home.

There was a large flat field next to the lighthouse and our massive generator was strong enough to power both the lighthouse and the cottage during storms.

"I have to do this, don't I?"

Felix placed his little head on my arm.

"Ugh, I can't refuse that face. But if I do this, I'm officially part of the town, which was totally not the plan. I moved here to be alone. I was going to be the mysterious lighthouse keeper witch who the town's children made up scary stories about." I grinned at Felix's exasperated expression. "I guess this is better, though."

Lars came over to the couch carrying two steaming mugs. He handed one to me and I sighed happily when I realized it was hot apple cider with whipped cream.

"You spoil me," I said, curling into his side.

He kissed the top of my head. "Only what you deserve. How're you feeling, sweetheart?"

"Sore, tired, but good."

"I'll give you a massage when you finish your drink."

"Be careful or I'll get used to this kind of treatment."

His scent sweetened, and he wrapped his arm around me. "As you should."

I smiled and took a sip of my drink. I wiggled happily at how good it was, earning me a low chuckle from Lars.

"So... I have an idea I wanted to run by you," I said.

"What's that?"

"The Harvest Festival is supposed to be tomorrow, but I guess the storm did some real damage in town and Main Street doesn't have electricity. So I was thinking..." I trailed off, my fingers twisted in my blanket. I wasn't used to this—wanting to be *social*. "I was thinking we could offer to have it here, in the field, and use the generator for anything that needs electricity."

Lars cupped my face, tilting it up to meet his gaze. "Yeah? You want to do that?"

I shrugged. "People seemed really excited about it, and it seems a shame to cancel it when we have the space here."

He leaned down and kissed the tip of my nose. "Stanley is going to be fucking thrilled."

"COME ON, people! Is no one following the proper setup maps from the Emergency Harvest Festival Relocation Binder? It's figure 17.3 in Appendix Three!"

"Oh, relax, Stanley!" Carmen shouted.

"He's in rare form today," Easton murmured in my ear.

I grinned. Stanley and the festival volunteers had rolled in early this morning, mowing a path through the field and figuring out the best way to hook things up to the generator. Most of the booths were set up—I'd seen Felix running around with a small knife from the pumpkin carving station—and the smell of pumpkin bread and apple cider filled the air.

My guys had been very protective, making sure at least one of them was hovering over me at all times, preventing me from doing anything too strenuous. I'd helped Ivy set up her rocks and paints before Easton insisted I step away and eat a snack.

I was finishing up my PB&J—Easton's arms wrapped around me from behind—when Stanley approached, trusty clipboard in hand. He'd swapped his usual gray cardigan with a festive forest green one with a crocheted leaf pattern. His husband, Harry, was wearing a matching one, which I thought was adorable.

"I notice you didn't complete the application for your festival booth," Stanley said with a look of deep disapproval.

Easton cleared his throat.

Stanley let out an aggrieved sigh. "Which I guess is acceptable since you're allowing us to use this space, although this field technically is town property—"

A low growl rumbled through Easton's chest, and I bit my lip to hide my smile.

Stanley huffed. "But I *suppose* that's beside the point. On behalf of the Starlight Grove Senior Committee for Overseeing the Committee for Town Festival Planning, we want to extend our gratitude to you."

"You're very welcome. You've done an amazing job organizing this on short notice. I've never seen such an incredible festival."

He puffed up with pride, and something about it reminded me so much of Felix I had to hold in my laughter.

Stanley tapped his clipboard. "Well, must be going. There's plenty more to do."

Easton and I watched him walk away and then burst out laughing.

"What the fuck was that committee name?" Easton wheezed.

"Oh, you mean the Senior Committee for Overseeing the Committee for Town Festival Planning? Seems like a perfectly normal name to me."

We were still laughing when Lars and Finn joined us. Lars had helped Lucy set up her booth before Carmen and Marisol had roped him in to set up their booth. I was pretty sure it was just an excuse for them to ogle his arm muscles, which... relatable.

"You get everything set up and up to code?" I asked Finn.

He leaned in for a kiss. "That took all of five minutes. The rest of the time was taken up by a very tedious lecture from Stanley. Char finally distracted him for long enough so I could escape."

"Well, everything is looking good. Will you guys do some booth crafts with me?"

Easton slung his arm over my shoulder. "Oh, I'm excellent at crafts."

62

OLIVE

"What do you think?" I asked Felix.

My guys and I were sitting in a circle next to the pumpkin carving booth. We each had a pumpkin and were keeping our final designs secret from each other, but I held mine up to Felix for his approval. I'd carved a cat face in my jack-o'-lantern. He cocked his head, meowed, and then sauntered away.

"I think he likes it," Finn said.

I grinned. "I think so. Now that I have Felix's approval, should we show each other?"

My guys nodded.

"Great, turn them around in one, two, *three*."

I blinked, brow furrowed, at the three designs in front of me.

Lars had gone with a traditional jack-o'-lantern, except its eyes were lopsided, and so was its creepy smile. But compared to the other two, it was a masterpiece. Because Easton had carved what I thought might be a... face? But it could also be some sort of monstrous demon. And Finn's design was so phallic it was bordering on pornographic.

"Umm, Finn?" I asked.

"It's the lighthouse!" he half-shouted. "See?" He gestured wildly at the lighthouse behind him.

I studied his pumpkin a bit closer. "Oh, is that... the cottage?" I pointed at the misshapen blob at the base of the "lighthouse."

"Yes," Finn said, defensively crossing his arms.

"Holy fuck," Lars said, turning Finn's pumpkin to face him. "I didn't realize we were making these kinds of carvings."

My shoulders shook from held-in laughter. "I can see the vision."

"Yeah, well, what is that?" Finn asked, pointing at Easton's pumpkin.

"It's Olive!" he said proudly.

The three of us stared at his carving. Pumpkin Olive had a triangle nose taking up most of her face, a gaping mouth that made her look like she was forever screaming, and a weird half-circle that might be... hair?

The bond filled with happiness, and we all burst out laughing.

"At least mine won't scar children," Easton said.

"I wouldn't be so sure of that," Lars laughed. He pulled me onto his lap, his strong arms surrounding me as he planted a kiss on my cheek. "Yours is definitely the winner, kitten, not that I'm surprised."

I snuggled into his chest, breathing in bright, fresh pine and feeling perfectly content. The storm had gone, leaving behind the perfect fall day. The sun was shining, the trees were showing off their bright red and orange leaves, and I was surrounded by people who loved me.

"We should probably move out of the way," Lars said reluctantly, his lips brushing against his bond mark on my neck.

I gave him one more squeeze and then pushed myself to standing. "We can put the pumpkins by the front door, as long as we turn Finn's around so the children don't see it."

He grumbled as he picked up his X-rated pumpkin but gave me a wink and kiss as we headed towards the cottage. Easton insisted on carrying my pumpkin because it was apparently too heavy for me. As we neared the door, I had a thought that stopped me in my tracks.

"Wait, we haven't really talked about what comes next for us. Do you guys want to live here?"

"Oh, I've already moved most of my stuff," Easton said, setting both our pumpkins down on the front steps.

"You what?" I spluttered.

He stood back to look at the pumpkin placement, completely unbothered. "We need to get a better closet system for everyone's clothes."

I looked at my other two alphas. "Have you also moved in without telling me?"

Finn leaned over to Lars. "What answer will be least upsetting, do you think?"

"Oh my god!" I did my best to sound put out by their high-handedness, but it was futile since they could sense my excitement through the bond.

Before my alphas could respond, Lucy headed up the path towards us. "Oh my god, what?"

"Oh, just the *tiny* detail that they've apparently moved in without telling me."

Lucy grinned. "Sounds about right. High-handed alphas. You can punish them later, but right now, I need to steal you for a second. Let's go inside—I have something to show you."

"You have something to show me inside my house?"

"Yes!" She opened the door and ushered me in, shutting the door on my alphas.

Before I could ask what was going on, she whirled around to face me, eyes bright. She pulled a large wrapped package from her over-sized tote bag and thrust it at me.

"Open it!"

I carefully ripped open the tissue paper, revealing a pile of gorgeous fabric. I lifted it, trying to figure out what it was. Lucy took it from me and held it up correctly so I could see that it was a cream dress with a deep v in the front. But attached to the shoulders was the most incredible cape I'd ever seen. It was also cream, but starting at the top of the cape were beautifully stitched autumnal flowers in golds, pinks, and reds. They continued down the cape, growing thicker until the bottom looked like a field of wildflowers. I'd never seen anything like it.

I looked back at Lucy, my lips parted.

"It's for you," she said, almost shyly. "I wanted you to have something fancy to wear."

My eyes filled with tears and I threw my arms around her, careful to avoid crushing the dress. "It's the most beautiful thing I've ever seen. Are you sure you want me to have it?"

She squeezed me back. "Of course. I've waited my whole life to have a sister, so this is a dream come true."

I held her a little tighter. "For me, too." I'd believed I would never have a family again. I'd never been so happy to be wrong.

We broke apart and I wiped my eyes.

"Put it on now!" Lucy said.

"Now?" This was definitely not appropriate festival attire.

"Yes. You have to show it off for me and your *bonded*." She waggled her eyebrows.

I laughed. "Fine."

Lucy had to help me put it on. It fit perfectly, and as I looked at myself in the mirror, I'd never felt so pretty. I twirled a little side to side. The cape made me look like a magical woodland fairy.

"I can't believe you made this," I breathed. "Lucy, it's the most amazing thing I've ever worn."

Her cheeks were pink as she beamed. "You look stunning. Your guys are going to flip. Let's go show them!"

"Oh, okay." I felt a little shy about going outside in this, but most people were in the field, not by the cottage. I could show my guys and then come back in and change.

Lucy held the front door for me and I followed her out.

"Happy birthday!"

I let out a small scream as what looked like the entire town gathered around the cottage, singing Happy Birthday to me. The crowd was filled with familiar faces—Ivy, Summer, and Lucy; Lars's moms —Frida, Harper, Isla, and Jo; Marisol and Carmen; Char, Rosie, and Gavin; Stanley and Harry; and so many more. And, of course, my guys were front and center.

My cheeks flushed bright red, but for once, the experience of being perceived didn't make my skin crawl. They weren't here to judge me; they were inexplicably here to *celebrate* me.

Easton bounded to my side and kissed the top of my head. "Happy birthday, baby."

Finn gripped my chin and gave me a firm kiss. "Just so you know, I'm spanking that ass later tonight for you hiding this from us."

"How did you even find out?" I asked.

Lars wrapped his arms around me. "Stanley asked Lucy if she was planning anything for your birthday. She was furious we hadn't told her." He gave me a pointed look, but I was trying to figure out how Stanley had known it was my birthday.

"He had your birthday from your job application," Finn said, reading the question on my face.

My chest ached when I caught sight of the mayor next to his husband, both of them wearing party hats. He was meddlesome and way too tenacious about town spirit, but I was touched he'd thought about my birthday.

The crowd parted, revealing Summer carrying a slightly lopsided but still adorable birthday cake in the shape of a cat. At that exact moment, Felix butted his head against my leg. I laughed and picked him up, and the two of us blew out the birthday candles together.

"It's vanilla cake with maple frosting," Summer said. "I wasn't sure what your favorite flavors were."

I leaned my head on Finn's shoulder. "I love maple."

The next few minutes were filled with the townspeople coming up to me, wishing me a happy birthday, and adding to a pile of presents forming by the door. My guys grounded me through the bond, keeping me from becoming overstimulated by everything.

"Alright people, listen up!" Stanley said. A hush fell over the crowd. "Each year at the Harvest Festival, we crown the Historic Starlight Grove Autumnal Harvest Celebration's Harvest Queen, and this year, the choice was clear. I am pleased to announce that our Harvest Queen is none other than our lighthouse keeper, Olive Autumn Harvest."

Lucy and Ivy pushed me forward to allow Stanley to place a crown on my head to much cheers and applause.

There were more congratulations and hugs, and Stanley launched into a lecture on how being Harvest Queen came with many responsibilities and he hoped I'd be prepared to take them on. Harry finally pulled him away, giving me a little wave over his shoulder.

As people started to disperse, returning to the booths to enjoy the final hours of the festival, my eyes caught on a massive alpha moving towards me.

"Oh my god, Gunnar!" I jogged a few steps and threw my arms around the man who had been like an uncle to me.

He caught me in his arms. He smelled like the sea, and it brought a lump to my throat. "Little Olive, all grown up," he said in a rough voice.

When we separated, I saw his bonded—Sarah and Anna— behind him. I let out an excited shout and hugged them, too.

"I can't believe you're here," I said, wiping at the tears in my eyes.

"Well, we needed to come check on you after meeting those idiots." He jutted his chin at my alphas who were standing back to give us some space. "I heard they wrecked your boat." Gunnar crossed his arms and looked distinctly unimpressed.

I pursed my lip. "Yeah, well, maybe not their finest moment."

The alpha shook his head. "Are you sure about them? Because I can get rid of them for you. Just say the word."

Sarah elbowed her alpha. "Do you not see those bond marks?" She gestured at the marks on my neck. They were still red and blotchy but would heal into silvery scars.

"I'm trying not to," Gunnar responded, making me laugh.

Sarah rolled her eyes before putting her arm around my shoulder. "He's feeling very protective of our little Olive," she said conspiratorially. "To him, I think you'll always be that little seven-year-old girl giving orders on your dad's boat."

"Probably." But I wasn't upset by it. I welcomed Gunnar's protectiveness, especially since I'd been the one to shut out Pack Christensen these past few years because I was so afraid to have any reminders of my parents. I'd ignored their invitations to come over for dinner, all their attempts to be there for me. But they were still here.

I swallowed the lump in my throat. "I'm sorry I disappeared."

Sarah wrapped me in her arms. "You never have to apologize, honey. You had just gone through the absolute worst thing, and we knew how much you were hurting." She sniffed. "I wish we had done more."

"You couldn't have done more. I was determined to be alone."

I sank into her embrace. She had been my mom's best friend, and hugging her felt like having my mom back, even if just for a moment. We pulled apart, giving each other watery smiles.

"Well, you're not alone anymore, Ms. Harvest Queen," she said, regaining her no-nonsense fisherwoman voice. "Make those guys drive you up the coast to visit us. We'll take you out on the boat so they can learn some basic life skills."

My lips quirked into a smile. "Gunnar is never going to let them live that down."

Sarah shook her head. "He and Jameson were best friends. Your dad isn't here to scare the shit out of those alphas, so Gunnar takes his role as surrogate dad very seriously."

This time, I couldn't stop a few tears from falling. "I miss them."

"I know, honey. I miss them, too."

We looked across at the festival. Carmen was leading an impromptu dance class between booths while Stanley shouted something about blocking the walkways.

"Your parents would be so proud of the life you've created here. I know I'm damn proud of you. And those alphas of yours might know shit about boating, but whew, they're hot. Good choice."

I snorted out a laugh. "Oh my god, Sarah."

"Psh, I might be old, but I have *eyes*."

I gestured for my guys to introduce themselves to Sarah and Anna. Gunnar remained silent, just stared them down, eyes blazing.

"That guy is scary as shit," Easton said once Sarah dragged her alphas into the festival.

"I still can't believe you crashed my boat," I said. *My Sweet Olive* had been rescued from the rocks and was now sitting in the marina, ready for repairs.

"You make one mistake," Easton said. I elbowed his side, which probably hurt my elbow more than him. He just wrapped his arms around me. "I was thinking—since we're a pack now, what's going to be our pack name?"

"Oh." My chest filled with excitement as it finally sank in that we were a *pack*. I hadn't dared to dream they would want forever with me, so I hadn't even thought about a pack name.

"We've got West, Ford, Andersson-Spring, and Harvest," Finn said.

"I'm happy with any of them," Lars said. "Maybe West because of the lighthouse? People in town already call it the West Lighthouse."

Easton groaned. "I would be Easton West. Everyone would call me a compass."

Lars snorted a laugh.

"It's better than Olive Autumn Harvest," I said. "My grandma on my mom's side was named Autumn, and I don't think my parents put together the whole *autumn harvest* thing."

"I love your name, though," Finn said. "Perfect for the Harvest Queen."

I smiled and stood on my tiptoes to kiss his bond mark, earning me a growl and a slap on the ass.

"You don't want to keep your name, Easton?" I asked.

His jaw hardened. "Definitely not."

I ran my hand through his long curls, wishing I could take away the pain of his upbringing. His expression softened, and he leaned into my touch, kissing my palm.

"Lars?" I asked.

"We could always hyphenate to be Pack Autumn-Spring," he mused.

I froze until a pulse of amusement reached me through the bond. I shoved him, laughing. "Please, no."

He chuckled. "Well, then. I think the choice is obvious. We'll be Pack Harvest to honor the omega at the center of our lives and the parents at the center of hers."

I sniffled as my eyes filled with tears. "Fuck, you can't just say things like that."

"Pack Harvest. I love it." Easton wrapped me in a tight hug, Finn

and Lars joining in until I was completely wrapped up with them—
drenched in their scents and surrounded by their love.

63

OLIVE

I SAT ON THE SIDE OF THE SANDY HILL OVERLOOKING THE beach. The festival had come to a close a few minutes ago, and I'd changed into sweatpants and one of Easton's thick sweaters. My omega was craving soft and cozy things, but I'd been sad to take off my gorgeous gown. It was the prettiest thing I'd ever worn, and I couldn't wait to find excuses to wear it again.

The sun was setting, streaking the sky with pinks and reds, and I lay back on the sand, uncaring that it would get in my hair. Bits of laughter and chatter reached me on the wind as everyone broke down the booths and cleaned everything up from the field. My guys refused to let me help since I was still recovering from my heat. I'd rolled my eyes, but the moment I sat down, exhaustion pulled at me.

I couldn't believe so much had happened this past week. I'd gone from devastated, thinking that Lars wanted someone else, to terrified I was going to lose my guys in the storm, to the happiest I'd ever been, bonding them and becoming a pack.

A quiet *meow* was the only thing alerting me that I wasn't alone. Felix lay down on my chest, stretching out regally like I was his personal throne. I scratched his ears.

"When I moved in, I had no idea I was letting such a diabolical scheming matchmaker into my home."

Felix purred.

"Thanks for bringing them to me." I had no doubt he knew what he was doing when he broke the tie at the town meeting. "And" —I swallowed around the lump in my throat—"thanks for choosing me first, Felix. Thanks for sticking with me."

His purr intensified, and he rubbed his head under my chin. We stayed there, quietly soaking in the evening, until Felix spotted something over my shoulder. I twisted around to follow his gaze and saw my alphas walking our way. Happiness swirled through me, amplified by my guys' emotions in the bond.

"You know you're always welcome here, Felix, even with them moving in. Anytime you want to stay, there will be space for you. But I'm not alone anymore, so I understand if you need to go." I wrapped my arms around him in a hug and squeezed lightly. "I'm sure you have plenty of scheming and matchmaking to do."

Felix purred and gave me one final bop with his head before hopping off my lap. He strutted past my guys as he headed back up the path towards town.

"What was that about?" Easton said, sitting down by my side and pressing my cold hand between his warm ones. Lars settled behind me and placed a blanket in my lap. I leaned into him, his purr vibrating through me. Finn sat on my other side, leaning in to kiss my cheek, scent-marking me in the process.

"I was just discussing important things with the mayor."

Easton squeezed my hand. "I'm sure the mayor and the Harvest Queen have a lot of official business to discuss."

A smile played on my lips. "So much business."

We sat in perfect silence, the emotions through the bond expressing more than we could put into words. Lars played with my hair, Finn fussed with the blanket, making sure I was warm, and Easton curled up against my side.

The sun slowly disappeared over the horizon, cloaking us in darkness. Little stars dotted the night sky. This was one of those quiet life moments that was so perfect I knew I'd treasure it forever.

Tears filled my eyes. "I love you all so much."

My guys held me tighter as the bond flooded with pure, bright love.

"We love you too, baby," Easton said, sounding a little choked up.

I lifted our joined hands and kissed them. "I'm so happy you stalked me."

"Wasn't stalking," he mumbled.

I just smiled and closed my eyes. The crisp breeze from the water brought the promise of winter, but I had my guys to keep me warm.

Today and every day in the future.

EPILOGUE

FELIX

My tail flicked side to side as I wandered through the remaining festival booths.

The grumpy sea creature omega was matched with her alphas. My work here was done. Of course, I would continue to monitor them. They clearly needed my guiding paw at all times.

I passed the rock where I'd stored my carving knife. You never knew when it would come in handy... when someone might need to be put in their place.

"Oh, sorry, Felix," a frazzled voice cried out as I narrowly avoided being stepped on.

I let out an irritated noise and turned my piercing gaze onto the culprit—the shy teacher omega. She was carrying a large box of rocks that blocked most of her view.

She set the box down on the grass and scratched my ears.

"I'm really sorry. Are you okay? I didn't see you there."

I leaned into her touch. Mmm, that was nice. The teacher omega always gave me treats. She kept some in her desk drawer in her classroom in case I slipped in after hours for a visit. She smelled like gingerbread, like Christmas.

Hmm... Christmas was just around the corner. I fixed the omega with my piercing stare and a little purr rumbled in my chest as a plan fell into place.

My tail flicked back and forth as I set off again, towards home.

Yes, this would be a very good holiday season.

The end.

Want to see how Pack Harvest spends Christmas Day?
Read the bonus scene here!

NEED MORE COZYVERSE?

Not ready to leave Starlight Grove? Curious about Felix's plans for Ivy Winter? Read *A Pack for Winter* by Eliana Lee, featuring Ivy and her pack.

And stay tuned: even more stories are coming! *A Pack for Spring* featuring Lucy Andersson-Spring by Emilia Emerson releases Spring 2026, and *A Pack for Summer* featuring Summer Pham by Eliana Lee releases Summer 2026.

See more of Emilia Emerson's Books here: emiliaemerson.com
See more of Eliana Lee's Books here: elianaleeauthor.com

ALSO BY EMILIA EMERSON

Curious about the Mafia book Olive and her guys were reading?

Check out *His Tesoro* by Emilia Rossi!

And don't miss Emilia Emerson's other Omegaverse Books:

Forbidden: Part One & Forbidden: Part Two

Cherished

ACKNOWLEDGMENTS

In February 2024, Eliana Lee messaged me with the idea of creating a low-angst omegaverse shared world. I immediately loved the idea but was resistant to say yes to a new project. I was in the middle of writing my first Mafia romance and was already overwhelmed with all the other books I wanted to write. But within a couple days, I couldn't stop thinking about Cozyverse. We started messaging ideas back and forth (each slightly more ridiculous than the last), and then the Instagram algorithm happened to show me Vaughn Designs's account. I messaged Eliana telling her I'd found our cover designer for this series we definitely were *not* committing to write, and the rest was history!

So my first thank you here has to go to Eliana: Cozyverse Mastermind Extraordinaire. I've always hated group projects, but collaborating on this world with you has been such a joy. You are genuinely hilarious, filled with brilliant ideas, and an incredible writing partner. This book was so much fun to write, and so much of that was because of you! I can't wait to be back in Starlight Grove with you for Spring and Summer, making obscure Gilmore Girls references and scheming up more Felix shenanigans.

To Rachel—for being an incredible writing partner, cheerleader, and beautiful friend. You inspire me to keep going when this whole writing adventure gets hard.

To Darcy—for being with me from the beginning and for being an incredibly thoughtful friend and writing partner.

To my wonderful beta readers, whose feedback helped make this story the best it could be: Aimee, Blair, Brit, Katherine, Jenny, and Robyn. I really couldn't do this without you. I'm so grateful I can trust you with my stories, these little pieces of my heart, at such a vulnerable stage of the writing process.

This book wasn't originally supposed to be about grief, but my characters have a way of taking the story exactly where it needs to go. Writing about Olive and Finn's grief made me reminisce a lot about my first year as a therapist. I was 22 years old (!), working at a grief counseling center. The work was devastating—my focus was working with clients who had experienced traumatic losses—but it was stunningly beautiful, too. We can't fix grief, change the past, or hold any certainties about the future. As a therapist, this often brought up deep feelings of helplessness. I wanted more than anything to take away my clients' pain, but all I could do was be with them in it. And it turns out, that was exactly enough.

My year at the grief counseling center was an age ago now—I feel like I've lived so many lives since then. But I will never forget those clients—the incredible people who trusted me, a young woman who had lived a lot of life in her few years but was still trying to figure herself out—to walk a part of their grief journey with them. If I could name them here and share their stories, you would know how stunningly breathtaking and beautiful and incredible they were. Since I can't, I'll just say this: I will forever carry imprinted upon my heart the ways my clients changed me. I faced some of my greatest fears with them, re-lived some of my darkest griefs, and learned so much about life and death and growing old and loving deeply.

My clients from that year will never read this, but to you reading this right now, I want to say: facing your own pain and darkness with a brave stance and eyes wide open is one of the most courageous things you can do. We live in a culture that, more than anything, fears that dark abyss of grief and death and dark emotions. If you've found yourself there, know that I'm right beside you. Holding your hand until you're ready to come back into the light, where the world is waiting to embrace you.

ABOUT THE AUTHOR

Emilia Emerson loves to embroider, take naps with her dog, read romance, and do projects around the house. Before becoming a full-time author, she was a mental health therapist and loves that writing romance allows her to explore worlds with guaranteed happily ever afters, cozy characters who love each other, and found families who overcome challenges together. She also writes Mafia Romance under the pen name Emilia Rossi.

Stay up to date on new announcements:

Website: emiliaemerson.com
Facebook Group: Emilia Emerson's Reader Group
Instagram & TikTok: @emiliaemersonauthor

Made in United States
Troutdale, OR
11/11/2024

24682345R00224